DATE DUE

The Lost Wagon

Books by Jim Kjelgaard

THE LOST WAGON

CRACKER BARREL TROUBLE SHOOTER

THE SPELL OF THE WHITE STURGEON

BIG RED

REBEL SIEGE

FOREST PATROL

BUCKSKIN BRIGADE

CHIP, THE DAM BUILDER

FIRE HUNTER

IRISH RED

KALAK OF THE ICE

A NOSE FOR TROUBLE

SNOW DOG

TRAILING TROUBLE

WILD TREK

THE EXPLORATIONS OF PERE MARQUETTE

OUTLAW RED

THE STORY OF THE MORMONS

The
LOST WAGON

JIM KJELGAARD

Dodd, Mead & Company · *New York*

Library of Congress Catalog Card Number: 55–7136

Printed in the United States of America

For Alma and Rob Zaun

Contents

The Lost Wagon

Pondering

WHEN HE had guided his plow halfway down the furrow, a bar-winged fly alighted just above Joe Tower's right ear. He felt it crawling, its presence irritating through the sweat that beaded his forehead and dampened his temples, and he knew that he should swat it away. When it was ready to do so the fly would bite him, and bar-winged flies drew blood when they bit.

He did not raise his hand because once again the devils which, at sporadic intervals, tormented him, were having a field day. The fly was a counter-irritant. He wanted it to bite. It was a time to be hurt because, after the fly bit him, there would be that much more satisfaction in smashing it.

At the same time he kept a wary eye on the mules. Though he was sometimes confused by the facts and affairs of his personal world, at the moment he had no doubt whatever about one thing. He hated all mules in general and these two in particular. They were big, sleek roan brutes with an air of innocence that was somehow imparted by their wagging ears and doleful expressions, but was entirely belied by the devil in their eyes. Twice within the past fifteen minutes they had balked, stepped over their traces, snarled their harnesses and kicked at him when he sought to untangle them. He had escaped injury because he knew mules. All his life he had handled animals, and most of the time he knew what they were going to do before they did it.

He felt the fly crawling around, and gloated silently as he awaited its bite. He mustn't harm the mules because a man simply never hurt his animals. But he could swat the fly, and so doing he

could relieve all his pent-up anger at the mules and, this afternoon, at the world in general.

Not for a second did he take his eyes from the mules, and they
seemed to know that he was watching them. Muscles rippled beneath taut hides as they strained into their collars and pulled as
though they had never had any thought except getting the plowing
done. Joe Tower's already tense nerves began to scream. The fly
didn't bite and the mules didn't balk, and unless something happened very soon, he felt that he would be reduced to babbling
idiocy.

Nothing happened except that the already hot sun seemed to
become a little hotter on his sweat-drenched shirt and his per-
spiring head and arms. But he had been scorched by so much
sun and had sweated so many gallons that he never thought about
it any more. Sun and sweat were a part of things, like snow and
ice. Nobody escaped them and nobody could do anything about
them, and Joe wasn't sure that anybody should want to. If the sun
didn't shine the crops wouldn't grow. Or if the sun did shine, and
there was no snow to melt and fill subterranean reservoirs, the
crops wouldn't grow anyhow. This basic reasoning should be obvious to anyone at all.

The rich brown earth turned cleanly as the plow wounded it,
and the scorching sun burned a healing scab over the wound.
Keeping intent eyes on both mules and waiting for the fly to bite,
Joe was not one man but two.

One of them felt a soul-filling peace. It was good to plow and to
have the nostril-filling scent of the newly turned earth, for these
things were symbolic. The earth was a vast treasure house, but the
treasure was not yielded freely. It was only for the strong, for him
who could sweat and strain and guide a plow. Such a person was
blessed beyond any others. But the other man who walked with
Joe was angry and resentful. He did not doubt his own strength
for he could plow as long a furrow as was necessary. He did dis-
like the forces, the petty forces that had nothing at all to do with
plowing, which kept him from doing it.

Joe's lean, six-foot body adjusted itself perfectly to the rhythm of the plow. Hairy, sun-browned arms gripped the handles with exactly the right pressure, and there was something almost lyrically smooth in the way he could, without using his hands at all, control the reins that were looped over the small of his back. Gray-streaked hair that needed cutting and black beard shadowed a face that might have been thirty years old or fifty, and was thirty-four.

To himself and his work he gave little conscious thought. He had plowed so many furrows that plowing came almost as naturally as breathing, and he had long since ceased even to think about his own physical proportions. What sometimes seemed an age ago and sometimes only yesterday, he had fancied himself as a dashing figure and very handsome. He had been nineteen then and courting Emma, and it was a foregone conclusion that the world was not only to be their oyster, but that it would be filled with the purest of pearls.

That had been yesterday, and yesterday was lost somewhere in the haze that every morning hung like a blue shroud over the low mountains that marched into the distance. This was today, and today meant work. But somehow, yesterday's dreams had not passed with passing time.

Yesterday's dream had become today's dream, and it was made up of things that a man might hope to possess—no unreasonable things, but ordinary things, like a sizable piece of good land, owned free and clear; an extra team of mules; a flower garden for Emma to fool around with, and maybe a small orchard down the side of a hill; some pretty clothes for Emma and for blossoming Barbara, and some toys for the younger ones; and most of all, freedom from the never-ending uncertainty about meeting the next payment. It seemed as though that shouldn't be too much for a man to want, yet most of it was still a dream.

Joe blew his breath upward to see if he could make the fly leave him and, when it did not, he became angrier. He was almost always a creature of the moment, and always the moments were filled with things demanding immediate attention. To the exclusion of all else, this one centered in a team of fractious mules, a fly that must bite soon and a strong sense of restlessness.

He came almost to the end of the furrow and still the fly contented itself with crawling around his temple and stopping now and again to buzz its wings or clean its fragile feet. Joe's tension increased and, had it not been for the anticipated senses of achievement that swatting the fly would give him after it bit, he would have swatted it anyhow.

They reached the furrow's end, he prepared to swing the team around, and that was the second the fly chose to bite him. It was a sharp and sudden pain, somewhat like the prick of a needle, but the pain did not ebb as a needle wound would have. The fly had pierced a blood vessel and would now bloat itself with blood. Joe Tower's hot anger passed the boiling point but, where another man might have cursed, he said nothing.

He let go of the right plow handle so that he could raise his hand and swat the fly. A surge of purest pleasure shimmered through him, for this was the second he had been awaiting. Just at that moment the mules rebelled.

Expertly, choosing precisely the right time, knowing not only exactly what to do but exactly how to do it, they stepped over their traces and swung away from each other. They plunged forward, dragging the plow on top of the ground. Instead of swatting the fly, Joe grabbed the reins with his right hand and pulled back hard.

The steel bits took hold, and the mule's jaws gaped open. But they were hard-mouthed, and Joe brought his left hand to the aid of his right while he fought back as stubbornly as the mules were fighting him. When he finally brought the team under control, the fly was gone and only a dull ache remained to prove that it had ever been.

For a moment Joe felt weak and spiritless, as though he had conceived some master plan which should have worked well but which instead had gone completely astray. Then, still eying the mules warily, he straightened them out and swung the plow around.

The silliness of what he had intended to do and the way he had intended to do it, struck him forcibly. He had actually made serious plans to relieve his own pent-up feelings by swatting a fly. He grinned and for a moment he rested.

His eyes strayed past the boundaries of his own farm to a green-clad hill where a little herd of cattle grazed. Joe looked wistfully at them. The cattle belonged to Pete Domley, and Joe had a sudden overwhelming conviction that Pete was the smartest man in Missouri. Instead of worrying about a farm, Pete had merely acquired a judicious assortment of bulls and cows and let nature work on his side. Beyond the slightest doubt, cattlemen had all the best of everything. It would be nice if all one had to do was cull his herds every season and sell the increase.

Joe could not let himself rest for long because the sun was shining, the ground was ready for working, and he had problems. He had bought his eighty-five acres for $600, of which he still owed Elias Dorrance, the banker, $400. This fall Elias would expect another payment. If Joe did not get the field plowed and planted he would have no crops to sell and therefore no money, and Elias was not noted for his willingness to wait. It was strange how things never worked out the way a man thought they would.

Joe had understood before they were married that Emma had not wanted to leave her father. Old Caleb Winthrop was a widower of uncertain temperament, gentle one hour and abusive the next. Emma had been devoted to him since her mother's death, and she had been able to forgive his harshness and his tyrannies because she deeply pitied his loneliness. She was even able to persuade Joe that old Caleb "didn't mean anything" and that "things would surely work themselves out" once they were all living together.

Joe had had his doubts, but he laid them aside, and after the wedding he gave up his small interest in a near-by farm and came to work for his father-in-law.

Things didn't "work themselves out." Joe stuck to his job for five long years, chafing all the time under the old man's constant criticism. Caleb had let it be understood that some day the farm would belong to Joe and Emma, but meanwhile it seemed as though there was nothing Joe could do right—or if he did anything right then sure as fate he'd done it at the wrong time. Emma, who'd been able to tolerate the old man's venom easily enough when it was directed against herself, suffered agonies when Caleb would start to mutter and then to shout over something Joe had done.

There had come a day when Caleb shouted at Joe a little too loud and a little too long. Emma asked Joe to step outside with her, there was something she wanted to say to him.

They walked away together toward the big tree over by the barn, and when they got there Emma turned to Joe and looked into his tired and angry eyes, and she put her hands on his arms and felt there the rapid tensing of his muscles as he clenched and unclenched his fists that were dug deep into his pockets.

"Joe," she said, "I was wrong. I should never have asked you to come here to work for Pa." The color rose up into her face. "I can't stand it when he yells at you. Something terrible happens inside of me. I—I *hate* him when he yells at you, Joe."

He took his hands out of his pockets and drew her close to him, and she put her head down on his shoulder and wept bitter tears. He moved his work-roughened hand tenderly over her soft hair, and he held her gently and rocked her a little because he felt she was trying to make a decision, a hard and painful decision, and he didn't want to influence her one way or the other.

When she quieted she talked again, blurting the words as though she had to get them out quickly—while she dared. "We can't stay," she said. "It's not right the way he treats you. And he won't change, Joe. He hates the thought of you getting his land, and he means to make you pay—not in money or work, but in other ways. Mean ways. It's not worth it, Joe."

A smile came over his face, and he held her away from him so she could see him and how good he felt. "I prayed to hear you say this, Emma. I've been wanting to leave for a long, long time, but I waited for you to come to it by yourself." He looked at her with all the love he felt and could never quite put into words. "I couldn't go without you, Emma, and I wouldn't force you to come —more especially because I can't offer you anything away from this farm. I'll have to work as a hired man till we can get together enough to buy us some land of our own."

Emma put her face down against his shoulder, and the words that came up were muffled. "I've got a confession to make, Joe. I knew you wanted to leave. I knew it a long time ago. But I was afraid to speak out against Pa. I guess I've always been afraid of Pa, not knowing it, thinking all the time I just respected him the way a daughter should. But hearing him yell at you, I found out something I never knew. I can get mad at Pa. I can get so mad at him that I'm not frightened at all any more. I could walk right up to Pa this minute and tell him we've had just about enough!"

She lifted her face then, startled by her own audacity, and said, "Want to see me do it?" And then, before he could say yes or no, she ran away from him back to the house, quick as a deer. Joe chased her, and when he came in panting through the door there she was standing in front of Caleb with her eyes blazing, and saying, loud and clear, "Pa, we've had just about enough!"

For eight years Joe had worked as a hired hand for other farmers. Being a menial did not trouble him at all, but he worried greatly over the fact that he was seldom able to offer his family more than the basic necessities of food, clothing, and shelter. Within his inner soul was a deep conviction that they deserved more. A great oak could not flourish in a flower pot, and human beings could not grow as humans should if they must always be restricted.

Last year Emma had overwhelmed him by producing $600 which, almost penny by penny, she had saved over the years. Two hundred had gone into the land and $400 into things needed for the land: mules, cows, harness, the plow, the harrow and a host of other things which never seemed very expensive when one bought them singly but which ate up money when purchased together. Now this wasn't working out. Though a part of Joe could be perfectly in tune with what he was doing, another part resented it fiercely. Good land was for good crops, and good crops were a joy to the heart and soul. But Joe looked over what he had already plowed and seemed to see there a row of dollar bills for Elias Dorrance. He thought uneasily of the way he lived, and wondered if his sons and daughters would have to live that way too. Then this feeling faded until it was only a vague irritation, and Joe became the complete farmer.

He guided the plow down another furrow and another. It was hard and hot work, but Joe licked his lips in anticipation as he forced himself to plow one more furrow. It pleased him to work as hard as he could, and sweat as much as he could, before he indulged himself because then the indulgence was appreciated all the more. Swinging back on still another furrow, he halted the mules in their tracks and walked to a leafy sycamore that spread its green branches where the plowed field ended. He pulled a handful of wilting grass aside and revealed a brown stone jug.

For two seconds, wanting to cheat himself of no part of this, he looked at the jug. Its earthen sides were beaded with little globules of water, and as it lay in the sycamore's shade it looked inviting. Joe knelt to pick it up, and the jug was cool to his hand. He pulled the corn cob stopper and held the jug to his lips while he took great gulps of cold water. It was part of the ritual, a measure of things as they must be. A man who had never been sweat-stained from hard labor could not know the true goodness of cold water. His thirst satisfied, Joe put the jug back and covered it with grass.

The day had been hard and somewhat frustrating, but it was with a sense of loss and resentment that he noted the long shadows of early evening draping themselves over the fields. The day couldn't possibly be ended, but as soon as he knew that it was ending he felt a rising pleasure. No man had a right to rest while there was daylight in which he might work, but anybody with half a lick of common sense knew that you couldn't work at night. When it was impossible to work, the whole time might be given to dreams, and dreams were a very important part of life, too.

Knowing very well that their day was over too, and that they were going to pasture, the mules stood meekly and made no attempt to kick as he unhitched them. Free from the plow, they stepped along as briskly as though they hadn't just finished pulling it for more than ten hours, and there was something akin to friendliness in their eyes when Joe drove them into the pasture, stripped their harness off, hung it on the upper railing, and shut the pasture gate behind him.

He turned to watch the mules frisk like a couple of colts across the green grass, then lie down and roll luxuriously in it. Not until tomorrow morning would he have to fight them into harness again, and that made him forget, in part, the trouble he had had with them today. He grinned at the mules.

There was a soft footstep beside him and Joe's oldest daughter was there. She was slim and tall, and almost startlingly beautiful. There was little resemblance to either Joe or Emma; Barbara was the re-creation of some ethereal being who had been in the family of one or the other perhaps 100 and perhaps 500 years ago. She had been one of the really awe-inspiring events in Joe's life. He was not naïve and he knew the ways of nature. But when he had courted Emma he had known only that he was desperately in love with her and that he wanted her always at his side. It had simply never occurred to him that they, too, should produce children; he hadn't thought that far. When Emma told him she was pregnant he had walked around in a half daze for weeks. He hadn't really believed it until Barbara's arrival.

Joe said, "Hello, Bobby."

She said, "Hello, Dad," and she added, as though it were an afterthought, "The chores are done."

Joe frowned. At the same time, since he was tired, he knew

some relief. Half the families around put their children to work
in the fields as soon as they were big enough to pull weeds, but
Joe had never liked the idea and he didn't hold with his womenfolk doing field work at all. Men were supposed to work the fields,
but almost as soon as she was big enough to do so, Barbara had
taken a hand. She liked to do things, and for all her seeming
slightness she was very strong. Just the same, even though he was
relieved because he would not have to milk the cows, swill the
pigs, and do all the other things that forever needed doing, Joe
didn't like it. But he spoke with the gentleness that Barbara inspired in him.

"You shouldn't be doing such chores."

She smiled, the corners of her eyes crinkling, and Joe thought
of Emma. "I like to do them and it won't hurt me."

Because he did not know what to say, for a moment Joe said
nothing. It was unreasonable because a man always had the right
to tell his children what to do, but secretly he was still more than
a little overawed by Barbara. Then the silence became awkward
and he asked,

"Where's Tad?"

"He— He's about."

Joe frowned. It was a foregone conclusion that Tad was about
because Tad, his eldest son, was always somewhere. Joe thought
of his children.

After Barbara they'd waited seven years for Tad. Then Emma,
Joe, Alfred, and Carlyle, had arrived in rapid succession. If Joe
understood any of them he understood Tad, for the eight-year-old
thought and acted a great deal like the father. A wild and restless
youngster, Tad was wholeheartedly for anything he didn't have.
As long as there was something he really wanted he was entirely
willing to work like a horse for it.

Where the field joined the forest, a white and black dog of
mixed ancestry panted into sight and stopped to look expectantly
back over his shoulder. Joe stiffened, waiting for what he knew he
would see now, and a moment later Tad appeared with Joe's long-

barreled rifle over his shoulder and a cluster of squirrels in his hand.

Joe's anger flared. Tad loved to hunt, which was not unusual because all normal boys did. But nobody eight years old had any business running around the woods with a rifle and more than once Joe had forbidden Tad to use his. Joe's face became stormy as the youngster drew near.

"What you been doing?"

Tad stopped, every freckle on his multifreckled face registering total innocence and his eyes big with surprise. Joe fumed. The boy was like him and yet they were not alike. Never in his life had Joe faced anything in any except a direct way. He did not know how to pretend, as Tad was pretending now.

"Huntin', Pa," the youngster said.

"Haven't I told you to leave that rifle alone?"

"You didn't tell me today."

"I don't have to tell you every day!"

"I didn't use but six shots."

Joe roared so loudly that the pastured mules looked curiously at him, "It's no matter if you used only one!"

"I got six squirrels," Tad explained. "Mike, he put 'em up a tree and kept 'em there. I just shot. Smacked every one of 'em plumb through the head."

"Give me that rifle," Joe snatched the weapon, "and get in the house before I tan your hide!"

"Yes, Pa."

The squirrels in his hand, the dog beside him, Tad trotted toward the house. There was nothing meek or subdued in his squared shoulders and upturned head, and for a moment Joe had an uncomfortable feeling that he had been tested by an eight-year-old. He scowled and shrugged the thought away while he felt a rising pride. Six squirrels with six shots was good shooting anywhere, and young ones wouldn't be all they should be if they didn't have a bit of the devil in them. He must keep the rifle where Tad couldn't reach it, though. Maybe this fall, or as soon as he could spare a day from the fields, it would be a good idea if he took Tad hunting with him. He really wouldn't mind Tad's using the rifle if he could be sure that it was safely used.

Barbara went to close the chicken coop. The rifle in his hand, Joe walked to the spring house, leaned the rifle against it, and dipped a pail full of water. He spilled some into a wooden bowl that stood on a wooden bench and sighed deliciously as he washed his face and hands. This, the final act of his working day, was one to which he always looked forward. It was as though, in washing away accumulated sweat and grime, he also washed away the troubles that plagued him. The end of the day was almost like being born again.

There was a new spring in his step and a fresh tilt to his head as he walked toward the house. He remembered Emma, not too clearly, as a lovely young girl. Now her figure was mature. Hard work, childbirth and worry had traced their own lines on her face. But to Joe there was something completely fitting and even refreshing about that. A tree could not forever remain a graceful young sapling. It had to grow, and became strong with growth, in order to withstand winter blasts, summer storms, fire, and other hazards that menaced it. Joe found in the mature Emma a solid strength and assurance that he could not remember knowing in the girl, and with it had come a deepening love. He met his wife and kissed her. Emma stepped back and smiled.

"Did you have a good day?"

"It was a good one."

Her eyes dwelt on the rifle, and her brows arched in question. "Did Tad have it again?"

Joe grinned. "Yup."

He took the rifle into his and Emma's bedroom, and hung it high on two wooden pegs driven close to the ceiling. For a moment he looked at it, frowning, and then he was satisfied. He could reach the rifle but Tad couldn't unless he had something to stand on. If he tried that, Emma would hear and stop him. Still, the boy was devilishly clever when it came to sneaking the gun out.

Tad was outside dressing his squirrels, and Barbara had gone down to the creek to gather a little knob of wild flowers for the table. As soon as Joe had settled himself in the chair, the four youngest children were upon him. Joe reached down to lift baby Carlyle into his lap with the other three, and they cuddled there like soft kittens.

"When I was out in the fields today," Joe began, "I met a big grizzly bear. He had a mouth this wide . . ."

He spread his hands to show the width of the grizzly bear's mouth and his fingers to demonstrate the length of its teeth. Gently, to their squealing delight, he tickled the four little ones and nibbled their hands and feet to show how the grizzly bear had mauled and bitten him.

Behind him, Emma stood at the window enjoying, as she did each night, the pure pleasure that Joe took in his children. She had loved Joe almost from the day she first set eyes on him, in the store where they had come together at the counter, she to buy calico for an apron, Joe to buy some nails for the repair of a fence. Something about the set of his shoulders and the powerful but easy way he moved caught her attention. Here was a man slow and sure and strong—slow of speech, slow to smile, but with an imp of mischief that could dart out unexpectedly from his eyes. When the storekeeper had held up for his attention a small jug of maple syrup from a shipment newly arrived, and had inquired, "Like one of these?" Joe's eyes had strayed to Emma and he'd replied, unblinking, "Sure would." Joe took the jug of syrup in his hand, hefted it for weight and again, looking into Emma's startled eyes, said "Sweet, no doubt of it." Then, absolutely overcome by his own impudence, he had slapped his money on the counter and run from the store, jug in hand, nearly falling over a box that stood in his path.

She smiled now, thinking of that casual beginning. Their marriage had not been easy, but it had been rich in tenderness and in sharing. The five years that they had lived with her father had been troubled and barren. Barbara's arrival had given them a center of relief away from Caleb. Barbara had been like an oasis in a parched land. Their feelings, that withered and died in Caleb's presence, could grow and flower when they were alone with their baby girl.

Joe had been bewitched by Barbara from the beginning. And each of his children had seemed miraculous to him in birth. He was a good man, a good father. True, there was a restlessness in Joe that sometimes frightened her. He liked to work, but to work for himself, for his own family. He had endured Caleb's domination with an inner rage that had seemed like a bottled-up tornado to Emma. Though he managed to conceal most of it, the fury of it had at times been revealed in his bloodshot eyes and white, set lips, in the way he strode out to the plow or pulled open the barn door—and it had caused a tight little knot of worry to harden inside of her. He wanted then, and he wanted now, to be on his own, his own man. The obligation of his debt to Elias Dorrance sat heavily upon him, more heavily than it did on Emma, because the furious independence that burned within him raged against the naked fact that the land was *not* his own, would not be his own until he had paid back every last dollar he owed on it.

Emma sighed a little, wishing that Joe did not chafe so under his debt. If Joe were less restless, she would be able to enjoy even more fully the home that in this one year had become so precious to her. Her eyes strayed now from the little mass of squirming and giggling humanity gathered about Joe's knees, and she re-examined lovingly, for the thousandth time, every bit of furniture in the room. Most of it had been made by Joe, and they had talked about it and planned it for where it would stand and how it would serve them. The little cupboard that held their best dishes had been polished with such energy that it gleamed as brightly as a copper pot. The curtains blowing in the soft breeze had been stitched by Barbara and herself after the young ones were tucked away for the night. The lamps were polished, their chimneys spotless. Everywhere in the room there was evidence of labor and tender care. Emma loved the room and everything in it. Her whole life was here in this room, with Joe, with her children. Life was hard, but it was rich and full, and if Joe did not have these flashes of restlessness, it would be well-nigh perfect.

Barbara came in and put her handful of flowers into a cup on the table and then, with quiet efficiency, she and Emma put the meal on the table and the four youngsters slid from Joe's lap to crowd hungrily around. Tad came in, his face and hands clean and his black hair slicked back with water. He carried the dressed squirrels on a piece of bark. Laying them on a wooden bench, he almost leaped into his chair. Emma smiled with her eyes and Joe smiled back, and the words they had whispered a thousand times to each other were heard, unsaid but understood.

Emma asked, "Did you get a lot done?"

"Quite a lot. But those darn mules—."

He told her of the trouble he'd had with the mules, but even while he spoke it seemed to be someone else talking. He could not understand it because it was past his understanding. To plow the earth and grow new crops was always good. By such deeds people lived and had lived since the beginning. But . . .

His every nerve and instinct, and his heart, told him that good land had magic in it. It had been maddening, as a hired hand, to be able to feel and touch this magic, and not to have it for his own. He had thought that having his own land would change all this, but it hadn't. Previously he had worked for wages while his employer reaped the benefit of his labor. Now he was merely working for Elias Dorrance. As before, all he could offer his family were the basic necessities. Joe looked down at his empty plate.

Emma's understanding eyes were upon him. She said, "Why don't you take a walk, Joe?"

"Now say! I might just do that! I might go down to Tenney's!"

"Why don't you?"

"I think I will."

Joe sought the star-lighted path leading to Tenney's general store, which was the center of half a dozen houses at Tenney's Crossing and the unofficial clubhouse for every man from miles around. Except for the church, which most men would think of visiting only on Sunday if they visited it at all, Tenney's store was the only meeting house. Joe looked at the star-dappled sky, and he was struck by what seemed the odd thought that he had never seen stars crowd each other aside.

Out in the shadows a bird twittered, and Joe stopped in his tracks. He knew all the local birds by their songs, and he could give a fair imitation of nearly all, but this one he could not identify and it mystified him. He decided to his own satisfaction that it was a vagrant mocking bird that had uttered a few off-key notes.

He was so absorbed in thinking about the bird that he reached Tenney's Crossing almost before he realized it. By the thin light of an early-rising moon he saw a man leaning at a slight angle against Frawley Thompson's house. Without too much interest he recognized a local Indian known as Lard Head, a nickname he had acquired from a passion for slicking his black hair down with lard. Lard Head's other consuming ambition in life was to get as drunk as possible as often as possible, and obviously he was drunk again. He was fast asleep standing up, and doubtless he would go looking for something else to drink as soon as he awakened.

Yellow oil lamps glowed behind the store windows, and Joe set his course straight. He saw Elias Dorrance come out of the store and linger in the shadows, waiting for him, and he felt a rising irritation. He disliked nobody simply because they had more than he, but he wouldn't have liked Elias Dorrance under any conditions. Elias, who lived by the sweat and toil of others, was an alien here in this place where most men lived by their own labor. The banker spoke,

"Hi, Joe."

"Hi."

"Got your seeding done?" Dorrance asked casually.

"Why don't you come see for yourself. Elias?"

He brushed past and into the store, not thinking about the fact that he had rebuffed the man to whom he owed money—and not caring. Elias Dorrance was not being neighborly; he was just checking in advance to find whether he'd get a payment this fall or whether he'd have to foreclose on Joe's farm. Either way it made no difference; no amount of sweet talk would keep Elias from getting his due and no other kind would insult him if he saw money in the offing. Elias was a sponge. He absorbed everything but had an amazing facility for disgorging whatever would not benefit him.

Joe put Elias from his mind and went into the store. A kerosene lamp burned in front and another in back, and in between was all the amazing variety of goods that a store such as this must stock. Lester Tenney sold everything from pins to farm wagons, and he always had exactly the right amount of goods. This was no coincidence, and anywhere except here Lester Tenney might have been a great merchant. He had an amazing insight into his customers' exact needs. Nobody had ever had to wait for him to put in a special offer or to bring goods from St. Louis.

A tall man whose gaunt frame made him seem even taller, Tenney was rearranging goods on a shelf when Joe entered. Wispy brown hair fought desperately for a hold on his balding head, but after the first wondering glance few people noticed anything except Lester Tenney's eyes. They were clear and blue, and very deep, and oddly similar to two pieces of clear blue sky. The storekeeper gave Joe a friendly nod and a cheery greeting.

"Good evening, Joe."

"Hi, Les. What's new?"

The storekeeper inclined his head toward a little knot of men gathered under the second lamp at the rear of the store.

"Bibbers Townley came back. For the past hour he has been enchanting we peasants with his adventures in the west."

"So?"

"Go back and listen," Lester Tenney advised. "It's worth it. The way Bibbers tells it, compared to him Marco Polo, Christopher Columbus and Daniel Boone were strict amateurs."

Joe looked with interest toward the men in the rear. Pete Domley, five feet two and taciturn, stood against the pot-bellied stove which, at this season, needed no fire. There were Yancey and Lew Garrow, lean and sun-scorched. Joe saw old Tom Abend, wild Percy Pearl, John Geragty, Fellers Compton, Joab Ferris and Lance Trevelyan. All these men he had known for years, and the years had brought them closer together. Side by side they had fought forest fires, battled to keep rain-swollen creeks within their banks, built a new house or barn for some unfortunate whose building had been destroyed by fire, hunted and fished together. Not one of them was the enemy of any other.

Joe saw them almost as he would have seen his family, and he felt pleased because they were present. His eyes strayed to the young man who sat on the counter, with his right leg cocked nonchalantly over his left knee, and he reflected that Bibbers Townley had changed very little.

Three years ago, then in his late teens, Bibbers had left Tenney's Crossing. But there had been some preliminaries attending his departure.

For days preceding his final farewell he had absented himself. He returned riding a fancy thoroughbred with a new saddle and he had also got hold of two new Colt revolvers and an apparently endless supply of ammunition. For two weeks, the guns prominent on his hips, he had swaggered around announcing to anyone who would listen that no hick town was big enough to hold him. He was, he said, a man of parts and he was going into the west where there was room for men. At the slightest provocation, and sometimes at none, he had drawn either or both of the revolvers and shot at any convenient target.

Joe edged unobtrusively up beside the Garrow brothers and looked with interest at Bibbers Townley. Before Joe was born, settlers had started going west. Four families from Tenney's

Crossing had gone, and Joe himself had considered going. But a man didn't pull up stakes and move that easily. At least, he didn't when he had six young ones to think about.

"And how do you think," Bibbers was saying when Joe joined the group, "I got this?"

He held up his right hand so the assembled men could see a white scar running diagonally from the base of his little finger across the palm to the base of his thumb. There was an uncertain silence, and Joe sensed a rising scorn among his friends. He chuckled silently. Tenney had told him that Bibbers had been talking for an hour, and evidently he had also been lying for an hour. But he could still hold his audience partly because he interested them and partly because, never having been west, they could not completely distinguish Bibbers' fact from his fiction. Then,

"You stuck your hand in the church poor box," Percy Pearl said smoothly, "and the parson had left his knife in it. You grabbed the knife instead of the money you thought you'd get."

Hot rage flashed the other's cheeks, and he braced his hands on the counter as though he were about to jump down. Percy Pearl stood cool, unflinching, and Bibbers settled back. Nobody knew how Percy Pearl earned his living. He never worked and he never farmed and he was often gone for long periods. But he always had a good horse and everything else he needed. However, since he never did anything questionable around Tenney's Crossing, it was just as well not to ask questions. Rumors were current that Percy was good with a knife and equally good with a gun, and nobody had any reason to doubt it.

"Do you want," Bibbers blustered, "to make something of it?"

Percy's shrug was cold as ice. "You asked me."

"Shut up, Percy," Lew Garrow urged. "Let him talk."

"Yeah," Fellers Compton seconded. "Let him talk."

"All right," Percy agreed. "Go ahead and talk, Bibbers."

"I got this cut," Bibbers said, sure that he had won an encounter which he had not won at all, "in a fight with Apaches. It was in Arizona territory. . . ."

For a couple of moments Joe listened with great interest to a lurid tale of a battle which Bibbers had had with eight Apaches. He shot six of them, and with the last two it was knife to knife. At that point the story became so absurd that Joe lost himself in his own thoughts.

Bibbers was a liar, had always been one. However, select ten groups of men from ten parts of the country and they would average out about the same. The fact that any part of the country could produce its quota of asinine braggarts was not necessarily a reflection on the country. Joe unleashed himself completely.

Suppose a man owned everything on his land and the land too? He'd still have to work, but he wouldn't have to work until his whole insides tightened into a hard knot, and inner forces built up so tensely that he seemed ready to explode! When things got that bad, if it were not for Elias Dorrance, a man could take an hour and go hunting or fishing or just walking. Would it ever be that bad if land was something between a man and his God, and not between a man and his banker? Would it be bad at all if he knew that his children were going to find opportunities which they could never have here?

Then there was the rest of it; the eternal wondering about the unknown! Wouldn't a man rid himself of that burden if he went to see for himself?

"One time in Sonora," Bibbers Townley was saying, and Joe listened with little interest while Bibbers regaled his audience with another improbable adventure. Joe stared beyond the stove, and saw only the vision that arose in his own mind. He broke into Bibbers' account of what he had done one time in Sonora.

"What about land," he called.

"Land? Land, my friend? Do you want to know how they measure land in the west? I'll tell you."

Immediately he started telling, all about how he had staked out land by riding for three days straight west, then three south,

three east, and three north. Finally he came back to the starting
point and all the land he'd ridden around was his. Joe spat dis-
gustedly.

"You thinkin' of goin'?" John Geragty asked Joe.

"I've been pondering on it."

"So have I."

Joe slipped away from the group and his feet were light on the
starry path. The curtains had parted, at least for the time being,
and he had seen the bright promise. He must hurry home at once
so he could tell Emma about it too.

CHAPTER TWO

The Discussion

FOR A MOMENT after Joe had gone, Emma sat silently at the table. She was lonely and a little depressed, as she always was when Joe left her. Even when he went to work his fields in the morning, she looked forward to the noon hour when he would be home for lunch. If he did not care to stop working long enough to come home but wished to eat in the fields instead, Emma carried him a meal whenever she could think of a plausible excuse for so doing. It was not always possible because Barbara insisted on doing it. Emma smiled wistfully. Barbara thought she was saving her mother work when in reality she was robbing her of a privilege.

"What are you smiling about, Mother?" Barbara asked.

"I was thinking of your father."

Barbara looked curiously at her and Emma made no comment. For all her lovely girlhood Barbara was still a child. She must live a few years before she could even hope to understand some things, and it would be futile to try to explain them now. Love was always a fine and beautiful thing, but the quick, fierce passions of youth were only the first flames. The smoldering fires that were fed by years of working and struggling together really welded it so that two, in actuality, did become one. But no young person would ever understand that. Only experience could teach it.

Emma glanced with studied casualness at her lovely daughter. Approaching her fifteenth birthday, for more than a year Barbara had had a large contingent of suitors. All were gawky youths who stumbled over their own feet, never knew what to do with their elbows, and were apt to stutter or stammer when disconcerted. Barbara accepted them with an almost regal poise the while she interested herself seriously in none, and that pleased Emma. She herself had married at sixteen, which was early enough. Emma thought with mingled pity and amusement of Lucy Trevelyan, whose fifteen-year-old Mary had been urged upon every eligible man in the neighborhood and who was now going around a second time. It was more than a question of just getting a man. It had to be the right man and, for Barbara, Emma wanted as much happiness as she had found with Joe.

Emma looked again at her daughter, who was staring dreamily across the table. After a moment, the youngster spoke,

"Why didn't you go to the store with Dad?"

"With all those men!" Emma was half horrified.

Barbara said thoughtfully, "I suppose it would be awkward. But you work very hard, too. If it relaxes Dad to go to the store, it should relax you."

Emma laughed. "I'd be as out of place there as your father would at a sewing bee!"

"When I get married," Barbara said firmly, "I'm going everywhere my husband goes. Everywhere!"

Tad snorted derisively, and left his chair to hone his beloved knife.

"Don't make fun of your sister, Tad."

"I didn't say nothin'," Tad protested.

"'I didn't say anything,'" Emma corrected.

"Yes, Ma."

"Let me hear you say it."

"I didn't say anything," Tad mumbled.

Emma turned from him and the incident had come, passed and was forgotten. She had about her a quality that demanded respect and attention, but which never left a sting.

In passing, Emma sometimes wondered at how much she herself had changed during the years of her marriage. From a gentle girl, much in awe of her father, admiring Joe from a distance and struck quite speechless when he asked her to marry him, she had acquired over the years both firmness and authority in her dealings with the children. Joe loved to play with his children when they were little, and he admired them as they grew older, but when it came to discipline he didn't appear to know how to go about it. With Tad he sometimes exploded, sometimes cuffed his ears and sometimes turned his back in despair. With the others he somehow subtracted himself, so that Emma was left in charge of discipline. Perhaps the trouble was that an ordinary reprimand would have seemed unsuitable to the wonderful creatures he thought them to be. Whatever the reason, over the years Emma had found that while all decisions regarding the children were discussed between Joe and herself, with Joe often playing a larger part than she did in the actual deciding, it was usually Emma alone who had to put the decisions into effect. She smiled ruefully. Nobody, not even Joe—*especially* not Joe—realized that Emma still had safely hidden away, some of the timidity of her younger years. Within the home, in relation to the children, she was undoubtedly a tower of strength.

Baby Emma slid from her chair to climb upon her mother's lap and lay her head on Emma's shoulder. Emma encircled her with a gentle arm.

She knew that Joe was in awe of Barbara, stood on just about an even footing with Tad, and regarded the other four as lovable, cuddly beings who were still too young to have any real identities of their own. But it was Emma who understood their hearts and, much of the time, their minds.

Proud of Barbara's grace and beauty, she still saw beyond it. Barbara was not, as Joe thought, fragile of body. She did have a generous nature and a delicate, sensitive mind that must either encompass all or reject all. There were times when Emma trembled for her and what the future might do to her. To Emma she was an opening bud, almost ready to bloom, and if blossoms were not tenderly nurtured they faced certain destruction. Emma hoped and prayed that the common sense and almost mature judgment which Barbara was already displaying would come to her aid when she most needed it.

Tad was a reflection of Joe, and yet he was not Joe. Behind Tad's wild impulses and rash acts, Emma saw the man to be. Tad would be a good man, like his father, and Emma knew that she was guilty of no heresy when she hoped that he might be even more capable and talented. Joe himself hoped that. He wanted everything for his children.

Baby Joe was a child of infinite patience. Given a problem, such as a knotted piece of string, he kept doggedly at it until every knot was untied and the string straight. Emma was grateful and happy for him, for she knew that the world never had enough people who were not afraid of problems. One day Joe would be outstanding.

Alfred was the soul of mischief. Quick and alert, he missed no opportunity for fun or pranks. Once, in all innocence, he had offered a present to Barbara and put in her outstretched hand a large black beetle. He had gone into gales of laughter when Barbara, who shrank from all insects, flung the beetle from her. Imaginative, Alfred was forever inventing games that he could play alone or in which all might share.

Carlyle had been born to laughter and an appreciation of the beautiful. From the very first, a bright butterfly, a stray sunbeam, a bit of colored ribbon, a colored leaf, had caught and held his fascinated attention. The first word he'd ever spoken had not been the traditional "mama," but "pretty." Emma treasured him greatly, and there was a tradition in her family that one of her ancestors had painted some of the world's outstanding masterpieces. Though she knew that she would never attempt to dictate the lives of her children, Emma had more than a faint hope that artistic talent would live again in Carlyle.

But it was the raven-haired child in her lap whom Emma cherished just a bit more than the rest. It was not because Emma saw her own image there, but because baby Emma was the sickly one.

She was subject to sudden, raging fevers that left her pale and weak. More than once they had despaired of her life. But she had always come through and no night passed that Emma did not offer up a prayer that she would always continue to do so. The child turned to smile sleepily at her mother.

"Time for bed, darling?" Emma coaxed.

"Yes, Mama."

Emma carried her into the living room, put her on a chair and returned to the kitchen to dip a pan of water from a kettle warming on the stove. Tenderly she removed the clothing from baby Emma's fragile little body, washed her daughter, put her night dress on and carried her into bed. She leaned over to kiss the child twice on each cheek and watched her snuggle happily beneath the quilts. This was a ritual that Emma herself must always perform. Barbara could put the other young children to bed, but Emma always had to take care of baby Emma.

Barbara had the giggling Carlyle in her arms when Emma went back into the kitchen. In passing, she patted the child's curly head and started to wash her dishes. Her china was carefully stored in the new cupboard and there it would remain until the children were big enough to respect it. Emma remembered poignantly one of her minor heartbreaks of years ago. The Casper family, departing for the west, had decided that their china was too frail to stand the trip so they'd given it to Emma. It was lovely, delicate ware that had come across an ocean, been used by the Caspers in New York, and brought by them to Missouri.

Emma delighted in its feel, and her heart lifted when she merely looked at it. Often she speculated about its history. It was ancient and expensive, the sort of china wealthy people of good taste would buy. Had it come from some castle in England, or perhaps Spain? Who were the people, now probably long dead, who had made merry over it? Delighted and thrilled, Emma had set the table with it. But Barbara, at the time their only child, was a baby then and she had pushed her cup and plate onto the floor where they shattered.

Emma put the rest away and used her old dishes until they, too, were broken. Joe, always handy with tools, had made her wooden plates, bowls, and cups. He had used hard, seasoned maple, and had worked endlessly with it until it was polished almost to the consistency of china. As each new baby arrived, Joe had made more table ware. They were almost alike, but not exactly so, and Emma had handled and washed them so often that every line in every piece was familiar. She knew by touch which plate, cup, or bowl, belonged to whom, and that gave her a good feeling. Just as it was part of Joe's life to respond intimately to the goodness in new-turned earth, it was part of hers to care for the various things that meant security for her family. Security, to Emma, meant no one big thing but a host of little ones.

She soaked her hands in the warm water, liking the feel of that too, while she washed the dishes with a soapy cloth. Rinsing them in clean water, she stacked them on the table beside her. She did it carefully, meticulously. Wooden dishes could not break, but it was part of her nature to be meticulous and nothing at all was so easy to get that one could afford to be careless with it. Besides, the dishes were precious. Joe had spent long hours, night hours when he could not work in the fields, making and polishing them. Where a less particular man would have called them good enough, Joe had worked on. He did not, he said, want to take the chance of any slivers finding their way into baby mouths.

Barbara brought the pajamaed Carlyle out for his good-night kiss and took him in to bed. She stooped for Alfred. Quick as a deer, he darted behind a chair and made faces at his sister. When Barbara went to the chair, Alfred, howling with glee, ran to his mother and clasped both arms about her. Emma turned to him. She herself was tired, and a bit out of patience, and she spoke more sharply than she ordinarily talked to any of the children.

"Go to bed now, Ally."

"Do' wanna."

"Alfred, go with Barbara!"

Meekly Alfred surrendered himself to Barbara's arms, and was carried into the other room for his bath. Emma shook her head to dislodge a wisp of hair that had fallen over her eye. There were rare occasions when she worried about Alfred too. She imagined that Percy Pearl must have been a great deal like him when he was a baby, and though she liked Percy, she would not want any of her children to imitate his way of life. Like everyone else, she really did not know how Percy lived. But there were rumors, and Emma suspected more. She comforted herself with the thought that there was really nothing to worry about. Thousands of children were mischievous. If all of them turned out badly, the world would be made up largely of bad people.

Emma dried her dishes as carefully as she had washed them and stacked them in the cupboard. She poured her dish water down the drain, an ingenious wooden spout that Joe had also constructed and which led into a cesspool beside the house. Vigorously she began to scrub her table and the wooden sink. In all their years together, except to praise her cooking, Joe had never once commented on the way she kept house. That had been a cause of minor dissension at first. Emma had worked for hours, hand-stitching the new curtains. Proudly she draped the windows, and when Joe came in he didn't even appear to notice. But the years had taught her much.

Joe regarded the house as exclusively her domain and the fields as his, though he always wanted to know what she cared to have in the family vegetable garden and sometimes asked her advice as to what crops he should plant. She warmed to him because he did, for it proved that he respected her. Concerning the house, his very lack of comment was approval. Emma poured clean water into her dish pans and scrubbed them while Barbara brought Alfred in for his kiss and took Joe. Carefully, Emma swept the floor and emptied the trash into the kitchen wastebasket, a hollow stump that Joe had further hollowed and so arranged that it had both a dust-tight bottom and a hinged cover.

Barbara came in with baby Joe, and after Emma kissed him, the girl took him to bed. Barbara re-entered the kitchen.

"Aren't you about finished, Mother?"

"Almost. Tad, take yourself off to bed now."

"Already?" Tad was testing the razor-keen blade of his newly honed knife.

"It's time. Take your bath and go to bed."

"Do I have to take a bath? I swam in the crick today."

"The 'creek,'" Emma corrected firmly. "If you swam you needn't bathe. But go to bed."

"It's too early," he complained.

"Tad!"

"Yes, Ma."

Tad took himself toward the bedroom and emerged, yawning, for his good-night kiss. After he had gone, Emma smiled covertly. Tad, at eight, resented his own childhood fiercely. He was in an almost ferocious rush to grow up so he could avail himself of what, in his own mind, were all the privileges of adulthood. But he still would not go to bed without his mother's kiss.

Emma seated herself at the table for the moment contented to rest. This, for her, was a time of contentment and soul-satisfying joy. She arose to each new day as though it were a complete new challenge that was sure to present its opportunities but might offer hazards, too. But the night always meant peace, and to know that her younger children were safe in bed brought happiness to Emma's heart. Now she knew only a little uneasiness because Joe was still absent. Barbara washed her hands and face, and let her satiny, tawny hair cascade down her shoulders.

"Are we going to the Trevelyans' barn dance Saturday night, Mother?"

"I think so."

"Would you mind very much if I did not go with you?"

Emma glanced curiously at her. "Why not?"

"Well, Johnny Abend asked if he could take me. So did Billy Trevelyan and Allan Geragty. It would be fun if you let me go with one of them."

Emma's eyes sparkled with humor. "And which of the three are you going to honor?"

Barbara wrinkled her nose. "Allan Geragty is a smart aleck. I don't like him."

Emma murmured, "Dear, a choice of only two escorts! Yes, you may go."

"Thank you. I believe I'll set outside for a little while, Mother."

"All right."

Barbara opened the door and closed it quietly behind her. Emma knew that she was going only to look at the stars, and that was good because all young people should have trysts with stars. They might never pull one out of the sky and have it for their own, but they could always try. Emma fell into a mood of sober reflection.

The years had brought her a fair measure of wisdom, and at thirty-two she knew a great deal which she had not known when, at sixteen, she became Joe's wife. Among other things, she knew now that her father had been a martinet. He knew, he thought, the only true way, and all about him must follow or risk his wrath. If Emma regretted any years of her married life, it was the first five when she had insisted that she must not leave her father. But she had honestly known of nothing else that she might do.

Since babyhood she had been under her father's influence, and in his opinion women must always take a secondary place. One by one, as her six older brothers attained their majority, they had quarreled with their father and left home. Then the old man had suffered a series of spasms, and now Emma wondered if they were not simulated spasms designed to keep his last remaining child at his side. But she had loved him and pitied him and remained under his influence. She had brought upon her husband five painful and unproductive years. But those five years had taught Emma the true measure of Joe's worth. In spite of old Caleb's abuse, Joe had given him the fullest help of which a man is capable. He had been in the fields from the first light of morning until the last lingering glow of twilight. And he had waited without a word of complaint until Emma herself was willing to leave. With a fresh surge of love and gratitude she thought about his patient waiting, more difficult for him than for many another. Because he had waited until she was fully ready, she had felt obliged to conceal from him the real anguish she felt when, looking back from the wagon that was carrying them away, she saw Caleb, a strangely shrunken, isolated figure, standing in the doorway of his empty home.

But it was not only pity for Caleb that tore at her. It was that her own roots ran deep, that Caleb's home had been her home for all of her life, that now she and Joe and Barbara had no home at all other than the quarters that would be given to them on the farm where Joe would be working. To be without her own home was a personal agony that she had shared with no one, but it was an agony that had enabled her to save and scrimp and put aside every penny until she could hold out her hands to Joe with enough money in them to buy a place of their own.

Now she held the spare copper lamp base in her hands, and with a soft piece of cloth she rubbed it and rubbed it until she could see mirrored in it the smiling, contented outlines of her own face. For a few precious minutes she dared to hope that, in spite of the troublesome debt, their most difficult years were behind them.

Barbara came in, stifling a yawn with her hand. "I think I'll go to bed too, Mother."

"Are you tired, darling?"

"Lazy, I suppose."

Barbara stooped to pick up a toy wagon—another of Joe's products—that Alfred and Carlyle had left on the floor. She put it in its proper place on a shelf, dipped a pan of water, and bathed herself. Night-dressed, she kissed her mother good night. Emma sat alone.

For eight years she had gone with Joe from farm to farm, where he worked for a house, food, and small wages. But he had always fed and clothed his family, and where other men had given up in despair, taken to drink, or even abandoned their families, Joe had still plodded on. Still, he was more than a plodder. Plodding was his way of making a good from what otherwise would have been a bad situation.

Just as she herself had wanted a home, Joe had wanted his own land, and to be his own master. Together they had worked and saved and sacrificed, until the day came when they were able to realize their ambition. For her it was the end of the journey. She had come home. The foundation of their life was laid. From here on all the work they did would be toward making their home and their land completely their own, forever. Yet she had seen as the year passed that Joe was somehow not content, and thinking about him now, a familiar fear began to tug at her again. She knew the wild fires that flared beneath Joe's placid exterior, and she was at a loss to explain them. The debt against which he fretted so angrily was to her bothersome but surely not intolerable. Bit by bit they would pay it off, and meanwhile they could live comfortably, each year expanding their little home to meet their expanding needs.

She started when she thought she heard his footstep, then sank back in her chair. Five minutes later the door opened quietly and Joe tiptoed in. Emma looked at his flushed cheeks and excited eyes, and for a moment she was startled. Men looked like that when they drank too much, but Joe didn't drink. However, he had surely partaken of some heady draught. Emma asked,

"Are you all right, Joe?"

"Oh sure. I'm all right. I was down at the store. Bibbers Townley's there. He just came back from the west."

He sat beside her, his eyes glowing, and Emma looked wonderingly at him. She had never seen him just this way before.

"Tell me, Joe," she urged.

He blurted, "How would you like to go west?"

A great fist seemed to have closed about her throat, and for a moment she could not breathe. After a time her breath came back, and her voice. But Joe was already going on, leaning forward tensely in his chair, his face eager and alive.

"There's land in the west, Emma! Land for us! For Tad, Joe, Alfred and Carlyle! Land for whoever Barbara and baby Emma might marry! It's for the *taking!*"

"There's land right here, Joe," she managed to say. "Our own land."

There was quick impatience in his voice as he repeated her words, "Our own land? I'll be able to pay Elias Dorrance $50 this fall, and out of that $40 goes for interest, and $10 off on what we owe."

"Still, it's something," she said hastily. "Ten off is something! Little by little, Joe, we'll make the land our own."

"How many years?" he demanded almost angrily. "How many more years will it take?"

She could not answer him, not only because she did not know the answer but because the question wasn't really a question. It was an accusation. He seemed to be accusing her of unwillingness to see something that was plain enough to Joe, that was right out there in front of them.

He was looking at her now, his whole face full of questioning. She avoided his eyes. "Let's think about it," she said. "The plowing and seeding's already done for this year. Let's think about it this year, and come next spring we'll talk about it again."

"Come next spring?" he asked vaguely. All of the glow faded from his face. Even his lips grew pale, and in the sudden quiet she could hear his breathing, quick and shallow and weary. He seemed spent, as though all the weariness of many weeks of work had been piled upon him all at once in this moment.

He rose and shuffled to the window. Directly overhead a lone star glittered, cold and unyielding, and he watched it silently.

Emma's heart ached for him, but what could she do? How could he ask her to do this terrible thing, to pull up her roots again and turn her back on all that they had so painfully, so hopefully gathered together into this little house? She couldn't do it, not even for Joe, even though she loved him as dearly as she loved life itself.

She went to him and stood beside him at the window. Soon he put his arm about her. She dropped her head on his shoulder and a shudder went through her, so that she held to him convulsively.

"Forgive me, Joe," she whispered. "I'm not brave and strong the way you think. I'm afraid, Joe. I love this house, and I'm frightened to leave it."

He held her close, and could find no words. A door had been closed between them, somehow, and he could not get through to her, to explain to her about the west. Maybe another year. Maybe. . . .

CHAPTER THREE

The Destroyers

JOE WAS so weary of body and brain that the things he saw shimmered behind a haze that was born of no weather, but in his own mind. He was detached from almost everything, a lone being in a lone world, and the only thread that connected him with anything else was the smooth handle of the ax which he carried in his hand. The ax was real as it could be real only to one who had just spent eleven hours using it. At the same time, and while he reeled with fatigue, Joe counted his blessings.

Now the oats were high and the young corn in tassel. The family vegetable garden was thriving, the hay was not yet ripe enough for the scythe, and there were many more trees to cut on Joe's sixteen acres of timber. Clearing all sixteen acres was a major task and one that Joe didn't even hope to complete for several years because he could work in the timber only when there was nothing else to do. However, he intended to chop and trim many more trees.

He was exhausted, but the restlessness that had possessed him a month earlier was now gone, and for the present he was contented. Preparing the land to grow crops and planting them had been hard work. But now it was finished and when the crops were harvested he would be able to feed his family and livestock through the winter. All the surplus must be sold to satisfy Elias Dorrance. Yet, for the moment Joe harbored no special resentment against him. Bankers were necessary, and Elias had helped Joe when he needed help.

Carefully, as a man who loves good tools will, Joe hung the ax on its wooden pegs in the tool shed, and then took it down again to test both bits with his thumb. An ax had to be razor-sharp, actually capable of shaving, if a man was to do good work with it, and whoever put a tool away in good shape would find it in the same shape when he needed it again. Joe found the ax so sharp that he must have honed it after felling the last tree. He grinned; he was more tired than he'd thought because he couldn't remember sharpening the ax.

He leaned against the tool shed's wall, giving himself to the luxury of doing nothing at all. He watched Barbara, serene and lovely, going toward the pig pen with a pail of swill and he knew a moment's sheer pleasure. He gave no thought to the incongruity of the scene, that anyone should be able to look graceful while feeding pigs, but felt only delight because he saw something lithe and beautiful.

Joe yawned. He had been very wakeful last night. Lying beside Emma, he had watched the moon wane and the first faint streaks of dawn creep like stealthy thieves out of the sky. Only then had he gone to sleep, and soon afterward it had been time to get up and go to work again.

He went to the well, drew a bucket of water, and washed his face and hands. Instead of going to the store tonight he would go to bed after the evening meal. The empty swill pail in hand, Barbara came to stand beside him and her slim figure was bent slightly backward, as though by a mysterious wind created by her own spirit.

She said, "You look tired."

"Now don't you fret your head about me!"

She smiled. "I will if I want to. How did it go today?"

"Good enough. How are the pigs?"

"Eleanor," Barbara said seriously, "keeps shoving Horace out of the trough. She won't let him eat."

Joe said dryly, "Eleanor has the manners of a pig, huh?"

She laughed, and Joe looked at her red-stained fingers. He knew without being told that Barbara, and probably all the rest except the babies, Alfred and Carlyle, had spent at least a part of their day gathering wild berries. Plucking and preserving wild fruit was a job the women folk and youngsters could do, and it was inevitable as summer itself. Joe fell back on a stock question,

"Where's Tad?"

"He went off in the woods by himself."

"Didn't he help you?"

"Oh yes. Mother made him."

Joe grinned inwardly. Emma seldom raised her voice to any of the youngsters and she never struck any of them. But somehow she managed prompt and unquestioning obedience to any order she issued, and that was more than Joe could do. There was about his wife a mysterious force which was always recognizable, but which Joe could not explain. It was strange, he reflected in passing, that this force did not carry over into anything outside the immediate family. It was strange that the thought of leaving the house should be so fearsome when in other respects Emma was so sure of herself. But he brushed the thought aside, as he had brushed it aside each time it came to plague him.

Joe entered the house and kissed Emma, and for the moment his weariness lifted. He wrinkled his nose.

"Something smells good!"

"Raspberry preserves. We'll try some tomorrow, but we can't now because it isn't done. We found good picking; some of those berries were as big as my thumb."

A black kettle in which simmered the fruits gathered that day was pushed toward the back of the stove. Spicy odors filled the room, and Joe knew that, when snow lay deep on the ground, Emma would bring her jams, jellies and preserves from the shelves where she kept them and they would be a little bit of the summer back again. Joe remembered the delights of winter morning feasts when all had spread pancakes a quarter inch thick with jam, and he smacked his lips.

The four younger children, their hands stained like Barbara's, rushed toward him and he braced himself to meet their charge.

The youngsters hadn't anyone except one another to play with and they always looked forward to his arrival. He plumbed his brain for a story to tell them or a little play to act out. Then Emma turned from the stove and spoke to the children:

"Your horses are trampling everything in the house and I won't have it. Tie them up again."

The happy youngsters returned to the game, obviously a game of horses that they had been playing, and Joe felt a swelling gratitude. It would be nice to rest, and Emma had known it. At the same time he felt a vast admiration for his wife; she had relieved him of any more responsibility without offending the children. It went to prove all over again what Joe had always suspected; for all their supposed fragility, and despite the fact that they were allegedly the weaker sex, women had strength and power about which men knew nothing. Strength and power, that is, when it came to dealing with their children. Regarding other things, though, such as making a sensible move in a sensible direction—but again he brushed the thought aside. He sank into a chair, and with a real effort managed to keep from going to sleep.

"How was it today?" Emma asked.

"I had a good day."

All things considered, he had had a good day. There was much about ax work that he enjoyed. An ax in the hands of a man who knew how to use it ceased to be a mere tool and became a precision instrument. To an ax man, an ax was much like a good rifle to a hunter.

"Are you going to cut more trees?" Emma asked.

"I'll work in the timber until the hay needs cutting."

That was all they said but that was all they had to say because the rest fell into a precise pattern. When the trees were felled and trimmed some would be split into rails for rail fences and the rest used for firewood. As soon as snow eliminated the danger of forest fire the brush would be burned. That was always a minor festival. The whole family turned out for the brush burning. The children watched, fascinated, while leaping flames climbed skyward through crackling branches. Then, while Joe raked the un-burned branches together and fired them, Tad and baby Emma built a snow man or a snow fort for the delectation of the rest. It usually ended with Emma and Barbara serving a lunch beside still-glowing coals and Joe always saved enough branches so everyone could have a dry seat.

Emma went to the door and called "Tad!" and as though the eight-year-old were on some invisible leash that attached himself to his mother, he appeared out of the lowering night. His seal-sleek hair proved that he had already washed at the well, but no mere water could suffice for Tad now. His face and arms were laced with deep gashes from which blood was again beginning to ooze, and there were fang marks on his upper forearms.

Joe said in astonishment, "What the dickens happened to you?"

"I caught a wildcat!" Tad said gleefully. "Caught him right in a snare I set myself!"

"Don't you know better than to fool around with wildcats?"

"It's only a little one," Tad said, as though that explained every-thing. "Not hardly big enough to chew anything yet. Got him in the barn, I have. I'm goin' to tame him."

"Get rid of him," Joe ordered.

"Aw, Pa!"

Joe was inflexible, "Get rid of him now! One thing we don't need around here, it's a wildcat!"

He caught up a lantern, lighted it, and with Tad trotting pro-testing at his heels, stamped out to the barn. The wildcat had al-ready seen to its own liberation. Tad had put him in one of the mules' feed boxes, covered it with a board, and weighted the board with a rock. The imprisoned cat had worked the board free and slipped away.

"Blast his ornery hide!" Tad ejaculated.

Joe said sternly, "What's that you said?"

"You say it."

"So you can too, huh? Get this, don't let me ever again hear you say anything that even sounds like a cuss word. And no more wildcats."

"It was only a little one."

"You heard me!"

Tad's face was stubborn, a little sullen. For a moment he said nothing and Joe repeated,

"You heard me!"

"Yes, Pa."

Joe lighted their way back to the house, blew the lantern out before he entered and hung it on a wooden peg. The gesture was automatic, and brought about by a lifetime of necessarily frugal living. One never stinted his family, himself, or his animals, in that order, on food. But one never wasted anything at all that cost money. Though the circuit-riding Reverend Haines often thundered to those of his flock who lived in Tenney's Crossing that money was the root of all evil, Joe had never believed that. Money was simply the hardest of all things to come by.

For once hardly savoring the food—and Emma had an almost magic touch with the plainest of viands—Joe ate because it was necessary to eat. Only vaguely was he aware of Barbara's keeping a watchful eye on the chattering younger children; of Tad, sullenly disappointed and still rebellious but not letting that interfere with his always prodigious appetite. He seemed closest to Emma, in whom everything else always seemed to center, and he knew that she was watching him while she worried about him. Before very long he would be asleep.

The youngsters slid from their chairs and went back to the bits of string they had been playing with. Obviously, for the time being, Emma's sadirons were horses because they were all tied at different places around the room. They wouldn't need him tonight, and Joe excused himself.

"Reckon I'll go see if the sky's still in place."

He rose from the table and stepped outside into the pleasant summer night. There was only blackness, unrelieved by any hint of moon or star light. Tad's dog came to wag a welcoming tail and sniff, and even while Joe petted the dog he thought that Mike wouldn't herd stock and he wouldn't hunt except with Tad. Therefore, in a land where everything had to earn its keep, he was useless. But young ones had to have something and Tad liked his pet largely, Joe suspected, because Mike could whip any other dog, or any other two dogs, in the whole country.

Joe breathed his fill of the night air, went back into the house, and for a few moments idly watched his four younger children at their play. Emma and Barbara were doing the dishes and, with a trace of sullenness still lingering about him, Tad sat at the table cutting a new sheath for his knife. Joe leaned against the door jamb and drowsed for a second. He seemed to be back in Tenney's store, listening to tales of unlimited land and unlimited opportunity in the west, and he saw his children with those opportunities before them. Joe shook himself awake.

He felt numb with fatigue as he took off his clothes and methodically hung them up. Though there were nights when he liked to stay late with the men at Tenney's store, tonight sleep was more inviting. But for a few minutes he lay wide awake and he knitted his brows because he was troubled about something. However, it was nothing he could clearly define and after a while Joe forced it from his mind. As soon as he did, he fell into a sound slumber. When he awakened, gray dawn again lingered behind the curtains with which Emma had draped the windows. Not for another three quarters of an hour would the rising sun change the gray to gold, and for a few moments Joe knew sheer contentment. Restful slumber had driven away the exhaustion and physical aches of the night before. Beside him, Emma still slept soundly.

Then, out in the lightening morning, Tad's dog barked. Emma came slowly awake, and turned to smile at him.

"Good morning."

"Good morning, darling."

He moved a little nearer, feeling the warmth of her body against his. Joe remembered his youth and bachelor days as a somewhat fruitless period, and he had not reached fulfillment until his marriage. Their life had never been easy. But it had always been good and this was one of the best parts of every day. For a little while they could be together in complete idleness, each happy because the other was near. They were rested and refreshed, ready to cope with the problems, big and small, that the day might bring. But in the morning, just before they arose, the big problems seemed small, and the small ones trifling.

"What's the dog barking at?" Emma asked drowsily.

"He's probably found a varmint out in the field. I'll go see. You rest a while yet."

Joe slipped out of bed, stretched luxuriously, stripped off his night shirt and put on his clothes. He went to the door, swung it open and stared stupidly at what he saw.

A rangy black steer stood in the center of the trampled corn patch, chewing placidly on a stalk of corn that projected like a green stick from its mouth. A herd of varicolored cows and steers were foraging listlessly or switching tails in what remained of the oat field. The vegetable garden lay in ruins. Though most of the cattle had filled their stomachs and were now contented to digest the rich fare they had eaten, a few calves and yearlings were still cropping eagerly at anything green that remained.

Joe's immediate reaction was a vast weakness, as though his body were no longer a solid thing but a liquid mass. He wilted like a melting candle, everything that had gone to make him suddenly dissolved, and only the feeble flame of a sputtering wick remained to prove that there ever had been anything else. Then he braced himeslf and fought back.

His whole life had been a struggle, with the odds tremendously against him. He'd been close to the breaking point only a month ago, when the desire to go west had swept around him like a flame, and he'd been forced to blot it out and forget it. Forgetting it had left him curiously empty and deflated. But he'd pulled himself together and knuckled down to the job of making this crop a good one. Now the crop lay before him, destroyed. A seething anger began slowly to gather in Joe's chest, and he held on to the doorframe to steady himself.

Emma appeared at his shoulder, and when he looked at her Joe saw that her face was pale. She said nothing but her comforting arm slipped about him. Joe said inanely,

"They're Pete Domley's cattle."

"I know."

Joe exploded, "I'll—!"

He wheeled, went back into the bedroom, and took the rifle from the pegs where he had hung it. His brain was on fire, so that priming and loading the weapon were mechanical functions which he knew nothing about but which he did well because he had done them so often. Not seeing anything else, aware only that destroyers had come to take that which rightly belonged to Joe's family, he leaned against the door jamb and took careful aim at the black steer. His finger tightened on the trigger when Emma's voice cut through the red mists that seethed in his brain.

"No, Joe!"

She looked almost ill, but there was desperation in her words that was far more effective than any physical barrier. She spoke again,

"It is not the way."

The red rage that flamed in his brain burned less hotly. He lowered the gun so that its stock rested on the floor, and looked from her to the destroying cattle. Then sanity reasserted itself. He put the rifle back on its pegs and said dully,

"I'll drive them away."

Joe strode toward the cattle with Tad's dog at his heels. He was well aware that it was futile to drive the raiders away for there was no more damage to be done. Yet he knew that the cattle did not belong where they were, and since there was no one else to chase them, he must.

The rangy black steer in the corn patch looked at him with mildly surprised eyes as Joe approached. He caught up a fallen corn stalk, slashed viciously at the animal's rump, and the steer galloped off to join those in the oat field. A blocky white and black cow with a calf at her heels bolted toward the end of the field and the rest followed. They crowded clumsily through the hedge that marked the boundary of Joe's land and went back into their pasture. There they all stopped to look, as though telling him that they knew they'd done wrong but informing him that they had a right to be where they were. When Joe did not pursue them any farther, the cattle wandered toward their water hole and Joe noted mechanically that there were many more than there had been. Pete had several herds which he kept in different pastures. Probably, guided by the mysterious senses which animals possess and which no man can explain, one or more of the other herds had come to join the cattle Pete kept here and together they had organized the raid.

Joe tossed his head furiously, and the veins in his head and neck were so taut that they stood out and throbbed visibly. The old restlessness returned with a force so overwhelming that it was almost impossible to resist it. He felt himself grow huge, and it seemed that if he took a step in one direction he would be right among the marauding cattle. A step in the other direction would be sure to bring him face to face with Elias Dorrance. There was no place to take his family where they would not be hemmed in and preyed upon by something. Unaccountably he thought of that night when he had walked to Tenney's store and looked at the stars that never shouldered each other aside. Joe voiced his explosive thoughts to the startled dog:

"This place is just too blasted small!"

The dog at his heels, Joe walked back to the house. Crushing disappointment was a luxury, and he had never been able to afford luxuries. And the past was forever lost, and now this belonged to the past. The fields could be plowed and planted again, and with luck the crops would mature before frost killed them.

Joe looked at Emma, still standing mutely in the doorway, and a hot knife turned in his heart. She seemed, with her eyes, to be asking him for forgiveness. If they'd gone west when he wanted to go, they wouldn't be faced now with the destruction of the whole summer's work. He could see in Emma's eyes the fear that things would get even worse than they were, that the new crop that Joe would start to plant now might be lost just as the present crop was already lost, and that they would go into the winter with no money, no feed for the animals, no provisions for the family.

He groped for words to comfort her, and could think of only, "I chased them. Everything's all right now."

"I—I'm terribly sorry, Joe." Her voice trembled.

"Now don't you go fretting your head! I'll get new crops in!"

She said uncertainly, "It's very late for new crops."

He forced what he hoped was a careless laugh, and wished he hadn't done so because she knew it was forced. Joe berated himself silently. Above all he wanted to soothe, to spare her, and there was no way. Their crops, their livelihood, was gone. It was more than a serious situation. It was a desperate one and she knew it as well as he did, but he tried.

"Now just don't you fret. Everything's all right."

She said, "Don't tell me that, Joe."

Though it was morning, with the day scarcely started, she turned tiredly to the stove. Joe sat down to await the meal she would give him. This was summer. Their ham, bacon, sausage, and other smoked meats, had long since been exhausted. Not until the advancing season brought weather cold enough to keep meat would they have any except the wild things they shot. Expertly, Emma mixed milk with eggs and scrambled them in a skillet. She laid slices of homemade bread on the stove until they toasted, and lathered the toast thickly with home-churned butter.

Flushed with sleep, Barbara emerged from the room where she slept with her sister and went outside to the well. When she came back, freshly washed, she had seen the havoc wrought by the cows. She looked at her mother's face, and at her father's, and was tactfully silent. She was young and healthy, and, in spite of the disaster, she looked radiant, and for some reason that he could not explain, Joe felt better. Elemental himself, he thought of elemental things. Though he could not have explained it, part of the awe Barbara inspired in him sprang from the fact that she was a lovely young woman in whom, symbolically, all the hope of the future lay. Certainly, without her, there could be no future. Joe started eating the heaping plate of scrambled eggs and toast that Emma gave him, and he was half through his meal when there was a timid knock at the door.

Joe said, "Come in."

The door opened and Pete Domley stood framed within it. Somehow he seemed to have shrunk to half his small stature, as though he were a dwarf that had come begging. His eyes were red from lack of sleep, and blue bags were pendant beneath them. Through the open door, Joe caught a glimpse of the white horse Pete had ridden here. For a second Joe's anger flared anew; if Pete had watched his cattle the crops would not be ruined. Pity for this small man who was usually as aggressive as a bantam rooster, but who now was so abject, stole Joe's anger. He said,

"Have some breakfast, Pete."

Pete came through the door, a slow and tired man. He said, "Lance Trevelyan told me last night they'd gone, Joe. They left their pasture on Twoaday Crick and just went. You can't always figure what critters will do."

Joe said, "I know."

"I thought sure," Pete said, "that they'd head for the high pastures above Twoaday. I looked there until almost sun-up."

"So?"

"So I'll pay you, Joe. You or Elias Dorrance, whichever way you want it."

Joe repeated, "Have some breakfast, Pete."

Pete sat down and Emma served him. Joe ate without speaking, and he watched Pete devour his breakfast listlessly. Beef in St. Louis brought fantastic prices, and probably in eastern cities it brought prices even more fabulous. Joe didn't know. He did know that the man who raised that beef on the hoof, and who was the primary provider of the markets, didn't get the most money. Pete, with seven young ones of his own, worked hard. Often he worked much for very little return.

Besides, Pete had ridden all night to find his missing cattle. Finally realizing the truth, he must have looked for them at other farms before he came to see Joe. No man could possibly ask more than that from any other man, and who knew what a fool steer would decide to do? The most a person looking for cattle in the black of night could do was guess, and if the guess went wrong, what then? Pete Domley hadn't eaten or trampled Joe's oats, corn, and vegetables. Pete's cattle had. There was, Joe felt, no more sense in crucifying Pete than there had been in nailing Christ to the Cross. Pete finished his breakfast, and after a moment's silence he said,

"Who'll I pay, Joe? You or Elias?"

"Neither, Pete."

Pete said stubbornly, "What's right is right."

"Look, you buy me some more seed and let it go at that."

Pete opened surprised eyes. "You going to plant again?"

"What else?"

"Well—You know where I live and the money will be there when you go to plant."

Pete mounted his tired horse and rode homeward. Moodily, with mingled pity and sadness, Joe watched him go. Pete wasn't really to blame. But he felt that he was. He had, however unwittingly, dealt mortal injury to his very good friend and that thought would forever haunt him.

Joe wandered out to his own ravaged fields, and as soon as he was in them he confirmed what he had known anyway. In the oat patch, a few bruised stalks strove valiantly to raise battered heads toward the sun. The corn was ruined and the vegetable garden was gone. What remained was not one twentieth of what was needed.

Joe caught the mules and evaded their striking feet and slicing teeth as he fought them into harness. Having run free for four days, the mules were not inclined to work again. But they had to work, for the man who commanded them was stronger than they. They plunged and reared when the harness was buckled about them, and kicked and squealed when they were once fastened to the plow. That was all they could do.

Joe guided the plow down the first long, straight furrow, and even as he did he assured himself that the second crop of oats would be better than the first for the second would feed on the bodies of the first. Joe reversed his mutinous team to start the second furrow, and when he came to the end it seemed, quite unaccountably, that the day should also be ended. Then he looked at the scarcely risen sun and knew that it had not yet started.

He steered the mules down another furrow, and angered more at himself than at them, jerked hard on the reins. The plow had gone a bit to one side, so that instead of being in rhythm with all the rest, the furrow curved away from them. Joe stopped and passed a hand over his sweating forehead. Twenty years or more ago his father had whipped him unmercifully for plowing a crooked furrow. From then until now he had never plowed one.

Joe turned the mules and straightened the furrow so that it matched the rest. From that time on, in order not to repeat the error, he had to watch himself and that made plowing twice the work. With an exhaustion equal to—maybe greater than—last night's, Joe saw the first long shadows of evening.

For the first time, rather than providing a refuge from problems, his house seemed to admit them with him. There was no peace and none of the calm that paid for a day's work. When dinner was over, the almost electric restlessness that tormented him mounted to supercharged heights.

"Do you know what?" he said fiercely, "I wish we could go to a good hoedown tonight! A real rip-snorter with everything in it!"

"Go down to the store and find out when the next one is and where," Emma urged. "I wouldn't mind going to a party myself."

Joe walked down the path toward the store, and in his mind, as he walked, he tried to create some of the camaraderie he would know when he reached it. He could not.

The sky might as well have been nonexistent, and he was scarcely conscious of the cool night air fanning his cheek. *It was not Elias alone. It was not his ruined crops alone. It was more that he couldn't stretch without bumping someone else's ribs.* Unless a person had enough money to start with, or was exceptionally lucky, he was lost here. It was not the way to live and certainly it was not the way for his family to live. Mechanically Joe strode toward the store and he was on the point of entering when a man moved toward him.

"Hi, Joe," Elias Dorrance said.

"Hi."

"I heard," said the other, "that you lost your crops."

Joe waited an interminable moment, until it occurred to him that, by now, everyone must have heard it. Then he said, "That's right."

Elias Dorrance asked, "What will you do now?"

"Plant more crops."

"The frost will get them."

"That's a chance I take."

"I'm sorry," Elias said. "I'm really sorry, and I know you're worried about me. You don't have to worry. You're a good farmer and a man of your word, and you're honest. I'll take another note until next fall."

"On what?" Joe asked.

Elias Dorrance's shrug was half seen in the night. "Your mules, your harness, your wagon, your livestock, your household goods. You can cover it."

For a moment Joe stood blankly, the offer not even registering. Then a slow anger that mounted by leaps and bounds grew within him.

He'd been overwhelmed when Emma gave him the $600 and told him that, at last, he could have his farm. He still could not understand how she had saved such a vast sum; Joe had never earned $600 in any one year. But every penny of it, everything they had, represented the combined sweat and toil, and almost the life's blood, of Emma and himself. Joe thought of Nick Johnson.

He, too, had had a farm financed by Elias and he'd lost a crop. The next year he lost another, and Elias had taken everything except the clothes the Johnsons wore on their backs. Now hopeless and defeated, Nick Johnson was again a hired man and his courage was so broken that he never would be anything else. Joe thought of Emma's cherished household goods, the few things his children owned, of the mules, the cows, everything upon which Elias had no claim. For a moment he had a savage urge to smash his fist into the banker's face, and Elias must have sensed it for he took a backward step. Joe bit his words off and spat them out,

"Elias, you can take a long running jump into the nearest duck pond."

Without looking back and without entering the store, he turned and strode through the darkness toward his house. A man who turned his back on the land almost turned his back on God too. But one who risked everything his family had was not a man at all. Joe entered the house. Emma was sewing at the table and she looked up, and concern flooded her eyes.

"Was there nobody at the store?"

"I didn't go. I met Elias."

Emma waited expectantly. For a short space Joe strode up and down the floor. Then he turned to face her.

"Elias offered to carry us another year. All he wants is a mortgage on everything that isn't already mortgaged to him."

Emma gaped, and Joe said quickly, "I told him to—I told him no."

She half rose out of her chair. "Joe, maybe you should have—"

"No!" he interrupted almost fiercely. "I won't do it! We're in debt as far as we're ever going to be! Some things will remain ours!"

There was a short silence while both pursued their own thoughts. Emma turned a worried face to him.

"Do you think you can make another crop?"

Joe looked at Emma and then he looked beyond her. Outside the night was black, but in his mind's eye he could clearly see the ravaged fields. In his muscles he could feel the ache of the plowing and the planting of the new crop. In the pit of his stomach he could already feel the pain and rage that he would feel if the new crop should be destroyed by frost.

Emma waited, and then she got to her feet with an anxious haste. "Pete Domley will pay for the seed, Joe. Barbara and I can help with the planting."

Now suddenly he didn't want to comfort her any more, nor to bolster up her hopes about the new crop. This was a time for facing facts.

"Emma," he said, and his lips felt dry and tight with the effort to control himself. "Emma, there's free land for the taking in the west."

She drew back as though she had been slapped. "That's a dream, Joe. A bright dream."

"It's not a dream," he said. "It's real land, and real people are going out there to live on it."

She clasped her hands in front of her, and he saw that they were trembling. Yet he made no move to go to her.

"We can't do it," she said. "Don't you see we can't do it? We've got six children to think about."

"Other people are doing it with children," he said doggedly.

"You can't make me do it!" she said wildly. "I'm not going to leave this house—not ever. We'll make out somehow. If need be, Pete Domley will take you on for a year—he owes you that after what happened."

The mighty storm that had been brewing in him broke now, and he lashed out at her. "I'm not going to be a hired man again, do you hear! I finished with that, and I'm not going back to it!"

His voice, harsh and loud, shattered Emma's self-control. She had always known that Joe could be angry, but never before had his anger been directed against herself. She went white, swayed for a moment, and then went unsteadily to the window. She stood clinging to the sill, staring out into the blackness.

He watched her in silence. Then he went to her, turned her around and made her look at him.

"Emma," he said through the pain in his throat. "You don't want me to be a hired man again, do you, Emma?"

Her eyes filled with tears and she tried to speak. No sound came, but she shook her head, No.

His voice grew humble now. He was deeply puzzled, and he begged her for an answer that he could understand. "Why are you so much against the west? Tell me truly. Tell me."

She found her voice. "I'm not against the west. I'm against leaving our home. I want to stay here. I—I hoped we could live here forever. I—I'm afraid, Joe."

He scowled, torn and uncertain.

"You've never been afraid before, Emma. We've been through a lot together, a lot of struggle and a lot of worry. We worried when baby Emma was sick, and when Tad fell out of the tree. But it's always come out all right."

"That was different," she stammered. "We—we were here among our own people. If we needed help, we could get help."

"Emma," he whispered. "Emma—I can take care of you. I can take care of the children."

She clutched him, buried her face in his neck.

"Emma," he said, "when we left your father, you were worried then, but you faced up to it, and life was much better afterward."

"We were younger then," she said. "Oh, Joe—we were much younger, and we had only Barbara. Now we've got six! Think of it, Joe! Six children, out in the wilderness!"

He forced her away from him. With his hand under her chin he forced her to look at him again. From the depths of his restless soul, from the center of his self, his yearning for an independent life poured out through his eyes and entreated her to understand him. His voice was hoarse with the intensity of his longing.

"Emma," he said. "I can take care of you. Trust me, dearest."

Something dissolved inside of her. She could not deny him any longer. He was begging her for his freedom to be his own man. He was begging her for space to grow in, and for their children to grow in. He was begging her to be brave for his sake, so that he could fulfill his deepest needs. Whatever her misgivings, whatever her terror, she must go with him into the unknown.

She put her hands on his shoulders and looked squarely into his eyes. "I do trust you, Joe," she said quietly. "We'll go west. We'll go just as soon as we can get ready."

CHAPTER FOUR

Mountain Man

MORNING LIGHT was dim behind the windows when Joe slipped out of bed. He moved carefully, making no noise, and after he had dressed he kept his shoes in his hand. A worried frown creased his brow, for last night had been a bad one.

It had started as soon as Joe came home from Tenney's store, where he had gone in the early afternoon to see Lester Tenney. He had counted on Les, a wise and good man, to advise him correctly and to give him information which he needed badly. Joe wanted to find out more about the west and, though he might have asked Bibbers Townley, he wanted the truth and nobody could count on Bibbers to tell the truth about anything.

Joe wanted to find somebody who had been west and who would give a reasonably accurate account of what it was like, and just as he expected, Les had known someone to whom he might go. At Hammerstown, fifteen miles from Tenney's Crossing, there lived a man named John Seeley. He was a farmer like Joe, and with him lived his ancient father. Grandpa Seeley could do little nowadays except sit in the sun in summer and nod before the stove in winter, but his mind had not decayed when his body weakened, and he knew as much as anyone else about the west. The famed Mountain Men, Jim Bridger, Jim Clyman, Kit Carson, had been his close friends. More than a dozen years ago, though he had not been a young man even then, he had helped guide the Mormon wagon trains on their incredible, desperate journey between Nauvoo, Illinois, and the valley of the Great Salt Lake.

Grandpa Seeley had lived in the west until just a few years ago, and probably he'd be there yet if his body had been equal to the task of keeping him there. Now he had no choice except living with his son. If Joe wanted to know about the west, Grandpa Seeley was the man who could tell him.

Joe went home, satisfied. But as soon as he arrived, his satisfaction turned to worry.

Young Emma, his second daughter, had always been subject to some mysterious ailment. The attacks came suddenly and without any warning at all. One moment the five-year-old would be playing with her brothers and sisters and the next she'd be gasping for breath while red fever spots flared in her cheeks and she was hot to the touch. Joe got home to find his daughter sick again.

It was a worrisome thing, and all the more so because there was nothing that could be done about it. The doctor whom Joe had once ridden all night to fetch had been no more helpful than the herbs which Granny Trevelyan gathered by the thin light of the moon's first quarter. The fever just had to run its course.

Emma was sitting in the cushioned chair, with young Emma clasped to her bosom, when Joe came in. He looked at them and knew. Emma had a love and devotion big enough to enfold everyone around her, except when one of her family was ill. Then whoever that might be got all she could offer. Joe grieved. He was burdened by an overwhelming sense of clumsy inadequateness, and though he knew he could do nothing he asked anyway,

"Can I do anything for you?"

Emma did not speak, but her lips formed the word No. For a moment Joe lingered helplessly near, still wanting to help but unable to do so. He knew that the words he said were not the right ones, but he said them anyway.

"The man I have to see is in Hammerstown. Shall I go tomorrow morning or would you rather I stayed here?"

Emma whispered, "Go ahead, Joe."

Joe tiptoed away from them. He could help a sick cow or mule, but he did not know what to do for his daughter, and he left his wife alone because it seemed that, by so doing, in some way maybe he was helping at least a little bit. A woman with an ailing child needed all her energies just to take care of it, and if she could be relieved of taking care of anything else, that was good.

Barbara took over, as Joe had known she would, and prepared the evening meal. It was as though Emma were still somehow in charge, for the children looked to Barbara as they did to their mother, and they obeyed her as they did Emma. Even Tad made no noise, and Joe felt a great humility. He was worried for the baby and her mother, but beyond feeling sorrow he did not know what else to do. He was glad that he was not called upon to run the household, for he would not have known how to go about it. He understood, as he had known since his marriage, that there are some things which only a woman can do.

That night he was lost. It was hard to remember when he and Emma had not shared the same bed. It was very lonely without her and very dreary, and because she wasn't beside him, sleep could not be good. At the same time, he reproached himself. He was a man, not a child, and men took care of themselves. They shouldn't need anything except themselves, but Joe knew that they had great need. His bed had been an empty one, and even though he had slept, it was not sound slumber.

Now, while shattered shreds of night battled with approaching day, he paused to look tenderly at his wife and child. They were still in the cushioned chair, and both slept. But even though she was not awake, Emma's possessive arms still wrapped her daughter securely. It was as though she were a high wall over which the peril that stalked the baby would have to climb before it could work real harm.

His shoes still in his hand, Joe took a long while to open the door in order to open it silently. He was hungry. But a man didn't think of his own needs if forgetting them meant that a feverish child and her mother could have another few moments of blessed rest. Besides, the hunger that tormented him was as nothing compared to the fever that burned baby Emma.

Joe closed the door as softly as he had opened it, easing it back on its hinges and letting the latch fall slowly. His shoes still in his hand, he walked a little way onto the dew-wet grass before he sat down to pull the shoes on and lace them. For a moment he sat still, undecided, while the dew seeped through the bottom of his trousers and against his warm seat. He could always go to Hammerstown when baby Emma was well again, and if he stayed home today there might be some little things he could do to help Emma. He might bring cold water for her, or perhaps she'd need something from the store. Joe made up his mind. Barbara and Tad could do whatever needed the doing, and every day that passed was one day closer to the frosts of autumn. There was no time to lose. Besides, only Emma knew how to help the sick youngster.

He did not cease to worry as he took a bridle from its peg in the barn and went toward the mules' pasture, but he was not so desperately troubled as he had been.

Joe hid the bridle behind his back as he approached the pasture. The mules looked at him from the corners of their eyes, then turned their backs and drifted toward the other side of the corral. Joe muttered under his breath. When they thought they would have to work, the mules were always hard to catch. Joe dropped the bridle beside the fence and returned to the barn. He stuck a rope in his belt and took a couple of handfuls of corn out of the grain barrel. The corn in a wooden scoop, he went back to the mule pasture, entered the gate, and lolled near it.

He thought again of the night in Tenney's store, and of Bibbers Townley telling about the west. In spite of the fact that Bibbers had been lying, the spirit of something bright and wonderful had been present. Joe thought of land, as much as a man wanted, free for the taking. He saw his sons planting grain for themselves, and not rows of dollar bills for some banker. He thought of his daughters happily married to strong men who needed, and had, space in which to grow.

The mules came, switching their tails and bobbing their heads, and the rising excitement that mounted in Joe kept him from feeling any resentment toward them. All his life he had looked for

something which he had never found, but he had never despaired
of finding it and he was still looking. If he had not been worried
about baby Emma, this would have been the best day he had
known in a long while.

The advancing mules stopped three feet away, and tried to
stretch their heads far enough to reach the grain scoop. Joe still
lolled idly against the fence, and seemed obviously uninterested
in the mules. They knew him almost as well as he did them, and
he mustn't act as though he wanted to catch them. Joe turned
away, rattling the corn as he did so.

They were upon him in a quick little rush, thrusting their enormous heads into the grain scoop. Sometimes when they were not
to be harnessed they were given a handful of grain, and Joe knew
how to allay their suspicions. They began to lick the corn with wet
tongues. Neither raised its head, for there was only a little grain
and each had to eat as quickly as possible lest the other get more
than a just share.

Joe worked his hand down to the rope in his belt, and when his
fingers closed around it, he brought the grain scoop closer. The
mules blew through their nostrils and followed. Then, seeing too
late that they had fallen into a trap, both tried to wheel and pound
away. Joe slipped the rope over the mare mule's head, took a half
hitch around a fence post, and stepped out of reach when the
mule slashed at him with her yellowed teeth.

Joe laughed. The mare mule was not less cunning and scheming
than her teammate, but the horse had a pounding, hard gait that
was difficult for a rider going only a short way and spine-shatter-
ing for a long ride. The mare had a gentle, rocking pace, and she
was the faster of the two.

The mare pulled to the end of her rope, but not far enough to
tighten it around her neck and choke herself, and she was looking fixedly at Joe when he came with the bridle. She stepped
suddenly forward, slackening the rope, and scuttled sidewise to
pin him between the fence and herself.

Joe laughed again, and brought the blunt end of his shoe hard into her soft belly. Her ears sagged reproachfully as she retreated and stood still. The mules always fought with their master, but it never did them any good because Joe remained master. She was docile enough as he slipped the bit into her mouth, strapped the bridle on, and led her through the gate.

The horse mule watched the whole procedure suspiciously. Then, as soon as the gate was closed and latched, and he knew that Joe wanted only the mare, he shattered the morning stillness with a far-carrying bray before trotting over to lick up the few grains of corn that had spilled on the ground.

Joe vaulted astride the mare and set himself for the lunge that he knew was coming now. He tried to make her keep her head up, but she got it down and bucked. Joe gripped her sides with his knees, and for a moment she pitched and twisted. Then she reared, trying to make him slide back over her tail, and when she did Joe shortened the rein so she couldn't get her head down again. She panted angrily, then obeyed the tug of the rein and started down the path toward Tenney's. Joe knew another moment of tormenting uncertainty.

He was a realist, and experience had taught him that nothing worth having came easily. Though he knew nothing about the west, he did know what wagon travel involved. At the best, it was not easy. Though he never doubted Emma's moral fiber, though he knew that once having decided to go she would spare herself nothing to make the trip possible and successful, was her physical strength equal to the hardships that they would almost certainly endure before they reached the land they wanted? Suppose baby Emma became desperately ill along the way and had only a wagon for shelter? Alfred, Carlyle and Joe were very young. Was Barbara equal to such a trip? Joe half turned the mule around, then turned her back and went on. He had taken upon himself the duty of digging out all possible information in advance. He had promised Emma to take care of her—and that meant he must prepare for every situation in which they were likely to find themselves. The sources of reliable information were few, but Seeley was one, and he meant to get to Seeley as early in the day as he humanly could.

The morning was lighter. But it was still too early for most people to be up and, save for Lard Head, who lay sleeping in front of the store, there was nobody around Tenney's Crossing. From the last house a little white dog ran out, yapped ineffectively at the mule, and scuttled back into the shadows when she lunged at him.

The mule broke into a fast canter and Joe let her run. Then, of her own accord, she slowed to an easy trot and walked on the upgrades. This was a wagon road, and sometimes wagons made the trip between Tenney's Crossing and Hammerstown when they were heavily loaded and in wet weather. The ruts on either side of the road were deep and uneven, and here and there they had been filled in with rocks. The bleached bones of an ox that had died on this road and been dragged aside were scattered about a grassy little dell.

The sky brightened, and Joe forgot his doubts. He felt light-hearted, almost gay, as he rode through forest broken by an occasional clearing. Little Emma, he assured himself, would be all right because she was always all right when her mother took care of her. And about the lost crops there need be no worry. If a man couldn't do one thing he could always do another, and the only really unfortunate men were those who wept, but did nothing else, when trouble came.

The mule had stopped cantering and trotting and was walking now. But she had a very fast walk, she covered ground much more swiftly than a walking man, and she was not fighting him any more. But Joe continued to watch her closely and to feel with his knees for any change in her. Mules were expert pretenders. They struck when it was least expected. However, if a man knew mules, they always gave some warning.

A mighty hunger mounted within Joe as he thought of the breakfast Barbara would prepare for her mother and brothers and sisters. But if he'd stopped for breakfast he would have risked

awakening Emma and the youngster. And he'd had to leave early
because time was important. He must find out about the west,
then take back to Emma everything he discovered.

They came to a long, gently slanting downgrade, and the mule
trotted again. A white-tailed deer with twin fawns at her heels
floated like a shadow across the road in front of him and stood
on the forested hillside. A singing pleasure rose in Joe, and he
slowed the mule as he passed because he wanted to look more
closely at the doe and her dappled babies. He wished that Emma
might be along, for she always enjoyed such sights, too.

Not until they were well past did Joe think that venison was
good eating, some of the best, and he was very hungry now. Well,
no doubt he would get something to eat at the Seeleys'. Joe had
never met them, but any stranger who came to your door should
be offered food because that was only common politeness. It was
unthinkable to send even an enemy away hungry.

A little more than two hours after he left his farm, Joe rode into
Hammerstown.

Save that the store was smaller and much more run down than
Tenney's, Hammerstown might have been Tenney's Crossing.
There were half a dozen houses, a church, and a log building that
served as a school and for any other public business that might
have to be transacted. The timber had been cleared away to make
fields, and beyond Hammerstown there were more farms. Two
men were just coming out of the store, and as soon as he was
abreast of them, Joe swung his mule around and stopped her.

"Can you tell me where John Seeley lives?" he called.

They regarded him with candid interest. "Straight down the
road. John's place is on top of the first hill. Somethin' we can do
for you?"

"You can tell me if the Seeleys will be home."

"They'll be home. Think you can find the place?"

"I reckon. Thank you."

"You're welcome, stranger."

Joe swung the mule back down the road and out of Hammerstown. A man with a yoke of oxen looked curiously at him as he passed and two children stopped to stare. Joe resented no part of it. People who lived in such places, and who seldom saw anyone except their near neighbors, were always frankly curious about anyone whom they did not know. The mule walked up the first hill and Joe guided her into the farmyard on top of it. It was more substantial than most farms, with a good, solid log house covered by a shingled roof. Obviously John Seeley enjoyed more than average prosperity, for there were glass windows on all sides of the house. Behind the house were a barn and sheds, and fields and forest beyond them.

A man with two teams of oxen was skidding a heavy drag of logs across a field toward the barn, and a boy about fifteen years old accompanied him. A bevy of small children crowded into the house's open door, and a shaggy dog that barked desultorily as it came, wagged toward Joe. The mule backed warily, and Joe kept a sharp eye on her. He had come to seek something from the people who lived here, and letting his mule kick their dog around was not the way to cement friendly relations.

A woman who, Joe thought, looked somewhat like Emma, came to stand in the doorway behind the children and at once Joe felt a little easier. Though he was usually ill at ease with strange women, he felt that he could talk to this one. He slid from the mule, holding the reins, and Joe said politely,

"I'm looking for John Seeley's place, ma'am. My name's Joe Tower. I come from over Tenney's Crossing way."

She smiled a warm welcome. "This is the Seeley place, Mr. Tower. My man's in the wood lot right now."

"There's a man and boy coming in. They have a drag of logs."

"That's my man and boy. Have you had breakfast, Mr. Tower?"

"No, ma'am."

"And you rode from Tenney's! I'll get you something right away! Just put your mule in back."

She hurried into the house and Joe led the mule toward the outbuildings. He'd brought a tie rope because, no matter how hospitable a host might be, one didn't just ask for corn to help catch his mule. Joe looped the rope around the mule's neck and tied her to a fence post before he slipped the bridle off. He turned to meet the man and boy who, by this time, were very near the barn.

John Seeley was a stocky, square-built man, and apparently he never made a fast move if a slow one would serve. But there was about him that which was as solid and dependable as the land he worked, and Joe warmed to him. He had an approving glance for the youngster who, Joe suspected, was a mirror of what the father had been twenty years ago.

"Are you John Seeley?" Joe asked.

"That's me," the other's voice was as deep as he was stocky. "What can I do for you?"

"My name's Tower," Joe introduced himself. "Joe Tower. I didn't exactly come to talk with you, but with your father. Les Tenney told me he's been west."

"And you," the other guessed, "aim to go?"

"I've been pondering on it. First I wanted to talk with somebody who's been there."

"I've been there."

"You have?"

"That's right, and I'll take Missouri."

"You didn't like it?"

"I like this better. Man, the west's no land of milk and honey. The rain's as wet there, the snow's as cold, the bugs bite as hard, and it's to heck and gone from any other place."

"How about free land?"

"There's that if a man has to have it."

"Depends on how you look at things, don't it?"

The other gave him a searching glance. "That's right. When do you aim to leave?"

"Don't know yet that I will leave. I just wanted to find out."

"Tell you what," John Seeley suggested, "I've been only once over the California Road or, as some call it, the Oregon Trail. But my father spent most of his life in the west. Talk to him; he'll be up soon. Reckon you saw Sophie?"

"That I did. She's kind enough to get me some breakfast and I can't say I'm sorry. Left before sun-up."

"Goshamighty! Fifteen miles with nothing to eat! Come in fast!"

Joe followed the other into his house, and sniffed hungrily at the good smell of pancakes baking and sausage sizzling. He knew a moment's envy. John Seeley must be very prosperous if he could afford sausage in July. To most people, by that time good meat was only a luscious memory or something to look forward to when the weather should again make it possible to keep meat. The children trooped out to play and the dog frolicked with them. Sophie Seeley filled Joe's plate with golden-brown pancakes and sausage patties, and his cup with coffee. Joe ate, and nobody spoke while he was eating because it was impolite to talk under such circumstances. When a man was hungry, it was most important that his hunger be satisfied.

Joe finished and pushed his plate back. He heard the lifting of a wooden latch, and his eyes strayed toward the door that was opening. Joe sat forward in his chair.

The man who came into the room was old as a rock and big as a hill. Taller than his tall son, Grandpa Seeley was stocky like John and straight. Snow-white hair tumbled down his massive head and rippled about his shoulders. A white beard strayed down his chest. His movements were firm and graceful. He came straight to the table and sat down, and not until he was seated, staring straight at Joe without seeing him, did Joe understand that his clear blue eyes saw nothing. Grandpa Seeley was blind and probably he found his way around the house because nobody ever moved anything.

His son got up and stood by the old man's shoulder. He did not raise his voice when he spoke,

"There's a man come to see you, Grandpa."

"Yes," the old man's voice had within it the blending of gentle winds, and stormy ones, and rippling streams, and strange bird songs. "Who is it?"

"My name's Tower," Joe spoke for himself while he reached across the table to grasp the old man's hand, "Joe Tower. I rode from Tenney's Crossing to ask you about the west."

"Glad to know you, Joe."

"I'd best get back to my work," John Seeley said.

He left, and Grandpa asked Joe, "What do you want to know about?"

"I—" Joe fumbled. He had come to ask about the west, and only now did it occur to him that he hadn't the slightest notion of what to ask. "I'm thinking of going there," he said lamely.

"You don't aim just to point your nose west and follow it?"

"No. That's why I came to see you. I want to find out how to do it."

"The west is a big place. What are your wishes?"

"A fellow named Townley told me he staked out land by riding three days in each direction and finally coming back to his starting point."

"Townley's a liar," Grandpa assured him. "Though some of the ranches and land grants in the southwest are most as big as the state of Missouri. They need a lot of land; takes maybe eighty acres to feed one cow in some of that country. You going in for cattle?"

"No. I'm a farmer."

"Oregon," Grandpa said. "Oregon's the place you want. Get yourself a quarter section there. That's all the land any farmer needs in that country."

"How do I get to Oregon?"

"Go out to Independence and get on the trail. Even if anybody in Independence can't put you on it, which they can, you won't miss it. Last time I was through, it was a few miles wide in some places and I expect it's wider now. With all the wagons that have gone through, people would have to branch out to find grass for their stock. Follow the Trail after you get on it and you'll be all right. But May's the time to start for Oregon. Unless you want to travel alone, you should wait until next spring."

"Can a lone wagon get through?"

"Sure, but it can be almighty lonesome. The prairies are a right sizable place to be in all by yourself. But you can do it alone. Some of the Mormon companies pushed hand carts all the way from the Missouri, and there were plenty of women pushing right along with the men. But, starting this late, you won't get through to Oregon this summer."

"How far can I get?"

"How are you traveling?"

"What's the best way?"

"Mules," Grandpa said decisively. "Next to them, oxen. Oxen will get along on skimpier grass, but they're slow. Horses are all right for riding but they don't stand up under a long haul."

"Is one team of mules enough?"

"That's taking a chance. You should have two, or anyhow one spare animal. Then, if you lose one, you can always get some place where they'll sell you another."

"How far can I get this season?"

"To Laramie, anyhow. With luck, and if storms hold off, you might get to Fort Bridger. But you can count on Laramie with time to spare."

"Can a man figure on finding something to do through the winter?"

"Any man who wants to work can find it. Tell you what, a little short of one day west of Laramie there's a friend of mine with a trading post. Name's Jim Snedeker. Tell him I sent you, and he'll give you and your mules a job. That is, always supposing you want to work for him."

"How about Indian trouble?"

"That's up to you. Ninety-eight out of a hundred Indian scrapes are not brought about by Indians, but by some mullethead of an emigrant who started a ruckus with them. If you don't bother the Indians, and don't let them bother you, you should have no trouble."

"What else will I need?"

"How many are going with you?"

"My wife and six young ones."

"Load your wagon heavy with eatables," Grandpa advised. "Carry plenty of flour. Take eggs; pack them in a barrel of corn meal and use up the meal as you use up the eggs. You should have coffee and whatever else you fancy in the way of eating. Take tools, the ones you'll need are the ones you need here. Go light on dishes and furniture. There's enough household goods been pitched out of wagons between Independence and the Wil'mette Valley to stock a city the size of St. Louis ten times over. You got a milk cow?"

"Two."

"Take both. You'll get some milk all the time. Hang the morning's milking in a pail behind the wagon. By night it'll be butter. Drink the evening's milking. Can you shoot?"

"Tolerable good."

Grandpa said, "There's still buffalo and I think there always will be, though they'll never be again like they were in '30 when we went into Santa Fe. But you can count on enough for meat. You got any money?"

"Very little," Joe confessed.

"Keep what you have. Take all of it with you and get as much more as you can. You'll need it."

Joe asked in some astonishment, "On the Oregon Trail?"

"On the Oregon Trail," Grandpa assured him. "Suppose a mule dies and you have to buy another? What if you have to stock up on flour?" For a moment Grandpa lost himself in the dreamy introspectiveness of the very old. "It's not like it was in the old days. A man didn't need anything but his horse and rifle then, and if he didn't have the horse he could always get one if he had

a rifle. The west has grown up. She's shed her three-cornered
pants and put on her long britches. Don't try it unless you have
some money."

"Is there anything else?"

"Watch the company you'll find. You'll run into soldiers, but no
constables or marshals, and you will find cutthroats. Take it easy.
Don't go too fast or too slow. Use the sense God gave you, and
you'll do all right."

"That's it, huh?"

"I've told you everything that's to be told," Grandpa assured
him. "If you can think of anything else, I'll try to answer your
questions."

"Can't figure another question," Joe admitted. "I should outfit
right, go to Independence, get on the Oregon Trail, and use common sense."

"That's the way."

"Thank you for your time. Thank you kindly."

Grandpa muttered, "That's all my time's good for now."

"What did you say?"

"Nothing important," the old man told him. He said, more to
himself than to Joe, "I'd like to do it over again, the way I did
it the first time."

Joe felt a sudden, warming kinship with this man whom he had
seen for the first time less than an hour ago. Grandpa Seeley was
going nowhere, not ever again in his entire life. But he had flung
his gauntlet in the face of a great challenge and he yearned to do
it again. Joe gripped the old man's hand again, and looked into
his sightless eyes. He said,

"You've given me a lot," and to the woman, "Thank you, Mrs.
Seeley, for everything."

She said, "Oh, I do hope nothing happens!"

"Nothing will. That is, nothing bad."

Joe fought his mule to a standstill, bridled her, mounted, and let
her choose her own pace home. The sun was high when he rode
into his yard. Her face tear streaked and her eyes red, Barbara

came to meet him. Joe's heart leaped in sudden panic; little Emma had been sick when he left. He said,

"What's wrong?"

"The cow!" Barbara choked back a sob. "Clover! She broke her leg while you were away and Pete Domley shot her!"

Barbara threw herself into his arms, and for the first time in years she sobbed like the little girl he had once known. Joe hugged her very tightly and stroked her slim back with his rough hand. The day had been a good one, and he had learned much that he needed to know. But he had not learned, he now realized with a poignant uneasiness, how to prepare a sensitive young girl for the hardships and dangers she must face in the long journey ahead of them.

CHAPTER FIVE

The Start

THE MULE pulled hard on the reins as she sought to reach a lush growth of grass near by. With a rough jerk Joe brought her back, and she stood meekly behind him. The mules could gauge his moods as exactly as he could theirs; they always know just how far they might go and when they'd better behave. The mule did not pull even hard enough to tighten the reins as she waited.

Barbara buried her tear-stained face in his shirt front and Joe held her fiercely close to him. Her body shook convulsively, and it seemed to Joe that every racking sob tore out of his throat too. He knew a moment of blank dismay because, though there were words that applied to the situation, he could not think of them. He did think of a doe whose hip had been shattered by a rifle ball, and he had a wild notion that there was some comparison between the stricken doe and his stricken child. Nobody had been able to do anything for the deer, either. Joe said,

"Don't cry, Bobby! Please don't cry!"

"It—it was awful!"

"I know, but would you want Clover to suffer? Pete did the right thing. If I'd have been here, I'd have done it myself."

Panting hard, Tad's dog came around a corner of the house and threw himself down in the shade. Tad followed, whittling on a stick with his knife and kicking at the shavings as they fell. He looked at his sobbing sister in her father's arms and scornfully expressed what he felt was a distinct superiority of all male creatures over all female.

"Huh! Cryin' about an old cow!"

Joe felt an immediate relief. He did not know how to comfort a broken-hearted girl, but at this moment he did know what to do about this freckle-faced son of his. He was relieved because Tad had provided him with an outlet for his pent-up feelings.

"Will you get out of here," he roared, "before I cut a hickory switch and use it to tan your ornery hide!"

Tad said, "I ain't doin' anything."

"You're walking around with a knife in your hand for one thing! For another you're getting too big for your britches! Now beat it, and if I catch you using a knife that way again I'll take it away from you until you show some sense!"

Head up, shoulders squared, Tad walked back around the house and Mike rose to follow him. Joe gulped, penitent because he had spoken harshly to Tad. But in some fashion that he did not understand the spell was broken and Barbara's near hysteria was no more. She pushed herself away from him, wiped her eyes with a handkerchief, and smiled tremulously. Joe had a sudden inspiration.

"Look, honey, go tell your mother that I have some things to say to her as soon as I've put the mule away. You might wait for me too. It's sort of a family matter."

For a second she said nothing and Joe had a momentary little panic because he thought she was going to start crying again. Instead, she repeated her smile.

"I'll tell her, Daddy."

She walked away and Joe was happy again. His master coup had been effective, and by sending Barbara to Emma he had at least taken her mind from Clover's tragedy. Barbara made pets of all the farm animals, and hers was a deep sensitivity. She could bear to see nothing she liked hurt. At pig-killing time, which was always in the fall, she made an excuse to visit her bosom friend, Marcia Geragty, and invariably she stayed away until everything was over. Though she was a willing and hard worker, nobody could count on her to help at the butchering—naturally the men always did the slaughtering—and sometimes Joe worried about her because obviously Barbara was destined to be a farmer's wife. As such, she would have to know a farm wife's tasks and taking care of meat was one of them. Joe knew another period of doubt and indecision.

Above all, he wanted for his children more and better opportunities than he had ever known. But, though Tad would be wild with joy at the very thought, was the west really a place for Barbara? She had grown up here; all her friends were here. Was it right to uproot her, to tear her away from everything she knew and loved? And—Joe still thought of her as very fragile—could she bear up under the hardships of such a long journey? Would the west offer her anything to compensate for what she would lose by leaving Missouri? Joe comforted himself with the thought that Barbara had a mind of her own. She could be counted on to express her sincere convictions at the forthcoming family conference.

Joe wrinkled his brow. He'd had his setbacks, but none comparable to the recent disasters. A whole crop ruined and a valuable cow lost. It seemed that the land over which he had labored so hard had rejected him completely. He knew a sudden wild urge to be away, to start immediately for Oregon where a man was his own master. Joe led the mule around a corner of the house and saw Tad leaning against the building.

Joe stopped and said gruffly, "Sorry I yelled, Tad."

Tad shrugged. "Clover's leg was broke. I saw it myself. What could you do except shoot her?"

"Nothing," Joe admitted, "but womenfolk don't—"

"Don't what?" Tad asked.

"They don't understand some things."

It was a lame explanation and one which, Joe felt, did not suffice. Women understood most things, and Joe knew of men who had died in agony while other men stood uncaringly near. That being the way things were sometimes, there was something mighty wholesome about anyone at all who could shed genuine tears over a dead cow. But Joe could think of nothing else to say.

Tad asked too casually, "What'd you find out this morning, Pa?"

Without answering immediately, Joe put the mule in the pasture, slipped her bridle off, and closed the gate. As far as he knew, none of the children even suspected that he and Emma were planning to go west. But Tad had a way of finding out much that he was not supposed to know; perhaps he had been lying awake, listening, the night Joe returned from Tenney's and talked with Emma. He turned to Tad and said,

"You come along and see."

The youngest children met him at the door, and Joe's heart lightened. The mysterious fevers attacked baby Emma without any warning at all. But they left her just as quickly and obviously she was well again. Joe knew that the youngsters wanted to play with him, but he felt that it was not a moment for play. They were on the verge of a profound uprooting that would affect the lives of all.

Barbara sat gracefully on a chair. Emma leaned against the sink, and Tad slipped unobtrusively past to make himself small in one corner. Joe glanced at the youngster and saw his eyes glowing and his face wild with excitement. He cleared his throat and wished desperately that he was a master of story-telling so that he might give his expectant family an exact word picture.

"I saw Grandpa Seeley at Hammerstown," he began. "He's an old man who's spent most of his life in the west and . . ."

In simple, unembellished language, he told them. He spoke of Oregon, where any family could live and live well on a quarter section of land that was free for the taking. He told of the Oregon Trail, which they would reach at Independence. The chances were good that they'd be traveling all alone, for most of the Oregon-bound emigrants started in May, and they might be very lonely. Mules were the best wagon beasts, but they really should have a spare team or at least a spare animal. They should take as much food as possible and that meant that most of their household goods must be left behind. However, selling whatever they could not take along would provide necessary funds. Even

though they took much food, they would have to depend on hunting for their meat. However, they would find buffalo and probably
other game animals. The chances were good that Indians would
not be a menace.

Joe told it honestly, adding nothing and holding nothing back.
He looked at Emma, who stood white-faced and calm, her back
against the wall; at Barbara, sitting dreamily with her chin in her
hand; at Tad, fairly vibrating with excitement. The younger
children, even Alfred who seldom sat still, seemed to have partaken of the solemnity of the moment and were listening intently.
Joe ran a hand through his shaggy hair.

"Well, that's it. That's the story and it sounded to me like a
straight one. I've told you everything I know."

"O'gon," Carlyle piped in his baby treble. "We go O'gon."

A moment's silence reigned.

Emma clasped her hands nervously in front of her, and then
disengaged them with an effort. "Was Mr. Seeley sure that we
can reach Laramie before winter closes in?"

"He said that we could do it with time to spare. We might even
make Fort Bridger if we're lucky."

Again her hands came together and held, her knuckles white.
"Did he say anything about the quarters we'll find there? I—I
should not like to live in an Indian tent in winter."

Joe smiled. "You wouldn't have to. Laramie's an Army post, but
we won't stay there. Just west of Laramie there's a trading post
run by a man named Snedeker. I can get a job with him for the
winter."

"We can't possibly carry enough of everything to see us
through. Are there places along the way where we might buy
new provisions?"

Joe said soberly, "Not too many. But we will be able to stock
up if we have to."

"Was—was he sure there'll be no Indian trouble?"

There were frequent occasions when Joe and Emma had the
same thought at the same time, and Joe had a fleeting, terrible

vision of his babies' fluffy hair adorning the smoky lodge of some fierce warrior prince. He hesitated before replying, then,

"He said we'd have no trouble if we don't bother the Indians and don't let them bother us." A deepening silence filled the room at the mention of Indians.

Then there was a knock at the door, and Joe opened it to face Elias Dorrance. Elias' horse was rein-haltered near by, and the banker said affably,

"Hi, Joe."

"Hi. Uh—come in."

The banker entered and bowed in turn to Emma and Barbara. "Mrs. Tower. Miss Tower." His glance encompassed the children and he turned to Joe. "I wondered if you've changed your mind?"

Joe squirmed inwardly, but at the same time he knew a small gratification. It was part of etiquette to offer any visitor a meal, but it was absolutely imperative to do so only if they came at meal time. Because his family was present, Joe controlled his anger. He said,

"No. No, I haven't."

"I see." Elias remained gracious. "I was merely riding past and thought this a good opportunity to see you. Well, I must be running along and it's good to see your charming family. If you care to talk with me, you have only to come to my office."

Elias bowed again and departed. Joe resisted an impulse to assist him out of the door with the toe of his shoe. Elias was not simply passing by. He had ridden out to see if there was any way he could get a mortgage on everything the Towers had left. Joe felt a cold and clammy thing that was not physical or born of any solid substance, brush his heart. He turned to see Emma staring fixedly at the four youngest children. Her glance roved to Barbara and Tad. Then her eyes met his squarely. The color that had left her cheeks came back to them now in a rush.

"Joe, I think it's time we told the children we're going to Oregon!"

"Hieee!" Tad shrieked.

Emma cast a reproving glance at him and Tad quieted. But his eyes danced and a beatific smile lighted his whole face.

"O'gon," Carlyle said again. "We go O'gon."

"It's Oregon, isn't it, mama?" little Emma corrected.

Emma said, heaving a deep and tremulous sigh, "Yes, dear, it's Oregon."

"I think," Barbara said, "that it's going to be just wonderful!"

Joe turned to look at her, startled because there was a quality in her voice that had never been present before. She spoke like an adult, but her eyes were wide with excitement and her cheeks were flushed. Joe shook his head. He had thought that, of all the family, Barbara might shrink from such a trip and all it involved. Joe said,

"Bobby, you really want to go!"

But Barbara was already lost in a dream and Emma answered for her daughter, "Of course she wants to go."

Joe glanced at his wife, sensing another feminine puzzle here which no man would ever figure out. He understood Tad's bubbling excitement at the prospect of new horizons and new adventure, but Tad was a boy and such a reaction was natural. He did not completely grasp, as Emma did, that Barbara was youth too. Youth was for daring, and exploring, and the farthest point on the horizon would always be alluring. Joe grinned at his youngest children.

"Any of you got anything to say?"

Little Joe asked, "How far is Oregon?"

"Quite a piece, Joe."

"Oh." The youngster devoted himself seriously to thinking about this new problem that had arisen.

The relief that Joe felt at the way his children had taken the news expressed itself in a minor outburst. Joe said, "Doggone it!"

Emma said, "Is something wrong?"

"I must have been in quite a fluster when I got here. Left the mare mule's bridle lying on the ground. I'd better go pick it up."

Tad said happily, "I'll go with you, Pa."

They left the house together and Joe felt strangely light, almost giddy, as he walked across the familiar yard. It was impossible to go to Oregon, but they were going. Joe grinned. There had been a great decision and a small one; they were going to Oregon and he must pick up a mule bridle.

"When we startin', Pa?" Tad breathed.

"Soon's we can get ready."

"Can Mike go too?"

"He can if he wants to walk all the way."

Tad breathed, "I'm goin' to walk, too! Can I shoot a buffalo, Pa? Can I?"

Joe said good humoredly, "For pete's sake, we're not out of Missouri yet—we haven't even started—and you talk of buffalo! Can't you wait until we see some?"

"Do you think we'll have Indian fights, Pa?" Tad asked breathlessly.

"We won't if I can help it." Joe was suddenly sober. "Tad, you and I have to be the men on this trip. You know that?"

"I know it, Pa! I know it and I'll do everything I can to help! Honest! Can I go tell Buster Trevelyan?"

"Sure."

With a wild whoop, Mike racing beside him, Tad was away. Joe picked up the mule bridle and glanced at the mules. They were standing together, nibbling each other with their lips. The mules usually quarreled over which was going to get the most of the choicest food, but they were genuinely fond of each other and Joe supposed that was a good thing too. Mules, hybrids that had no future because they were incapable of reproducing their own kind, must feel desperately frustrated at times.

A meadow lark sang from the top of the fence and Joe answered it, imitating almost perfectly the bird's sweet call. The meadow lark called again and Joe talked back to it. He wondered if there would be meadow larks in Oregon and hoped wistfully that he would find them there for they were a totem bird, a symbol of good luck. Nothing could be too bad as long as there was a meadow lark about. Joe had always fought against killing them for any reason, though now and again some of his neighbors shot or snared some to eat.

Joe answered a bobwhite that called from a corner of brush, and a red-winged blackbird that perched on a swaying reed down near the creek. He had always cherished a secret desire to play a fiddle, or almost any kind of musical instrument, but he'd never been able to do it. His one talent, besides farming, was imitating bird calls and he enjoyed himself with those. Yancey Garrow, who could play the fiddle, had even said he'd trade that for Joe's ability.

A pang assailed Joe when he looked again at his raided fields, but it was the ache any good farmer would feel when good crops are destroyed. He no longer felt completely in tune with these fields; they'd lost their power to hold him and make him do their bidding. Joe's thoughts remained on Oregon, and the constant urge to be doing something must be devoted to making that trip a success.

He took the bridle to the barn and carefully hung it on its proper peg. When his eyes strayed over the harness, which was kept in the barn except when the mules were working every day, he noted a frayed tug strap and knew that he would have to replace or repair it before they started. There'd be few leather shops on the Oregon Trail and they'd be far apart. Because it was part of his nature to want everything the way it should be, he cleaned accumulated litter out of the mules' stalls. All summer long, night and day, the mules were in the pasture, and it never occurred to Joe that he'd done a useless bit of work because the mules wouldn't be in their stalls this winter.

The younger children were playing in the yard, and Joe entered the house to find Emma alone. Lost in thought, she was standing at the stove, touching it here and there as though to memorize the feeling of it. She swung around guiltily when she heard Joe behind her.

"You gave me a start," she said.

"You won't like leaving the stove behind?"

"It's a good stove," she said defiantly. "But my grandmother didn't have one, and she got along just fine. I guess I can, too."

Joe sighed, and his eyes moved around the room to other things that would be left behind.

Seeing him Emma stamped her foot. "One thing I know, Joe Tower. I'm not going to eat myself up regretting all the things we can't take with us. Those are *things*, not people. The people we love best, our own children, are going to be right with us. So let's not get all in a fuss about any old stove."

He chuckled. Then, seeing the slight quiver of her lips, he spoke softly. "But also let's not do too much pretending that things don't bother us when they really do. It's a good stove, and you'll miss it."

Her throat worked for a moment, then hastily she changed the subject. "About the cow, Joe—I'm grateful to you for making it easy for Barbara."

He said with honest surprise, "*I* made it easy for her?"

"She saved her tears for you, didn't she?"

"Yes. But—"

She said quietly, "One of the reasons I love you so much is because you really don't know why a little girl would rather cry on your shoulder." She took out a handkerchief and blew her nose. "Pete butchered the cow properly."

Joe said, "Well, it will be a lot of jerky and pickled beef to take along."

She smiled tearfully at him. "Who in this family would eat Clover, Joe? I asked Pete to take the beef down and sell it to Lester Tenney. We can use more money, now that we're Oregon-bound."

Joe scratched his head. "Guess you're right. I couldn't enjoy the beef myself and we do need money." Money. And provisions. A barrel of corn meal, Seeley had said. All the eatables they could carry.

"There's a lot of planning to do," he said to Emma.

"A lot of planning," she echoed, nodding, with an effort at crisp composure.

Go to Independence, Grandpa Seeley had told him. Get on the Oregon Trail and use common sense. It had all seemed so simple, but there was more to it than that. For instance, though they probably could camp beside the wagon much of the time, suppose there were stormy nights and they had to sleep inside? Provision would have to be made for it. The wagon itself would have to receive a thorough checking, with faulty parts replaced. The box would almost surely have to be built higher, and a canvas cover fitted tightly. Every item that went along, from the smallest to the largest, would have to have its own place. All of it had to be planned, and Joe had planned none of it.

Barbara came out of the room she shared with little Emma and Joe's spirits rose. At the same time, he was puzzled and slightly amused. Only a short time ago he had held Barbara in his arms, completely crushed and wilted. Now there was no trace of that, but only the sheer loveliness, intensified by excitement, that almost always walked with this girl and that imparted itself to whatever or whomever she encountered. She smiled.

"Why don't you go fishing and do your pondering, Daddy? You won't be working the fields this afternoon."

Joe looked gratefully at her. All women seemed to know all men better than any man understood any one woman. Emma knew that he needed solitude sometimes for thinking about his problems. Like her mother, Barbara seemed to know it too.

"Now say," Joe said, "I might just do that."

Not for a long while had he taken the time to go fishing, though he had often wished mightily that he could go. When he fished, he knew a serenity of soul and peace of mind that he found in doing nothing else, and it made no difference whether or not he caught anything. The mind of a true fisherman is not on petty subjects, and suddenly Joe knew that he must go.

"Hurry up, Pa!" Tad called in the door. "I've got the worms all dug and the poles all ready."

"I thought you'd gone to see Buster Trevelyan?"

"I did see him. He helped me dig worms."

Joe felt that somehow he must be a very shallow and easily led person. His daughter had suggested that he go fishing. His wife had told him the same thing, though she had not needed to speak. Now his son appeared with fishing tackle and bait. Joe hesitated, and Emma urged,

"Go ahead. You won't get any work done today anyhow and fishing will be good for you."

"Well, we might get a mess of fish."

He left the house, followed by the jubilant Tad, who had two poles with lines, floats, and hooks attached to them slung over his shoulder and a hollow branch containing worms in his hand. Mike tagged amiably along, bristled hopefully when a neighbor's dog crossed Pete Domley's pasture, and relaxed sadly when the dog kept on going. Mike didn't care what he fought, or where or when, as long as he could fight, and Joe looked at his son's dog with a new eye. Mike had never been an asset on the farm, but he might be one on the Oregon Trail.

Tad led the way to a long, still pool bordered by sycamores and willows. Joe took his pole, baited, cast, and watched his bobber float with the gentle current. He eyed a school of minnows that were swimming in the shoals and looked again at his bobber. The minnows in the shallow edges of the pool were quiet, therefore nothing had been chasing them for a while and it was Joe's guess that the fish wouldn't bite well today. If the bass were feeding, the minnows would be more nervous and alert. Joe asked his son a question that had been on his mind.

"How'd you know I'd go fishing this afternoon?"

"If we're goin' to Oregon, you sure wouldn't be workin' the fields."

"Is that the only reason you knew?"

"Nope. I just kind of thought it was a day for you and me to go fishin'."

"Did your mother or sister tell you to get the worms and tackle?"

Tad said indignantly, "Now, Pa, you know they wouldn't be tellin' me to take you fishin'!"

Joe knew that he was not telling the truth, and that Emma must have told him to dig worms and arrange fishing tackle, and for a moment he felt a slight annoyance. Then he relented. If anyone told the strict truth all the time, Joe felt, they'd be very hard to live with. Tad's was a harmless deception. The worst the youngster had in him was a streak of wildness, and he'd outgrow that. The Oregon Trail, Joe reflected, might take some of it out of him.

Joe relaxed on the stream bank, giving himself completely to thoughts of this new venture and at peace with himself and the world. In his wood lot were both hickory and oak that he had felled last year and left to season. For a share of the timber, John Geragty would work it into proper sizes at his saw mill. Maybe it would be a good idea to carry a spare reach for the wagon and spare axles. They could always be slung underneath without adding too much to the load. Since they couldn't take everything with them—or nearly everything—they would have a lot to sell or trade. The kitchen stove for one thing. He swallowed a lump when he thought of Emma standing at the stove, touching it lightly with her fingertips. Then he made himself go on with his planning. The planning, right now, was a whole lot more necessary than the stove. They would have to sell the stove. Stoves were none too plentiful in this country and lots of farm wives cooked over fireplaces. The stove should get them a new wagon cover, which Les Tenney carried in stock, and something else besides. Now—

Tad yelled, "Pa! Your line!"

Joe awakened with a start to see his bobber gone down and his line moving slowly out into the stream. He yanked on the pole, lifted a two-pound bass clear of the water, and brought it, flopping, to the grass beside him. Mike, who had been asleep in the grass, awakened with a throaty bark and came over to inspect the catch. Joe shoved him aside, and Tad said approvingly,

"Gee! That's a nice one!"

"It's not too bad," Joe agreed. "Mike, get away!"

He slid the bass onto a willow stringer that Tad cut and put it back in the water, weighting one end of the stringer with a rock. Then he gave all his attention to fishing. While he had been thinking of Oregon, the bass must have started feeding for the minnows were more alert now. Even as Joe watched, a school of them darted this way and that while something dark and sullen lunged among them.

Two minutes later Joe caught another bass, and before the sun started to set, he and Tad had fourteen. Joe borrowed Tad's knife, which was always razor-sharp, and knelt beside their catch.

"I'll show you a trick," he promised.

He scaled the fish, removed their heads and fins, and made a clean cut down the back. Deftly, needing only a moment, he worked the flesh away and left the bones. Tad knelt near by, watching and admiring every move, and Joe said patiently,

"Move a little away, will you? I'd sure hate to slice you up along with these fish."

Tad grinned and moved a couple of inches back. Joe worked on. When he was done he had only boneless fish, with all the offal left behind, and there had been no waste of anything. Joe smacked his lips.

"You cook something out of a fish when you cook the bones into it," he said. "Wait'll you try these."

"Maybe Mom will fix them tonight, huh?"

"Could be. Let's go find out."

Pete Domley's white horse was tied outside the door, and Pete came from the house to meet them. Joe handed the filleted fish, which he was carrying on a slab of wood, to Tad.

"Take these to your mother, will you? She'll want them soon if we're going to have them for supper."

Pete Domley glanced down at the pile of fish and sniffed hungrily. "They look downright good. It's a long while since I've had time to get any for myself."

"Maybe you'll stay and help us eat these?" Joe invited. "There's plenty."

Pete grinned. "I might just do that. Sorry about the cow. She stepped in a chuck hole and broke a front leg. There just wasn't anything else to do."

"I know. Thanks for taking care of it, Pete."

"Emma said to sell the beef to Les."

"Yeah, and I reckon she's right. Nobody here would eat it."

"Les gave me twenty-three dollars and seventy cents, cash money. I gave it all to Emma."

"You should have kept something for your trouble."

"It wasn't any trouble. Emma says you're going to Oregon?"

"That's right, Pete. We are."

Pete said seriously, "I don't know but what it would be a good move for anybody. Yes, I'm sure it would be."

"Why don't you come along?"

"I probably would, if I was fifteen years younger. But I'm pushing fifty, and I've chased a lot of will-o'-the-wisps in my day. Guess I'm getting chicken-hearted."

"Oregon's no will-o'-the-wisp."

"I know, but by the time a man gets to be my age he thinks everything is. I stick to what I know, and I can't make out any place unless I think so. I don't think I'd make out in Oregon. Want to sell me your standing hay?"

"I'll give it to you."

"Don't be so open-hearted; you're going to Oregon and you'll need money. Besides, I winter a lot of stock and hay's worth money to me. Would twenty-five dollars be right?"

"Right enough with me."

"Good. I'll cut the hay when it's ready for cutting. I swear, Joe, you look like a kid again."

"I almost feel like one, Pete. Doggone, it's not that I don't like

Missouri. It's just that I sort of felt myself batting my head against a brick wall here, and now we're going to Oregon."

Pete nodded wisely. "The world would be just as well off if all men hit down a new road when the old one ends blind. Only most of us lack the courage to get off paths we know. Especially when we're older. I envy you."

"Don't be so darn philosophical, Pete. Come on. Let's go in and wait for something to eat."

Pete Domley finished his meal and rode away. A great restlessness gnawed at Joe, and he felt his usual imperative urge to be doing something. Only now it was a happy anticipation, and not a frustrating tenseness. Joe glanced at the lowering sun, decided that at least an hour of daylight remained, and a moment later Tad joined him.

"Hey, Pa, let's be doin' somethin'. Huh?"

"Sure. Let's bring some of that oak and hickory in from the wood lot."

Joe was amazed. Ordinarily Tad could be forced to work only under threat of immediate punishment. Even then, unless he liked it, he would not keep at whatever task was assigned him unless he were watched every second. That he should offer of his own free will to help was itself a minor revolution, and proof that he was infected with what Joe was beginning to think of as Oregon fever.

They caught and harnessed the mules. Joe shouldered a peavey —a logger's hook—and let Tad drive the mules to the wood lot. Joe used his peavey to roll half a dozen of the seasoned oak and hickory logs over a long chain, bound the chain around them, and hitched the mules to it. In the gathering twilight, Joe and his son walked side by side while the mules dragged the logs back to the house. They unharnessed the mules and let them frolic in their pasture.

The logs lay ready to be taken to John Geragty's saw mill. Joe gave them one final glance. When they were sawed into boards he would use part of them himself. Part John Geragty would take as pay for his labor, and the rest would be sold or traded for all the things they needed and did not have for their trip to Oregon. It was the first short step.

Joe felt a surging, happy restlessness, but he had no wish to go to the store. It seemed as though, somehow, his family had become a unique group that had nothing to do with anybody else and were no part of anyone else. They were going to Oregon while all the rest were staying here, and that set them apart. Joe wanted to stay with them because of this new-found and delightful kinship with each other.

He watched Barbara and Emma folding Emma's wedding dress, a long white, frilly thing, between clean curtains. Obviously the dress was destined to be part of the contents of a trunk that yawned on the kitchen floor. Joe got up to lend a hand; the dress could be folded much more compactly and thus occupy less space.

"Now you just sit down," Emma ordered. "This is not a mule or an ax."

"I was just trying to help."

"Not with this." The glance she gave him was one of mingled tenderness and amusement.

Tad sat at the table, working expertly with a whetstone as he put a razor edge back on his knife. Carlyle, still so young that the use of his legs was new to him, wobbled precariously across the floor and grasped Joe's knee. He paused, his fascinated eyes riveted on something, and when Joe looked he saw a fish scale that clung to his trousers and reflected rainbow tints in the lamp light. Joe lifted the youngster into his lap, and Carlyle bent over so he could continue to watch the fish scale.

"Come on," Joe invited the other. "I know a story."

His little fist closed, Alfred came to stand before Joe. The youngster's eyes danced, a grin parted his lips.

"Present for you," he said, extending his closed fist.

Joe reached to take it, but when Alfred opened his fist there was nothing at all there and the child howled with glee. Joe looked intently at his hand, and he pretended to slip the gift into his pocket.

"Thanks," he said seriously, "that's just about the nicest present I ever had!"

Alfred looked puzzled. Dainty little Emma and sober Joe came to him, and Joe gathered all of them into his lap.

"Went fishing today," he said, "and the first thing you know there was an old man with long white whiskers standing right on the bottom of the creek . . ."

He improvised as his story unfolded, telling how the old man's white whiskers hid an enormous mouth into which fish swam. Every now and again, probably because he was angry, he spit a fish at Joe or Tad. Baby Emma looked suspiciously at him and Tad turned with a knowing grin, but all remained interested. Finally the biggest fish of all came along and had trouble getting into the old man's mouth. There, and at once, he grew half again as big. When the old man tried to spit that fish he couldn't; he could get only half of it out of his mouth. Neither could he take it all the way in. The last Joe saw of him he was walking up the bottom of the creek with the fish still half in and half out of his mouth.

Carlyle went to sleep in his arms and little Emma rested contentedly against his shoulder. Little Joe frowned while he considered this new problem, a fish stuck in an old man's mouth, and Alfred yawned. Emma came to clasp baby Emma gently to her and she put the child to bed. One by one, Barbara took the rest.

Joe sat nervously in his chair, too tense to sleep and not knowing what to do. The night-to-be seemed an interminable time, and morning would never come. Joe thought of a hundred things he must do and he ached to be doing them so they could start for Oregon.

"You better go to bed," Emma told him

"I couldn't sleep."

"Neither can you stay awake until we start for Oregon." She came to his side and ran her hand through his hair, thinking, *He is part boy, part man. Like a boy, he can't wait to start. Like a man—like Joe,* she corrected herself, *he wants to make everything*

double-safe for his young ones. Only, can he make things safe? Is
there any safety in the wilderness?

Her hand stilled, then resolutely took up its stroking again.
"Tomorrow's another day," she said.

Joe grinned. "Could be you're right. I'll turn in."

He was awake with earliest daylight, and lay staring at the thin
dawn that lurked behind curtain-draped windows. It was a happy
awakening, and the day held more true promise than any Joe
could remember. He had, he felt as he lay beside Emma, been
born all over again. But he had hurdled childhood and been born
as a wholly new kind of man with nothing mean or petty in his
life. Emma stirred beside him and Joe's hand stole out to clasp
hers. For a moment they lay side by side, anticipating events-to-
be by living their greatest adventure in their minds.

After breakfast Joe and Tad skidded more seasoned oak and
hickory logs in from the wood lot. He took the box from his wagon
and drove the stripped-down wagon up beside the logs. Loading
them was really a two-man job, but one man could do it.

Joe slanted and braced two short logs against the wagon and
used his peavey to roll one of the heavier logs toward them. He
rolled one end a short way up one of the leaning logs and braced
it with a chunk of wood. Going to the other end, he rolled that
up and blocked it. By alternating ends, and rolling each a short
way at a time, he finally loaded the log onto the wagon. Tad stood
impatiently near.

"I'll help you, Pa."

Joe shook his head. "Not with this."

"Aw, I can handle a peavey."

"Nope. If one of those logs rolled on you, there wouldn't be
enough left to scrape up."

"Let me help!"

Joe said patiently, "You watch and see how it's done. Maybe the
next time you can help."

Tad squatted on his heels and watched, sulking. Joe loaded the
wagon, chained the load, and climbed on top of it to drive through

Tenney's Crossing to John Geragty's saw mill. There was plenty of timber to be had for the taking, but never a surplus of seasoned oak and hickory. John would have no trouble selling it for a good price, and therefore he would take his pay for sawing in lumber instead of money. Joe drove up to the saw mill, and John Geragty came to meet him.

"Hear you're goin' to Oregon," he greeted.

"You hear right, John. Who told you?"

"Everybody knows it by this time. The Crossin' hasn't had this kind of news to chew on since Casey McManus was lynched."

"Hope the chewing's good," Joe grinned. "Got some seasoned oak and hickory. Want to work it up for me?"

"What do you need?"

"Boards for a wagon box and a new reach and axles. Wouldn't do any harm to have an extra tongue, too."

"Cash deal?"

"Share."

"I don't know," the other said doubtfully. "You want to buy the metal for your axles?"

"Sure."

"Then it's a deal. We'll split the timber half and half. If you don't need all yours, I'll sell it for you. Bill Logan's buildin' a new barn and he wants good lumber."

"Good enough."

Joe drove home with his empty wagon, and the mules pricked their long ears forward when they came in sight of the pasture. Two saddle horses were tied to the fence, and Joe recognized one of them as Percy Pearl's fine thoroughbred. The other was a blocky paint owned by Watson Charters, a quarrelsome man who was greatly impressed with his own importance. Largely because nobody else would take the job, which meant that they might have to embarrass their neighbors, Watson Charters was the local constable and he did a great deal of work for Elias Dorrance. Charters came forward to meet Joe, closely followed by Percy Pearl. Joe jumped down from the wagon.

Charters produced a penciled document, obviously one he had written himself, from his pocket and began to read it:

"I hereby restrict and enjoin you, under clause A, article 13, of the laws of the State of Missouri, from removing from this property, or causing anyone else to remove from this property, any grasses, crops, or other article that takes root from the ground. I—"

"Wait a minute," Percy Pearl interrupted blandly. "I didn't understand. Read it again, Watson."

The constable looked annoyed, but started reading, "I hereby restrict and enjoin you, under clause A—"

"Now isn't that something?" Percy said admiringly. "He wrote it all by himself, too. Reminds me of some of the literary masterpieces I myself created when I was a student in the sixth form at Carrodale. Only Watson's is sheer genius. 'Grasses, crops, or other article that takes root from the ground.' Banishes immediately any lingering doubts one might have that they're rooted in the air. Who besides Watson would have thought of such a thing?"

Watson Charters said, "You'll have to be quiet, Percy."

"No, I won't have to be quiet. Article 1, Bill of Rights, the Constitution of the United States. That's an interesting document, too, in its own little way. Of course there's no comparison between that and yours."

"I am here," Watson Charters said, "to—"

"Yes, Joe," Percy said piously. "We are both here to see that justice is not made to grovel in the muck. Justice! May it ever be supreme! Watson is here to inform you that you cannot sell your standing hay to Pete Domley or take any more timber from your wood lot. The reason? Our friend Elias wishes to sell it himself."

"It's not his!" Joe roared. "Darn his picture! I cut that wood myself and Elias hasn't any right to the hay!"

"Sell that hay or take any more wood," Watson Charters said, "and I'll jail you."

Percy Pearl's hand moved as smoothly as a bit of rustling silk. Seemingly plucked from nowhere, a pistol appeared in it. The pistol blasted. As though it were blown by the wind, Watson Charters' hat lifted from his head and spiraled to the ground, a hole in its brim. Percy Pearl remained unruffled.

"How clumsy," he murmured. "But I still don't understand you, Watson. What are you going to do if Joe sells more wood or the hay?"

"Now look, Percy, I'm just—"

"I know," Percy soothed. "You are a selfless and devoted man who is just doing his duty with no thought of personal compensation, except maybe a third of whatever else Elias can steal from Joe. But what did you say you're going to do to Joe?"

There was a silence while the muscles worked in Watson's jaws. "I'm not goin' to do anything to him," he said gruffly. "Elias can handle this himself."

He mounted his blocky horse and rode away. Percy Pearl looked at Joe, and a delighted chuckle escaped him.

CHAPTER SIX

The Party

A HUGE sycamore with a massive, hollow trunk grew about twenty five yards from Joe's barn. It was a very old tree and taller than most sycamores. Because it was all alone, and received no shade or interference from other trees, it had many branches and all of them were alive. Full-leafed, the sycamore cast comfortable shade over a wide area.

Joe had his forge and anvil set up beneath the tree. Barbara stood ready to work the forge's bellows and the horse mule was tethered near by. Putting new shoes on both mules was the last necessary job before they could start for Oregon, but Joe was pensive as he prepared to go about the task.

For a while after deciding to go to Oregon, heightening excitement and enthusiasm of the older members of the family had communicated itself to the younger. Carlyle still wanted to know, at least fifteen times a day, when they were leaving and how soon they would arrive. Joe, Emma, and Alfred, had come to accept the journey as a matter of course. But Tad remained the only one whose spirits had not been even slightly dampened.

Leaving for Oregon remained a glorious adventure. But all except Tad had discovered, when it came time to decide just what was going with them and what would have to stay behind, that to break off an old life and start a new one would cause even more wrenches than they had expected. A house was big, and if another room were needed, one could always be added. But a wagon box had definite limitations.

Joe had taken the wooden handles from his hoes, rakes, and

peaveys. Of his harrow, he was taking only the metal parts and he had even removed the wooden handles from his beloved plow. There was little likelihood that he'd be using some tools on the Trail and he could replace the missing wood when they got to Oregon. Even so, his tool box was filled. They had to have an ax or how would they chop wood? He might need his screw drivers, awls, chisels, augers, wrenches, saws, any time at all. They couldn't be made more compact than they already were. Naturally, the rifle had to be in working order. Joe had limited himself strictly to that which they could not do without on the Trail or would need for starting a new life in Oregon, and he sold or traded everything he could spare. It had cost him a pang to part with hammers, chisels, wrenches, and other tools which he had used so many years that their handles were worn to the shape of his hand. But he was more keenly aware of the sacrifices made by Emma and Barbara.

With an eye to Barbara's future needs, Emma had packed the wedding dress and a few other items which could not be classed as utilitarian. For herself she had taken only her sturdiest dresses and had packed only necessities for each of the children. As a final indulgence, and only after a deep inner struggle as to whether or not she was doing the right thing, she had packed the first pair of baby shoes each of the children had worn.

Helping her mother, Barbara had quietly slipped two of Emma's prettier dresses into the trunk and Emma had promptly removed them. Barbara had packed a battered rag doll that was greatly treasured by little Emma, a string ball that was Joe's plaything, a set of fading wooden blocks with animals pictured on them for Alfred, and a bright picture that Carlyle adored. She had argued Emma into accepting these by reminding her that, though the children would have toys in the wagon, they would become tired of them. Then these could be brought out and they would arouse complete new interest.

Those were some of the minor problems. But there had been major heart-breaks too and Joe knew that only one of them centered around the stove. Emma was equally proud of an exquisitely made chest of drawers which probably had been brought to Missouri by a trading party sent out by the migrating Mormons. They had left the Mormon Trail and had come into Missouri for food, and because they hadn't any money they traded the goods in their wagons for bacon or grain. Joe had traded a shoat for the chest of drawers some six or eight years ago.

Emma said nothing about leaving it behind, but because Joe knew her he knew what it cost her to do so. Then, with sudden inspiration, he had pointed out that the chest of drawers could be lashed inside the wagon and would be a convenient storage place for the clothes they would need day by day. Emma had paid him with a grateful smile, but that was not what Joe thought about right now.

He'd been repairing the wagon when he went to the house for a drink of water. Chance had taken him past the kitchen window, and unseen by her, he had observed Emma sitting at the kitchen table. Arranged on it was all her lovely, delicate china. Joe spent an uncomfortable moment watching her adore with her eyes and caress with her hands the most exquisite and beautiful things she had ever owned. Then he had slipped away as quietly as he came, and when he went to the house an hour later the china was all back in the cupboard.

It had stayed there while the days passed, and Joe said nothing because he could think of nothing to say. Emma was fighting day by day, wanting to keep the china and yet knowing that she could not. Finally, and only yesterday, she had asked Joe, all too casually, if he would take it over and give it to Helen Domley.

Doggedly, Joe continued his preparations to shoe the mules. He hadn't given the china to Helen Domley. He had carried it to John Geragty's saw mill, nailed a box together, tenderly packed each piece of china in sawdust, covered the box, and sneaked it into the wagon. Now he worried because it seemed that, somehow, he had both deceived Emma and cheated Helen Domley.

Barbara asked, "Is something the matter, Daddy?"

"Nope," Joe evaded. "Start the bellows will you, honey?"

Barbara hesitated a moment and Joe waited. The past days had wrought a change in his daughter, making her all the more difficult to understand. At times she seemed to have a new maturity, as though she were already a woman, and at others she was a trembling child. But she had never expressed anything except enthusiastic interest in the forthcoming trip. She began to work the bellows steadily, neither too fast nor too slow, and the smell of the hot charcoal in the forge was a good thing.

With a pair of iron tongs, Joe held the mule shoe he was fashioning in the glowing charcoal until the shoe partook of the fire's color. Still gripping it with the tongs, a blacksmith's maul in his right hand, Joe shaped the shoe on the anvil.

Some people didn't care how they shoed their mules; they simply nailed shoes on and let the hoofs grow out to fit them. Joe had never believed in such slipshod methods. He gave painstaking consideration to the temper and weight of the shoe, and the conformation of the hoof it was to fit. Correctly shod draft animals did not go lame easily and they worked harder because they were comfortable. Joe trusted no one else to shoe his mules for him.

He looked critically at the shoe, then reheated it and gave it a slightly wider curve. The mule's hoofs were nearly alike. But they were not exactly alike and each shoe must be designed accordingly. Finally satisfied, Joe plunged the shoe in a pail of tepid water and approached the mule.

The mare mule, at shoeing time, literally went wild. She became so terrified that she had to be dragged to the forge and roped and hog-tied after she was there to keep her from injuring the blacksmith. But the horse had a streak of vanity that took peculiar directions. He was proud to wear new shoes, and after they were nailed on he spent hours walking about to test them. Usually a full day passed before he no longer gave his new-shod hoofs any attention.

When Joe approached, the mule lifted his rear hoof voluntarily and held it. He did it gracefully, taking all his weight on his other three legs and never at any time endangering Joe. Joe tried the shoe, and when he saw that it was a perfect fit he nailed it on. The mule swung his head to look approvingly at his hoof. Joe rose and wiped the sweat from his forehead.

Everything except the mule shoeing was done. The wagon had a new box, and all the parts that had seemed even slightly weak or worn had been replaced. They knew exactly what they were going to take along, and among other things they were going to take six of Emma's best hens plus a rooster, and there was a place for everything. New, double-thick canvas covered the wagon, and Joe had even arranged a canvas drop curtain so that, if it were necessary to camp inside, the male and female members of his family could have their own compartments. Joe had ninety-eight dollars in cash, and an uneasy feeling that it would not be nearly enough. But he did not know how to get any more.

As soon as Pete Domley came—and he should be here any minute—they could rope and shoe the mare mule. There they could start, and the sooner the better. Joe had dreamed of the Oregon Trail so many times that, if he wasn't on it soon, he felt that he would begin braying like a mule himself. He smiled at his daughter.

"I think we'll leave tomorrow morning, Bobby."

"Oh, Daddy! May I stay with Marcia tonight?"

Her lambent eyes glowed with pure delight, and Joe noted with approval the fire in her voice. Though it was not an unmixed blessing, Barbara felt all of everything that touched her. Her temperament, Joe felt, was not unlike the glowing fire in the forge. He said,

"It's all right with me if it is with your mother."

"Are you happy, Daddy?"

"Sure am! I— What the dickens!"

Pete Domley's white horse had appeared on the path leading from Tenney's Crossing, but Pete was not alone on the horse. Ahead of him, clutched firmly in Pete's strong hands, was Tad. Pete was also packing a rifle, something he seldom did unless he intended to go hunting. He reined his horse to a halt beside Joe.

"I figure this is your business!"

"What's my business?"

Pete said firmly, "Tell him, Tad."

Tad's face was sullen and angry, with every freckle livid. He stared almost haughtily at his father and Joe's eyes narrowed. He said,

"That's my rifle too, huh?"

"Right."

Tad snapped, "If a man's goin' west he'd better know how to fight Indians. And I didn't hit him."

"That's right," Pete agreed, "but you couldn't have shoved a knife blade between the place where that bullet hit the wall and his head."

Joe felt hot anger rise. "Who did he shoot at?"

"He came into the Crossing lugging your rifle," Pete asserted, "and before anybody could stop him he took a shot at Lard Head."

"I didn't take a shot at him," Tad denied. "If I had, I'd of hit him."

Joe said grimly, "Bobby, you go help your mother. Pete will work the bellows for me when we shoe the mare."

The girl left, not looking back, and Joe faced his son. "Get off that horse."

Tad obeyed, but his chin was outthrust and his eyes flashed. Joe flexed his right arm.

"Take down your britches."

Tad's pants slid around his ankles, and Joe grasped him with his left arm and turned his bare buttocks upward. With carefully measured force Joe brought the palm of his right hand down, and the mule turned to look curiously on this strange scene while Pete's horse danced skittishly. Tad's normally pink seat assumed a fiery hue, but he did not cry out. Finished, Joe set the boy gently on his feet.

"If ever, except in your own self-defense, you shoot at another man, be he red, white, yellow, or black, you're going to get this over again and three times as hard."

Tears welled up in Tad's eyes, but his jaw was still outthrust and his shoulders were squared as he walked away. Joe scratched his shaggy head in wonder.

"I'll be doggoned! Can you tie that one?"

"Nope," Pete admitted. "I can't."

"What would you have done?"

"Same thing you did, Joe. I will say, though, that it's some of the neatest shooting I ever saw. Lard Head was standing against Frawley Thompson's fence, and that bullet whistled close enough to curl his hair. I'll bet there's one Indian scared sober."

"Was he drunk?"

"He's always drunk."

"Makes no difference," Joe declared. "That kid of mine has to have some respect for people, Indians included. And he's got to realize that rifles are dangerous."

Pete said dryly, "I kind of think he's beginning to. Shall we bring your mare mule in and shoe her?"

"Reckon."

They roped the mare mule, dragged her to the forge, threw her, and shoed her. She struck viciously when they let her up, but Joe had expected the attack and he dodged it. They put both mules back in their pasture and Joe looked uneasily at the house. Emma never struck any of the children, and Joe had just administered Tad's first spanking. If there were to be repercussions, they might as well be faced right now. Joe said,

"Excuse me a minute, Pete."

"Sure."

Joe walked nervously toward the house. Beyond much doubt, they would start for Oregon tomorrow and he had had few arguments with Emma. He felt uneasily that beginning their trip with a quarrel would be a bad omen, and sure to bring bad luck. Joe quailed when he looked in at the door, for Emma bristled to meet him.

"What did you do to Tad?"

Joe braced himself, then became a little angry. "I paddled his hinder for him, hard as I wanted to lay it on!"

"If you hadn't, Joe Tower, I'd have paddled yours! The idea! Shooting at that poor, besotted Indian!"

Joe asked in astonishment, "You're not mad at me!"

"I would be, if you hadn't done a father's duty!"

He put his hand on her shoulder for a moment, and gave her a wry smile. "Did Tad tell you?"

"Tad hasn't been near the house. Barbara told me." She wilted into his arms. "Oh, Joe, do you suppose—?"

Because he knew her so well, Joe knew what she was thinking. At eight years of age all youngsters were harmless, but at eighteen some might be bad and some good. Joe crushed his wife to him.

He said, "We'll teach him. It's just that he has to learn some things the hard way."

"Oh Joe! I'm glad we're going! Oregon will be good for him!"

Joe's heart skipped a beat with delight at hearing her say this. "It will give him a chance to work his vinegar off. I'm not so sure he could do that if he stayed here. He'd want a farm of his own, and Elias would have to loan him some of the money to buy it, and the first time Elias pressed him there'd be fur flying. It wouldn't be Tad's either."

They felt a tender intimacy, a closeness that made them cling together. Joe cleared his throat. He had deceived her, and now he must undo that deception.

He said, "I didn't give your dishes to Helen."

"But," her eyes puzzled, "I asked you to."

"I know. I made a box for them and put them in the wagon instead."

A little anguished shadow flitted across her face. "I couldn't bear to have them broken."

"They won't be broken," he assured her. "The Casper's broke because they just didn't know how to pack. We're taking eggs too, aren't we? Every piece will get to Oregon with us."

The anguished shadow faded and she cast him a glance of purest love. But doubts remained, and she was a bit ashamed.

"We have so much to carry and so little room."

"There's room for that little box. You'd like to have your dishes, wouldn't you?"

"I'd love to!"

"Then they're going to Oregon with us. I'd better get the rifle. Left it outside."

Joe walked out to get the rifle, which was still leaning against the sycamore, and he returned to the house with it. He smiled whimsically. The pegs in his and Emma's bedroom were no longer a safe place for the rifle; they hadn't been in the first place or Tad never would have been able to smuggle the weapon out of the house. Joe set his jaw. Tad would have to use the rifle; it was an indispensable part of any man's equipment on any frontier. But he would have to use it properly. If he didn't, if there was any more irresponsible shooting, he'd feel the flat of his father's hand again.

For the time being, Joe hung the rifle back on its pegs. He turned to smile at his wife.

"The mules are shod, and there's not a darn thing to do except start for Oregon."

Emma clasped her hands together, her one gesture of apprehension. "It doesn't seem possible, does it?"

"Nope. Seems like there must be a hundred things to do yet. We'd best remember to catch your hens and rooster while they're on the roost tonight. Oh my golly!"

"What's the matter?"

"I left Pete standing outside!"

Joe went to the door to call Pete, and just as he did so Yancey Garrow rode up on his gaunt brown horse. He held a package across the saddle in front of him, and his fiddle case was over his shoulder. Grinning, he dismounted.

"Lucy thought you might like to take this along. It's a ham and a side of bacon."

"You butchering now?"

"We always," and Yancey voiced what Joe knew was a bald-faced lie, "kill one hog in summer." Joe gulped. With the possible exception of John Seeley, who could afford it, nobody butchered in the summer. But the Garrows had wanted their departing friends to enjoy ham and bacon. Joe said,

"That's right good of you, Yancey."

"It's nothing," the other said airily. He carried the package of meat into the house.

Emma greeted him. "Hello, Yancey."

"Hi, Emma. I swear you get prettier every day. How you ever fell for an old he-coon like Joe is something I'll never understand." He shifted the fiddle to his other shoulder. Pete stood in the doorway, and seemed to be waiting.

"Play something, Yancey," Emma pleaded. "Play some music for us."

"Sure. What do you want to hear?"

"Anything."

Yancey Garrow took his fiddle out of its case, tucked it under his chin, and drew the bow across it a couple of times. He began a lively rendition of "Yankee Doodle." Her face flushed with pleasure, Barbara emerged from her room.

"Long while since I've danced with a girl as pretty as you are!" Pete Domley declared. "Come on, Bobby."

He whirled her around the room while Yancey increased the tempo of his music. Grinning, Joe took Emma in his arms. A shadow darkened the door and Fellers Compton was there.

"Stretch my ears and call me a jackass!" he breathed. "You people get the best ideas of anybody in Missouri!"

He had a wrapped parcel in his hands and he put it down on the table. "Caroline put up too much strawberry preserves and she hopes to unload some of it on you, now that you're going away. Keep playing, Yancey. I'll be back."

While Joe danced with Barbara and Pete Domley with Emma, Yancey played "Oh, Susannah," and then another of Foster's songs. Putting his fiddle aside for a second, Yancey dipped himself a drink of water. Barbara's and Emma's eyes were glistening, for the air was tense and expectant. This was the way most parties started. Yancey put the gourd dipper beside the bucket of water just as old Tom Abend drove up with his wife, his three youngest children, his two married daughters, their husbands, and their children.

"Fellers said we might come over here to see what's goin' on," he greeted.

"Right good idea," Joe said.

Tom continued, "One of my boys shot a buck last week, and we made jerky. Lot more'n we can use so I brought some for you to take along."

"Thanks, Tom."

Joe saw Tom's amiable wife and daughters chatting with Emma. In addition to jerky, meant to go along with the departing wagon, they had brought four pies, several pounds of butter, some fresh venison, and two lanterns. Yancey swung into the plaintive melody of "Ben Bolt" and Joe found himself dancing with one of Tom Abend's daughters while her husband danced with Emma.

The neighbors came on horse- and muleback, in wagons and carts, and on foot, with those who lived nearest arriving first. All bore gifts, and all explained that they simply had too much at home. The Towers would really be doing them a favor to take some of it off their hands. In addition, all brought whatever had been ready for a hoedown in the making. They overflowed the house and spilled out into the yard, but somebody had stretched a rope between the house and the barn and hung lighted lanterns on it. Tonight there would be no thought of saving lantern oil. Tonight was for fun.

Yancey played until he was tired, and then Les Tenney spelled him. While not as expert a fiddler as Yancey, Les knew a great many tunes, variations on those tunes, and when he could think of nothing else he improvised his own music. Joe saw Barbara dancing with Marcia Geragty, but only for a second. Grinning, two of Tom Abend's big sons separated the girls and danced them away. Dancing with eight-year-old Celia Trevelyan, Tad was having a wonderful time and even the babies danced with each other.

Inside the house, the table groaned under its weight of food and a huge pot of coffee, and those who were hungry could help themselves to as much as they wanted any time they wanted it. But nobody lingered inside for very long. Old Tom Abend tapped Joe on the shoulder.

"My sons-in-law got a coon treed behind the barn. They want you to come help shake it out."

"Sounds like fun."

"It will be."

Joe followed old Tom out of the light cast by the hanging lanterns and into the dark shadows cast by the barn. Tom's two husky sons-in-law stood beside the barrel of whisky that they had set up on blocks of wood and tapped. The crowd around the barrel increased as more men slipped away from the dance, and cups rattled as they were filled and passed around. Old Tom said clearly.

"We'll drink to the Tower family and Oregon!"

"All right!" they chorused. "To all the Towers and Oregon!"

Joe stepped back into the shadows, raised the cup to his lips, and managed, unseen, to spill it onto the grass. But he felt as though he had drunk all of it. His feet were light and airy, and his head seemed clearer than it had ever been before. He laughed unrestrainedly, and rejoined the party just in time to choose Emma as his partner for a square dance which Lance Trevelyan was calling;

"Alamen left and you git around,
Hand over hand like a merry-go-round."

As the dance gathered tempo, all the younger children were put to sleep in either the beds or in whichever wagon was not already crowded with sleeping youngsters. Joe danced on, and at intervals cups again rattled behind the barn while the barrel became lighter.

Because it seemed to him that the dance had just started, Joe was amazed when the sun rose.

CHAPTER SEVEN

Independence

THE LAST hour the Towers spent at their old home was a time of bustling confusion and great activity. Joe shook hands with all the men, and stood awkwardly while all the women kissed his cheek and wished him well. The women gathered about Emma, and tears flowed as they embraced. Joe gulped, more than ever realizing the enormity of the task they had undertaken and what it involved. The people gathered about were the friends of a lifetime, and living together had cemented more than superficial friendship. There was love too, and respect, and Joe had a sudden wild desire to ask everybody to go with him. He tried not to look at the weeping Emma, and knew a lighter moment when he saw Tad, knife at his belt, swaggering before the younger set. Then he saw Helen Domley with Carlyle in her arms and turned away so no man would see the tears in his own eyes.

Under no circumstances could Joe have described exactly how they started for Oregon; he saw the over-all picture but not the details. He did know that the mattresses, the last articles to go into the wagon, were carried there and placed exactly right by an army of willing workers. The same army literally overwhelmed and hitched the mules, and tied the placid cow to the wagon's rear. Joe's four younger children, still sleepy, promptly went to sleep on the mattresses. Tad, who had already asserted his determination to walk all the way to Oregon, refused to ride and Mike stayed at his heels. Barbara walked hand in hand with Marcia Geragty, and Emma was in John Geragty's wagon. Nobody else was going to Oregon, but the Towers would have plenty of company for at least the first part of their journey. Not everybody could see them off, for some had to return to their work. But most went.

The mules, overawed at being caught and harnessed by so many expert muleteers, were completely tractable. They strained willingly into their harness when Joe gave the order. Ahead, behind, and one both sides, rode or walked the people they were leaving. One by one they had to turn back and start in the other direction, and the last to turn was Marcia Geragty. Though Joe could not be positive about many other details of their leave-taking, he was never to forget the parting of his daughter and her best friend.

They were walking ahead of the wagon, still hand in hand but not shoulder to shoulder. They were not looking at each other. Suddenly, and Joe thought that no word passed between them, they stepped off the road and embraced. Joe stopped the wagon so Barbara could climb in, and because he did not want her to know that he saw tears in her eyes, he stared straight ahead. Emma came from John Geragty's cart to climb up on the wagon seat beside Joe and the last thing the Towers heard from any of their Missouri friends were the Geragtys shouting,

"Good luck, and God bless you!"

Except for the stubborn Tad, who obviously intended to make good his boast that he would walk all the way to Oregon, Joe's family was in the wagon. The accustomed routine of the youngest children had been interrupted sufficiently to keep them sleepy and subdued. The others spoke little, for Joe, Emma, and Barbara, had stayed up until the dance ended. In addition, for the first time each in his own way was beginning fully to realize that they were definitely on the way. They thought of all they had left behind, and wondered about what was to come. There seemed so much to wonder about. Yet everything they might expect to find had only a vague shape in their minds. Emma reflected, as she moved with the jogging motion of the wagon, that to wonder vaguely about a vague future is in itself a tiring thing, more tiring even than a hoedown.

At the first night's camp there was much to do, and all of them too weary to do it. But Joe did cut wood for a fire, and chain the mules so they couldn't break away and go home, and tether the cow in a place where she could find good grazing, and feed Emma's poultry. He was glad that he had to do no more. Emma spread out some of the remainders of last night's feast, but no one had much interest in eating. At the same time no one regretted any part of last night. A rousing hoedown was the right way to take leave of your friends.

The little ones nodded over their food and then, with the familiar faces of Emma and Barbara hovering over them and the familiar arms of Emma and Barbara holding and hugging them, they snuggled down into their places in the wagon as if nothing here were in any way new or different. Joe made a pallet for Emma and one for Barbara, and then he and Tad rolled up in their blankets and lay down a few feet away.

Tad fell asleep in an instant, and slept so deeply that he snored a little, something he did only when he was completely exhausted. The occasional snort, emerging at intervals from the bundle of blanket that was Tad, brought a smile to Joe's face as he lay beside him. That young one was going to live this trip to the hilt, every minute of it. For a moment Joe felt good that Tad was to have this tremendous adventure while he was still so young. But the good feeling gave way almost at once to a medley of thoughts that shouldered each other out of the way for his attention— thoughts of possible accidents, and plans to be made—plans that would be revised from day to day according to the hazards and needs of the moment. As the land beneath them changed, they would all need to change, to make the best of whatever might come, to adapt themselves to each day's demands on them. The older ones would have to fend for the younger ones. He thought of Emma and Barbara and Tad, and his heart warmed at the thought of their courage and their loyalty. And then his heart froze at the thought of the dangers that might overtake them. And so, with this turmoil of feelings in his breast, Joe Tower slowly, reluctantly, unwilling to leave his problems unsolved, dropped off into an uneasy sleep.

Barbara looked up at the stars and at the soft depth of the night sky. She thought there was something eerie and yet wonderful about sleeping in the open with her whole family around her. Tonight we are God's children, she thought. We are closer to God here, with no roof between us and Him. How fragrant was the night air! How mysterious and beautiful was the soft rustling of grass and brush, stirring in the gentle summer breeze! The scratching of a field mouse, the chirp of a cricket—everything was full of life and promise for the future. She stretched luxuriously, thinking of great mountains and wide, wild rivers, and of vast western plains where they would meet strapping farmers and ranchers, some of them, perhaps, with tall handsome sons, sons with strong arms and laughing eyes. She grinned at herself then, and curled into a ball and dropped off to sleep, wondering whether the grass would be as fragrant in Oregon.

Emma lay staring into blackness. Without a familiar tree or rooftop silhouetted against it, the sky was a vast and awesome thing. It was limitless, remote and indifferent. Her family was a few scattered scraps of humanity, fallen down here to rest on the unfriendly ground under the distant, disinterested sky. She twitched when a cricket chirped and, shivering, drew the blanket closer around her. She wanted to go to Joe, and to lie close to him, but she dared not show him that she was afraid. From this point on, for the children's sake, she must be the woman they thought her to be—endlessly resourceful and forever serene. Her eyes ached with staring, and she hungered for the familiar walls of their little room, or failing that, at least a familiar fence, a familiar tree, a familiar anything. Then she thought of the babies, of their dear familiar faces now placid in slumber. She thought of Barbara's familiar grace as she walked beside the wagon, of Tad's familiar bounding and leaping as he led his dog a merry chase. And she thought of Joe, of his familiar voice as he talked to the children, of the strength of his arms as he helped her down from the wagon, and of his willing, unstinting devotion to all of them. She knew then that all the dearest and most familiar parts of her life were right here, all around her.

Tears welled into her eyes, and she let them run down over her cheeks, and she prayed that she would be strong enough and brave enough, and that they would reach Oregon alive and well and that, on the new land, they would all be happy and at peace.

By the next morning the passing of time had already started to heal their wounds. With baby Emma and little Joe beside her, Emma chose to walk for a while. Alfred and Carlyle, swelling with pride at being elevated to a place of such importance, rode on the seat beside Joe. Barbara danced down the trail, filling her arms with summer-blooming flowers. With Mike always at his heels, Tad left the road for the more exciting country on either side. He would disappear for an hour or more, but he always reappeared, sometimes waiting ahead of the wagon and sometimes running to catch up with it.

After three days and a few hours on the road, they came at last to Independence. Everybody except Tad chose to ride.

Joe took a little firmer grip on the reins, and he felt a growing tension that he tried to conceal. He had been born only five miles from Tenney's Crossing, and until now, never in all his life had he been more than forty miles from his birthplace. He knew Tenney's, Hammerstown, and the other settlements and he felt at home in them. But he had never been to a city. Joe smiled nervously. Maybe, if a man realized all the implications in all the decisions he made, he would decide some things differently. It was one thing to decide to go to Oregon, but quite another to go, and Joe was honestly frightened because he had to pass through a city.

He set his jaw and growled inwardly to himself. He had no quarrel with anyone in Independence. There was no reason why anyone there should quarrel with him, and whoever minded his own business usually got along all right. But he had never seen, or imagined, such imposing buildings or so many people living near each other. A little excitement stole his nervousness and he said to Emma,

"Quite a place, huh?"

Her voice was shocked, "Joe, did you see what those women were wearing?"

"Nope."

"I never heard of such a thing! I'm glad we're not going to live here!"

"Don't worry," he said gently. "We're not going to live here. The tight pants some of those men got on wouldn't last too long if they got off in the brush, huh? Don't the place smell sort of funny?"

"Yes it does. And isn't it exciting?"

"It's a real big place. Lots of houses."

"Oh yes, and—I don't know, Joe,—it makes me feel crowded."

"Is this Oregon?" Alfred wanted to know.

A high-piled heavily loaded wagon drawn by six oxen came up the street they were going down, and two women riding side saddle swerved around it. Next came a cart—Joe had never seen one just like it—driven by what must be a dandy of the town. The cart was pulled by two high-stepping perfectly matched bays and trailed by two black and white dogs of a curious breed. They looked somewhat like hounds, but they weren't hounds. Mightily Joe wished that Percy Pearl or Les Tenney was along to explain these wonders to him. Joe gasped,

"Oh my gosh!"

He was too late. The two coach dogs swerved from the cart to take Mike, one on either side. There was a shrill yelp as Mike slashed the first one, and a scream of pain as he got the second. The two dogs streaked back to their cart and the driver made a U turn that brought him up beside Joe's wagon.

"Is that your dog?" he demanded furiously.

"Now, see here. Your dogs tackled—"

"Is that your dog?" the other repeated.

Joe's anger flared. "Yes! What do you aim to do about it?"

"Give you a horsewhipping."

He took a ridiculous little whip from a socket in his cart and shook it threateningly. Joe caught up the long-lashed bull whip that he sometimes used on the mules.

"If you want to play—"

The lash snapped within an inch of the other's ear and the mules jumped nervously. With a practiced hand, Joe held them in. He faced the dandified youngster in the cart.

"Smart thing for you to do is leave me alone, stranger. Your dogs started the fight."

"You barbarians from the back country—!"

"That'll be enough too."

Without another word, the outraged young man wheeled his cart and drove on. Joe started the mules, and for a second he remained furious. Then he chuckled.

"Give me a horsewhipping, huh! He couldn't break a soft-shelled egg with that little switch!"

Tad came alongside the wagon and looked into it, grinning and starry-eyed. "Gee, Pa, that was great! Why'nt you tease him into fightin'? You could of cleaned his clock like nothin'!"

"There'll be no fights anywhere if I can help it. Speaking of that, keep your dog on a rope while we're in Independence. It might save trouble."

"Aw, Pa—"

"You heard me." Joe tossed the youngster a length of rope. "Use this."

Joe drove on and all except Mike, who sulked under confinement or restriction and who was doubly offended now because there were plenty of dogs on the street, marveled at the sights and sounds of a bustling metropolis like Independence. There were more ox, horse, and mule teams on any one street than

passed through Tenney's Crossing in three months. Joe didn't like
the place because he preferred the open country and villages, and
he'd be just as happy when he got out of it. But it was interesting,
and since they had to go through anyway, they might as well
look. Somewhere was a ferry that would take them across the
Missouri, and Independence was the last great city they'd see.
Except for Salt Lake City—and the Oregon Trail did not go
through there—everything between Independence and Oregon
was still settlements, missions, and army and trading posts.

They passed the houses and a row of shacks, and beyond them
came to the corrals. The stock traders of Independence did a
thriving business, for many of those going over the Oregon Trail
came to Independence by river boat, horseback, stage, or on foot.
Then they bought the wagons that were to carry their goods over
the Trail, the beasts that were to pull the wagons, and in some
instances goods to carry in them. Some of those who came from
the east did not know how to handle stock, so that frequently it
was footsore or sick by the time they arrived at Independence.
Thus they had to replace their animals anyway.

However, most of the wagons started over the Oregon Trail in
spring, with the first ones leaving as soon as the grass was green
enough to furnish good grazing. Naturally the heaviest stock sales
occurred when there were the most emigrants wanting to buy,
and now some of the corrals were empty. But there were still more
oxen, horses and mules than Joe had ever before seen in one
place.

He halted his team abruptly as a man holding one end of a rope
in his hand raced into the road. On the rope's other end was a big,
dappled-gray, fighting-mad mule. Just as the man stumbled and
fell, Joe handed the reins to Emma and leaped from the wagon.

The gray mule was pounding toward the fallen man when Joe
came between them and seized the lead rope. Instantly the mule
transferred its anger to him, and Joe dodged aside. He shortened
the rope as he did so, getting closer to the gray mule. It was, he

saw, as much frightened as angry and Joe spoke soothingly. At the same time, his anger rose. Some men should never handle mules, and obviously the man now picking himself up out of the road was one of them.

Bit by bit, never making a fast move and always sure of himself, Joe calmed the mule. He got his hands on the halter's check strap, and continued to utter soothing words with his mouth the while he talked with his hands too. He did not look around when the man who had been mishandling the animal said defiantly, "I quit!" and stalked off down the road. His departure seemed further to reassure the gray mule.

"Howdy, friend."

Joe turned to face a man as tall as he was, and as wide through the middle as he was tall. He had sparse hair, shrewd eyes, a pudgy nose, and flabby lips behind which gold teeth flashed. A frayed, unlighted cigar was clutched firmly in his teeth, Joe said, "Howdy."

"You're a mule man, huh?"

"Just wanted to keep that idiot from getting killed."

"You shouldn't have bothered; sooner or later he'll get killed anyhow. He told me he could gentle some mules."

"He must have used a club."

"He did. You Oregon-bound?"

"Yup."

"You'll never make it this season."

"I know that."

"How about taking the job you just saw left vacant? I'll pay you well. My name's Jake Favors."

Joe said, "I'm Joe Tower and I'm on my way to Oregon."

"And I have to get some mules gentled. Tell you what, if you can break me in a team of six, I'll give you ten dollars a head."

Joe grinned. "Have to get to Oregon."

"How much do you think it's worth?"

"Fifty dollars a head."

Jake Favors raised both hands in mock horror. "Man! I can't sell mules for fifty dollars a head!"

"You must be a mighty poor salesman."

"Tell you what. I'll lose money on it but I'll give you twenty five dollars a head for breaking in a team of six that will work together."

Joe hesitated. Certainly a hundred and fifty dollars more would be a godsend. It would assure them of enough money no matter what happened, but it took time to break mules properly. However, it would take less time if Joe could choose his own mules. He looked at the corral from which the gray had come.

"That your stock?"

"That's part of it."

"And I pick my own mules?"

"Any you want."

Joe said doubtfully, "I could wagon break six, but somebody else will have to polish 'em off."

Jake Favors looked narrowly at him. "What do you mean?"

"I'll break six to harness and teach them to pull together, gee, haw, stop, and back. It'll take more practice before they're really a fine team."

"Why can't you make 'em fine?"

Joe looked him straight in the eye. "I haven't got time."

"Do I pay you before you start or after you finish?" There was more than a trace of sarcasm in the question.

Joe said grimly, "After I finish. But I also want a clean place to camp and feed for my stock."

Jake Favors said, "You've made yourself a deal. Drive into the meadow behind the corrals and make camp. There's a good spring rising under the apple trees, and it's far enough from the corrals so you won't get much smell."

Joe swung his team off the road and onto the dusty, dry ground adjoining the corrals. A little way farther on the wagon wheels ground clean grass, and Emma looked nervously back at the city.

Independence had its allure, but she had her children to think of and who knew what evil lurked in a place like this? She asked,

"How long do you think it will take you, Joe?"

"I'm going to try to make it in three weeks, but it might take longer."

"Isn't that cutting our time very short?"

"I doubt it. I figure that we can make thirty miles a day. We'll be in Laramie well before the fall storms hit and we certainly need the money."

Emma moved uneasily and murmured, "Yes, we need it."

Because it was secluded and out of the city, she was less nervous when Joe swung the team into the grove of apple trees. There were eight of them that had had no attention, and as a consequence they bore knotty little apples that clung tightly to the branches with a few ripened ones on the ground. But the place was clean, and the spring that rose in the center of the trees and trickled itself into a reed-bordered rill, was cold.

Joe got down from the wagon seat and turned to help Emma. Leaping gracefully from the rear, Barbara turned to catch the younger children in her arms. Carlyle looked with intense interest at a red apple that had fallen from one of the trees and lay gleaming in the grass. Little Emma smoothed her dress and Joe looked soberly about. Alfred turned a disappointed glance on his parents.

"Is this Oregon?" he wanted to know.

Emma said, "It's a long ways to Oregon, Ally."

The youngster wandered down to the rill, and stooped swiftly to catch a green frog in his hands. He cupped it there, and the rest gathered around to marvel at this prize. Tad said impatiently,

"Let's make camp, Pa."

Joe warmed to his freckle-faced son, so unpredictable and wild one hour and so dependable the next. He reflected with a sense of gratification that Tad had been no trouble whatever on this trip. Maybe the trek was already beginning to take some of his wildness. Joe looked around at the camp site.

Since they were going to be here for some time, and not just overnight, they could have more comfort than overnight camps afforded. There were stones lying around and a good fireplace might be fashioned from them. He said,

"How about gathering stones for a fireplace, Tad?"

"Sure."

The youngster went willingly to work, and after she had tied the cow securely, Barbara helped him.

Joe unhitched the mules and staked them. His eyes lighted on two chunks of wood that had been cut from a felled apple tree. He pointed them out to Emma.

"Suppose I borrow some boards from Jake Favors and lay them across those chunks? We'd have a passable table. Plenty of wood around. Might make us some benches, too."

Her heart leaped at the thought of a real table again, but she subdued it quickly. "You don't want to take time for that, Joe. A table's the last thing in the world we need to bother about."

He looked at her sidewise and winked solemnly, and she was caught between laughter and tears. His look told her more plainly than words that he knew what the small domestic comforts meant to her, and that he didn't intend to be prevented from wasting an hour for her comfort.

Barbara and Tad had collected a good heap of stones, and Joe started building a fireplace. Emma knelt beside him.

"Let me do this."

"Aren't you tired?"

"I've done nothing except ride for three days," Emma said scornfully. "You can leave the camp to us."

"Well, if you're sure you can make it—"

Emma's eyes twinkled, "We're sure."

Joe left and walked to Jake Favors' dingy office. The stock dealer rose to meet him.

"Wonder if I can borrow boards to make a table and benches?" Joe asked.

"Sure," Jake Favors agreed. "If chairs would do as well as benches, I have some."

"They'll be fine."

"Don't you be wasting your time with them, though. I want you to work on mules." He bellowed, "Sam!"

The biggest, slowest-moving colored man Joe had ever seen shuffled into the office. When he smiled, gleaming white teeth flashed in an enormous mouth. He rolled friendly eyes at Joe.

"Sam," Jake Favors directed, "make a table for this gentleman's family and take some chairs down. If they want anything else, you get it. All right?"

There was a long pause and Sam said, "Shu-ah." For a moment Joe was torn. He'd wanted to build Emma that table with his own hands. Then he realized that time was a precious thing for all of them, and he'd do best to leave it in Sam's hands.

Sam ambled off toward a lumber pile and Jake Favors turned to Joe. "You want a free hand, huh?"

"Yup."

"Well, you've got it."

"I'll take a look at your mules."

Joe strode toward the corrals. Wagon and pack stock was worth whatever the dealers could get for it, and what they could get depended on how much prospective purchasers knew about what they were buying. A good, well-broken work mule was worth a hundred dollars or more. Because they didn't know any better, some emigrants paid that much for any mule at all. Harnessing them after they parted with their money was their problem, but obviously Jake Favors knew someone who wanted six good mules. It was also evident that whoever wanted them had no intention of buying unbroken stock; he must know something about mules.

For three hours Joe did nothing except study mules in various corrals. Mules have a wide range of temperament; some respond swiftly to handling and some remain stubborn. If Joe could choose six that were gentle, his task would not take so long. But there were other considerations. Since these mules were intended to work as a team of six, they must be intended to pull heavy loads and no mule is fitted for heavy work until it is five years old. Also

—Joe felt that he was being fairly paid and was conscious of his obligation to do a good job—a matched team would probably be easier to sell than an unmatched one.

With extreme care he selected the animals he wanted.

Emma looked covertly up from the fireplace she was building to see where Joe had gone, and when she discovered that he remained within sight of the camp, she felt a rising relief. Reason told her that there was nothing to fear in Independence, but she was afraid anyway. Her whole life had been spent in sparsely settled country; she had never been in any town bigger than Tenney's Crossing. Here she felt hemmed in. Even so, and in spite of fears, she was excited. Emma mulled over a plan that was forming in her mind while Barbara and Tad brought more stones. Barbara knelt beside her mother.

"I'll help you."

"All right, dear."

For a while they worked in silence, fitting the uneven stones so that they made a solid fireplace. Then Emma voiced her plan,

"Barbara, before we leave, you and I are going shopping in some of these big stores."

"Oh mother! Really?"

"We'll go."

The girl sighed, "That will be wonderful!"

Emma worked on, secretly relieved and at the same time puzzled. She had thought that she understood her daughter thoroughly, but apparently she didn't. Emma herself wanted desperately to shop in Independence, but knew that she'd never dare go alone. She'd expected Barbara to be a little afraid too, and thought the two of them might lean on each other. But there had been only happy and eager enthusiasm in the girl's voice. Barbara had a self-confidence and self-assurance that Emma had never possessed, and that was good.

"Ahm heah to help you, ma'am."

Emma turned, a little startled, but when she saw the enormous colored man, she smiled. She had an instinctive perception that enabled her to understand people, and there was no harm in the colored giant. Emma looked at the load of boards, a load that any ordinary man would have found difficult to carry over his shoulder, that Sam held almost effortlessly under his arm. The Negro said,

"Ahm s'posed to make you a table, ma'am."

"Well, let's see," Emma smiled again. "We shouldn't have it too near the fire. How about over there under the first tree?"

"Shu-ah, ma'am."

At a snail-like pace, the colored man carried his load to the shade of the first tree and began building a table. Tad came with more stones and Emma told him,

"That will be plenty, Tad."

"Can I help you, Ma?"

"There doesn't seem to be anything to do right now."

"Can I go up by Pa? He might need help."

"Yes, but be careful."

"I will," and Tad raced off with Mike leaping at his heels.

Emma glanced at her younger children, who were still occupied with their captive frog. Somewhere they had found a discarded jar, put wet grass in it, and were keeping their pet there.

Little Emma said, "Now we must give him some bread."

"They don't eat bread!" Joe said scornfully. "Frogs eat worms and bugs."

Little Emma said, "Ugh!"

Emma and Barbara took the mattresses from the wagon, laid them on canvas brought along for that purpose, and arranged comfortable beds. The big colored man came to stand beside them again.

"Ahve got youah table an' chaihs."

Emma looked up, a little surprised. She had noted the pace at which Sam moved, and decided in her own mind that they would be fortunate to have a table within the first week, but it was all built and the chairs stood around it. Emma smiled her delight.

"I do thank you. That's a real fine table."

The colored man smiled back. "Ah'll fetch you some fi' wood."

He ambled off while Emma and Barbara busied themselves arranging cooking utensils and the wooden dishes on the table. Emma shook her hair back. She recognized, with a trace of shame, that she was far more contented here, even in this strange spot, than she had been while traveling. The road was a gypsy life. Even though they slept under the stars and cooked and ate in the open, for at least a short time this was home. Emma planned in her mind the meals she would make.

Barbara suddenly exclaimed, "Mother!"

Emma followed her daughter's anguished gaze, and she suppressed a gasp. The rooster and six hens hadn't been out of their crate since they'd been put into it, though Joe had cleaned the crate every day. Now, somehow, the crate had come open and the six hens were scuttling about the grass while the rooster flapped wings that longed for exercise.

Barbara said, "We must catch them quickly!"

"No," as always, Emma rose to the occasion. "Leave them alone and do nothing to frighten them. They'll roost somewhere tonight and we can catch them easier."

She kept an anxious eye on the chickens as she mixed bread dough. The chickens were very precious and Emma did not know whether or not they could be replaced. But she would not let her children know that she worried or they might be troubled too. Barbara got a pailful of water from the spring and started peeling potatoes. Emma cut a generous chunk from the ham Yancey Garrow had given them and got it ready for baking. Sam returned with a huge armload of wood.

"You want a fi'?" he asked.

"Oh, thank you. If you will, please."

The Negro built a fire in the fireplace and Emma dismissed him. Tired of playing, the younger children had cached their treasured frog somewhere near the spring and were lying listlessly in the grass. Twilight came, and with immense gratification Emma saw the chickens go back into their crate. It was a good thing, for certainly they could not ride all the way to Oregon without being out of the crate, and if they would go back of their own accord they could be freed every night.

Not until twilight started to fade into night did Joe and Tad return.

"By gosh!" Joe exclaimed. "You really have a camp set up!"

Emma said, "The colored man helped a lot. Anybody hungry hereabouts?"

"Hungry as a bear and three cubs."

"Good."

She put the food on the table, cutting generous slices from the ham and serving the children first because Joe wanted it that way. There was milk for them, coffee for Joe and herself. Emma placed a heaping plate of fluffy biscuits beside the potato dish. Joe ate in silence, noticing the new gaiety in Emma's face and manner, and he thought that maybe now she was feeling better about the whole trip. He finished, leaned back in his chair, and sighed happily.

"I've got the six picked."

"Did you have any trouble?"

"Nope. Just had to look over a lot of mules. Got me six blacks, alike as six peas in a pod. Put 'em together in a little corral, and there won't be a prettier six-mule team in Missouri."

"Ma," Tad spoke up. "Pa says it's all right with him if I go into town tomorrow."

Emma said doubtfully, "I don't know—"

"He'll come to no harm," Joe assured her.

"Well, if your father thinks it's all right, you may go."

"Oh gee! Good!"

Emma put little Emma to bed and washed the dishes while Barbara took care of the other children. Barbara sat alone, dreaming, and for a little while Joe and Emma sat side by side before the dying fire. Their hands met, and they did not speak because speech was unnecessary. Joe was thinking of Oregon, of good land, free for the taking. And Emma was thinking how good it felt to be camped in this one place, and to know that they would be in the same place tomorrow evening again. The live coals cast a bright glow over them.

The next morning, shortly after sun-up, Joe left for the corrals. A half hour later, with Mike on a leash, Tad set out to explore Independence. Emma worried, but reassured herself. If Joe had said that Tad would be all right, he would be. She heated water in her dish pans, emptied it into a tub, and scrubbed the clothes they'd been wearing. This was a fine opportunity to catch up on all chores such as washing and mending. Emma wondered how she would do her washing on the trail ahead. But there had to be a way and she would find it. Barbara, brushing out the wagon, leaped lightly to the ground and unwrapped the cloth that bound her hair.

"There was dust half an inch thick," she grimaced. "I don't see how we picked all of it up in this short time."

"It will gather," Emma said thoughtfully, "and I don't know what we can do except clean it out."

"What are you going to do now, Mother?"

"There doesn't seem to be anything." Emma, who must always be busy, knew a feeling of disquiet because there was no task at hand. "Let's take the children for a walk."

Joe and Alfred scampered ahead, overturning stones and picking up worms for what was probably the best-fed frog in Missouri. Little Emma gathered daisies, wove them into a chain, and proudly presented it to her mother. Carlyle stared, wholly entranced, at a horde of bright orange butterflies that clung to a wet place on the ground. Barbara strolled gracefully beside her mother while they talked of events to be. Then it was time to get lunch. Joe came, but there was no sign of Tad. He'd been permitted to explore the town on condition that he be back for lunch.

"Do you suppose he's in trouble?" she asked worriedly.

Joe muttered, "He just forgot. Doggone that kid! I'll—Say! What the dickens!"

Across the meadow came a large and determined woman whose

right hand had a firm grip on Tad's right arm. Mike sulked behind, ears flattened and tail drooping. Emma gasped. Blood crimsoned Tad's upper lip and had spattered from there onto his shirt. His nose was still bleeding. The woman approached the group at the table and pushed Tad toward them.

"Is this your little beast?" she said fiercely.

Joe knew a rising concern and a quick flash of anger, but he controlled himself. "This is my son."

"Keep him here or I'll have him jailed for assault!"

Joe asked wonderingly, "Who did he assault?"

"First my Jeremy, then my Tommy, then my George! They—! All of them have bloody noses!"

"They called me a hayseed," Tad muttered grimly.

The woman turned on her heel and strode away. Tad stood expectant but defiant, awaiting the punishment he knew he would get. His eyes widened when Joe said quietly,

"Wash your face and come have some lunch, Tad."

"But, Pa—"

"When it's three to one," Joe explained, "it's not entirely sensible. But neither is it assault. Besides, didn't they call you a hayseed?"

Emma controlled a smile.

The days passed, and because there was little to do, Emma began to find them tedious. She still cherished a desire to shop in Independence, but she had given up hope of doing it, for Joe was working all day long and there was no one else whom she would trust with the children. Because Barbara knew how her mother felt, she contained her own crushing disappointment and said nothing. Then the bomb exploded. Joe came to lunch, but instead of rising and going right back to work, which was his usual routine, he lingered at the table.

"Your afternoon off, Emma," he said cheerfully. "I'll wash the dishes."

"But—"

"I'm going to let the mules rest this afternoon," he ran a hand through his shaggy hair, "and I've been doing some pondering. I pondered that you and Bobby might like to see some of Independence. Go ahead. Take some money along so you can buy yourselves something."

Emma felt a leaping excitement which immediately conflicted with a strong sense of duty. She wanted desperately to go even while she thought of numberless reasons why she should not.

"Go ahead," Joe laughed. "It's all planned."

"Well, if you're certain—"

"I'm certain, and I'll take care of the kids. Now hurry up and get started."

Emma put her arms around Joe's neck in a quick, tight hug. Barbara, astonished at the unusual show of emotion, giggled, and then followed suit.

Emma and Barbara dressed in the wagon, and for the first time Emma regretted desperately the fact that she had not brought one of her prettier dresses. But she did the best she could, and her heart leaped when Joe looked admiringly at her. Emma glanced at her daughter, radiant in a simple brown dress, and pride swelled within her.

"Have a good time," Joe called as they departed.

Emma was completely in the grip of excitement. Firmly she clutched her purse, in which five dollars reposed. She would not put it beyond city people to snatch a woman's purse if they could. Then she began to worry about her appearance. She felt awkward and out of place, and when a young man stared hard at her she blushed, for she decided that she was betraying her rustic upbringing. Then she knew that the young man was merely exercising the right of all young men when lovely girls are present, and that he was staring at Barbara.

They stopped before a store in whose windows a variety of groceries were arranged, and after a moment they entered. Emma began to feel more at ease. The man who came forward reminded her of Les Tenney.

"Is there something I may do for you?" he asked.

Emma murmured, "We thought we might just walk about and—

and not decide for a while." She looked him firmly in the eye and he bowed, and moved away. Reassured by the success of her first encounter, she held her head high.

They passed a glass counter that was divided into compartments, and each compartment was filled to the top with candy. Then they went down the other aisle and out on the street again. Emma gave herself wholly to the spirit of the thing. There were stores in which nothing except drugs were sold, others that dispensed only clothing and shoes. They examined a hardware store and when Emma looked at the gleaming new tools she thought wistfully of Joe, and how he would love them. She envisioned Barbara in a dazzling gown that sold for the staggering price of thirteen dollars. Carefully they examined the latest in kitchen ware and utensils.

Then their day was done. They had spent an afternoon in Paradise and their souls had been lifted. Their eyes had been filled with visions of beautiful, incredible things. They had had a glimpse of another way of life, and it was exciting, but it was not their own. Emma knew that they would have to stock up on provisions before they left Independence. But as they trudged wearily wagonward, they went again into the first store they had entered and Emma made her only purchase of that day.

"Give me," she said, pointing at a mound of horehound candies, "five cents' worth of those."

Finally Joe's work was done. With the six mules in harness and Jake Favors riding beside him, he took a heavy wagon through Independence. Joe turned the wagon where Jake wanted it turned, halted the mules when that was desired, backed them, made them trot and canter. Back at the corral, without a word of protest, Jake Favors paid him in gold and looked him squarely in the eye.

"Want to stay and work for me?"

"Can't. I have to get to Oregon."

"It's late in the season, and almost 700 miles to Laramie. You'll have to have smooth going all the way to get there ahead of the fall storms. If the storms don't get you, the Indians might. There won't be anybody else heading out this late in the year. You're all alone, a lost wagon."

"We'll get there and we're not lost."

"I'll make it thirty dollars a mule and promise you work all winter."

"Have to get to Oregon."

"You emigrants for Oregon," lamented Jake Favors, who had grown wealthy selling them horses and mules, "don't have a lick of common sense among the lot of you!

The Towers broke up camp, and returned to Jake the boards and chairs they had borrowed. Barbara scoured the camp site for toys and scraps of clothing the young ones might have dropped in the grass.

Emma stood quietly for a moment looking at the charred stones of the fireplace where she had prepared so many meals in the past three weeks. She reflected that the spot where a woman prepares meals to feed her family has the oddest way of becoming precious. Even though she wanted, just as much as Joe did, to move on now to their final camping site, to the land on which their new home would stand, she had a queer little hankering to stay on here under these trees.

When the wagon began to move away from the apple trees, she looked back, winking angrily to dispose of the tears that came into her eyes. Joe, without turning to look at her, laid his hand, just for a moment, over hers.

CHAPTER EIGHT

The River

JOE AND Tad, jackets buttoned and wool caps pulled down over their ears, were gathering buffalo chips for fuel. For the first part of their journey, wood had been theirs for the taking. But for the past ten days there had been very little, and Joe supposed that this was partly because there never had been very much in the first place and partly because emigrants preceding him had cut down what there was. Joe tried to put this vast prairie in a proper perspective.

The change in terrain had been gradual. No one day, or even the whole trip so far, had revealed any startling differences. The hills in Missouri were low and rolling and so was this country. But the Missouri hills had been forested, and with very few exceptions the only trees they'd found here had been growing along river or creek bottoms. Yet, each day had brought its own changes. But Joe had to think of the whole trip, and get the over-all picture, to place them correctly. When one traveled only twenty or thirty miles, each night's camp seemed much like the one preceding it. But each had differed, and much more startling than any physical change in the country they'd traveled was the sense of going a great distance.

Tenney's Crossing had been warm and friendly, with neighbors always at hand, and not until they reached Independence had they in any sense of the word felt alien. Going out of Independence, they'd passed homesteads and settlements and felt at home there. But here there was only the prairie, a vast thing that stretched on all sides. They were all alone, wholly dependent on their own resources, and with no one else to whom they might turn. It was, Joe felt, much like being suspended in space. He didn't like the country and he was more than a little afraid of it. But he hadn't mentioned his fears to Emma.

Buffalo chips in both hands, Tad put them in the sack Joe was carrying. Joe glanced at him but made no comment. Tad seemed to be looking for something, and sooner or later he would mention whatever he sought.

"How come?" he said finally. "How come, Pa?"

"How come what?"

"All this dry buffalo manure around and no buffalo."

"I don't know that myself," Joe admitted.

"We've come a right smart ways without seein' any, ain't we?"

"We sure have."

"Wouldn't you like to see some?"

"Yup."

"So would I. Do you think we'll get all the way to Oregon without findin' any?"

"I don't know."

"How far are we from Oregon?"

"A long ways. Now if you'll stop asking questions, and start gathering buffalo chips, we might get enough."

"Sure, Pa."

Mike, who had adapted himself to wagon life, sniffed eagerly at a bunch of grass in which a jack rabbit had rested. Mike had had a wonderful time stalking rabbits and prairie chickens, though he hadn't caught anything as yet, and Joe looked worriedly at the dog.

Perhaps Jake Favors had been doing something besides trying to hire a man who knew mules when he advised them to winter in Independence, for the Trail had been anything except easy. It was easy to stay on, of course, for all one had to do was follow the Platte River and the tracks of the wagons that had gone before. Or, at least, stay near the Platte. There must have been a great many emigrants this past season, for the grass was cropped short by their animals and in some places it hadn't grown back. In all such places—the mules had to eat well if they were to work hard —it had been necessary to swerve to one side and find grazing. It wasn't always easy because others had the same idea and that, Joe knew now, was one of the reasons why the Oregon Trail was several miles wide in some places.

However, though sometimes grass was hard to find, it could always be found and that was a minor problem. A major one was that they were far behind the schedule Joe had hoped to keep. It was just short of 700 miles between Independence and Laramie, and Joe had counted on making the trip in thirty-five days at the very most. However, they were already out thirty-two days and certainly they had a long way to go. Joe didn't know just how far, for his calculations had been completely upset.

Even for the first two weeks out of Laramie, Joe had not been able to cover his hoped-for thirty miles a day. They'd been delayed by the necessity of finding grass for the stock. Then had come near disaster.

Joe had awakened one morning and turned over for another few minutes' sleep, for by the look of things it couldn't possibly be time to get up. The morning was almost as black as the night had been. Then Joe came awake with a start. As soon as he did so he knew that it was past the time for getting up and that they were facing a storm.

Heavy, black clouds covered the sky so deeply that the sun could find no crack to break through. Emma had come from the wagon to join Joe and for a few seconds they had stood near each other while each gave comfort to the other. They shared a weird and terrible feeling that they were really lost on the endless prairie whose ceiling was now an even more fierce plain of clouds. Then they hurriedly started a fire and cooked breakfast before the forthcoming rain made it impossible to do so.

They'd scarcely started when lightning flashed and thunder boomed in a wild and awful way. All about was space, with no sheltering trees or hills, and thunder filled that space. The clouds opened up and cold rain sluiced down. Joe was grateful for the double thickness of canvas on the wagon. Except for Tad, who still refused to ride, his family would be dry. A wetting wouldn't hurt Tad as long as he kept moving, and if Joe had to put him there by main strength he would sleep in the wagon at night. But heavy rain turned the Trail into a quagmire.

From that moment, the movement of the wagon had become slow and torturing. Wheels sank halfway to the hubs. The mules strained and slipped as they sought a solid footing, and only Joe's expert driving kept them on their feet. They had to go on because it was unthinkable to stop in this morass. There was no house, and as far as Joe could see, no material for building one. For two days following the rain they had to nibble at cold food because the soaked buffalo chips, the only fuel, would not burn. Their clothing and almost everything inside the wagon was mud-crusted and there was small use in cleaning anything because five minutes afterward it was sure to be muddy again. The cold wind following the rain was within itself evidence that this was bitter country where snow would lie deep.

Worst of all, their provisions were running low. Grandpa Seeley had advised him to load the wagon heavily with food, and Joe had followed the advice. Before leaving Independence he had bought more, but his family had always had hearty appetites and travel stimulated them. Joe had shot a few jack rabbits, which even Mike found difficult to chew, and a few prairie chickens which were delicious. But, though jack rabbits were numerous, everybody else who came this way must have been shooting prairie chickens, too. They were so wary that it was almost impossible to get a shot at one now.

Joe continued to pick up buffalo chips the while he continued to worry. They were so slowed by the mud that sometimes it seemed that they camped one night almost in sight of last night's camp. Probably they traveled farther than that, though Joe estimated that they hadn't covered more than eight miles any day they'd been in the mud. He'd been able to buy almost nothing at Fort

Kearney; their commissary was low and the men there were already on short rations. They'd told him he had enough to last to Laramie, but they hadn't known about bad travel conditions.

They filled the sack with buffalo chips, bent their heads against the cold north wind, and Joe quenched a rising uneasiness. Probably there would be no very deep snow for several weeks. But any snow at all would be sure to slow them up and they could afford no more delays. The thought of his children going hungry clutched at him with an almost physical pain. It was by no means certain that anyone else would come this way before spring again made for good travel conditions, and even if somebody did come the chances were good that they'd have nothing to spare. Tad spoke from the muffled depths of his jacket collar.

"Think it will snow, Pa?"

"No. I don't think so."

He had halted the wagon on a grassy knoll that offered good drainage and at least they'd be out of the mud tonight. The tethered mules and the cow were eagerly cropping grass. Emma's chickens, that had come to regard the wagon as their real home, were scratching vigorously in the dirt. With night, they would go into their crate to roost. Emma and Barbara, who had refashioned two of Joe's old pairs of trousers to fit them—articles of clothing neither would have dreamed of wearing near Tenney's Crossing but which were practical here—were arranging their cook ware. They awaited only the buffalo chips.

"Here we are!" Joe sang out.

He plucked a handful of dry grass for tinder, arranged his fire, and lighted it with a sulphur match that he took from a corked bottle. The flames climbed hungrily through the grass and ate more slowly into the chips. Joe remembered the roaring wood fires they'd had back in Missouri, and he stirred uncomfortably. It was necessary to cross these plains before they could go to Oregon, and there was nothing anyone could do about them except cross. But Joe was just as happy that they were not going to live here. Grandpa Seeley had known what he was talking about when he spoke of the plains' vast loneliness.

Emma looked wistfully at the fire. "I kind of miss a wood fire."

"We'll get some," Joe promised. "There must be wood somewhere, and the mud can't last forever. Soon as we get out of it we can travel a lot faster. Don't you worry."

Emma laughed, and Joe knew that it was a forced laugh. "I'm not a bit worried! I didn't expect luxuries all the way."

Tad, who had slipped away, darted back to the wagon. His eyes were big with excitement.

"Hey, Pa!"

"Yes?"

"There's some animals just over the next knoll!"

Joe's heart leaped. "What are they?"

"I dunno. They look sort of like deer, but they ain't deer."

Joe got his rifle and turned to Emma. "You and Bobby feed the youngsters and have your own supper, will you? Expect Tad and me when we get back." To Tad he said, "Show me where they are!"

Tad tied Mike to the wagon wheel and led the way up the knoll. He slipped down the other side, and Joe noted with pride that he walked carefully. He avoided rustling grass and stones, anything at all that might make a noise. Joe reflected that, one day, Tad would be a wonderful hunter. Tad crawled up the opposite knoll as carefully as he had descended the first and stopped. He pointed.

"They're just on the other side," he whispered. "There's four of 'em."

"Come on, son."

They dropped to their hands and knees and crawled very slowly. Nearing the crest of the knoll, they wriggled on their bellies. With only their heads showing, they looked down the other side of the knoll. Tad whispered,

"There they are!"

The knoll sloped into a shallow gulley that was about three hundred yards long by two hundred wide. Joe saw the animals, a big buck with three does, and though he himself had never before seen any, he knew from the descriptions of people who had been west that they were pronghorns, or antelope. His practiced hunter's eye told him that they were already suspicious; they had either seen Tad or else they had seen Joe and Tad. They were grazing nervously near the far end of the gully, hopelessly out of range.

"They were a lot closer before," Tad whispered.

"Sh-h! Maybe they'll come nearer!"

Joe lay perfectly still, trying desperately not even to wink an eye as he watched the antelope. By sheer force of will he yearned to draw them closer. One of them, just one, and his family would have enough food again. One of the does slashed at another with an angry hoof, and they drifted a little farther away. Joe began to worry. In another twenty minutes it would be too dark to shoot. He whispered,

"We have to do something!"

"Yes?"

"Do you know right where they are, Tad?"

"Sure."

"Can you slip down this knoll, see if you can work around behind 'em, and scare 'em toward me?"

"Sure, Pa."

Tad slipped away and Joe concentrated his fierce, yearning gaze on the antelope. He must not miss. They had to have one of the antelope, and the thought made him tense. Joe forced himself to relax so that he would be able to shoot more truly. Minute by minute, the night shadows lowered. The rifle's sights were already beginning to blur when the antelope moved.

They sprang away suddenly, but instead of running toward Joe, they quartered across the gully. Knowing that they were still out of range, but wanting desperately to get one, Joe aimed at the running buck. He squeezed the trigger, and the rifle belched red flame into the gathering twilight. But the antelope continued to run.

Joe stood up, sweating, and it was as though a heavy weight was suddenly upon his heart. He felt a little nauseated, and he wet dry lips with his tongue. It seemed, somehow, that he was guilty of a terrible and unforgivable sin. But even while he berated himself, Joe knew pride when Tad appeared where he should have been. The youngster had done his part exactly right. It was no fault of his if the antelope had run exactly wrong.

Tad panted up the knoll to join him. "Missed, huh?"

Joe said glumly, "I missed."

"Oh well," Tad remained cheerful, "they weren't very big anyhow."

They wandered back to the wagon. Emma, who had heard the shot, came running expectantly toward them.

"Missed," Joe said, and he took refuge in Tad's alibi. "They weren't very big anyhow."

"It's nothing," she said, and Joe thought he detected a catch in her voice. "There'll be other opportunities. You come and have your suppers now."

She had kept their plates warm near the dying fire, and she gave Tad one. The youngster stood up to eat while Emma brought Joe's plate. He looked down at it, potatoes, biscuits, butter, jerked beef that they had bought in Independence, and a cup of coffee. They were his usual full rations, and he said,

"Doggone, I just don't feel hungry. If you'll put this away, it'll be all the lunch I want tomorrow."

Tad said, "I ain't hungry neither, Mom."

"Now see here!" Emma's voice rose and there was a convulsive sob in it. "Barbara wasn't hungry, Tad isn't hungry, you aren't hungry—! What's the matter with all of you! You've got to eat— you've *got* to!"

Carefully, Joe put the plate and the cup of coffee on the ground. He caught her in his arms and held her very close to him, and she leaned against him, tense and trembling, without making a sound. His arms tightened about her, and he whispered so even Tad couldn't hear,

"My darling! Oh my darling!"

"I—I'm sorry, Joe."

"Emma," his voice was firm, "I know it's hard. But we'll get out, and I swear that to you by everything that's holy to me!"

Her eyes seemed like live coals as she looked at him.

Miserably Joe said, "Tad, you eat. If you're going to scout up more game you'll have to."

Barbara, who had been putting the younger children to bed, jumped from the wagon to stand comfortingly near her mother. Joe said gently,

"Your mother and I have some things to talk over, honey."

She said uncertainly, "All right."

Joe said, "By the way, you take your meals too, Bobby."

"I really wasn't hungry."

"You'd best take 'em anyhow."

He picked up the plate of food and the cup of coffee and led Emma into the shadows away from the fire. Gently he turned to face her.

"How much did you eat?"

"I—I wasn't hungry."

He cut a slice of meat and used the fork to try to put it into her mouth. Her self-control went, and she broke into deep, painful sobbing. "Why did you bring us to this terrible place?" she choked out. "What right did you have to take us away from our home? You—a father—to bring six children out here into this mud—four helpless little ones—this—this horrible *wilderness!*" The words were torn from her, her whole body shook with the violence of her feelings. "You were willing to take a chance, weren't you? But how about *us!* What if we starve to death out here! How will you feel when there is *nothing* to eat—nothing for the babies, nothing for any of us? Joe, Joe, what have you done to us!"

Now the sobs racked her so that she could speak no more.

Joe had placed the cup and plate on the ground, and now he stood silent, alone, his head hanging low. He made no move to touch her. Under her lashing all his courage had fled. He did not know his own mind. Likely he was all wrong to have come out here. He was lost, and his family was lost with him.

She dashed the tears furiously out of her eyes, and then suddenly she saw him. As though she had been blind before, seeing only the children, their hunger, now she opened her eyes and saw Joe. She saw what her attack was doing to him. Helplessly, she looked at his stooped shoulders, at his hands hanging lifeless. A knife of pain turned in her chest. Everything that Joe had done, he had done for all of them. The trip was to bring all of them to a new and better place. If Joe had more hankering than other men had for an independent life, didn't that make him a better father too, a man for the children to look up to? Why, she was attacking the very courage that made Joe Tower the fine man that he was, the fine father, the brave and loving husband.

Her fears did not disappear, but something bigger and more important than fear flowed into her. Her sobs stopped. She went to Joe and put her arms around his neck.

"I've been going on like a loon, Joe," she said.

He raised his face, and looked at her, bewildered.

"Seems as though sometimes I get an overdose of feeling, and an underdose of sense." She laughed shakily. "We're going to a better life, Joe, and no matter what I say, I know that from the bottom of my heart. No matter what we have to go through on the way—we'll look back at this, my darling, and have a good laugh over it, some day!"

An enormous relief came to his face. His shoulders straightened, and he took her in his arms. "You do trust me, Emma?" he asked, huskily.

For answer, she kissed him on the lips. The kiss told him everything he needed to know.

He took up the plate of food, divided the food exactly in half and, dutifully, he and Emma finished every morsel. They each drank exactly half of the coffee, smiling tremulously at each other over the rim of the cup.

They returned to the children then.

Joe brought a bucket of water and a handful of sand from the Platte, and they scrubbed their dishes clean. Back in the wagon, Joe let the drop curtain fall, removed his mud-stained outer garments, and lay with his sons curled close on one side of the curtain while Emma joined her daughters on the other. It was the best arrangement now; the fire offered little comfort and there was no point in just standing around outside. Joe looked to his rifle, and made sure that it was within easy reach of his hand. They had seen few Indians so far and all of them had been peaceful. But they might run into hostiles.

Underneath the wagon, Mike moaned fretfully in his sleep as he dreamed of some happy hunt in which he and Tad had participated. Joe felt a little easier. The dog ate his share of food and so far he had been unable to get any for himself. But he was courageous, and almost certainly he would give the alarm if anything tried to approach them in the night. Joe pulled the quilts up around his chin and settled into the warm bed.

"There was a little wagon going to Oregon," he began.

On both sides of the curtain little pairs of ears were attentive, and eyes stared expectantly into the darkness of the wagon. Joe continued his story.

By sheer coincidence the little wagon in the story had the same number of children in it that this wagon carried. But the mules were stubborn and would not pull. Even a carrot dangled in front of their noses would not make them move. They wanted to go back to Missouri. Finally the children in the little wagon had a happy inspiration. They stood where the mules could hear them —these mules could understand children talk—and had a great argument. They wanted to go back to Missouri too. But the mules did not know the right way. Calling good bye to the mules, and assuring them that they were going to Missouri, the children started walking toward Oregon. The mules looked at each other, decided they'd been wrong, and followed the children all the way. When they got there, they liked Oregon so well that they no longer wanted to go anywhere.

On the other side of the curtain little Emma said sleepily, "That was a nice story, Daddy."

Little Joe yawned prodigiously and Alfred and Carlyle snuggled a bit closer to their father. Tad whispered,

"Pa."

"Yes?"

"I'm sorry we didn't get us an antelope."

"So am I."

"But we'll get one, huh?"

"Sure we will. Don't talk any more now. The kids are going to sleep."

"All right, Pa."

Joe tried to sense whether, on the other side of the curtain, Emma still lay awake. He had a feeling that she did, but he did not want to whisper to her and risk awakening her if she was asleep. He stared at the blackness over him.

Grandpa Seeley had told him as much as any man could tell another about going to Oregon. But no man could really know unless he tried the journey himself; how could Grandpa Seeley have forecast the rain and the sea of mud? Joe stirred uneasily. He had, in a very real sense, appointed himself the guardian of seven lives and he knew very well that those lives were now in danger. Their supplies were dangerously low and it was still an undetermined distance to Laramie. In that moment Joe wished mightily that they had never come, and he knew that, if he could, he would turn back. Now they might better go on. Laramie was certainly closer than Independence or Kearney and there was nothing for Joe at Kearney. The die was cast. They had made their choice.

The curtain rustled and Emma's hand came through, searching in the dark for her husband. Tenderly, Joe took the proffered hand, and she whispered,

"Joe, it will be all right."

He whispered back, "Yes, darling."

There was silence while their hands remained clasped. Joe thought, with anguish, of all his wife had endured. No part of it had been easy for her, but nothing else was as bad as the mud. It clung to everything, found its way into every part of the wagon, and even into the food. Normally a tidy housewife, the unconquerable mud revolted Emma's very soul.

Expressing a hope that was nothing more than a hope, he whispered with an effort at certainty, "Things are going to get better soon, Emma."

For answer there was only the comforting pressure of her hand.

Wind rustled the canvas cover, and Joe still stared into darkness. They were only on the first lap of their journey, with a very long way to go. Certainly, before they ever reached Oregon, there would be more hardship and danger. Joe's hand still in hers, Emma fell asleep.

In the middle of the next morning, the laboring mules finally pulled the wagon onto dry ground. Joe heaved a tremendous sigh of relief, and the mules bobbed happy heads up and down and trotted. Emma turned gleeful, excited eyes on her husband. Back in the wagon, for the first time in a week, Alfred voiced childish glee.

"Is this Oregon?" he asked.

"Not quite, Ally." Joe felt like laughing.

"Let's have us a game," little Joe urged.

Just before they entered the mud, Carlyle had discovered a bed of small round pebbles. They were some sort of quartz, Joe didn't know just what because he had never seen them before, and when held to the light they were translucent. The youngsters had devised a fascinating game wherein, unseen by the rest, one hid a few pebbles. Then all the rest had to guess how many there were, and the one who came nearest held the pebbles next time.

Alfred asked, "How many stones I got?"

"Six," baby Emma guessed.

"Four," little Joe said soberly.

"Five," Carlyle hazarded.

"Nope." Alfred was shaking with suppressed mirth.

"How many do you have?" Barbara asked.

"Not any!"

Alfred burst into laughter and little Joe protested seriously, "That is not the way to play this game!"

Emma looked brightly at Joe and he smiled back. They were still a lost dot on a vast prairie and their situation had not changed materially from last night's. But they were out of the mud. They had met and defeated a slimy, vicious enemy that had done its best to drag them down, and their spirits lifted accordingly.

Emma breathed, "This is wonderful!"

"Like riding on feathers," Joe agreed and he called back to his daughter, "How do you like this, Bobby?"

"Oh, it's grand!" Her voice was gay, but there was a strange undertone in it that Joe could not understand. He looked quizzically at Emma. She lowered her voice.

"Barbara isn't really in the wagon, Joe. She's gone to Oregon ahead of us."

"Oh," he said, only half understanding.

She said softly, "Our little girl has grown up, Joe. But she isn't so grown-up that she can't dream, and I hope she never will be. What were you thinking of when you were her age?"

"You," he said promptly.

She became a little coy. "You hadn't even met me!"

"Just the same I was thinking about you. Doggone it, Emma, I didn't have a very good life before I met you. Oh, I don't mean it that way at all. I had everything most other people did, but it just seemed that I was lost. There was nobody at all I could tell things to, or share with, and the first day I saw you I knew I could never leave."

She said, "Oh, but you *did* leave, running out of that store like a streak, with the maple syrup jug in your hand!"

They laughed heartily, for the sheer joy of laughing, and back in the wagon the children laughed too. But they had not kept their voices low enough. Barbara had heard, and she knelt staring dreamily out of the open flaps. All behind her was forever behind, and she knew that. What—and who—would lie ahead? Emma, who knew her daughter, was right. Barbara's spirit had winged past the slow-moving mules and taken her to Oregon long before the rest would ever get there.

Despite the mud, Tad had not forsworn his announced intention of walking every inch of the way to Oregon. He hadn't had a bad time because of his weight; places where the wagon bogged down, he could skip over. Where the Trail was too muddy, Tad sought the knolls and rises on one side or the other and often these were short cuts. Now, the faithful Mike close beside him, he was waving from a knoll about a hundred yards ahead and his voice carried back.

"Hey, Pa!"

"Yes?"

"Come on! Look!"

"I'm coming! Hang on to your shirt!"

He drove to the foot of the knoll, looked in the direction Tad indicated, and knit his brows in wonder. Three hundred yards farther on, almost squarely in the center of the Trail, was another wagon. It was oddly still and only half real, a ghost that haunted the Trail. Its once taut canvas cover sagged, and the back flaps gaped emptily. Emma turned puzzled eyes on Joe.

"What do you think it is?"

"I don't know. Let's drive down and see."

As he drew nearer he knew that, though doubtless this wagon had once had a driver, it contained no people at all now. Tad, racing toward it, stopped uncertainly and waited while Mike bristled beside him. The youngster had been halted by sight of the oxen that had once drawn this wagon, but that now lay dead in their yokes. Joe stopped the mules, handed the reins to Emma, and walked slowly toward the wagon. His courage restored by his father's presence, Tad kept pace with him. Joe looked at the oxen, dead too long to have any hope of discovering what had killed them. He swung up to look into the wagon and, as he had expected, found it empty.

"What do you think happened?" Tad asked in awed tones.

"I don't know."

"Indians?"

"Could be."

"Shucks!"

"What's the matter?"

"Why couldn't they have waited until we came along?"

"Don't talk foolish!" Joe ordered sternly. "Besides, if it was Indians, they'd have taken the wagon too."

"Unless," Tad pointed out, "they were driven away by people shooting from other wagons."

"That could be too, and maybe some fool driver just drove his oxen to death. Anyhow, we'd better be moving."

"My guess is sick or poisoned oxen," he explained to Emma when he got back on the seat and took the reins. "There aren't any bullet holes in the wagon cover."

"Oh, I do hope that whoever was in there is all right!"

"They probably are," Joe reassured her. "Probably picked up by another wagon."

They drove on, sobered by this evidence of certain accident, and possible tragedy, along the Oregon Trail. The hard trail continued; rain country was definitely behind. But a cold north wind still blew and Joe urged on the mules. There was no summer weather behind that wind and he had no desire to be caught out here when snow fell. For a moment they rode in silence, and it seemed that there was something alien among them. Even the children were still, and Emma turned to Joe, vaguely puzzled.

"Do you hear anything?"

"By gosh, I thought I did."

"I too."

There was a distant, muted throbbing that came to them in discordant tempo, like a wind that blows in blasts instead of with steady force. But the wind around the wagon was still steady and still from the north. Joe twisted uneasily on the wagon seat, for it seemed to him that there was much he should know about this that he did not know. He had a sense of danger, which was silly, for no danger threatened. The mules bobbed uneasy heads.

"Hey, Pa!"

Tad's voice was desperate and wild. Running hard, the youngster appeared on a near-by knoll. Joe stopped the team and waited, while fear's cold fingers caressed his spine. Tad's jacket was open, his face sweat-streaked, and he had run so far and so fast that he gasped for breath.

"My gosh!" he yelled. "Must be a million of 'em!"

"A million what?"

"Buffalo!" Tad gasped. "And they're headin' this way!"

"Get in quick!"

"How about Mike?"

Joe leaped from the wagon, cradled the dog in his arms, handed him up to Emma, and helped his exhausted son. He cracked the bull whip over both mules and gave them free rein.

"Hi-eee! Get up there!"

The mules sprang forward, jerking their traces tight, and the whip cracked over them again. They broke into a wild gallop while the wagon jolted over some unseen obstacle. Joe braced his feet and shouted to Emma,

"Get in back!"

She slid over the seat into the wagon box, and crouched down, drawing the children close to her while Joe cracked his whip again. He breathed a silent prayer as he did so. Though he knew nothing about buffalo stampedes, he had seen cattle run wild. Surely this must be worse.

Then the mules needed no whipping, for the first of the buffalo were in sight. Up a knoll they surged, and down the other side. Tightly packed, those in front could not have turned if they would, for those in back forced them on. A flowing, brown sea of beasts, the noise of their hoofs drowned all other noises and the very earth seemed to shake.

The mules were racing for their lives now, and they knew it. Curbing them not at all and letting them choose their own course, Joe risked one sidewise glance at the stampeding herd. There were a vast number of buffalo, Joe could not even guess how many, and they were going to cross the Oregon Trail. Above the thunder of their hoofs Joe heard Tad's scream,

"Pa!"

"What?" Joe roared back.

"Can I use the rifle?"

"Yes!"

Some great and terrible thing, some mighty force, bumped the wagon and sent it slewing sidewise. Joe slanted the reins forward, as though by so doing he might give the mules more speed, and willed wings onto their hoofs. He heard the rifle's spiteful crack. Then the mules slowed of their own accord and he knew they were safe, but by a very narrow margin. The wagon had actually been bumped by one of the running buffalo. Joe drew the panting mules to a halt and looked back to see the great herd still running.

"Got one!" Tad gloated. "Got one and there it lays!"

"You were a long time shooting," Joe complained.

"Shucks, didn't want to shoot one out of the middle. The rest would have pounded it to bits. I wanted to get one of the rearmost so we'd have somethin' to eat."

Joe turned to look at his son with surprise and admiration. "That was right good thinking!"

Pale and shaken, Emma took her place on the seat beside Joe. Barbara wiped her face with a handkerchief. Too young to appreciate the danger they had avoided, the younger children stood with open mouths, staring at the fleeing buffalo. Joe squeezed Emma's hand.

"What on earth could have brought that on?" she gasped.

"I don't know. Maybe hunters started the herd and it just didn't stop."

"How terribly close!"

"Too close!"

Tad asked eagerly, "Can I take the rifle and go see my buffalo, Pa?"

"Go ahead."

He watched closely while Tad climbed out of the wagon and Mike leaped after him. Before leaving the wagon's shelter, Tad reloaded the rifle and Joe nodded approvingly. Tad was no fool. The buffalo was down, but nobody had proved that it could not get up and Tad wanted to be ready if it did. Joe continued to watch, not joining Tad because this rightly belonged to him. It was a prize worthy of note, and because he himself had brought it down, it would help shape Tad's manhood if nobody else interfered. Joe gave the youngster time to reach and admire his game, then swung the mules to follow.

Barbara shuddered, but braced herself. "Can I help you with it, Daddy?"

Joe said gently, "I don't think so, Bobby."

"Then I'll take the youngsters for a walk. It will keep them out of mischief."

"Wanna see the buffalo!" Alfred protested.

Emma said, "Ally, you go with Barbara."

Joe stopped to let Barbara take the younger children and drove on. The buffalo was a fat cow with a big hump, and Joe thought curiously that he had never really known before how large buffalo can be. He looked at Emma's happy eyes, and knew what she was thinking. The Tower family still had problems, but short rations was no longer one of them.

Tad asked, puzzled, "What are we going to do with it, Pa?"

"Guess we'll have to butcher it like we would a beef."

He hadn't any pulleys to hoist the enormous carcass into a tree, and there weren't any trees to hoist it into. Joe bled the animal. Unhitching the mules, he used them to turn the carcass over on its back. Tad had shot better than he knew, for the buffalo was a barren cow and that was always the best eating. Joe began at one haunch, Tad at the other, and they skinned the dead beast.

The freed skin was dropped on both sides, so that no dirt would cling to the sticky, warm carcass. Emma brought her carving boards and containers from the wagon.

Joe scratched his head, at a loss as to just what they should take and what they should leave. Somewhere he had heard that the hump was the best part of any buffalo, and certainly they'd want the liver. The rest of the meat would have to cool and season before it would be fit for use, but the liver they could eat tonight. However, before they could do anything about the hump, the carcass would have to be made lighter.

Expertly Joe sliced around one of the haunches, and he was surprised when he lifted it quite easily. It weighed, he estimated, no more than a hundred pounds. Maybe buffalo looked bigger than they were. Joe laid the haunch on a carving board and Emma stood ready with her knife.

"You finish what you're doing," she told him. "I'll take care of this."

She began slicing the haunch into steaks. Joe and Tad separated the other haunch, and opened the belly cavity to get the liver. Of the front quarters they took only the choicest parts, and Joe used his saw to cut out the loin. He rolled the lightened carcass over on its side and sliced experimentally at the hump. He was surprised to find a ridge of bone there, and he stood to look down on it. Joe tried again, and failed, to remove the hump. He shrugged. Evidently, whoever had said that the hump was a choice part of any buffalo, didn't know what they were talking about.

Joe, Emma and Tad worked with the meat, throwing away all tissue and bone and keeping only what was edible. Because they were working under adverse conditions, and without all the tools they needed, it took them longer than it would have taken to prepare a steer's carcass. But when they were finished, every meat box was filled and there was still much of the buffalo left.

That night, the first in many, they camped among trees and had wood for their fire. Joe ate what seemed to be a vast quantity of buffalo liver, took a second helping, and was ashamed of himself. But Tad had four helpings and Emma and Barbara each had two. It was good eating, but there seemed to be in it a certain quality that enabled one to eat large quantities and still want more. Joe said happily,

"Have some more, Joey? There's plenty."

"I might try another little piece."

Little Emma said, "I'm stuffed," and Alfred and Carlyle shook their heads. They sat around the festive board, completely relaxed and happy. Last night, after the crushing disappointment of missing the antelope and knowing they had more mud to face, near despair had reigned. Tonight they were on hard ground, with a wood fire, and there was more than plenty for everyone. They would get through.

The next day the sun shone, and the day after that. But a cold wind still blew in from the north and there was a promise of things to come. It was a sinister promise, freighted with bitter and cold meanings, and Joe hurried the mules as much as he could. He gave thanks because the Trail remained dry and they could make good time. When he came to the river he stopped for a few minutes.

It was a willow-bordered, slow-moving river that emptied into the Platte, and it seemed a gentle thing. The tired mules halted in their traces and Joe got down from the wagon seat. Mike and Tad beside him, he walked back and forth on the bank of the river and tried to find an answer to the riddle which he felt must exist here. The Trail went into the river and out the other side; other wagons had forded it. But there still seemed to be a question, and Joe was puzzled because he could see no reason to question. He could not see the bottom of the river, but it was muddy. How many other muddy rivers and creeks had he forded?

"Reckon we can make it?" he asked Tad.

"Other wagons made it."

"Well, we can too."

He climbed back onto the seat and picked up the reins. The

mules stepped forward, then suddenly sidewise. Joe's heart missed
a beat and he let them go, for now he saw why he had had an
instinctive fear of this river.

When the other wagons crossed, it must have been low, perhaps little more than a trickle. But, doubtless due to upcountry
rains, now it was in flood and had undercut its banks. Where other
wagons had found a safe ford, he found only a treacherous shell
of dirt. The wagon lurched sickeningly, threatened to tip, then
came out of a hole into which the right front wheel had fallen.
The mules strained with all their strength, swung back toward
solid ground, and Joe breathed his thanks because he had mules.
Horses or oxen would have gone right ahead, leaving the wagon
hopelessly mired and perhaps drowning themselves. Mules did
their own thinking.

For a brief second that lengthened into eternity, and while the
mules strove mightily to move it, the wagon stopped. Then it was
moving again and Joe felt sick. The right front wheel had gone
down, and the right front wheel was still down while the wagon
dragged on its axle. The wheel was broken, and he had a spare
for everything except wheels. Then he stifled his fright.

The mules came to safe ground and stopped, their sides heaving. Joe stepped from the wagon to see what he knew he would
find. The rim was broken, and the spokes. There was no possibility
of repairing the wheel. Tad joined him, then Emma and Barbara.

"Why don't you fix it, Pa?" Tad asked.

"I can't." He looked levelly at Emma. "Are you afraid to stay
with the youngsters for a while?"

She looked at him, unable to answer.

"I'll leave the rifle with Tad."

"What are you going to do, Joe?"

"The only thing I can do, ride back to that abandoned wagon
we saw and take a wheel from it. The mules won't be hauling a
wagon and I should be able to make time. If I leave now, I can
get a long way before dark."

She gritted her teeth. What must be, must be.

"I'll fix you some lunch."

"Thank you, darling. Tad, walk with me, will you?"

"Sure, Pa."

Tad beside him, Joe walked up the river bank. He swallowed hard. If there were a fort, or even a house—But there wasn't any and he couldn't build any. Joe turned to his son. He looked down in the wide, trusting eyes, and he felt both proud and fearful.

"Tad, you must take over."

"Sure, Pa." His face was eager.

"I don't think you'll have any trouble. But if you do, if anyone at all comes, don't try to defend the wagon. Walk away and let them have it."

"Suppose they come after us?"

"Then," Joe said grimly, "shoot and shoot to kill!"

Tad blinked once, and then he said soberly, "Yes, Pa."

Joe took from his box the tools he needed, and strapped them to the horse mule's harness. Emma pressed a parcel into his hands.

"Here's food." Suddenly her eyes misted over, and her mouth trembled, and then stopped. "You—you watch yourself, Joe. Be careful." She managed a smile.

"I'll be all right," he called as he rode away. "I'll be back before you know it."

They watched him ride away, the younger children merely staring. But Barbara and Emma had a sudden sense of weakness, as though their strength were going with him. Tad set his jaw and clutched the rifle.

Joe turned once to wave.

As soon as he was out of sight, the loneliness and desolation, the terrible emptiness of this wild place, struck Emma Tower like a solid blow. She shivered and kept her face averted because she did not want her children to see what was written there. Gazing down the Trail, she thought she saw Joe again and knew she had not. He had gone on a lonely, dangerous ride, and for a moment

she entertained the soul-chilling notion that she would never see
him again.

Then she banished such thoughts from her mind. She was here,
halfway between Missouri and God only knew where, because
she had confidence in Joe's ability to take care of his family and
himself. She loved Missouri and she would have been perfectly
contented to stay there. But she loved Joe more, and she knew
all about the desperate longings and wild undercurrents which
were within him and which he must constantly battle. She knew
about the opportunities he had always sought but never had, and
of his hopes for his children. If Oregon was the answer to that,
then Oregon it would be.

Now, for another moment, all she knew was that she had been
deserted and that it was terrible. Had she been alone, she told
herself, she might have wept, for she felt like weeping. Then she
knew that that was wrong too. Had there been no children dependent on her, she would have gone with Joe. But the children
were here and she rose to the occasion.

"Tad," she called, "you and Barbara pick up some of that driftwood along the river and bring it in."

She watched them as they left to do her bidding, her lovely
daughter and the son who was so like his father. Tad had the long
rifle over his shoulder and he would not go out of sight of the
wagon. Every second or so he looked toward it. Tad returned with
all the wood he could carry, two small pieces clutched under his
arm and dragging a larger piece.

"Tad," Emma told him, "if you would leave the rifle here you
could carry a lot more wood."

"No," he demurred.

"Yes you could."

"No. Pa told me to watch over things and I aim to do it."

She almost smiled openly, but stopped herself in time. A
daughter of Missouri, she knew something about rifles and she
had seen her son aim from a jolting, careening wagon and stop a

running buffalo with one shot. Suddenly, though she could not help worrying about Joe, the emptiness was not a complete vacuum and she no longer felt deserted. This, while not normal, was no extraordinary situation. The Towers might be here instead of in a proper house. Wherever they were, they would take care of themselves.

The chickens scratched in the grass. Tethered in good grazing, the gentle cow stood patiently while Emma milked her. She marveled. Though the cow had walked all the way from Missouri, and could graze only when the wagon stopped, she still gave almost a third as much milk as she had given at home. Emma petted her affectionately. She was a very good cow, one that would be of some use after they got to Oregon.

Tad laid the fire. Lying on the windward side, he shielded it with his body and started the blaze with only one match. The match bottle he corked carefully and put exactly where it belonged. Emma watched fondly and a little wistfully. Some time, she thought, the world might be in such a condition that an eight-year-old could be a boy without having to be a man. Still, if there was any lack in his life, Tad did not seem to be aware of it. He had been left with responsibilities, and he was accepting them. And he fairly bristled with his newfound self-importance.

The three youngest children had become a herd of stampeding buffalo and baby Emma was the wagon they were trying to cut off. Young Joe entered so enthusiastically into the game that he made himself the buffalo that had bumped the wagon, and baby Emma took a seat in the grass. At once the adventuring wagon became a wailing child who was gathered up and comforted in Barbara's slim arms.

Emma baked bread, broiled buffalo steaks, and divided the milk, giving each of the youngest children a double portion and Barbara and herself a half portion. She liked coffee with her evening meals. But they were low on coffee, she wanted to save what there was for Joe, and it was by no means certain that they would be able to buy any at Laramie. Even if some were avail-

able it would probably be expensive, for every pound of everything except meat had to be freighted in wagons or carried on the
backs of pack animals.

Barbara and Emma washed the dishes, put them away, and
Emma gathered her children around the fire.

"Tell us a story," Alfred begged.

Emma had never been good at story-telling, and she felt a swift
pang of longing for Joe. "Let's sing."

She had a sweet and clear soprano, and Barbara's voice was as
lovely as Barbara. They sang "Yankee Doodle," the first song
Yancey Garrow had played for them and one Emma had learned
at her father's knee. It was the marching song of American soldiers
in the Revolutionary War, and Emma's father had fought in that
war. There was discord at first, but even Carlyle caught the
rhythm and carried his end fairly well. They went through the
same song four times because the children were entranced with
their ability to sing it, and then Tad rose to peer into the enfold-
ing shadows of early evening.

"The fire should be out, huh?"

Emma said, "Yes. But let's make our beds first."

She said no more and was grateful because Tad and Barbara
said nothing. The four youngest children knew only that the fire
was going out. They did not know that a blazing fire can be seen
a very long way at night, and who could be sure what savage
beings prowled this lonely land?

Tad tied Mike to the wagon, and Emma knew why he was
doing it. Some nights Mike was apt to go prowling, and that was
all right as long as Joe was with them. Nobody worried then, for
nobody doubted that Joe would hear, in time, any danger that
stalked them. But tonight Mike must not prowl, for they depended on him to warn them.

Emma let the drop curtain fall and took Barbara and baby
Emma on her side. She peered around the curtain to see Tad,
who had chosen to sleep near the partly open flaps, arranging the
powder horn and bullet pouch where he could reach them in an

instant. The rifle he laid beside him. In the night, when none of her children could watch, Emma's hand stole forth to grasp a long-bladed knife. She took it to bed with her, and only then did she pray.

She lay sleepless but unmoving in the darkness. The wind rustled the wagon cover, and she heard the cow moving about. A leaping fish splashed in the river. The coyotes began their chorus. These were all familiar noises and they could be dismissed as such. Emma waited tensely for the one sound she hoped she would not hear; the dog's challenging bark. She whispered through the curtain,

"Tad?"

"Yes, Ma?"

"Go to sleep now."

"Yes, Ma."

Tad stopped his restless wriggling, sorry because he had kept his mother awake. Very carefully, not making a sound, he rose and peered through the back flaps. He couldn't see anything, but he thought he saw something and cold fright gripped him. He lay down, knowing that he must not sleep and wishing mightily that Joe was here. Everything always seemed so safe and secure then, but everything was so terrifying now. He leaped at a noise, then identified it as Mike's grunting. Tad nodded sleepily, and he was half awake and half asleep when he heard the thunder of horses' hoofs. They were sweeping down on the wagon; and opening the back flaps, Tad saw them coming. There were at least forty of the Indians, and even though his father had told him not to defend the wagon, he had to defend it now. He shot, saw the leading warrior pitch from his horse, and reloaded the rifle to shoot again. Trembling, he came completely awake and lay shivering for a moment. What he had heard was only the wind plucking at the wagon cover. Now lulled by the sound, Tad settled back into bed. He thought of Buster Trevelyan, back in Missouri, and hoped that some day he would see Buster again so

he could tell all about his hair-raising adventures on the Oregon
Trail. He heard a night bird call, fought himself to wakefulness,
then went to sleep with his cheek on the rifle.

After an eternity, morning was upon them. Cloud banks surged
in the sky, and the sun could not break through them. The north
wind seemed keener and colder than it had been before. Emma
dressed the babies, glanced at Tad to make sure that he had
dressed himself warmly, and took up the duties of the day.

She made the longest possible ceremony of breakfast. Even so,
after it was all done and the dishes washed, the endless day faced
her. She glanced wistfully at the river, and thought of all the
clothes that must be washed. However, this was not the time for
washing. There were more important affairs.

Her children about her, shadowed by the rifle-carrying Tad, she
walked a little way down the Oregon Trail. But she did not
walk very far because Carlyle's legs would not carry him far. As
slowly as possible she returned to the wagon, and the youngsters
shrieked with delight as Mike bounced after a jack rabbit that
speedily left him behind.

Emma built up the fire while Barbara organized a game of
hide-and-seek among the children. Emma took her needle and
thread and mended some of Joe's trousers, and she took some
small comfort from this much contact with him.

Even though she dreaded it, she was glad when night came
again. All day long the youngsters had had to be kept busy and
happy, and there were only her own and Barbara's resources upon which to draw. Though she feared what the night would bring,
at least the youngsters would sleep. Emma put them to bed, and
again, in the darkness, she took the long knife in bed with her.
She whispered of her weariness and terror to Joe, and hoped that,
somehow, he would hear her and come back. Grimly she fought
exhaustion, and set herself to listen as she had listened all last
night. It was still dark inside the wagon when she heard Mike's
challenging bark.

She awoke in sudden panic, terrified by the thought that she had let herself sleep. The knife clasped tightly in her hand, she sat up in bed. Barbara awakened.

"What is it, mother?"

"Hush!"

She heard the back flaps rustle, and she peered around the curtain to see Tad, rifle in hand, climbing out of the wagon. Emma slipped past the curtain and stepped carefully over her still-sleeping sons. It was still dark inside the wagon, but dawn's first faint light had come. Emma leaned over the rear.

"What is it, Tad?"

"Stay in the wagon!" he hissed.

She saw him crouching, holding Mike's muzzle so the dog could not bark again and peering intently in the direction the dog was looking. Emma tightened her grip on the knife and made ready to fight for her children's lives.

She did not weaken, or feel herself go limp, or give way to tears, until she heard Tad's happily shouted,

"It's Pa! Pa's come back!"

CHAPTER NINE

Storm

JOE HAD stopped only to let the mules rest and graze, and wherever that was he nibbled a cold snack from the food Emma had prepared for him. Then he slept, but he had purposely brought no blankets and he built no fire, because he did not want to oversleep. Though he was tired enough to doze wherever he lay down, the cold always awakened him.

Never for an instant did he forget the fact that he had left his family camped, undefended, along the river. He must return to them at the earliest possible moment, for they were his to protect. Therefore, he let the mules have only the barest minimum of grazing and rest, and he drove himself as hard as he drove them.

Though he slept little, he remained alert to the things about him. No man should travel in this country without a rifle, and he had left the rifle with Tad. Should any personal emergency arise, he would have to meet it as best he could. He didn't expect any; they'd come all this way and needed the rifle only for food. Joe smiled wryly. It always seemed that, when one lacked something, the need for it arose. He cantered the mules around a knoll, and both came to a sliding halt while they pricked their ears forward and blew their nostrils.

No more than sixty yards away, staring intently at them, was an enormous bear. Joe swallowed hard. He was familiar with the little black bears of Missouri, but this was no black bear. Joe remembered vaguely that he had heard of white bears, or western grizzlies, and the bear was of a pale color. They were savage things and enormously strong. Certainly this one looked as though it could kill one or both of the mules without exerting itself unduly.

Joe swung the mules, who needed no urging, and galloped them to the right. Glancing behind, he saw the bear running and for a moment he thought it was racing to cut him off. Then he grinned weakly and relaxed. All bears, he remembered, have rather poor hearing and sight. They have a keen sense of smell, but the wind had been blowing from the bear to Joe. Probably the grizzly hadn't even been aware of his presence until the mules started to run, and then he was as frightened as the mules. Or, Joe thought, as frightened as one Joe Tower.

Reaching the abandoned wagon, he first gathered two piles of flat stones. One he arranged beneath the wagon's axle; the other he piled a few feet in front. He had remembered to cut a prying pole when he passed the grove of trees in which they had camped. Using one pile of stones as a fulcrum, he inserted the pole beneath the axle and lifted. Raising the front end of the wagon, Joe drove a forged stick over the prying pole to hold it. Then he built higher the stones beneath the axle.

When the wheel no longer touched the earth, he took it off. Lifting the wagon's other side, he took that wheel too, and packed both on the horse mule. Should they break another wheel, he would not be caught without a spare.

On the return trip he rode hard, pressing the mules and stopping only twice. From a distance he heard Mike's bark, and he advanced cautiously. Tad did have the rifle, and Joe had no wish to resemble, however remotely, a prowling Indian. Then he heard,

"It's Pa! Pa's come back!"

Joe threw caution to the winds and rode openly, and now his weariness seemed in some magic fashion to evaporate. He had been very worried about Emma and the youngsters; in his mind they had been the victims of raiding Indians, one or all of the younger children had fallen into the river and drowned, one of the great white bears had raided them, they hadn't known how to start a fire and thus were cold; these and a dozen other disasters had overtaken them. To know that none of his fears was realized drove worry from his mind and furnished complete relief.

He wondered at Tad as he put the mules to a trot. Back in Missouri, given a rifle and told to stand guard, Tad might have shot at anything, including noises, that startled him. Obviously the Oregon Trail, and perhaps the spanking Joe had given him, had taught the youngster much that he needed to know. Joe saw the wagon and his wife and son, and he called,

"Hi!"

"Hello, Joe!"

Emma's greeting was a glad one, and her voice revealed none of the terror she had endured.

Lithe as a fawn, lovely even though she was dressed in cumbersome garments, Barbara leaped from the wagon and waved excitedly,

"Hello, Daddy!"

"Hi, Bobby!"

Joe rode up to the wagon and halted his mules. He looked down at Tad. "Everything was all right, huh?"

"Yeah. Nothin' came."

Joe laughed. "You never have luck, do you?"

He looked at Emma, and saw in her eyes everything that she had not put into words. Traces of terror and loneliness lingered there, and he knew that she had prayed for him. But happiness because he had finally come back was driving the rest away as surely as the rising sun dispels morning mist.

"Have you had breakfast?" Emma inquired.

"Yup. Had a snack down the trail a ways."

"But you're in here almost before daylight. I'll fix something for you."

Emma built up her fire and put water over to boil for coffee. She made her spider—a skillet with legs—ready and laid three eggs beside it. Joe looked concernedly at them.

"Better save those for the kids, hadn't you?"

"The children aren't lacking anything and I have eight more eggs. Every hen but one has laid every day."

"They must like wagon life." He winked solemnly at her.

"I'm sure they do," she replied, dimpling. "It's a good life—for chickens."

The children looked up at the sound of their parents' hearty, soul-easing laughter.

Joe unlashed the wagon wheels, lifted them from the mule, leaned them against the wagon, unharnessed the mules, and tied them where they could graze. He was in high spirits and the world was good again. He sat before the blazing fire and partook hungrily of the breakfast Emma prepared for him. The younger children tumbled out of the wagon and ran to their father. Carlyle and baby Emma snuggled contentedly in his lap while they ate their breakfast, and young Joe and Alfred braced themselves one on either side.

Almost at once Joe was restless again and he felt an inner urge to be moving. He had lingered in Independence far too long, gentling a six-mule team for Jake Favors, and a wet trail and a broken wheel had set them farther behind. Now the north wind blew steadily, and the clouds were black and angry. But the mules had been working hard and it was hazardous to go on unless they grazed and rested. There was a long trail still ahead, and the team must be in condition for it. However, he could replace the wagon wheel.

There were no flat rocks here, but the river bank was piled high with driftwood, ranging all the way from slender branches to huge trees that had come down on the swollen current. Joe found a prying pole, used a chunk of wood for a fulcrum, and lifted the wagon. While Barbara and Tad sat on the end of the pole, holding the wagon in place, Joe blocked the front end with more wood. He replaced the broken wheel and busied himself with his ax.

Comparatively little of the driftwood was green; few growing trees had been uprooted by the high water. Of the dead trees, some were water-logged and these he passed by. He wanted only dry and buoyant wood that would help keep the wagon afloat when they crossed the river, and when he found such a piece he chopped it into the lengths he desired. Leaving each piece where he chopped it, he prowled up the river bank looking for still more suitable wood and a place where they might ford.

He found where the bank sloped easily into the water, with no sharp drops and no undercutting. Joe threw a chunk of wood in, watched it drift gently downstream, and knew the current was not a swift one. He tried to gauge the depth with his eye, but the river was too muddy to let him do it and there might be hidden obstacles on the bottom. Joe glanced back toward the wagon, decided that he could not be seen from it, and removed his clothing.

He shivered in the raw north wind, but walked slowly into the water. The bank and the river bottom both seemed solid, and Joe could feel no hidden obstruction that might get a mule in trouble. Much warmer than the air, the water rose to his chest and then to his neck. He swam, but the deep part of the river was only about twenty feet wide and he could wade again. Joe climbed up onto the far bank. He inspected it carefully, and when he was finished he knew that he could take the wagon across here.

Joe dressed and trotted back to the wagon. The cold wind and the water had left him numb, so that he had to move fast in order to restore circulation. But before he came in sight of the wagon he walked again. Emma had emphatic ideas about proper deportment in cold weather, and none of her notions included stripping naked and swimming a river. Joe whistled as he strode up to the wagon. He'd had little sleep for two nights, but was not unduly tired.

"Everything's smooth as a tub of lard," he called cheerfully. "I found a new ford. Can you catch your chickens?"

"Oh yes. They're tame."

"Give me an hour or so, then catch them and load everything on the wagon. The Towers are about to move again."

He took the whiffletree from the wagon, let a chain drag behind it, and harnessed the mules. Joe drove them up the river bank, gathering the wood he had cut as he came to each piece, binding as big a load as the chain would surround and dragging it to the ford he had selected. When all the wood was piled there, he returned for the wagon.

The youngest children remained inside, peering curiously out the front or back, while Joe, Emma, Barbara and Tad lashed wood beneath the wagon box, on both sides of it, and even to the tongue. Joe stepped back to grin at their handiwork. There was so much wood tied to the wagon that only the wheels and cover were visible. It was not absolutely essential; the wagon itself would have floated. But Joe wanted to keep water out of the box and away from the load.

"Never thought we'd have to build our own ship out in the middle of this—wish I knew just what it is and where it is. But we're on our way to Laramie. Let's launch."

The mules walked gingerly down to the river, taking their time and testing what lay ahead before they put their full weight on it. With only the lightest pressure on the reins, Joe let them have their own way. Nobody could make a mule go where it didn't want to go and nobody could hurry a mule that wanted to be cautious. They entered the water, waded out until it lapped their bellies, and continued to move carefully. Then they were swimming, holding their heads high so no water could trickle into their ears. They waded again.

Safe on the opposite bank, Joe and Tad untied the ropes that held the wood on, and they threw as much as they could reasonably carry into the wagon box. Not forgotten was that long and dismal stretch where buffalo chips were the only fuel. Should they again strike treeless trail, they would have firewood.

That night they camped just across the river, within a stone's throw of the ford where the wheel had broken.

With dawn, the first snow lay on the ground. It was light and powdery, little more than a white dust that did not hide completely the grass on the near-by knolls but seemed to cover entirely those farther away. Little snow devils, picked up by wind, whirled across the trail and filled ruts while leaving the crown between them brown and naked. Joe hurried the mules, and wished mightily that he had saved some grain for them. Mules worked better when they were on grain, but all they'd been able to carry from Independence had been used up two weeks ago. The rest of the trip to Laramie would necessarily be forced, with no time to linger on the way and since there wasn't any grain, the mules would have to work without it.

Tad trotted beside the wagon and fell behind. Joe waited for him.

"Better get in."

"I aim to walk. I'll keep up."

Joe felt his anger rise, but he held it in check. Tad had been mighty brave and mighty helpful and he was entitled to be treated with respect. "We're going to make time, Tad. We've got to now."

Tad was silent, and the struggle he was undergoing showed plainly on his freckled face.

Suddenly, without a word of comment, he climbed into the wagon and settled himself where he could watch out the back end. Joe's heart swelled with pride. Emma had told him that his daughter had grown up, and now he knew that his son was growing, too. Fiercely proud, Tad had fully intended to walk all the way to Oregon. But he had seen the need, and had placed the family's welfare above his own.

Joe said, "Keep your eye peeled for antelope, will you? Holler if you see any and I'll hand you the rifle."

"Sure, Pa. You want buffalo too?"

"Can't stop to butcher a buffalo right now."

Joe kept the mules at a fast walk except on upgrades and trotted them on all the down slopes. The mules were big, but their hoofs were slender and much smaller than a horse's. Therefore, though this light fall did not bother them, they would have harder going than horses found should there be deep snow.

Clouds ruled the sky until almost noon, then they broke and the sun shone for a few hours. There was little warmth in it and the north wind still blew. But all the snow melted, leaving them a clear trail, and there had not been enough snow so that its melting left mud in its wake.

That night they stopped half an hour before their usual stopping time because, though speed was important, grass was just as necessary and there was rich grass at this spot. The mules and the cow could eat their fill and be ready for a long trail tomorrow. The next day they started at dawn, and the day after that. On the seventh day after the first snowfall they met a rider coming east. Joe looked around to see where his children were, and he made sure that the rifle was in reach. Then they drew nearer and he saw that the rider was a white man.

He was small, not much taller than Pete Domley, and his horse, a clean-limbed sorrel, seemed huge in comparison. The man wore a wool cap, a buffalo skin coat with the hair still on, and cloth trousers that were tucked into high-laced moccasins. A luxuriant black beard fell a third of the way down his chest. He carried a long rifle crosswise on the front of his saddle, and strapped behind was a small pack.

Joe sat forward on the seat and he felt Emma move with him. The children crowded forward, staring with frank curiosity at this, the first man they had met since they were a couple of days out of Kearney. There might have been others near the trail, but if there had been any, they hadn't met them. Now they were going to meet, and for a little while the country seemed neither so lonely nor so vast. Joe halted the mules and the rider stopped his horse beside them. Though he was small, his voice was loud and blasting,

"Migosh! Emigrants! What'd you do? Get lost?"

"Yep!" Joe laughed for the sheer joy of laughing and because it felt so good to meet someone else. "Plumb lost!"

"You must have. Do you know how far behind the rest you are?"

"We left late."

"You don't figure on gettin' to Oregon this season, do you?"

"Just to Laramie. How far is it?"

"A piece up the Trail. I left there yesterday at midmornin'."

"Then we should make it in tomorrow?"

"I don't know," the rider said doubtfully. "You could if you was ridin' horses, but you'll have to make them mules step some with a wagon behind 'em."

"It's almost noon," Emma spoke up. "Why don't we lunch here and ask Mr.—"

"Gaystell, ma'am," the rider swept off his hat and bowed to Emma. "John Gaystell, and I'll be right proud to join you in a bit of lunch. I didn't expect to see any white folks this side of Kearney."

Joe stepped down, turned to help Emma, and stood aside as Tad and Barbara alighted. Joe caught the younger children in his arms and helped them down; they could descend without his help but this was faster. He was swinging Carlyle to the ground when he heard Emma say,

"My daughter, Barbara Tower, Mr. Gaystell."

"Pleased to know you, miss. Say, more wagons goin' to Oregon should carry freight like you! Dress up the country no end!"

Barbara blushed and Joe grinned. The men of Missouri were outspoken, but few of them were as candid as John Gaystell.

While Tad climbed back into the wagon and tossed wood to the ground, Joe unhitched the mules but left them in harness. He slipped their bridles and picketed the team where they could find good grazing. When he was finished, Tad had the fire started and Barbara and Emma were preparing lunch. John Gaystell slipped unobtrusively over to stand beside Joe, and startled him by lowering his voice to a whisper.

"You goin' to winter at Laramie?"

"Why?"

"None of my mix. Sure none of my mix if that's what you want to do. And the soldiers at Laramie are a decent sort. But you don't get that many men together without findin' one or two who might not be so decent. And—that daughter of yours is a right pretty girl."

Joe said, "Figured on wintering at Snedeker's."

"That'll be better. That'll be a lot better."

Tad gazed with mingled admiration and awe at this man of the west who had met them on the Trail. Barbara and Emma peppered him with questions which he was trying gallantly to answer. Was Laramie a big place? Yes, it was quite a fort. Were the houses good? Good as you'll find anywhere. Were there any white women at

Laramie? Yes, John Gaystell looked roguishly at Barbara, and a whole passel of young soldiers. What were the women wearing? He stumbled on that one, but finally declared that they were wearing dresses.

Joe's spirits mounted. For long, lonely weeks his family had seen only each other, and at times it seemed that they were the only people in a huge world. Living in close intimacy, everybody had long ago learned not only what the rest were going to say next, but almost what they were going to think next. Meeting a stranger, someone with a different viewpoint, was a stimulating and heady as a glass of sparkling wine.

John Gaystell had been in Oregon, and as soon as he completed his mission in Independence, he was going back. It was, he told them, a wonderful country where the Towers might have their choice of land, and they could find it as close to or as far away from neighbors as they wished. The Trail was long but not too difficult, and they had already covered a lot of it. If they started from Snedeker's as soon as the grass was green enough to provide food for their stock, they should get to Oregon in time to plant some crops. There was perhaps some danger from white men but little from Indians; though there were rumors of another uprising, none had materialized and John Gaystell thought none would. The Indians were not inclined to bother people who minded their own business and stayed on the Oregon Trail. They might, however, become angry if what they considered their private hunting grounds were invaded. Joe must be careful where he went. They could ford the Laramie River, the Trail crossed about a mile below the fort, and they could rest at the fort. Snedeker's was a few miles west of Laramie.

John Gaystell looked longingly at the last three biscuits on the plate and licked his lips.

"Have another one?" Emma invited.

"No thank you, ma'am," he refused politely.

"Let me butter them and you take them along for your evening meal. We'll have fresh ones tonight, anyway."

"Well, ma'am, if you want to do that—Those biscuits are better than any cake I ever tasted!"

John Gaystell mounted his horse, waved good-by, and rode east toward Independence. The entire family watched him go, until he was out of sight. Joe hitched the mules and drove on up the Trail. Now, and at last, he knew where they were and they were very near Laramie. If they did not get in tomorrow, they certainly would the next day.

That night they camped very close to the river, and in the middle of the night Joe awakened to a sense of wonder. Either something was present that should not be, or there was something lacking that should be, but not until he had lain for a moment did he deduce that the wind had died. It was a wierd thing; for weeks the north wind had been their constant companion. Very quietly Joe parted the back flaps and looked out.

The wind had stopped but the snow had started. The ground was already white, and huge, feathery flakes whirled earthward so silently that they did not even rustle against the taut wagon cover. Joe went back to sleep. This was going to be more than a dusting. Probably it was the season's first heavy snowfall, but there was no reason to worry. They were near Laramie and they could reach it.

Joe was awakened a second time by Emma's light touch on his shoulder, and he opened his eyes to find that dawn had come. He sat bolt upright, looking into his wife's troubled face, and without being told he knew why she had roused him. It was the fever again, the mysterious malady that plagued baby Emma. Joe dressed, heartsick and afraid. There was nothing he had been able to do before for his daughter, and there was nothing he could do now. But always before baby Emma had been in a safe, warm house. Here they were far out on the plains, and facing a storm. He peered through the curtain to see the child in her mother's arms. Joe whispered,

"There's sure to be a doctor at Laramie."

He threw wood out the back flaps, climbed after it, and built a fire. He brought the cow in and milked her. Her coat buttoned tightly around her, Barbara prepared breakfast. Tad came to the fire, and Barbara took food to the younger children. When she returned, her eyes were clouded with worry.

"Mother wanted only some milk."

"Do you think you can keep those youngsters busy today, so they won't bother your mother and sister?"

"Yes."

Joe said gently, "Try your best, Bobby. We're going into Laramie today."

"I'll help drive," Tad offered. His lifted face was pale with determination.

Joe rested a hand briefly on the boy's shoulder. "I'll need help."

Inside the wagon Emma cradled the sick child against her breast, and she prayed as she always prayed when baby Emma was sick. "Dear Lord, spare us our little girl. She is a good child, Lord, and will grow up to be a good woman. We'll take care of her, Lord, and do the best we can for her, if only you'll pull her through again, as you did before." She rocked the child gently, and her thoughts went on after the prayer in a kind of formless argument. Little Emma hadn't asked to come out here in the wilderness. They had brought her, and now she was sick. For one wild, horrible moment she thought of baby Emma dying and being buried out here in the limitless plain, and her breath stopped. But no, no, no—she would be well again, she would be well and laughing and running in the tall grass. Emma bent her tense, determined face over the feverish child, as though by sheer will she could drive the illness away, banish the fever and the pain. And in her mind the prayer continued, over and over: "Dear Lord, spare us our little girl."

Snow fell so thickly that the mules, tethered only fifty feet from the wagon, had their coats plastered with it and were dimly seen shapes against the white background. They shook themselves when Joe approached, and the harnesses knocked off such snow as still clung to them. Joe backed the mules into place, hitched them to

the wagon, and climbed up beside Tad. He crossed his fingers as
he did so.

Once he had driven two mules, pulling a ton of weight in addition to the wagon, fifty miles in the course of a day. But the mules
were grain-fed and rested, and they hadn't had to pull their load
through snow. This team had worked every day, had had no grain,
and they were tired. Joe picked up the reins and started them at a
fast walk. The wagon wheels made crunching noises in the new
snow, and the mules blinked their eyes against the storm. Joe
stopped at noon only long enough to build a fire so Barbara could
cook a meal. Hastily, Joe gulped his food and looked into the
wagon.

Barbara had kept the drop curtain down, and Joe, Carlyle and
Alfred, on one side of it. She had served their meal there, and
they were eating hastily too so they could snuggle back beneath
the warm quilts. Joe parted the curtain to look at Emma, and he
knew a sudden sense of loss because it seemed that she had gone
away from him. Her whole physical and spiritual being were with
the sick baby, and Joe swallowed hard. He had a sudden, wild and
dreadful notion that his youngest daughter looked the way angels
must look. Joe stepped outside, wiped his sweating forehead, and
set his jaw. They would get to Laramie tonight.

The snow fell neither faster nor more slowly, and Joe breathed a
sigh of thanks because there was no wind. Without wind the snow
could not drift, but there was no assurance that the wind would
not blow again tonight or tomorrow. If it did, if he had to stop
and shovel through deep drifts, they might not get into Laramie
for two or even three days, and with the child feverish such a de-
lay was intolerable. She must get in out of the storm and feel the
good heat that comes only from a stove or fireplace. Joe kept the
mules at a fast walk but he did not let them trot or canter. Whether
or not they got into Laramie depended almost entirely on how
skillfully he handled the team.

Seven inches of snow covered the ground, but where it lay
smoothly on both sides, the Trail itself was deeply rutted with

crowns between the ruts, and snow followed the road's contours. It was easy to see, and mules had a feeling for trails that horses and oxen did not possess. But the mules were walking more slowly now, and when they came to a slight rise Joe halted to let them breathe.

Tad said, "They're gettin' tired, Pa."

Joe heard Emma crooning to her sick daughter. "They can go on," he said. He drove to the top of the rise, halted again, and handed the reins to Tad.

"Hang on to them, will you?"

He took the pail from the wagon and milked. The cow stood patiently and let him do it, then backed to the full length of her lead rope and looked at him questioningly. It was time to camp and the cow knew it, but Joe merely petted her and handed the milk up to Barbara.

"Can you feed the youngsters and yourself in the wagon?"

"Yes, Daddy. We'll have milk and there's buttered biscuits left."

"Good." Joe looked at his wife. "How is she?"

Hollow-eyed, Emma looked back at him.

"Very feverish. Is there any chance of getting out of the storm?"

Little Emma's cheeks were almost translucent, and she twitched in her sleep. Joe swallowed hard, and again had a strange feeling that angels must look this way. Joe forced cheer into his voice.

"We'll be in Laramie soon. Don't you worry."

Snow was falling faster; the tracks they'd made coming up the rise were half filled and there was no indication that the storm would lessen. Joe took the reins from Tad and the weary mules plodded on. Joe tried to peer down the Trail and could see only a few feet, but that was not because of heavy snow. Night was coming. Joe stopped the mules again.

"Reckon you could keep them moving?" he asked Tad.

"I reckon. What are you goin' to do, Pa?"

"Make darn' sure we stay on the Trail."

Joe handed the reins to Tad and leaped from the wagon into the snow-filled twilight. Mules had an instinct for the trail. But men had a keener one and to get lost now might be fatal. Joe walked to the head of the team, and the mules flicked their long ears forward while they sniffed him anxiously. They, too, knew that it was past the time to stop. Joe turned his back to the team and called to Tad,

"All right."

He walked fast enough to keep ahead of the laboring team, and his heart caught in his throat because he had to set a very slow pace. The mules were straining hard to do work that under ordinary circumstances would not have been excessive. The night was wholly black now.

Joe stopped suddenly, aware that they had come to another river only because he heard the soft purling of water. Two more steps and he would have walked into it. His heart pounded, and he trembled. John Gaystell had spoken of the Laramie River, and had said that it could be forded. Suppose there was another river that could not be forded, one Gaystell hadn't mentioned? Joe hesitated, then got his rifle.

He stood on the river bank, pointed the rifle straight up and, when he shot, the muzzle blast illumined only falling snow. Too weary to do anything else, the mules only started nervously when the rifle roared. Joe listened intently, keeping his mouth open the better to hear. Then, after what seemed like hours and could have been no more than fifteen seconds, in the distance he heard an answering shot. Ten minutes later a hail sounded out in the darkness.

"Hall-oo!"

"Hall-oo!" Joe called back.

He heard a shouted, "Where are you?"

"Across the river! Can we ford?"

"Yes! Do you see my light?"

"No!"

"Stay where you are! I'll come over!"

A horse splashed in the river and came toward them. Suddenly, and almost unbelievingly, out in the swirling snow Joe saw the lighted lantern that the rider carried. He called,

"I see you now!"

"Come straight toward me! I'll wait!"

Joe climbed to the seat, took the reins from Tad, and drove the mules in the river. They walked more briskly now, and Joe thought that no man can, for very long, deceive a mule. They knew that their journey was nearly over, and that not too far ahead they would find both food and shelter. Perhaps they smelled the fort.

Out in the river, as they drew closer, Joe saw a mounted trooper holding a lantern high. The soldier walked his horse back across the river. Two other cavalry men waited there, and the soldier with the lighted lantern paused beside the wagon.

"Good Lord! Who hits the trail on a night like this?"

"Had to get to Laramie," Joe explained.

"You're almost there. How are your mules?"

"Worn out."

"Follow us. We'll take it slow."

Joe followed the troopers up the trail, and the lights of Laramie shone through the storm. Guarded by armed soldiers, the gate was open and Joe drove through into the stockade. The sergeant with the lantern came beside the wagon again.

"Can we get quarters?" Joe asked. "We have a sick youngster with us."

"Want to go to the hospital?"

"No!" Emma said.

One of the soldiers rode ahead, and Joe swung his tired team to follow the sergeant. Lamp light brightened windows, and Joe halted the mules. The sergeant dismounted.

"Here you are. Bring the youngster in."

Joe helped Emma from the wagon and into an officer's quarters, where the soldier who had ridden ahead had lighted an already-laid fire. There were cots and blankets, and Emma unwrapped the shawl that enfolded her sick baby. She looked around her at the kind anxious face of the soldier standing ready to help, at the good, stout walls of the room they were in, at the warm fire where all the children would soon be gathered, and at Joe, hovering over her now, wanting so much to protect her, to protect them all. A smile of hope lighted her face.

"She'll be all right now, Joe. She needed the fire and a real rest. She'll have it, now."

"Do you want the doctor?" the sergeant asked.

Emma said cheerfully, "We really don't need him right now. Would he come later if she should take a turn for the worse?"

"Certainly."

Barbara entered with Carlyle, and the sergeant swung to come face to face with her. For a moment, but only for a moment, he lost his brisk military bearing while a delighted grin flickered across his lips. Emma watched, and now that she was no longer under tension she could afford to be mischievous.

"Sergeant—?"

"Dugan, ma'am."

"Thank you, Sergeant Dugan. We're the Tower family and this is our daughter, Barbara."

"You sure are welcome, miss!" Sergeant Dugan breathed.

Joe brought the rest of his sleepy, fretful family in, and left Emma and Barbara to put them to bed while he went outside with Sergeant Dugan. The soldier examined the mules with the practiced eye of a man who knew animals.

"They certainly are done," he agreed. "We'd better take them to the stables where they can have hay and grain. The cow can go in the corral."

Thankfully, Joe permitted the soldiers to take care of the mules and the cow.

The Towers had come through the first portion of their journey. That much was over now, and his family was safe and out of the storm. He wanted to be with them, to watch them bask in the warmth of the fire, to share with them the well-being of this wonderful, though temporary, shelter.

CHAPTER TEN

Snedeker's

THE TOWER family, Joe thought with a smile, had never been as well off as it was right now. Baby Emma had come through her illness, and was thriving. They hadn't been assigned an orderly, but most of the time among the soldiers who were off duty, they had from four to fifteen. Joe's smile widened and his eyes sparkled. Some of the officers and noncoms had their wives with them and some of the enlisted men had squaws to whom, Joe presumed, they were married.

But Laramie was an isolated fort. Most of the soldiers were young, out for a taste of adventure, and they found little enough. Even patrols into Indian country became monotonous after one made a sufficient number of them, and winter duty at the fort was routine.

Bringing Barbara among so many lonely youngsters who hadn't expected to see a girl until emigrant trains started coming through in the spring created a situation which had all the explosive potentialities of a match held too near an open powder keg and was, at the same time, amusing.

Wood was the fuel used at Laramie, but Joe hadn't had to cut or carry any. The wood box was always filled, and at least five times a day some youngster who had elected to wear his country's uniform dropped in to see if the Towers didn't need any more. The water pails invariably brimmed over, and they were always full because the men of Laramie had decided that nothing but the freshest water was good enough. When Barbara went to the sutler's store, she was always attended by an escort large enough to form a good-sized patrol and she could not carry even the smallest parcel back. Every evening, until Emma shooed them out, their quarters overflowed with soldiers eager to do anything at all as long as they could be near Barbara.

Joe did not worry about her; any soldier who offered an insolent remark, or even an insolent look, to Barbara, would have been overwhelmed by a sufficient number of her protectors. But, aside from the fact that Joe wanted to winter at Snedeker's and not at Laramie, the affair had its more serious aspects. Only last night Privates Haggerty and Jankoski, vying for the honor of walking closest to Barbara when she went to the store, had left each other with blackened eyes and bleeding noses and they'd promptly been clapped into the guardhouse for their pains. Probably there would be other fights; Joe understood that Private Brown did not gaze with a kindly eye on Corporal Lester. Lester had filled the water pails just as Brown was on his way to do it.

Joe chuckled out loud. Sitting across the breakfast table from him, Emma raised an inquiring eye.

"I was thinking of those two crazy kids, Haggerty and Jankoski, and the fight they had over Bobby last night," he explained.

"Sh-h." Emma nodded toward the bedroom in which Barbara still slept. "She'll hear you."

Joe lowered his voice. "I didn't mean to talk so loud. It looks to me, if we don't get Bobby out of here, as though the Army will be at war with itself."

"Yes, dear," Emma smiled abstractedly and Joe saw that her mind was elsewhere. He leaned back in his chair, looking idly at his empty plate. Then he rose to get his coat.

"Are you going out?" Emma asked.

"Yes. I'm getting the wagon back into shape."

Emma asked casually, "Joe, do you know anything about this young man, Hugo Gearey?"

Joe shrugged. "I've seen him around."

"But you don't know where he came from?"

He was a little surprised. "Why should I?"

"Can you find out?"

"Now look, I can't just walk up to Gearey and ask him where he comes from and what he did there."

"You might," she pointed out, "ask Sergeant Dugan or Sergeant Dunbar."

He looked closely at her. "Why do you want to know about Gearey, Emma?"

She avoided his eyes. "Just a woman's curiosity. Will you find out?"

He said reluctantly, "I'll ask Dugan or Dunbar."

Joe left, and Emma sat alone at the table. After such a long time on the Trail, the past three days at Laramie had been unbelievable luxury. Their quarters were warm and snug, with adequate housekeeping facilities. The roof was wood instead of canvas. Best of all, there had been three days of blessed relief from worry and tension. For the first time since leaving Independence Emma slept restfully because she was positive that they would have to respond to no alarm in the middle of the night. Because they did not have to rise with the sun and travel all day, there was leisure for sewing, washing, and preparing meals as Emma thought they should be prepared. However, though Laramie provided surcease from the rigors of the Trail, it brought its own problems.

Emma did not agree with Joe's notion that there was no reason to worry about Barbara. Most of the young men who overwhelmed her with attention were more amusing than otherwise. Except that some of them were a little older than the swains who had so awkwardly wooed Barbara in Missouri, they did not differ greatly from the Tenney's Crossing youths. They blushed easily, sometimes stumbled over their own feet, and while they devoted themselves to Barbara and wanted to admire, they were content to do so from a distance. Barbara could wither them with a frown, or send them into ecstasy with a smile. Emma poured a second cup of coffee, a blissful extravagance, and thought about Private Hugo Gearey.

Emma thought he was about twenty-six, not old, but still older than most of the other privates. There was about him a fine courtliness and courtesy which within itself spoke of background and good breeding; he knew exactly what to say and exactly when and how to say it. His was a charm that attracted men and captivated women. Emma had never before met such a person, and she knew that all of Gearey's charm and courtliness had been fully noticed by Barbara.

But though Emma was old enough, and wise enough, to base her final appraisal of anyone at all on other than outward characteristics, she could not suppress an uncomfortable feeling that Gearey's eyes were cold and that they betrayed an inner weakness. Most of all, with no war on, she wondered what a person of his obvious breeding and background was doing, as a private, in a fort like Laramie. She conceded that he might be out for a bit of adventure, but most of the youngsters who were at Laramie for that reason alone were from three to seven years younger than Gearey. Though there were a few older privates who kept their own counsel and doubtless had their own reasons for being where they were, most of the enlistees who were making the Army a career were non-commissioned officers by the time they were Gearey's age.

The bedroom door opened and Barbara appeared, sleep-disheveled but lovely.

"Good morning, Mother."

"Good morning, dear. Did you sleep well?"

"Oh!" Barbara stretched her young arms for the sheer pleasure of doing so. "I had a heavenly rest!"

"I'll get your breakfast."

"I'll get it, Mother."

Barbara washed, put two slices of bacon in a skillet and knelt before the fire place. She broke an egg over the sputtering bacon, brought it to the table and buttered herself a piece of bread. Emma smiled at her daughter.

"Have you reflected upon your ardent suitors' fist-fight of last night?"

Barbara said scornfully, "Yes, and it was so silly! I couldn't stop them, and I was just mortified when they insisted on fighting that way!" Her face clouded. "Do you think they'll keep them in the guardhouse very long, Mother?"

"I suppose they'll be out before they're both old men."

Barbara grinned, and said happily, "It's been such fun!"

"It would be," Emma admitted dryly, "with fifty or more unattached young men ready to grovel at your feet every time you make calf's eyes at them."

She laughed, "Oh Mother, none of them are serious—it's really all fun!"

"I don't know about that. How many proposals have you had?"

"Only seven so far. Johnny Parr, Michael Dilling, and Pete Robbins want to come to Oregon just as soon as their enlistments are up. Albert Johnson asked me to go to Baltimore with him, after we're married of course! His father has a store there, and I can be a clerk in it. Rodney Burr, he's from Maine and he talks so strangely, has wonderful plans for starting a shipyard in San Francisco. Robert Smith and Dan Jankoski want to get married right here."

"What did you tell them?"

"Mother, what *would* I tell them? I don't want to marry any of them!"

"I hope you didn't hurt their feelings."

"I refused as nicely as I could."

Emma looked down at the table, gratified. Barbara was no longer the half-child half-woman who had left Missouri. The Oregon Trail had given her a new maturity and poise. Barbara finished her meal and folded her hands thoughtfully under her chin. She stared across the table and for a moment she did not speak. Then,

"Mother, there's a dance tonight in the mess hall. May I go?"

"Do you mean you can single out just one escort?"

"Hugo asked me," she said dreamily. "He—he's so different. I—I just can't explain it. He simply makes the others seem like children. His home is in New York City, and it will take me at least a year to tell you all the things he's told me about it."

Emma murmured, "Hugo must talk fast."

"He does, Mother!" she said eagerly, missing entirely the double meaning in Emma's remark. "He's the most interesting young man I've ever met!"

Because she knew she dared say nothing else, Emma said, "Yes, dear, you may go."

"Thank you, Mother."

Though Emma would not have left her youngest children alone on the prairie, she felt safe to leave them in Tad's care at the fort. That night, to the music of a very good five piece band, she danced in Joe's arms. She waited for him to tell her anything he might have found out concerning Hugo Gearey, and when he said nothing she knew that he had forgotten to ask. In turn Emma danced with Sergeants Dugan, Dunbar, and a variety of others. She watched the young men trying desperately to dance with Barbara.

Emma noted that she was with Hugo Gearey for two dances out of three. She did, then, want to dance with him. Soldiers watched the pair, jealous and suspicious. Emma danced again with Joe, and she knew that he was very tired. She smiled at him, clasped his hand a little more tightly and glanced again at Barbara.

"We can go," she whispered. "The dance is finished in another fifteen minutes anyhow."

"Wouldn't you like to see it out?"

"No, darling."

Back in their quarters, Joe stifled a yawn and washed up. Emma sat at the table, glancing alternately at the flickering oil lamp and at her husband.

"I'm really not tired. I'll wait for Barbara."

She wilted into Emma's arms and muffled her heartbroken sobs. Emma resisted an impulse to go to the window and look out. She knew the dance was over, but Barbara had not appeared. Then, a half hour later, she heard them at the door. Emma waited, not sure as to whether or not she was doing right. She tried not to listen to their low-pitched voices. But there could be no mistaking the sharp sound of someone's face being slapped.

The door opened and Barbara rushed in. Her cheeks were red, her eyes were furious. She saw her mother and stopped uncertainly, closing the door behind her.

"Mother!"

She wilted into Emma's arms and muffled her heartbroken sobs. Emma held her strongly and caressed her tenderly. Barbara drew back and plastered a handkerchief to her face.

"Oh, Mother," she sobbed. "I thought he was so wonderful! He's horrible, Mother, *horrible!* The things he said! And then he tried to—to—" There was a fresh burst of sobbing.

"Thank God you found out," Emma said quietly. "I've been afraid of that young man from the beginning. But I knew you'd have to discover it for yourself."

"But he was so charming, Mother, so—so *charming!*"

"Exactly," said Emma, dryly.

A spasm of fear crossed Barbara's face. "Mother," she whispered, "don't tell Daddy."

"Don't you want him to know, dear?"

"No! I'd be so ashamed. I should have known better. I acted like such a *fool,* Mother!"

Emma smiled softly. "You're not exactly very old or experienced, Bobby."

"Oh, I know, but—I'm so ashamed, Mother. *Please* don't tell Daddy."

Emma nodded gently. "Whatever you say, Bobby. We'll keep it a secret, then."

Barbara thanked her with a passionate hug. Then she permitted Emma to wash her face and put her to bed.

For a little while Emma sat on the edge of her daughter's bed, holding the moist and weary hand and stroking it, until finally the girl's nervous breathing steadied and softened, and Bobby was asleep. Sadness that was partly happiness filled Emma's heart. Bobby had been hurt, but pain could be a teacher, too. And she had not been hurt so much as she might have been, had she not discovered the true nature of Hugo Gearey. Through this shock and this pain, their lovely Barbara would grow.

Joe was thoughtful. For three days he had watched, secretly but vastly amused, while every unattached young man in Fort Laramie vied for Barbara's company. He knew that Barbara was lovely, but he knew also that no young girl could have come to Laramie, in the dead of winter, without creating something of a ripple. The isolated young men there, like isolated young men the world over, were girl-hungry, and any girl who came among them would have been a queen. But few, Joe told himself smugly, would have had the complete reign that was Barbara's.

He had seen her respond with laughing gaiety and delight. But this morning, when three soldiers called for her, she was not her usual radiant self. There had been more than a trace of soberness in Barbara's manner. Joe wondered why it was there and if he should do anything about it, but decided that Emma would have told him if it was anything of importance. He did remember that he had forgotten to ask about Hugo Gearey, and was sorry he had forgotten. He must not forget again; Emma wanted to know.

Joe had taken advantage of their time at Laramie to repair the wagon and to rest and feed the mules. Though they had by no means become fat they were in good shape and they compared very favorably to any mule team in the stables. The mules were ready to go, and the Towers had better go on. There were civilian employees at Laramie, but the soldiers did the woodcutting, carpentry, stock tending, and all the work Joe liked. Though they could winter at Laramie if they wanted to, and occupy the quarters they had now at least until the lieutenant whose rooms they were using returned, it would be an idle winter and they would have to buy what they needed. There was little possibility of working for wages, or even of paying with labor for what they needed.

The younger children were playing in the snow and grizzled old Sergeant Dunbar was romping with them. Dunbar had spent his life in the army. It was his first love and there'd never been time for any other. But Dunbar was almost through. A veteran of many years' service, he was fast becoming too old for active duty and now he wore a haunted look. The army could no longer use him and there were no wife and children to care about him. Facing a cheerless future, for the time being Dunbar was forgetting it by fall in love with Joe's four youngsters. He was with them every second he could spare, and he forever invented games for them to play. Joe stepped outside. Dunbar arose from the snow fort he was building for the babies.

"Good morning, Mr. Tower."

"Good morning, Sergeant. Have you seen my daughter?"

Dunbar grinned. "She and about a platoon of lovesick soldiers have gone somewhere. They cluster around her like flies around a honey jar. I don't blame them. If I were thirty years younger, I'd be with her too. But there's safety in numbers. You needn't worry about her."

"I'm not worried. How about my freckle-faced son?"

"He's been spending his time at the stables, listening to tales of Indian fights. Hope he doesn't believe all of them."

There was a vast tenderness and a mighty longing in Dunbar's eyes as he watched the playing children. He had lived his life as he saw fit and, given the same circumstances, probably he'd live it over again the same way. Joe looked keenly at him. Dunbar's army service had hardened him without making him callous. But only now, when it was too late, did Dunbar think about all he might have done and hadn't. He looked upon the children with the almost desperate longing of an older man who wished they belonged to him.

Suddenly remembering, Joe asked, "Sergeant, can you tell me anything about this Hugo Gearey?"

Dunbar looked frankly at him. "Why?"

Joe, vastly talented when it came to minding his own affairs, squirmed. But he felt that he should not say that Emma had asked him to find out.

"I just wanted to know."

Dunbar's eyes were grave. "Has Gearey been sparking your daughter?"

"As far as I know, they all have."

"Is there—?" Dunbar waved his hands.

Joe said, "No. There isn't."

Dunbar nibbled his lower lip. "Gearey isn't the best soldier nor the worst. He hasn't been in a fight yet so I can't tell you how he'd act there."

"Where does he come from?"

"New York's his home and," Dunbar became impulsive, "Mr. Tower, I'm going to tell you because I believe you know how to respect a confidence. Gearey comes from a wealthy home. He's here now because he got in trouble."

"What sort?"

"Girl trouble."

"Oh."

He looked gravely at the snow, and thought about Emma's powers of discernment. To Joe, Gearey had been just another soldier. Emma had suspected him, and she was right. Joe must be sure to tell her what he had found out so Emma, in her own way, could tell Barbara. Dunbar broke the silence.

"Are you staying with us?"

"No. I reckon we'll winter at Snedeker's."

"The noises you'll hear at Laramie will be hearts breaking," Dunbar assured him. "Going on to Oregon when the weather breaks?"

"That's right."

"I've a notion to do that myself. My time is up in June. You know, I used to dream of going back to Boston and spend my time smoking a pipe and wearing slippers when I got a pension. Now I know I'd be lost in Boston."

"Why don't you come to Oregon? I hear it's a big country."

"Sure," Dunbar smiled. "I'll stake a claim near you and spend all my time playing with these kids."

"The kids wouldn't mind."

"Neither would I," Dunbar said earnestly. "Wish I could see my way clear. When are you leaving?"

"Tomorrow morning, I reckon."

"You won't have any trouble. A patrol went down yesterday and broke a track. I'd ride with you myself if I wasn't expecting a load of freight."

"Then you do get freight in winter?"

"Oh sure. But it's three times as hard to get it here in winter as it is in summer. Three times as expensive, too. The summer rate per pound between here and Independence is a little short of ten cents. The winter rate is almost thirty-two cents."

"Whew! And I need supplies!"

"Laramie's the place to stock up," Dunbar assured him. "You'll buy anything here at just what it would cost you in Independence plus freight, and you'll get summer freight rates on what's here now. That's a lot better than it was. I've seen the time when coffee and sugar were $2 a pound at Laramie, and flour sold for $40 a hundred. It still does at some of the trading posts. The mountain men who run them know how to get an emigrant's last nickel. That's why it's better to stock up here."

"Suppose an emigrant without any money comes through?"

"Plenty of them don't have any, or at least they say they don't. They get enough to see them through. One purpose of this fort is to help emigrants, and letting them starve isn't helping them."

"You run away now, Daddy," little Emma directed. "We must get our fort built."

"Orders from a superior officer," Dunbar grinned. "I'd better report for duty."

Unostentatiously, Joe re-entered their quarters. He frowned worriedly as Emma looked up from behind her mending.

He said, "I found out about this Gearey. He seems to be no good."

Her eyes revealed nothing. "Thank you, Joe."

"We'd best keep Bobby away from him, don't you think?"

She smiled briefly. "There isn't any need to worry."

Joe looked at her in consternation. Then he said uncertainly, "I thought I'd better tell you before I go down to the stables. I'll be back in an hour or so."

"All right, dear." She continued sewing placidly.

Joe left with an uncomfortable feeling that, somehow, he'd been a little silly. He shook a puzzled head. Before she'd known anything about him, Emma had worried about Gearey. Now that she knew her suspicions were justified, she didn't seem to worry at all. Joe decided again that he never would understand women. But he comforted himself with the assurance that Emma would handle the situation in her own sensible way.

Joe walked on to the stables. He'd shod both mules again, but it was easier here. Laramie had a complete blacksmith shop as well as a full complement of men who knew all about handling fractious mules, horses and oxen. Though she'd put up her usual fight when it came her turn to be shod, the mare mule hadn't had a chance. Both mules had new calks on their shoes, and that would give them better footing in snow.

At the far end of the stockade, surrounded by the usual crowd, Barbara was inspecting the fort. She, Joe thought, had had a wonderful time. Emma had been happy too. Sergeant Driscoll's Latin wife, who had known the gaiety of Mexico City and the excitement of Santa Fe, was withering in this lonely place and she had seized eagerly the opportunity for relief that Emma's presence afforded. A pretty, vivacious woman, Ynez Driscoll spoke glowingly of the colorful places she had known and listened attentively when Emma told of Missouri. Emma's and Ynez Driscoll's backgrounds were worlds apart, and for that very reason each found the other's tales fascinating.

Joe reached the stables. One of the stable detail, a red-haired private whose name Joe did not remember, grinned at him.

"Good morning, Mr. Tower."

"Good morning, son. Can I borrow a currycomb and brush?"

"You don't need any," the redhead assured him. "We've already groomed your mules."

"Well—thanks."

"Look them over," the redhead invited.

The mules turned friendly heads and blew through their noses when Joe approached the stalls in which they were tied. The stable detail had not only groomed them, but had done so with all the painstaking care they'd have lavished on the colonel's horse if they were readying for a parade. Every hair was in place and the mules' coats shone. The red-haired private, who had followed Joe, lingered a little way behind him and tried to be very casual.

"Are they all right?"

"They're fine. I'd say they're absolutely perfect. And I'm certainly obliged to you."

"It's nothing—nothing at all.—Uh—May I ask you a question?"

"Sure."

"Are you going to winter at Laramie?"

"I'm afraid not. We're going down to Snedeker's."

A concerted moan of despair arose from the stable detail, and Joe was surrounded by young soldiers who presented what they hoped was forceful argument. Laramie was bigger, better, and more comfortable, than Snedeker's. It had a lot more to offer; Snedeker's was just a trading post with the main store fortified in case Indians attacked. For that matter, suppose they did attack? Could Joe, Jim Snedeker, and whoever else might happen to be around Snedeker's post, defend Joe's family? Snedeker's was lonely, too. Joe should consider everything very carefully, then do the sensible thing and winter at Laramie. Of course not, they answered indignantly when Joe asked if Barbara had anything to do with their fervent desire to see the Towers remain where they were. They were merely thinking of what would be best all around.

Joe left the saddened detail and walked to the sutler's store.

Money was hard to come by, and even with what Jake Favors had paid him he hadn't any too much. But money was not more precious than anything else, and just ahead was a season that, even in their leanest years, the Towers observed faithfully. Joe prowled among the counters. He bought an exquisite shawl that probably had come to Laramie from Santa Fe and to Santa Fe from Mexico. Carefull, making sure that he was not observed, he tucked the wrapped shawl into a small box that fitted into his tool box. After that he got Emma, and together they returned to the store.

They walked through the store while she chose Christmas presents for the children. There was a bracelet of hammered silver set with turquoise, another product of Mexico, and Emma bought it for Barbara. Thinking of Tad, Joe looked wistfully at the rifles. But rifles were expensive, they dared not spend that much, and Joe nodded approval when Emma selected a hatchet. There was a doll for little Emma, small bows with blunt arrows for Joe and Alfred, and a wooden horse, probably carved by some soldier and brightly painted, for Carlyle. They put the gifts in Emma's trunk, and then returned to the store for supplies.

The next morning, mournfully attended by every soldier in Laramie who could possibly break away from whatever he was doing at the moment, Joe drove his mules out the stockade's west gate and on down the Oregon Trail. Some of the soldiers trooped after them and Barbara walked with her swains. Regretfully, the escort turned back after Barbara had climbed into the wagon.

For two hours, following the track broken by the cavalry patrol, they traveled in comparative silence. After lonely, hard weeks on the Trail, they had sojourned for a brief time in the comparative gaiety and certain security of Laramie. Now they were back on the Trail, with nobody knowing what really lay ahead, and the thought was a sobering one.

Barbara did not look back. Her experience with Hugo Gearey had left its mark on her. For all his charm he had been disrespectful and—and nasty and—well, just horrible. Color rose into her face at the thought of his arm pulling her roughly against him, of his lips pressing, demanding—Oh, how she hated him now! Yes, hated him, *hated* him!

Yet, as the wagon jogged along, the face that intruded again and again between Bobby and the scenery was none other than the face of Hugo Gearey.

Watching her daughter, Emma noticed that something had changed. Barbara's eagerness for what was to come seemed somehow dimmed by the events at Laramie. She sat quietly, submissively, lost in thought. What was going on inside that lovely young head? Emma sighed. No one could guess, and least of all, perhaps, Barbara herself.

There was about a foot of snow. But though the weather had not been bitterly cold, it had lingered below the freezing point. There had been no thaw, and therefore there was no crust to break. The snow was still soft, and the wagon left deep ruts in its wake. The mules pulled steadily, and Joe swung them from side to side so that they might take turns walking in the already-broken trail left by the cavalry patrol. A pair of crows winged across the Trail, alighted in a solitary pine, and cawed raucously. About to answer them, Joe was halted by Tad's excited,

"Pa, look!"

To one side was a small cabin built at the base of a knoll, and as Joe turned a buffalo came from behind the knoll to stare curiously at the wagon. Another followed, and another. Then the rest of the herd came in sight and twenty-two buffaloes stood in the snow. Tad gulped, and looked longingly at the rifle, but they'd bought beef at Laramie and had all they needed. To shoot a buffalo now would be only for the sake of shooting something, and a waste of powder, shot and meat. Joe did not believe in that. The buffalo herd watched the wagon for a moment, then fell to pawing snow so that they might uncover the grass beneath.

Joe grinned, and he heard Barbara chuckle. Emma turned in the seat for a better look as they drove past. Sighting the buffalo brought back things that had been, and once again put them in tune with a roving life. The children began to giggle and chatter as they started a game. Tad leaned against the seat, staring intently at what lay ahead and on both sides, but saying nothing.

Rested, and on not too difficult a trail despite the snow, the mules set a brisk pace. Joe let them have their way, watching them only casually. Mules had what some people—who knew a little about them but seldom drove them—called a sense of humor. Others, better acquainted with mules, knew that they were merely full of deviltry. They did delight in confounding their drivers but they liked to have the advantage of any situation. It was a lot easier to snarl a harness when they were hitched to a plow than it was with a wagon tongue between them, and they knew it. Only occasionally, when the driver became too lax, did they try any tricks when they were pulling a loaded wagon.

Mike, who had padded steadily behind or at one side of the wagon, bounced ahead suddenly. He bristled, and a deep snarl rumbled in his chest. Keeping in the tracks of the cavalry patrol, he ran about fifty feet down the trail and halted. Joe stopped the wagon.

"Call your dog," he told Tad.

"Gee! What's comin'?"

"I don't know. Call your dog."

Tad whistled. Reluctantly, stopping every few paces to look over his shoulder, Mike came back to the wagon. Joe handed Tad a piece of rope.

"Better tie him."

"Aw, Pa. Suppose—"

"Tie him."

Tad jumped into the snow and tied the rope around Mike's neck. Still bristling, tightening the rope, Mike strained down the Trail. Joe watched closely. Mike was an enthusiastic hunter as long as he hunted nothing larger than jack rabbits. He was not afraid of bigger game but he was smart enough to know that some things were too big for him, and therefore he paid little attention to them. Obviously he now scented either something that he wanted to hunt or something that offered prospects for a rousing battle, and presently the mules scented it too. They lifted their heads, cocked their ears forward, and watched ahead. Joe glanced at the rifle, and made sure of the exact location of his powder horn and bullet pouch.

Presently three Indians mounted on small brown horses came around the knoll that had hidden them and advanced toward the wagon. Two nondescript dogs trailed them. Joe took the reins in his left hand, leaving his right free should whatever happen next demand action. He looked keenly at the approaching riders.

They were wild, proud, startling. They wore full-length buckskin trousers, moccasins, and buffalo-skin coats. Fur hats were pulled over their black hair. They sat their little horses with an easy, insolent grace that few white men ever achieve. Their one concession to white men's ways was the long rifle that each carried over his saddle bow.

Looking to neither side, betraying by not so much as the flicker of an eyelid the fact that they saw the wagon and its occupants, they swerved around and continued down the trail. Even Mike's savage lunge at their dogs, a lunge that was halted only because Tad reefed full strength on the rope, did not disturb for one second the dogs, horses or riders. Without a single backward glance they disappeared around another knoll, and Joe halted the wagon to let Tad get in.

"Gee!" Tad gasped. "Was that a war party?"

"Must have been," Joe asserted.

But he knew it was not. Though he was unfamiliar with western Indians, Joe had heard that war parties bedecked their cheeks with war paint and wore scalp locks. That might and might not be true. A man heard a lot of things and he was silly as an ox if he believed all of them. However, a war party would not have ridden so nonchalantly up the Trail where they were so easily seen. Probably they were just three Indians going to Laramie, but Tad wanted desperately to find great adventure on this journey and it would do no harm to let him think that he had at least brushed elbows with it.

"You're smart, Pa!" Tad breathed.

"Why do you say that?"

"Suppose old Mike had been loose, and pitched into those dogs like he wanted to? First thing, wham! They'd 've tried to help their dogs and we'd 've had a nice fight on our hands!"

"Sure thing," Joe agreed.

He smiled to himself because of the disappointed down pitch in Tad's voice. The youngster ate, slept, and traveled with a mighty dream of a fight with Indians. He could have his dream, but not, if Joe could possibly help it, the fight. He wanted to reach Oregon, and anything that interfered with that goal was, at the very least, an unpleasant annoyance. Anything that put his family in danger, if there was a way to keep them out, would be an unforgivable error.

They stopped for lunch, went on, and there were two hours of daylight remaining when Joe smelled wood smoke. Five minutes later, he saw Snedeker's.

The post was at one side of the Trail, in a group of pines, and scattered pines grew on snow-clad hills that rolled away from the post. The main building, a solid structure of heavy logs, was the center of a group of buildings which probably served as warehouses, stables, and quarters. About two hundred yards away, a little bunch of horses that were grazing in the snow raised their heads to watch the mules come in. They were Indian ponies, thin and gaunt. An old mule grazed all alone, and in a pole corral at one side were three nice-looking saddle horses. Probably they were personal mounts for whoever lived at Snedeker's.

Joe swung his team off the Trail and up to the post. Silence lay all around. Joe stopped, and hoped his grin concealed the nervousness he felt when he turned to Emma. Laramie was a town complete within itself; compared to Snedeker's it was almost a city. Joe swallowed hard, already doubting the wisdom of wintering here when they might have stayed at Laramie. He comforted himself with the thought that they could still go back. He gave the reins to Emma and jumped from the wagon.

"I'll go find out about things."

The post, he saw, had small windows and all of them were high off the ground. The door was massive, hand-hewn timber that was liberally scratched and gouged, and Joe frowned as he looked at it. A craftsman himself, he decided that the door had been made by a poor or sloppy worker. Then he saw that the battered door had never been made that way; the cuts and gouges had been put there by ax blades and bullets. No bullet had gone all the way through, but certainly Snedeker's had been under attack. Joe lifted the latch and walked into the gloomy interior.

The building was long and low, with a wooden floor built well off the ground. Only with difficulty could anyone from outside reach the small windows, but due to the raised floors, anyone on the inside could stand at them and shoot out. There were counters and shelves, but they were not heavily loaded. Over a huge stone fireplace in which chunks of wood crackled was a rack with six long rifles in it, and at one side was a pile of cured buffalo robes. Unlighted lanterns hung from the ceiling beams, and here and there smoke-blackened candles clung by their own melted wax to saucers.

"Can I help you, sir?"

Joe saw him then, a lean young man with straight black hair. Supple as a bull whip, he had risen with easy grace from a chair near the fireplace. He wore a cloth shirt, trousers, and leather shoes. His face was thin, with high cheek bones, and the brown eyes that were fixed steadily on Joe were humor-lighted. Joe fidgeted. This young man, and he could not be more than twenty, reminded him almost uncomfortably of Percy Pearl.

Joe said, "I'm looking for Jim Snedeker. My name's Joe Tower."

"I'll call him, Mr. Tow—"

Before he could finish, an apparition came through an open door toward the rear of the building. Tall, it was thin to the point of gauntness. A fur hat sat on its head, and uncut gray and black hair straggled from beneath the hat. It was dressed in an ornate fringed buckskin shirt and buckskin trousers. Its feet were bare. Above a gray stubble that covered its leathery cheeks were eyes so pale and blue that they seemed to have no expression at all, but to be oddly like drifting blue smoke. Its expression was a snarl, and its voice matched the expression.

"Want to see me, eh? Go ahead an' look."

"I'm looking for Jim Snedeker."

"Who you think I am? Pres'dent of the Unitey States?"

Joe controlled his rising anger and prepared to state his mission. But before he could speak, Snedeker spoke again.

"You an Oregon emmy-grant?"

"That's right."

"Where's your booie knives?"

"What?"

"Your booie knives, man! Last emmy-grant I saw off the Trail had six of 'em an' a revolver stuck in his belt. Where's yours?"

"I haven't any."

"You're a heck of a emmy-grant." Snedeker addressed the youth, "Ain't he a heck of a emmy-grant, Ellis?"

The youth winked at Joe. Snedeker saw him do it and glared.

"Don't you go doin' that behint my back! Wuthless pup! I see you do it!" He turned to Joe. "This Ellis Garner, he sets around here all the time 'stead of movin' his rear a mite! Kids nowadays ain't wuth the powder to blow 'em up! Ain't that so, Ellis?"

"Jim, this man—"

"Shut up!" Snedeker whirled on Joe. "What do you want of me?"

"Did you know a man named Seeley?"

"Yeh. I knew him. Shif'less old coot. What about him?"

"He said you'd give me a job."

"I might." Snedeker stroked his stubble. "I might at that. You drink?"

"No."

"Why the blazes don't you? Ever'body else does."

"None of your blasted business!" Joe exploded.

"Why you—!" Snedeker sputtered like a boiling tea kettle. "Ain't no man talks thataway to me!" He strode to the rifle rack, seized a rifle, and aimed it at Joe. "Take that back!"

"Put that popgun down before I take it away from you and spank you with it!" Joe roared. "You crazy old goat! I wouldn't work for you if you were the last man on this Trail!"

"You got just fifteen seconds," Snedeker warned.

"Why you—!"

Joe was angry as he had been only once or twice in his life. In Missouri, the code was hospitality. Here, where there was so much space and so few people, that code should have been much more powerful. Snedeker did not have to give him a job, but by all the rules of humanity he should have offered food and shelter.

"I won't tell you again!" Snedeker breathed.

Joe grasped the rifle's muzzle, twisted it aside, and brought his right hand back to deliver a smashing blow to the other's chin. Suddenly he found the rifle in his hands. Snedeker reeled away from him, roaring with laughter. Joe stood dumfounded, not knowing what to think. When the old mountain man straightened, his eyes were no longer the color of smoke. They were friendly.

"Lordy, lordy!" he chortled. "You win!"

"Win what?"

"The job you asked for, man! Sort of knowed when you spoke of Shoshone Seeley that you was all right; Shoshone wouldn't ask nobody to stop here 'thout they was. But they's a lot of half-witted Injuns 'round here, an' some even more half-witted emmy-grants will be stoppin'. They'll bluff you out of your eye teeth if you let 'em, an' I can't have nobody who lets themselfs be bluffed. Will say, though, that you might show a mite more sense. Thutty-five a month for you'n your team, quarters, and found for yourself. All right?"

"It's all right with me."

"Good," Snedeker pronounced, "on account that's all you'd get anyhow. Your folks with you?"

"They're in the wagon."

"Bring 'em in, man! Bring 'em in! Anybody with the sense of a jack rabbit wouldn't leave his folks set in the wagon on a day like this!"

Joe brought his family in and introduced them to Snedeker and Ellis Garner. The children went to the fireplace, and stood gratefully in its warmth. Barbara smoothed her tumbled hair with her hand. Snedeker nudged Joe and he looked at Ellis Garner. A smile of purest joy glowed on the young man's face.

"He's a woman chaser," Snedeker said in a whisper that carried clear across the room. "Chased one here all the way from Maryland. But, lordy, lordy! She sure didn't have the shine of *that* filly!"

CHAPTER ELEVEN

Winter

IN THE time he'd spent at Snedeker's, Joe had learned a great deal.

Snedeker was a Mountain Man, one of that rare breed who had waded every stream in the west in their search for beaver. They fought every tribe of Indians that showed fight, went without hesitation where they wished to go, and spent incredibly long and dangerous months with only their rifles and their resourcefulness as protection. Then they took their furs to some wild fort, or some wilderness rendezvous, and in a few days spent all the money they had earned in a whole season of perilous living.

The heyday of the Mountain Men spanned only a brief sixteen years when no gentleman was really dressed unless he wore a beaver hat. Silk replaced beaver, and broke the fur market. But though their livelihood was gone, the Mountain Men weren't. Some returned to the east. Some guided wagon trains across country that they knew as well as the emigrants knew their own back yards. Some simply disappeared, gone in search of what they considered wild and free country. And some, like Snedeker, merely transferred their way of living to other pursuits and lived much as they always had.

At their first meeting, Snedeker had enraged Joe. Now Joe understood him, and with understanding had come both liking and respect. Throughout his adult life Snedeker had bowed to no will except his own, and he saw no reason for changing his ways. But, though his outward air was that of a grizzly bear with a sore paw, inwardly he was soft as a marshmallow. A shrewd bargainer, he seemed to have an instinctive knowledge of how much money emigrants carried and how much they were willing to spend. But no penniless emigrant had ever been turned away, though Snedeker would not outfit them clear to Oregon. Whether they were east- or westbound, he gave them a couple of days' supplies and sent them to Laramie where, as Snedeker knew, they became the government's responsibility.

Joe had lost his misgivings about wintering at the post. No war party could take Laramie, but neither could any take Snedeker's. They'd already tried it and succeeded only in running off a few horses. Taking their trail, Snedeker had brought back the stock he'd lost and a number of the Indian ponies as well. Besides, according to Snedeker, there was small danger of an Indian attack in winter. The tribes that came to Laramie wintered on northern hunting grounds, and their ponies had to exist as best they could. Since no western Indian would think of going into battle without a mount, they made war in the spring after there was sufficient grass to fatten and strengthen their horses. The three the Towers had met must have been strays, or possibly they had to go to Laramie for something they needed.

On a wind-swept hill about a half mile from the post, Joe sank his ax cleanly into a pine. Expertly he measured his next strike, and when the ax sank in, a large chip of wood broke out. Wasting not one blow of his ax or a half ounce of strength, Joe felled the tree cleanly and rested a moment. He glanced over to where Ellis Garner had another pine two-thirds felled. Joe nodded approvingly. There were tricks to handling an ax. When he and Ellis had started felling trees, which Snedeker needed to enlarge his post, Ellis had had a lot to learn. But under Joe's expert guidance he was learning fast, and, given a year or two of experience, he would be a good ax man himself.

Ellis stopped chopping and grinned across the space that separated them. "You must pick the softest trees."

"That's an ax you have in your hand," Joe gibed. "Not a feather. Don't use it like one."

"Yes, teacher."

Joe grinned and went back to work. He had grown to like this slim and soft-spoken youngster, but at the same time he worried about him. Where Ellis came from Joe didn't know and he hadn't asked; one didn't inquire too deeply into anyone else's past life. Probably he was from somewhere in the east and he had been to school; that showed in his manner and his choice of words. But there was within him an undercurrent of irritability, and at times he was moody and fretful. Somewhere behind him there seemed to be a memory that hurt. Increasingly, Joe compared him to the suave and polished Percy Pearl, who never farmed, never worked for wages, but who always had everything he needed. Not that there was anything suave or polished about Ellis—on the contrary, he was impulsive, often unpredictable. But he had Percy's quickness and dry humor and, like Percy, he gave you the feeling he might go after anything he wanted, and get it, without being too critical of ways and means. Percy was an outlaw and Ellis might become one. But that was his business unless Ellis's affairs should become too closely entwined with the Tower's.

Joe frowned as he worked. Ellis had taken more than a casual interest in Barbara, which was not unusual because Joe had yet to meet the young man who was not attracted to his daughter. They were together much of the time, and they took long walks. Joe thought of Hugo Gearey, who was at Laramie because of girl trouble in New York. Snedeker had said that Ellis had followed a girl all the way from Maryland, and what sort of trouble was he in? Why was he here at an isolated trading post?

Joe trimmed the branches from his tree, leaving a smooth trunk. He felled and trimmed another pine and looked toward the tethered mules. They were still in harness, but their bridles were slipped and Joe had tied them out of the bitterest wind. He glanced down the slanting, ice-sheathed furrow that led to the post. The day after their arrival, new snow had added six inches to that already on the ground and there had been light falls since. Joe had driven the mules through it to break a track, and had dragged one log down the broken track. Succeeding loads had widened and packed it, so that now the mules were able to pull as many logs as could be hitched on.

The weather had turned cold enough so that Joe's nostrils pinched when he stood still, and a little rime of frost formed about the muzzles of the tethered mules. That wouldn't hurt them as long as they didn't have to stand on a short tether for any great length of time, and if they did not stand at all when they sweated. There was little danger of that in such weather; the team had only to walk to the place where they were cutting pines and the logs were not hard to pull down the icy slide. Joe sank his ax into the felled pine's stump and walked over to Ellis.

"How are you doing?"

"All right."

Joe stood, feeling the goodness he usually felt after a day of hard and productive labor. At the same time he felt a swelling relief and a rising little happiness. Tomorrow was a very special day.

Joe said, "Don't seem like tonight is Christmas Eve, does it?"

Ellis murmured absently, "No, it doesn't."

"Let's go in."

"Suits me."

Joe bridled the mules. He drove them to the felled trees and laid his long chain across the slide. His ax swinging from his hand, Ellis joined him. They used peavies to roll logs into a compact pile and bound the chain around them. Knowing that their work would be done as soon as they had dragged these last logs down to Snedeker's building site, the mules needed no urging or even driving. Joe looped the reins over the mules' harness and walked companionably beside Ellis. Glad that the day's work was over, the younger man slashed restlessly at the icy slide with his ax.

Joe said caustically, "Tenderfoot!"

"What's wrong now, teacher?"

"Axes are for cutting wood, not ice. I'll bet you nicked it."

Ellis shrugged. "Live and learn. I won't do it again."

He seemed irritable, depressed, and Joe stole a sidewise glance at him. "A penny for your thoughts."

"You'd be cheated," Ellis grinned sheepishly.

"Say, what are you so gosh darn low about?"

"I'm not low. Are you coming over tonight?"

"The kids will be over. I have work to do."

"Don't you ever think of anything else?"

"Can't. When you're an old man like me, with a bunch of youngsters looking to you, you won't be able to either."

For a moment they walked in silence while Ellis's introspective mood enfolded him like an invisible cloak. He said suddenly,

"Joe, what do you think of women?"

For a moment, because he was puzzled, Joe did not answer. It was more than a casual question, and behind it lay something that Joe failed to understand. When he did answer, he said very gently,

"I know about only one woman, son. And I think the world of her."

"Do you believe in love?"

Joe said firmly, "I most certainly do."

"Do—do you think it's right—? Oh, darn it! I'm all at sea!" he steadied. "Joe, I'm giving it to you straight. I'm going to marry Barbara if I can! Do you have any objections?"

Shocked surprise rippled through Joe and his heart turned cold. He felt numb. He had always known that Barbara would marry some day, but that day remained in the distant future and there was no need to worry about it now. Joe thought of the young man who walked beside him, and of how very little he knew about him. Again he thought of Snedeker's reference to Ellis as a woman chaser and he had a great urge to ask Ellis to tell him so that his own doubts might be cleared. But because he did not know how to ask, Joe said only,

"Have you asked Barbara?"

"Yes."

"What did she say?"

"She didn't say no."

Joe pondered, trying to straighten this in his mind. He knew a little more about Ellis than he had known a moment ago. Wherever he had come from, and whatever he might have done, he had not tried to evade this issue. He had given it to Joe straight, as a man should, and that was a large point in his favor.

Ellis repeated, "I asked if you had any objections."

Joe said quietly, "I'm her father, Ellis, not her master. I'm not going to choose a husband for her."

"Thanks, Joe."

There was another silence, and Ellis said thoughtfully, "Joe—"

"Yes?"

"There's a New Year's dance at Laramie. Will you let Barbara go with me?"

"Laramie's a long ways off."

"We'll go one day and come back the next. She can stay with Sergeant Driscoll's wife overnight."

"Have you asked her?"

"She said she'd like to go."

"You'll have to ask her mother."

"I know. She said I'd have to have your permission and her mother's."

Joe hesitated, then thought of Emma's wisdom. She would know exactly what to do, and Joe said,

"It's all right with me if it is with her mother."

"Thanks again, Joe."

They left the logs beside those already at the new building site, and Ellis wandered toward the main post where he lived with Snedeker. Joe stabled the mules and fed them hay and grain; animals that work hard should eat well. He filled his lungs with the crisp air and turned toward the quarters Snedeker had given him and his family. Joe frowned as he did so.

Laramie, staffed by soldiers and with the best freighters at its command, was still strictly utilitarian. Though their quarters at

Laramie had been comfortable, they had not afforded what Joe was beginning to think of as the luxuries they'd had in Missouri. Snedeker's necessarily offered less than Laramie. The cabin was wind- and weather-tight, but it was crude. Built as quarters for men, it had a large kitchen served by a fireplace and a larger bunk room with ten bunks and a bigger fireplace.

By stretching buffalo hides from ceiling to floor, Joe had divided it into three rooms; one for Emma and himself; one for Barbara and little Emma; and one for the four boys. Each had privacy, and using their own mattresses and quilts on the bunks added to their comfort. But it still lacked conveniences and Joe thought Emma was beginning to feel the strain. She looked tired and worn, or was that his imagination? It couldn't be, he decided. Tad was seldom in the cabin except for meals and Barbara helped her mother. But the youngsters could go out for only short intervals, and keeping four children happy in such a place would be a strain on anyone.

Joe opened the door, entered, and closed the door quickly to keep the cold wind out. He stamped snow from his boots. The youngsters rushed across the floor to meet him. They clustered about his legs while he removed his jacket and hung it on a wooden peg driven into the wall. Barbara waved from the fireplace. Joe kissed Emma and after one swift glance at his face she stepped back to raise an inquiring brow.

"Is something wrong?" she asked softly.

He murmured, "Wait'll the kids are gone."

"You sit down," Emma urged. "We'll have buffalo steak again for supper."

She spoke a little tiredly, and Joe said nothing. Snedeker had a limited supply of sugar, flour, salt, coffee, and all the other staples and these he sold to Joe for just what they cost at Laramie. Joe's own quota was free, for that had been part of their bargain, but he had to pay for what his family used. The meat that went with it, for which Snedeker charged nothing, was buffalo, elk, antelope, bear, and bighorn. Because there was more buffalo than anything else, they ate it most of the time and Emma was wearying of it. All they had in addition was such milk as the cow gave. Emma's chickens, in a shed by themselves, hadn't laid for weeks.

Emma went back to her work and Joe sank down in a chair. He'd told the children a story every night, usually centering it on something he had seen or done while felling trees, and the subject was wearing thin. Unable to think of any new slants, he assured them that his knee was a big black horse and bounced each of them in turn. Tad, who had a supernatural talent for appearing whenever there was anything to eat, raced in just as Emma and Barbara put the food on the table.

Every night, as soon as the dishes were washed, all of them usually went over to while away a couple of hours with Snedeker and Ellis. Given a free hand to do as they wished, the younger children played with Snedeker's few trade goods; they were few in winter because few Indians came to trade. They brought their buffalo robes in spring, but by that time Snedeker would have more goods. This night Joe and Emma did not put their coats on and the younger children looked questioningly at them.

"Go with Barbara," Emma told them. "We'll stay home tonight."

Barbara, who knew some things that the youngsters did not, winked knowingly at her parents and dressed the younger children. They trooped out into the night, and Joe and Emma were left alone. Joe stared moodily into the fire while Emma waited expectantly. Joe said,

"Ellis wants to marry Barbara."

She bit her lower lip, but did not register the astonishment that Joe had anticipated. He nodded; probably she'd already known.

"It isn't unexpected," she said.

"What do you think about it?"

Emma hesitated. "Barbara hasn't accepted him."

"How do you know?"

Emma said, "She'd have told me."

Joe pondered. "He seems like a good enough young man, but

we don't know a blasted thing about him. I wouldn't want Barbara to get in a mess."

"What did you tell him, Joe?"

"That I am Barbara's father, not her master. I can't tell her who to marry." He scowled, wondering if he'd done right. Emma laid a comforting hand on his arm.

"What else *could* you have told him?"

"Nothing."

She sighed. "That's right. All we can do is help guide Barbara."

"There's another thing. Ellis wants to take her to a New Year's dance at Laramie. He said they'll go one day and come back the next, and Barbara can stay with Ynez Driscoll overnight."

"What did you say to that?"

"I said he'd have to ask you."

Emma said hesitantly, "It may be a good idea and it may not. I'll have to think about it." Joe saw that she had clasped her hands together, and that the knuckles showed white. Unquestionably she was worried about Barbara and Ellis, more worried than *he* was. Joe knew, too, that Emma would leave no stone unturned to learn more about Ellis before things went much further, and he suspected that she would learn about Ellis not by asking questions of Snedeker, but by talking with Ellis himself.

The fire blazed brightly, casting shadows on the rough-hewn beams that supported the ceiling and on the uneven floor. There was a spot of dirt on the floor, and Emma stooped mechanically to brush it up. Joe looked fondly at her, and knew that she had already borne trials which only a strong person could bear. His brow clouded when he thought of trials still to come.

He said, "It's been a hard road, Emma, and a long one."

"We didn't expect it would be easy, Joe." And then, because she saw he needed something more from her, she said, "We've been lucky, Joe. We're through with the worst weather—we won't need to move again until spring. Meanwhile—why, we're just as comfortable here as we could be in our own home!"

He smiled wryly, and held her eyes with his own honest glance.

"It's *not* our own home, though, and nothing will ever feel like home again until we've stopped moving, and planted crops, and have our own roof over our heads."

He had said what was in her mind, so there was no need for further speech on that subject. She came to him and kissed him lightly on the forehead.

He jumped to his feet and grabbed her in a furious hug. "Emma, my fine girl!" he declared. "When we get to Oregon I'm going to build you a house that will make our other house seem like a chicken coop!"

She looked at him with all of her love and faith, and with laughter in her eyes. "With five acres of flower garden and a square mile just for the chickens!" she said. They laughed uproariously, ridiculously. Then Joe remembered something.

"Excuse me a minute."

Joe went to the wagon, and took from the tool box the one parcel that had been there since leaving Laramie. Very gently he gave it to Emma.

"Merry Christmas, my dear."

"Joe!" She held the package tenderly, caressing it with her spirit before she did with her hands, for she knew the gift could never be forsaken or forgotten. She heard Joe say,

"I only wish it was half as fine as you are."

Her hands trembled as she opened the package and gazed with rapt eyes at the scarf. Emma, who had seen little except hardship since leaving Missouri, brushed this truly beautiful thing with her hands and pressed it against her cheek. In the exquisite scarf she saw all her hopes and dreams come alive.

She said, "I have something for you, too."

She gave him a watch, a thick silver watch that had been made by some German craftsman and had somehow found its way to the sutler's store at Fort Laramie. Joe gazed at it, not believing what he saw. Watches were luxuries, thus they were only for those who could afford luxuries. Joe turned the key. He held the watch to his ear so he could hear its ticking.

In the middle of a wilderness, on their way to another, owning only what they could load on a wagon, they sat very close and knew the true spirit of Christmas. They watched the minute hand, amazed at how slowly time passed when you were looking at it, and then they laughed again, free and hearty laughter that can be born only of hope and faith in the future.

Joe said, "I'll have to get busy."

A lighted lantern in his hand, he went to a small pine he had already marked and chopped it cleanly. From behind the cabin he took a bucket of sand that he had saved for this purpose, and thrust the tree upright in it. When he re-entered the cabin, popcorn snapped in Emma's skillet and for one of the few times since leaving the farm, her trunk was open. There were parcels and jars on the table. Her new scarf worn proudly on her shoulders, Emma looked up from the fireplace.

"Canned pumpkin." She indicated the jars. "I brought it all this way so we can have pumpkin pie tomorrow."

"Oh boy!" Joe smacked his lips.

The cabin seemed to have come alive with the spirit of Christmas. The rafters had a softer glow. Through their minds ran strains of gay music they had heard, but it was so real that it semed to be heard again in the cabin.

Emma asked, "Pop some more corn, will you?"

"Sure thing."

While Joe knelt before the fireplace, Emma threaded a needle and strung popcorn on the thread. She draped it gracefully over the tree, then opened a parcel and took colored ornaments from it. They were the tree ornaments Emma had had from her mother, and she'd treasured them for years. The tree sparkled in its new-found glory.

Emma had wrapped the children's presents carefully and separately, and had written their name on each. She arranged them beside the tree, then took another armful of wrapped presents out of the trunk. Joe looked at them, surprised.

"What are they?"

"Barbara's presents. She knitted hats for you, Mr. Snedeker, and Ellis."

"I never saw her knitting."

"How could you when you're away all day long?" She was impatient now. "Do you want to call them, Joe? Bring all of them."

"Right away."

Not bothering with a coat, Joe ran across the short space that separated their cabin from the store and entered. A wolf pelt draped over his shoulders, Tad was leading his brothers in a march among the counters and baby Emma was playing with a string of bright beads she had found. Snedeker tilted on a chair beside the fire, watching the children. Barbara and Ellis sat together on the opposite side of the fireplace, and Joe did not look too closely at them. Ellis had told him that Barbara hadn't said no, and it *did* seem that they sat pretty close together.

Joe called, "You're all coming over to our place."

"Run along, kids," Snedeker told them. "Your maw wants you."

"You too, Jim."

"Me? What would she want me for?"

"Come over and find out."

"I'll be doggone!" Snedeker exclaimed. "Fust time in thutty years a white woman's wanted to see me! You sure?"

"I'm sure. Come on."

Barbara rose and Joe's eyes were drawn to her. He had always known that his daughter was lovely. Now she seemed radiant, and she floated across the rough wooden floor to her father. Barbara's voice was an angel's breath.

"Look, Daddy!"

Around her neck she wore a golden chain, and on the chain was a ring set with a red stone. Joe gazed with intense interest for never before had he seen such a stone. It caught and trapped the lantern's light, and the fire's glow, and captured within itself some of the crimson that warmed Barbara's cheeks. The stone seemed alive and fiery, and though he knew little about such things Joe knew that it was precious.

"What is it?" he asked.

"It's a ruby," Barbara told him. "Ellis gave it to me."

"It was my mother's," Ellis said eagerly.

Joe looked at him askance. "Do you think you should give it away?"

Quick anger flashed across Ellis's face. "I think I should give it to Barbara."

"Well." Ellis's response unsettled him, and for a second Joe debated the possible facets to this situation, then lost himself in the spirit of the evening, "Come on. Emma's waiting."

He led them to the cabin, stood aside as they entered, and heard Emma's sincere, "Merry Christmas! Merry Christmas, everybody!" Joe glanced at Barbara and Ellis, standing close together. The younger children, all of whom had remembered Christmas in Missouri but none of whom had thought of it on the Oregon Trail, stared wide-eyed at the tree. Joe fidgeted, glad because Emma knew just what to do. She addressed the wondering children,

"Santa Claus was here and he left something for everyone." She picked up a wrapped gift. "Carlyle."

Emma put the package in his hands and helped him open it. Staring at this gaily painted wonder, the baby toddled off to cradle the horse in his lap. He moved the movable legs and stroked the silken mane. Alfred stood breathlessly, his mouth open and his eyes shining. Little Joe was excited and baby Emma danced. Tad stood as he saw the men standing, but what he felt showed in his bright eyes.

"This *must* be Oregon!" Alfred exclaimed.

The adults smiled gently while Alfred stared in fascination at his bow and arrows. Joe opened his present, and two arrows whistled across the room. Her face wholly blissful, little Emma cradled the doll in her arms and began crooning to it. Tad's eyes glowed when he tore the wrappings from his hatchet. He tested the blade with his thumb and immediately began honing it.

Lost in this unforgettable evening, Barbara slipped the silver bracelet over her slim wrist and held it up for all to see. She smiled her thanks at her father and mother. Emma picked up another package.

"Ellis. Barbara made it for you."

He took the knitted hat. It was of two colors, with a buffalo head worked into the front and a silver tassel. He tried it on, then slipped it off. The glance he gave Barbara was filled with infinite tenderness, and nobody except Barbara heard his low-voiced thanks.

"Jim."

"Lordy, lordy!" Snedeker breathed.

Spellbound, he looked at the hat. Then he took his battered headpiece off, opened the door, and threw it into the snow. The new hat he smoothed over his shaggy locks, and reached up to touch it as though he could not believe it was there. Snedeker strode across the floor, threw both arms around Barbara, and kissed her. Barbara blushed.

The whistling wind played with the shingles on the cabin and plucked at the chinking in the logs. Absorbed in their presents, the youngsters scarcely glanced up. A coyote on the ridge behind the cabin began to yell. Then the outside noises quieted for a moment and Emma's clear voice sang,

> "God rest ye merry, gentlemen,
> Let nothing ye dismay—"

Joe joined in the centuries-old hymn, then Barbara and Ellis, and the children. Jim Snedeker retreated to the background. He took his hat off and stood silently, and in that moment he revealed completely the man within his hard outer shell. Emma led the next carol,

> "The first Noel the angels did say,
> Was to certain poor shepherds in fields as they lay;"

Outside, the wind howled louder, and the coyote yelled again. But they seemed strange and far-off noises that had no relation whatever with the cabin or with those inside it. The spirit of the season was theirs, and they were one with Him who had died for them. The last notes of the last carol still trembled in the cabin when Emma smiled graciously,

"Jim, you and Ellis are to have dinner with us tomorrow. There'll be pumpkin pie and roast antelope."

"Wait a bit, ma'am," Snedeker protested. "Did you say antelope?"

"Yes, Jim."

"Reckon not," Snedeker decided. "You just wait a bit. Don't leave your hosses gallop away an' I'll be back."

He put his new hat tenderly on his head and left the cabin. Presently he was back, with a huge smoked ham dangling from his right hand. It was one Snedeker had been hoarding for his own use, and the last ham at the post, but he gave it freely.

"Better Christmas dinner than antelope," he affirmed.

Emma's eyes shone with her pleasure at the prospect of a traditional Christmas feast. "Oh! Thank you, Jim!"

"Welcome, ma'am! Plain welcome! I ain't had a Christmas like this sinst I was eight years old. Well, I'll be shaggin' along. Comin', Ellis?"

"Soon."

Ellis lingered until the children were in bed, then bade a reluctant good night and prepared to leave. Emma got her coat.

"Would you mind walking me to the store, Ellis? I do need a bit of sugar."

"I'll be happy to, Mrs. Tower."

"Let me—" Joe began.

Emma said quickly, "No, you stay here, Joe. I'll get it."

Ellis held the door for her and they stepped into the brisk night. Emma waited for him to join her.

"Brr! Isn't it cold?"

"It certainly is."

She sensed his uncertainty, his embarrassment, and did her best to put him at ease.

"Come. Walk beside me."

She slipped her hand through his arm and drew him a bit closer.

"You're a tall young man, Ellis. Your mother must be very proud of you."

There was wistfulness in this voice, "I haven't any mother. She died when I was eight."

"Oh." Emma's sympathy was immediate and sincere. "I'm sorry! Do you remember very much about her."

He said simply, "I'll never forget her. We lived in Baltimore."

"Was it nice there?"

His voice was dreamy. "While my mother was alive, we had a big house and there was always fun. But she went, and then my father died when I was twelve and—"

He paused suddenly and turned to look shrewdly at her. "Any more questions, Mrs. Tower?"

In the darkness, Emma blushed. But she carried on determinedly. "You've expressed a desire to marry Barbara," she said frankly, "and you want to take her on an overnight trip to Laramie. Naturally, I intend to find out a great deal more about you, Ellis."

"Very well!" he said, angry now. "Here are some facts." He began speaking rapidly and distinctly, shooting out the facts as though he were making a legal report. "When my father died my Uncle George was the executor. There was always enough money, but Uncle George and I didn't get along. He wanted me to go into his bank. I didn't care for that. For a year I went to Columbian College—that's in Washington, Mrs. Tower, and then . . ."

He broke off sharply, and there was a long moment of silence. When he spoke again, his voice was quiet and ashamed. "Forgive me, Mrs. Tower. You've a right to know everything about me that you want to know. You've already found out one bad thing about me—I have a quick temper and an unpleasant one. I want to apologize."

"That's all right, Ellis," Emma said serenely. "Let's go on from here. You were at college in Washington, you say?"

"Yes, ma'am," he said humbly. "I met a girl in Washington, Mary Harkness. I was in love with her. When Mary's folks decided to come west, there seemed to be nothing left for me in the east. I came along. It seemed the right thing to do. I had enough money to buy a horse and everything else I needed."

"What happened, Ellis?" Emma whispered.

"When we got to Laramie, Mary married a man named Jeremy Blake. They went on together."

Emma's voice was very gentle. "Did it hurt?"

"I wished I could die."

Emma said, "You must understand that not all women are good, Ellis, any more than all men are. After enticing you to come along, and then marrying someone else—"

"I haven't made myself clear, Mrs. Tower. She did not entice me to come along; I came of my own free will and entirely because I wanted to. Nor was Mary in any sense of the word bad or deceitful. She is fine, loyal, and good. She simply didn't want me."

Emma's heart beat happily. Ellis had chased a woman all the way from Maryland, Jim Snedeker had said. Now Emma knew the story. She asked,

"What did you do then, Ellis?"

There was a faint trace of remembered bitterness in his voice. "I went to work for Jim. I knew there would be nothing for me at his post, but the way I felt then there seemed to be nothing for me anywhere. I just worked along, without much hope or any plan at all. Then you brought Barbara."

"And she means much to you?"

He said firmly, "I'm grateful Mary made the choice she did."

She took his arm. "Come along, I must get my sugar." She stopped at the entrance to the store. "Oh, Ellis. One more thing. About that New Year's dance at Fort Laramie. I want you to know that I think it's a splendid idea."

"You do!"

"Certainly. Young people should enjoy themselves, and Barbara will be perfectly all right with Ynez Driscoll." She was rewarded with a smile of the purest gratitude and delight.

Emma bought a pound of sugar, which she really had not needed, and went back to the cabin. Contentedly she slept beside Joe, and was still drowsy when he awakened. She knew when Joe got out of bed to start both fires, then crawled back in to wait until the cabin warmed. She heard the children giggling in their beds.

They breakfasted, and Emma and Barbara began to prepare the Christmas dinner. Except that they would have had turkey instead of ham, everything would have been exactly this way back in Missouri. But so long had they been out, living from what they had in the wagon and building fires under every possible condition, and so much longer had they been at Snedeker's, eating wild meat and stretching other foods as far as possible in order to save money, that this seemed to be scaling the utmost heights of luxury. They baked the ham and pies, and Emma opened three jars of string beans that had also been saved for this occasion. There were no potatoes. But there was feathery-light bread and butter.

It was a memorable Christmas dinner, one that was never forgotten by any of the older people who partook of it. Emma had brought spices for the ham, and Joe carved and served pink slices of the steaming delicacy. When everybody had eaten as much as they could, there was still a full third of the ham left. But Emma's three pumpkin pies had been eaten to the last crumb.

Tad went out to test his hatchet, and after the dishes were washed Barbara and Ellis took a walk in the snow. Emma and Joe watched the young couple as they left. Emma had told her husband of her talk with Ellis. His response had been an uneasy one.

"He's mighty hasty, seems to me."

"Mighty young, too," she had reminded him.

Still enthralled with their presents, the youngsters played busily.

Snedeker took a blackened pipe from his pocket, filled it with vile-smelling tobacco, and offered the tobacco pouch to Joe.

"Smoke?"

"No thanks. I never got the habit."

"Lordy, lordy. No smokin'. No drinkin'. What do you do, Joe?"

"I like to hunt and fish."

"Of both you'll find a heap in Oregon," Snedeker assured him. "Though 'tain't an' never will be like 'twas. I remember—"

Joe and Emma listened while he spoke of the west that used to be. He spoke of Blackfeet, Sioux, Pawnees, and of battles with them. He created word pictures of virgin creeks which, until the Mountain Men came, had known no white man's tracks. There were so many buffalo that the plains were black with them and the thunder of their hoofs drowned even a shrieking wind. Snedeker told of vast herds of deer, elk, and antelope. He told of colorful camps and rendezvous.

"I seen it all," he continued, "and 'tain't so many years it took to see it. The like will never be again. The west is growin' up. Buffalo hides have took the place of beaver. Emmy-grants, crazy for land, are pourin' in like a falls off a mountain. Mebbe, when you come to think of it, that's right too. The west was made for people, not buffalo. Do you know they's even crazy talk of a railroad an' wire line clean across the kentry? Yep. Five minutes after somebody in New York says it, somebody in San Francisco will know what he said. I misbelieve that'll ever be; don't see how it can be. But when the buffalo go, an' they's sure to go, they'll be lots of things. All the gold they found in Californy won't be a acorn's wuth to what will be found. I don't mean gold, nuther. They's ore beds in the west for the whole kentry ten times over. They's farm land thick with wild grass, an' that'll grow crops jest as good. They's a galore of timber, enough to make all the cities an' towns what'll ever need be made. The emmy-grants who've gone ain't made a dent in the west. Some day Oregon alone will have twicet as many emmy-grants as have been over the Trail in the past ten years, an' they'll be room for 'em. They'll be cities on the west coast to shade anything what's on the east." He became wistful. "The west will be tamed, but I'm right glad I ain't goin' to live to see it all tamed. I wouldn't like that a'tall."

That night Joe went happily to bed, for Snedeker's discourse had been a great comfort to him. He had left Missouri because he needed room and opportunity for his children, and he was getting into the west while there was still plenty of both. When the millions came, providing they came at all in his time, he would be too old to care and the children would be young enough to adjust.

Rising in a cloudless sky, next morning's sun brought little warmth. Overnight the weather had turned very cold, so that a thick glazing of frost lay on the windows. Since there was a great pile of logs at the building site, and no special hurry about getting any more, today Joe and Ellis were to see if they could find some buffalo. By all means they were to bring in something, for meat stocks at the post were low. If they couldn't find buffalo, they were to try for elk or deer. Should they discover a herd of buffalo, they were to shoot as many as possible. Though there was a limit to the meat that could be used, Snedeker could hire squaws to cure the hides. There was a steady market for buffalo robes in the east, but it was not necessary to send them east in order to realize a good profit. Oregon-bound emigrants would pay four dollars each for buffalo robes right at the post.

Ellis rode his horse, Joe mounted the mare mule, and each man carried a rifle. Without speaking they mounted the ridge behind the post and went into pine forest. A deer flitted among the trees and Joe raised his rifle. But the deer was gone before he could get a shot.

"Let's try for buffalo first," Ellis suggested. "We can always pick up something else if we don't find any."

"All right with me. Have you hunted buffalo?"

"Yes. There are meadows back here where we'll find them if there are any around. They stay there because of good grass and it's out of the wind. If we find a herd, take those on the outside first."

A little while later Ellis held up his hand because it would be unwise to speak, dismounted, and tied his horse to a tree. Joe slid off the mule and tied her. He followed Ellis through the pines and looked down on an open meadow.

Sixteen buffaloes moved sluggishly about while they scraped for grass with ponderous hoofs. Ellis Garner's rifle came up as easily as though it were an extension of his own arm. He sighed, shot, and a buffalo dropped heavily. Ellis indicated another cow that stood on the fringe of the herd and reloaded.

They shot six before the rest scented blood and pounded clumsily away in a cloud of flying snow. Ellis watched the fleeing herd until it was out of sight. Joe warmed to him. Whatever Ellis might be, he was no deliberate killer. He had shot buffalo because it was part of his job, not because he loved to shoot. Joe suspected that a flying buck or lurking elk would have been game much more to his liking.

Ellis asked, "Want to bring a sled up while I skin these? If we both leave, they'll be nothing but wolf bait."

"I'll help you."

"It's no job. You just slit them up the belly and around the legs, cut a slot for a rope, and let your horse pull the skin off. I'll be done by the time you're back."

Joe said, "Tad shot a buffalo on the way to Laramie and it took us a long while to skin it. Where'd you learn this trick?"

"Jim taught me."

Joe rode the mare mule back to the post, harnessed the team and hitched them to one of Snedeker's bobsleds. He followed the tracks they'd made going in and saw the six buffalo carcasses, rawly naked already freezing. Ellis was walking about, beating his hands together to warm them.

"Better take some of the humps," he said. "It's one of the best parts."

Joe scratched his head. "I heard that too, but I couldn't even cut it out."

"I'll show you."

There was a ridge of bone over the hump, but it did not go clear through. Ellis inserted his knife, cut deftly, and lifted out a three-pound chunk of meat. Under Ellis's direction, Joe did the next one. They took the humps, the livers, half a dozen hind quarters, the loins and the tongues, and laid them on the fresh hides.

While they loaded the meat on the bobsleds, Joe was silent, preoccupied by his confused feelings about Ellis. The young man was undoubtedly a hard worker when he wanted to be, and he was friendly and respectful—when he wanted to be. But always Ellis gave you the feeling he was going to do exactly what he wanted, and if that thing happened to be unfriendly, why that was the time for a person to watch out. He had an impulsive way of speaking and acting. Ten to one he'd tell you just what he thought about something, even if the telling might cause some folks real embarrassment. That was honesty, of a kind, but it could be cruelty, too, and Joe wasn't exactly sure which it was in the case of Ellis. As for Barbara, Ellis seemed smitten, sure enough, but would he be respectful and take good care of her on the jaunt to Laramie? Emma seemed confident, but Joe was deeply uncertain, and the uncertainty made him grim and silent as they loaded the last of the meat.

The next day the cut wood, and Joe glanced questioningly at the sky. The sun still shone, but there was something in the air that Joe could not analyze. It was a faint but startling thing, like the sudden rustle of a leaf when there is no wind, and it seemed to grow stronger as day followed day. But there was only an uneasy feeling and nothing tangible to furnish evidence that something grim and terrible did lurk behind the sun.

On the last day of the year, the rest of the Towers watched Ellis, riding his horse, and Barbara, mounted on one of Snedeker's with her dancing dress carried in a pack behind the saddle, start down the Trail for the New Year's dance at Laramie.

CHAPTER TWELVE

Barbara and Ellis

WHEN BARBARA TOWER mounted Snedeker's blaze-faced brown horse, she was a little afraid. All her life she had been accustomed to farm animals of various kinds, and she had an inborn understanding of them as well as deep sympathy for them. But her riding had been confined to the placid farm horses of Missouri, and now she felt this high-strung creature quivering beneath her and eager to go. Holding the horse in, she bent down as though to examine the length of her stirrup.

She was not afraid of the horse, but she trembled lest she do something wrong while Ellis was watching. Expertly, he wheeled his horse and came to her side.

"Shall I shorten the stirrups?"

"No, I was just looking. I think they're about right."

She warmed to this young man who thought it his place to offer her small courtesies. Except for Hugo Gearey, all the other young men she'd ever known would have waited while she herself did whatever was necessary. Experimentally, she reined the horse about and he responded at once. That restored her confidence. The horse was spirited but he was thoroughly broken and without being forced he would heed the wishes of his rider. She fell in behind Ellis and they walked their horses out to the Trail. They turned to wave good-by to Barbara's watching family, and the Towers waved back.

The weather was crisp and cold, with a steady north wind that crimsoned both young people's cheeks. But they were not cold because they were dressed for the weather—Barbara wore her heavy brown coat, cut down trousers, and had a wool scarf over her head—they were young, and the prospect of an exciting dance provided its own spiritual warmth.

At least once a week and sometimes oftener, cavalry patrols had been down the Trail. The patrols always stopped at Snedeker's, but they were always commanded by some noncommissioned officer with a strong sense of duty and a stronger realization of what would happen if he was in any way derelict in that duty. Therefore, much to the chagrin of the young privates who made up the body of the patrol, and who wanted to stay near Barbara, they never stopped for very long. However, because of them the Trail was packed, and Ellis dropped back to ride beside Barbara.

He wore a buffalo-skin coat, heavy trousers, and loose moccasins over two pairs of wool socks. Behind his saddle was a parcel with necessary toilet articles and a change of clothing, and Barbara had noted that too. The men of Missouri went to dances and parties in their work clothing, and civilians who attended dances at Fort Laramie seldom bothered to change greasy buckskins or whatever else they were wearing. But Ellis was going to make himself presentable and she knew he was doing it for her.

Many things about Ellis appealed to her, yet when she asked herself how she felt about marrying him, no answer came to mind. Actually, although they had been together a great deal, they had not talked very much and she knew relatively little about him. He seemed outspoken enough with her mother and her father, but when he was alone with Barbara he tended to become tongue-tied. And since she herself had trouble with words in his presence, their conversations were usually halting and uninformative.

She could not help thinking, from time to time, of Hugo Gearey's witty and fascinating talk, of the hours when he had regaled her with countless stories and anecdotes. She remembered, too, although she brushed the thought angrily aside, the feeling of his arms about her, of his lips on her lips. He was a horrid person, but she could not deny that he had remained in her mind, and his poise and charm, deceptive though they were, made Ellis's long awkward silences more disturbing than they otherwise would be. On the other hand, when Ellis looked at her with his whole heart in his eyes she tingled. She was woman enough to be thrilled by his devotion, even though she wasn't at all sure of her own feelings toward him.

Ellis's Kentucky thoroughbred, a sleek and powerful animal, kept its head high and ears forward as it looked interestedly at everything on both sides of the Trail. Though he was not boastful, Ellis could not conceal the pride he took in his horse and occasionally Barbara wondered whether he would ever take that much pride in anything else. The wool cap she had knitted for him was pulled down over the left side of his face to shield his cheek from the wind, and he turned toward her.

"How do you like it?" he asked.

It was meant to be a gay and informal question, but somehow it was stilted and formal. Barbara tried to respond gaily and for the moment could not.

"This is fine!"

She smiled, and when he smiled back she could not help thinking that he had a warm and nice smile. Yet she felt restrained, and could not understand her feeling. When Ellis asked her to go to the dance, it had seemed a wonderful adventure and she had gone to bed each night hoping that he would get her father's and mother's permission. Now that they were actually on the Trail and started toward Laramie, she had misgivings. She had gone out with young men before, but never for overnight, and she wondered suddenly what her friends back in Missouri would say if they could know. The thought should not disturb her but it did. For the moment the young man beside her was almost a stranger, and she thought that she had been ill-advised to go with him at all.

She shifted her hands, and when she did so the rein brushed

her mount's neck and he turned half around. Barbara knew a sudden rush of embarrassment. She had been holding the reins too loosely, and not paying enough attention to what she was doing. As a consequence she had blundered, and in Ellis's eyes she must be less than perfect. But when she turned to explain her error, he was looking the other way. Barbara began to relax.

A coyote flashed out of a copse of brush and raced down the Trail. With a spontaneous whoop that startled her momentarily, Ellis was after it. Barbara reined her horse to a slow walk and watched, her eyes shining. Ellis rode his big horse as though he were a part of it, with every move of horse and rider perfectly coordinated. She watched the coyote outdistance him. Laughing, he came back. Barbara laughed, too, and suddenly it seemed that all the ice between them had melted.

"Didn't anyone ever tell you that a horse can't outrun a coyote?"

"King could. I was holding him back. Didn't want to frighten the poor little coyote to death."

They laughed wildly, as though at some huge joke, and the horses bobbed happy heads as they went down the Trail at a fast walk. Ellis turned to watch six elk disappearing into a pine thicket. Barbara stole a covert glance at his profile.

She'd given Ellis a great deal of thought. Certainly she wanted to get married. But there should be more to marriage than the simple act of a man and woman exchanging vows and living together. Her own parents' marriage was far different, she reflected, than other marriages she had seen among their neighbors in Missouri. Her parents had a special kind of feeling for each other that was much more than physical, more even than their satisfaction in sharing their home and their children. They laughed together and they worried together, and one could be happy for no reason except the other had enjoyed himself, the way Emma was happy when Joe would come back refreshed from an evening at Tenney's store. It was a kind of blending and merging, with each one willing and eager to give up his own private world in order to build a sort of combination world. She couldn't quite get it into words, but it did seem like a real melting and fusing of two destinies into one destiny. Barbara herself had never met any man who made her feel like blending and merging her life that way, and she wondered whether something might be lacking in her.

Barbara remembered vividly the night Ellis proposed to her. When they'd first arrived at Snedeker's, she had heard Jim Snedeker refer to Ellis as a woman chaser and she had thought little about that or about Ellis. Most of the boys she knew chased girls. But as day followed day, unaccountably she had found herself watching for Ellis. Working in the cabin, she would glance out the window to see if he was around. When he asked her to go walking with him, she was happy to go.

They were strolling on a dark, moonless night when—and she still did not know how it happened—she was in his arms and his lips were on hers. Ellis's embrace was not like Hugo Gearey's and his lips had a different meaning in them. She could yield to this kiss and still feel safe, and somehow deeply stirred in a new way, a mysterious way. Barbara felt her knees tingle, and her body went strangely limp. A thousand times since, in memory, she had heard his whispered,

"I love you, Bobby! Will you marry me?"

And her reply. "I—I don't know, Ellis."

For a few days after that she had avoided him and secretly had been a little afraid of him. But she had always gone back because there was something about him that drew her back.

Now, as she studied his profile, she knew that her answer was the only one she could have given. She hadn't known and she still didn't know. Ellis turned suddenly and Barbara glanced quickly away.

"Race you!" he said.

"Oh, Ellis—"

"Come on!"

He touched his knees to his horse and Barbara accepted the challenge. Side by side they thundered down the Trail, and

Barbara let the reins slacken while, with an almost fierce will, she urged her horse on. She wanted to win. But she could not win. Her mount was good, but Ellis's was better. He drew ahead, widened the gap between them, and as soon as he was ten yards in the lead he stopped and turned to grin.

"I win!"

"You should, with that horse."

Ellis said, and Barbara had an easy feeling that her father would have said it in almost the same way, "He's as good as there is. It's the sort of horse a man should have. Want to ride him?"

"I'd love to!"

They changed mounts, Ellis holding hers even while he shortened the stirrups for her. Barbara felt the huge horse beneath her and knew a sudden wild thrill. She had heard of the delights of horsemanship, but until now she had never really tasted them. The horse stood still but, standing, he communicated his surging, latent power to his rider. Barbara had a giddy feeling that, if she let him run and did not restrain him, he could run clear to the end of the world. The horse turned its head to look at her with gentle eyes, but he responded at once when she wanted him to. His gait was so soft and easy that Barbara had a strange sense of floating, and she had not ridden a hundred yards before she knew that this horse was hers completely, and that he would do whatever she wanted him to do. She turned a teasing face to Ellis.

"Let's race now!"

They were off again, Barbara little more than a feather's weight in the saddle while the horse seemed to develop an eagle's wings. It was purest joy, unmarred delight, but when Barbara thought she had left Ellis far in the rear and looked around, he was almost at her heels. She had the better horse, but he was the better rider. Barbara reined her horse to a walk.

"I win!"

"You'll win anything with King. How do you like him?"

"He's wonderful!"

"He certainly is."

Again they rode side by side, all softness gone and easy intimacy reigning.

Ellis passed her a slip of paper. "Your dance card."

She unfolded the paper and read, "First dance, Ellis. Second dance, Ellis. Third dance, Ellis. Fourth dance—" There were twenty dances, with Ellis as her partner for every one. She looked at him in mock indignation.

"I'm supposed to fill my dance card!"

He grinned. "No harm in hinting, is there?"

"You're impossible!"

"I've always been."

They laughed again, and the horses pricked their ears forward. Following their intent gaze, the pair saw a cavalry patrol come around a hill and, when they drew nearer, Sergeant Dunbar greeted them. Barbara warmed at the sight of her old friend.

"Hello!"

"Hello!" they called in unison.

The patrol reined in, the six privates who accompanied Dunbar gloomy and sullen because they would miss the New Year's festivities at Laramie. For the moment, Barbara recognized no familiar face among them.

Dunbar's eyes twinkled as he glanced from Barbara to Ellis. "Going to Laramie?" he asked.

"Um-hum," Barbara said happily. "We're going to the dance there."

Dunbar barked, "Jankoski and Gearey, stay in line!"

Barbara found herself face to face with Hugo Gearey. At sight of him her heart lurched.

He removed his hat and bowed. Then, turning to Dunbar he said, with strict military formality, "Sergeant Dunbar, may I have five minutes alone with Miss Tower? I have an important message for her."

Dunbar scowled. "Barbara, is it your wish to talk with Private Gearey for five minutes?"

Barbara was torn. She knew that Gearey was not to be trusted, yet with all these men around to protect her—and if he did have a message—

She replied primly, "Five minutes should be ample."

Gearey behind her, Barbara rode on down the path until they were out of earshot but still in full view of the others.

Then she turned to him. "Well?"

He chewed his lip. "Can't we get out of sight of those blasted—"

"Your message?" she interrupted.

He saw that she would not be swayed. He drew a deep breath. "Barbara—I never got to see you again, to apologize for the ugly way I behaved that night. I want you to know that I have the deepest regard, the deepest respect for you. I hope you'll give me an opportunity to prove this. May I see you—soon?"

His voice was deep and warm. He seemed so terribly in earnest. Could it be that she had misjudged him? She wavered, and he saw that he had gained ground.

"I won't urge you now," he said humbly. "But I'll come down to Snedeker's when this patrol is over, and—" He dropped his voice until it was little more than a vibrant whisper, "You will see me, Barbara? Just for an hour?"

Again she hesitated, some inner devil prompting, "*You are not promised to Ellis. Why not see him—just for an hour?*" She tossed her head and said, with an effort at indifference, "Possibly. I don't promise." Then she reined her horse around and galloped back to the others.

Ellis watched her coming with burning eyes, and he glared murderously at Gearey. Hugo's face was noncommittal and entirely friendly as he took his place in line. The meeting had been, for Hugo, a great piece of luck.

Barbara saw that Ellis was on the verge of an outburst, but she felt he had no right to one, and she would not placate him. She averted her gaze to look at Dunbar. He asked, "Your family is at Snedeker's, eh?"

"That's right," Barbara smiled, "and they'll love to see you."

"Can't stop on the way down," he said regretfully, "but we'll surely do it on the way back. How are the youngsters?"

"They've missed you."

A happy smile lighted Dunbar's face and he said to Ellis, "Take good care of this young lady."

"I will," Ellis assured him. His eyes swept Gearey once more, and again Barbara saw that there was something explosive in Ellis, something a girl ought to worry about.

They went on, walking their horses most of the time but trotting them occasionally. Clouds spanned the sky and the sun disappeared, and when it did the cold seemed more intense. Barbara thought of the lunch that her mother had packed.

"I'm hungry," she said.

Morosely he replied, "It isn't noon yet."

"Let's eat anyway."

"Your wish is my command, Your Highness." There was resentment still in his voice.

Ellis dismounted, helped Barbara dismount, and rein-tied the horses. He made his way to a stand of pine a few feet off the Trail, broke an armful of the brittle lower branches from them, and started a fire beside the packed snow. Barbara moved into its circle of warmth and unpacked the sandwiches. She thought they were roast buffalo, but when she opened them she saw that they contained the last of the Christmas ham. She knew a flush of gratitude toward her mother who, when sending young people out for a royal time, would also provide them with a royal feast.

"This is good!" she called to him, but Ellis was eating silently, scarcely aware of the food at all.

Barbara laughed, took a generous bite, and ate hungrily. Ellis finished his sandwich and took another. He was about to eat it when he straightened and looked down the Trail. When he turned to her, his face was serious.

"I don't like it."

She said airily, "What don't you like?"

He moved away from her studying the sky and the movements of the branches. "The wind's shifted from north to east."

"Can't the wind change its mind?"

"Bobby," he was very earnest, "we're in for a storm. We'd better ride."

She was uncertain. "Are you sure?"

"I'm dead sure!"

He helped her repack the sandwiches and returned them to her saddlebag. She felt a rising concern and a little fear. But after he helped her mount his horse and she looked down at him, she steadied. There was going to be a storm because he had said so. But he seemed calm, and somehow she felt that he would know what to do about it.

"We're going to make time," he told her. "I've put you on King because he'll follow me and I know he'll keep up. If you need anything, say so."

A cold chill brushed Barbara's spine when they were again moving. The wind, that had fanned their left cheeks since they'd started, was now full in their faces and Barbara bent her head against it. She had an overwhelming sense of something terrible about to be. It was as though a great, grim beast lurked in the overcast sky and was preparing to pounce on them.

Ellis set off at a canter, and Barbara's mount kept close at his heels. She sensed a difference in the horse. He too knew that a storm was on the way and he feared it. But he had an animal's blind faith in Ellis. The wind's whine became a savage snarl, and Barbara bent her head further. She looked up when Ellis shouted, and it was terrifying because he had to shout.

"Are you all right?"

She shouted back, "I'm all right."

"Don't worry."

She voiced her fear. "Don't—don't you think we'd better go back?"

"We'll never make it!"

The first snow came, a barrage of wind-driven pellets that stung

her face and left her gasping. The day turned to twilight, and
when she raised her head she could see only a few feet on either
side. Just ahead of her, Ellis was a snow-shrouded figure. Time
became meaningless, measureless. They moved on and on for
how many minutes or hours she could not tell. The fury of the
wind increased and breathing became more difficult. Barbara
wanted to cry out and knew that she must not. The cold touched
her body and seemed to penetrate her very bones. She was aware
of Ellis shouting, and it seemed that he shouted from a very long
way off.

"Give me your reins!"

Without question she put the reins in his outstretched hand and
clung to the saddle horn. The horses were walking now, fighting
the storm. Barbara knew a stabbing panic. Was this the end?
Would this be the end of her life, before she had fully lived? The
cold numbed her, so that there was no longer much feeling in her
hands and face. She almost slipped from the saddle. Then she was
aware of Ellis shouting again, and she saw him standing beside
her.

"Get off!" he repeated.

She slip into his arms and felt them close about her. He carried
her. She still heard the wind but it did not blast her nor was snow
falling on her, and she knew they had found shelter. Dimly she
saw the doorway through which they had entered, and felt herself
being very gently set down. Ellis's shout rang very loudly because
he had not remembered that there was no longer need to shout.

"Can you stand up?"

"Yes!"

She stood on shaky knees while Ellis brought both horses in and
closed the door. It was very black now, but when Ellis struck a
match she saw that they were in some kind of cabin with a big
pile of buffalo robes in the center. The match flickered out. She
heard him fumbling in the darkness. Then his arms were around
her again and his voice was very gentle:

"We're all right now."

"Wh—where are we?"

"In one of Jim's storage shacks. Come on."

She let him guide her, and tried with her numb fingers to help him when he began removing her snow-crusted outer clothing. He struck another match so he could see her shoes, unlaced them, took them off, and eased her down on a pile of buffalo robes he had arranged. He covered her with more robes, but she lay shivering and it seemed that she would never be warm again. The cabin lighted as he struck still another match, led the horses to the opposite wall and tied them to a pile of buffalo robes. She shivered and said fretfully, between stiff lips,

"I'm cold."

Then he was beside her under the robes, giving to her chilled body the warmth of his own. Gratefully she snuggled very close, while the horses stamped inside and the wind screamed outside. Ellis put both arms around her. Sleep claimed Barbara.

When she awakened, it was still black night inside the cabin and the wind still screamed outside. Barbara felt warm, snug, comfortable. She put out an exploring hand to touch Ellis, and he responded instantly, taking her whole hand and wrist into his warm, sensitive fingers.

"Are you awake, Barbara?"

"Ellis," she whispered. "You saved our lives."

He pressed her hand gently and held it undemandingly in his own. "I've been lying here thinking," he said. "When we were out in the storm, I wasn't sure we could reach this cabin. Suppose we hadn't come through? I was lying here trying to figure out what was the thing I would most regret. Know what I decided?"

"What?" Sleepily content, she awaited his answer. How strange —or perhaps it wasn't so strange—that in this barren cabin, in utter darkness and isolation, when they had narrowly escaped death, that Ellis should be able to talk to her so openly, so easily, more easily than at any time since she had met him. "What would you most regret, Ellis?"

"I would regret that I had not known you longer, had more

time with you. I would regret that I hadn't told you more about myself, even the bad things. I want to tell you everything about myself, Barbara. Whether you say yes or no to me later on, I want it to be on the basis of all the truth. May I tell you about—about before I came to Snedeker's?"

"Please," she whispered.

He told her, then, about his gentle laughing mother, and his loving but unreliable father who had made too much money gambling and had lived too fast and died too young. And he told her about his Uncle George who had not only stolen most of the family property but had tried to rule Ellis with an iron rod, had disrupted all his plans and made a fool of him before his friends, and who had ended up by receiving a punch in the jaw from his outraged nephew. He told her of his one good year at college, of his falling in love with Mary Harkness and his following her across the country. He told her of his moodiness (which she already knew) and of his quick temper (which she already knew) and he told her that he was ashamed of his temper and that he recognized that it was a remnant of his childhood, and that most of the time it was unjustified, and that he couldn't promise to get rid of it immediately but that he would keep on trying until he did. He spared himself nothing, and only by reading between the lines was she able to see a young man buffeted and lonely, but eager for friendship and love, with a wealth of devotion to offer, a true humility and a burning desire for truth and honesty above all things.

How different was this blurted, forthright account from the smooth, polished presentation of a Hugo Gearey!

He had stopped talking and now they lay quietly, looking up into the darkness. He had confided all of himself, placed all of his faith in her understanding. And even now he asked nothing, made no demands. Ellis Garner was an amazing young man. She felt that there was much, much more to know about him, but everything that she already knew she could respect. She turned to him.

In the darkness, their arms found each other and their lips met.

This, Barbara thought, was a dream come true. This was what she thought of when she thought of marriage.

Thus, out of the storm, was born their love.

After Barbara and Ellis left, Joe went back to his woodcutting. He worked steadily, almost savagely, but for the first time in days there was no joy in labor. Joe felled and trimmed another tree and immediately attacked the next one. He shook his head doggedly, knowing that he missed Barbara and Ellis but not wanting to admit it to himself. He looked anxiously up when the wind shifted from north to east but he did not recognize the meaning behind its shift. He was uneasy about the clouds. He decided that Barbara and Ellis must be in Laramie. At the same time, he knew that he was merely trying to reassure himself about some peril that he sensed but could not see. They couldn't be in Laramie by this time even if they'd galloped all the way.

Shortly before noon, the wind began to scream and Joe knew. Mounting the mare mule, he held his ax very tightly and drove both mules at a dead run all the way back to the cabin. But before he got there, the snow started.

It fell in grotesque, distorted curtains that were bent and twisted by the howling wind. Joe stabled the mules and fought his way out of the stable toward the store. Flying snow plastered his clothing, and he was a white wraith when he reached the door. Joe entered.

"Jim?"

"Yeah?"

"Can we get down the Trail?"

"No, man! We'd be lost in the snow afore we went twicet and arrer shot."

"But those kids—"

"Don't bust a button," Snedeker advised. "That Ellis Garner, he's nobody's fool. He'll know what to do."

"I'm going anyhow!"

Snedeker walked to the rifle rack, took a rifle from it and

grasped its muzzle with both hands. "Try it an' I'll lay you out with this."

"We can't get through?"

"We can't, an' you got the rest of your family to think about."

"I—"

"Stop fussin'. Even the sojers that went down a while back haven't showed up. They had to den in the snow. No sense throwin' your life away. When the snow stops, I'll go with you. Now git to your cabin an' act like you had some sense."

Joe stumbled through the wind-driven snow and only dimly could he even see the cabin. He opened the door and needed all his strength to close it against the wind. Though it lacked hours until nightfall, Emma had lighted a lantern and her face was white in its glow.

"Joe, the youngsters—"

"They had horses. They'll be in Laramie by this time."

He spoke what he hoped was the truth and knew was not. Emma knew it too but she said nothing. Joe removed his snow-plastered hat and coat and walked to a window. He couldn't even see trees that grew no more than sixty feet away. Joe clenched his fists so hard that nails bit into palms, and his throat was very dry. No human being could fight such a storm, and if Ellis and Barbara were not in Laramie . . .

Tad sat on the floor, busily carving wooden knives for Alfred and Carlyle. Little Joe watched soberly, but when he reached for Tad's knife, Tad drew it away.

Tad said with unaccustomed gentleness, "No, you might cut yourself." He said casually, "Ma, the storm seems to be lettin' up. Bobby an' Ellis will be all right."

Holding baby Emma on her lap, knowing that Tad wanted to reassure her, Emma said wanly, "Yes, dear."

The afternoon was endless, but the night was worse. Joe forced food into his mouth and swallowed. But it was tastless fare; he had ears only for the wind that blasted the cabin and thoughts for nothing except Barbara and Ellis. That night he lay beside Emma, listening while the storm raged. He could not sleep and he knew that Emma was wakeful too. The night was a week long, and Joe started at an alien sound. He sat up in the darkness. Then,

"Joe?" It was Snedeker.

"Yes?"

"Come on. We kin go now."

Joe slipped out of bed and dressed, and Emma stood beside him. She brought his hat and coat, and her eyes held the prayer that she had whispered all night. Joe pressed her hand, and when he opened the door he saw that the snow had stopped. A gray ghost in the darkness, Snedeker stood on snowshoes. There were two more pairs strapped to his back and another leaning against the cabin.

He knelt to lace Joe's snowshoes, and swung down the Trail. Joe followed awkwardly; he had never worn snowshoes and he found them hard to wear. Snedeker dropped back beside him.

"Don't fight 'em," he advised. "Walk on 'em. You'll get the hang of it.'

Joe said grimly, "I'll keep up."

He began to sweat as he strove to keep pace. Snedeker was older than he but Snedeker had worn snowshoes for years. Joe took his hat off and brushed his sweaty face with a gloved hand. He would keep going if it killed him, and judging by the way his legs were beginning to ache it might do just that. Snedeker dropped back to offer him a chunk of meat.

"Pemmican," he said. "It'll stay by a man."

Joe ate and, from the food, he took a new store of strength. He fought his way to within six feet of Snedeker while the sun rose on a heaped and drifted world.

"Did you know the storm was coming?" he called.

"Don't be an idjit, man. Think I'd of let those kids go if I had?"

They went on, and it seemed to Joe that he had walked forever and must continue to walk. It was his curse for letting two young-sters, two who were scarcely more than children, risk their lives in this terrible white hell. But when he looked at his watch he discovered that he had been walking for only four hours. Then they mounted a knoll and Snedeker stopped to point.

At the foot of the knoll, two riderless horses were churning through a drift. Behind them came two people, the leader dressed in a buffalo skin coat and a silver-tasseled hat while the other wore Barbara's heavy brown coat. Forgetting that he did not know how to snowshoe, Joe ran, and he was neck and neck with Snedeker when they reached the pair. The winded, tired horses stopped to rest. Joe leaped into the trench they had broken to fling both arms about his daughter.

"Bobby!"

"Hello, Daddy! Was Mother worried?"

"A mite," Joe admitted. He looked at her weary face and hugged her again. "How did you ride out the storm?"

Ellis said, "We never reached Laramie. The snow caught us close to that cabin under the knoll." Joe remembered the cabin; they'd seen buffalo near it. Ellis finished, "We had to spend the night there."

An iron band tightened around Joe's heart. He gulped and wondered how he would tell this to Emma.

"No fireplace thar," Snedeker asserted. "No wood nuther. How'd you keep warm?"

Ellis said, "We spread buffalo robes on the floor, covered ourselves with others and lay together to keep each other warm." He looked squarely at Joe. "It was the only way."

Their faces were weary. But somehow they were shining and happy and there was only innocence written upon them. Joe's heart sank again. Barbara edged very close to Ellis, took his arm, and laughed.

"We ate the rest of mother's lunch for breakfast, Daddy! Ham sandwiches for breakfast are wonderful if you're hungry enough!"

Joe said sympathetically, "It must have been a terrible night."

"Best night of my life." Ellis smiled with his whole face. "I asked Barbara again and this time she said yes."

"Lordy, lordy," breathed Jim Snedeker.

CHAPTER THIRTEEN

Spring

SPRING WAS heralded by a soft and gentle south wind. It ruffled the pines and stooped to caress the snowbanks. Crusted snow softened and water gathered in every little ditch and depression. Ice melted from Joe's log slide, leaving last year's dead grass brown and forlorn between snowbanks. Walked on all winter, and getting the sun's full force for half a day, the snow in the cabin yard melted and the younger children could play there.

Inside the cabin, the door of which swung open so they could watch the children, Emma and Barbara were mending clothes. A pair of Joe's trousers in her lap, Emma's needle flew as she stitched a patch over a torn knee. She had had some forebodings concerning worn-out clothing and the availability of new cloth, but she needn't have worried. There had been bolts of cloth at Laramie. Even Snedeker had some in stock and he had assured her that most trading posts carried it.

Across the table, Barbara was mending one of Tad's shirts. Emma looked at her daughter and smiled.

"It's almost the last one, isn't it?"

"It is the last."

"Good." Emma breathed her fill of the balmy air that came in a gentle stream through the door. "Isn't this weather wonderful?"

"It's heavenly!" Barbara sighed.

Emma hid a smile. Barbara had walked light-footed and light hearted for most of the winter, and nothing had worn a plain face since the night of the storm. She saw beauty in everything, even the cabin's rough-hewn rafters, and Emma had done nothing to mar her joy. Hurt would come to Barbara as it came to every-one, but hurt, work and struggling were some of the catalysts that fused a marriage. Emma worked busily on.

She was happy for Barbara and Ellis, but she knew that Ellis retained a streak of wildness. That was not extraordinary; no young man worth his salt is contented to plod along like an ox or a cow. Emma had been pretty much satisfied with her son-in-law-to-be since Christmas Eve when she'd talked to him and she felt reasonably sure he'd outgrow his wildness, but she did not discount the possibility that Ellis's temper and impulsiveness might lead him astray, or cause the engagement to be broken before he'd had time to outgrow it. She laid the mended trousers on the table and thrust her threaded needle into her apron front. Barbara finished Tad's shirt and hung it on a peg.

"That's all, Mother."

"We do seem to be caught up." Emma glanced critically at Barbara's mending and found it good. "But let me show you something."

She went to her trunk and from it took three partial bolts of gingham, one blue, one brown and one tan, and unfolded a strip of each one as she laid them on the table.

"What do you think of it?"

Barbara's eyes sparkled. She touched the cloth with gentle fingers and stroked it.

"It's lovely! What are you going to do with it?"

"Housewives need house dresses, darling."

"But, Mother you've several now."

Emma laughed. "It's you I'm thinking of. You didn't suppose I was going to let you come all the way to Oregon to languish in a cabin, did you? I bought this from Lester Tenney two days before we left."

"Mother!" To Barbara every evidence that she would some day actually be married to Ellis had a kind of magic in it, and she touched the cloth again, a benediction. Life was full of the most beautiful promise. Even the small threat that Hugo Gearey might come again to plague her had been dispelled by news of his transfer. The future held no blemish.

Knife on one side of his belt, hatchet on the other, Tad came into the cabin. He looked at Barbara with a smile that was half a leer, and Emma knitted vexed brows. Tad seemed to derive a vast amusement from Barbara's and Ellis's engagement, but what Emma did not know was that, one evening when they thought they were alone, Tad had happened on Ellis kissing his sister. He hadn't made his presence known, he had slipped away as quietly as he came, and he had never told anyone. Why any man should kiss a girl at all was beyond his comprehension. Why Ellis, to whom Tad had looked up but who had since fallen several notches in Tad's estimation, should bother kissing Barbara, was a complete mystery. But it was a hilarious mystery and one that had furnished Tad no end of private amusement.

"Hi," he said.

Emma said, "Tad! How many times must I tell you to wipe the mud from your shoes before you come in?"

"Oh, yeah." Tad looked down at his muddy boots. "Well, I was goin' right out again anyhow."

He scooted out the door and Emma sighed, "That boy can't sit still a minute!"

She went to the door to see where he had gone but he was already out of sight. The younger children, supervised by little Joe, were building a house from stray pieces of wood that they picked up in the yard. Emma looked down to where Joe worked, and for a moment her eyes dwelt warmly on him.

She went back inside to cut the patterns for Barbara's house dresses.

Joe, Ellis and Jim Snedeker, were notching the logs that Joe and Ellis had cut and brought in. An old man, Snedeker was by no means feeble. Though not as active as either Joe or Ellis, he had used an ax for more years than Joe was old and he made up in skill what he lacked in agility. Though Joe was the best ax man of the trio, Snedeker notched almost as many logs as Ellis.

Joe worked willingly, happily, for this was work he liked. But within him was again a mighty restlessness and he kept his face turned to the south wind. Every tiny variation in it became almost a personal issue, for they had set out from Missouri to build a new life in Oregon and nothing must interfere. When the snow melted grass would grow, and the snow would melt if the south wind blew. As soon as there was enough grass they could be on their way.

Near where they were working, a group of quaking aspens, their trunks and branches already colored with spring's green hue, trembled in the wind. A hare hopped among them, crouched at the base of a tree and sat perfectly still. A happy canine grin on his face, ears pricked up, Mike ran through the soggy snow to give chase and the two disappeared. Snedeker rested his ax on a log.

"Wish I'd kep' count of the piddlin' little critters that dog of your'n has took after, Joe. He has done naught else sinst you fetched him here."

"He's been chasing them all the way from Missouri," Joe said. "The darn dog's probably run far enough to get him to Oregon and back six times over. But he hasn't caught anything yet."

"That don't stop his tryin'," Snedeker grunted. "Puts me in mind of a trapper I knowed. He ketched more beaver'n anybody elst, an' when nobody in the hul show could find buffalo, he could. But what he wanted was a white b'ar. The place was thick with 'em, but his medicine wasn't right for white b'ar. Ever'body elst run on 'em, but not Piegan Kelley. Got so he'd rush through his traps, skin out his pelts, an' rush off to find a white b'ar. Finally he found one. B'ar found him the same time. When I come up the b'ar was layin' dead as a stone an' Piegan was almost so. But he was grinnin' like a coyote that just ketched an antelope kid. 'Got my b'ar,' says he to me, 'I can die happy now.' He did, too. That's the way 'twill be with your dog."

The aspen branches rattled more violently. Joe looked toward them. Quaking aspen quivered even when all other trees were still, and Joe had never known why.

"Why do aspens shake, Jim?" he asked.

"They're soft. I figger their branches ain't tight's other trees."

"That isn't the reason at all," Ellis dissented. "The Cross on which Christ was crucified was made of aspen, and since then all aspens have trembled."

"Whar'd you l'arn that?" Snedeker demanded.

"I'm just naturally smart. Besides, I saw it in a book."

"Book l'arnin'," Snedeker pronounced gravely, "don't do nobody no good. Gives 'em fancy ideas in a plain kentry. You ought to tell the missus that, Joe."

Joe grinned. Emma had been teaching Tad and baby Emma the fundamentals of English, arithmetic, and spelling. It had helped her pass the time and, in spite of Snedeker's ideas on the subject, it would help the youngsters too.

"Your freckle-faced young 'un's comin'," Snedeker said.

Mike came racing back to leap on Tad. The dog frolicked around him, wagging his tail furiously. Tad pushed him away and Mike fell in at his master's side. Joe smiled. Mike hadn't earned his keep in Missouri or on the Trail either, but it was a comfort to know that he was there and he was a companion for Tad.

"Can I take the rifle an' go huntin', Pa?" Tad asked.

"It's pretty slushy."

"I'll mind my step."

"Well, go ahead. But don't go too far."

Mike padding beside him, Tad trotted back to get the rifle. Snedeker looked after him.

"Ain't you scair't to let him tote a rifle?" he asked Joe.

"I would have been back in Missouri, but not here. He's learned a lot."

"Likely little sprout," Snedeker asserted. "I mind the time—"

Snedeker was off on a long, rambling story about a young Mexican they'd found in Santa Fe and Joe listened with half an ear. Missouri, somehow, seemed very far off and unreal, as though they'd never lived there except in a dream. Oregon was the only reality, and they had already covered a good part of the Trail. If they started from Snedeker's as soon as travel conditions permitted, they would reach Oregon long before those who started this spring from Independence. There would be plenty of time to find land they liked, build a cabin, and probably to plant some crops.

"—the kid went to Texas," Snedeker finished. "The last I hear about him he's doin' right well for hisself stealin' hosses an' cattle in Mexico an' runnin' 'em over the border. Joe, you ain't payin' me no mind!"

"Oh—Oh yes, I heard you. Jim, when can we expect grass?"

"Emmy-grants," Snedeker grumbled. "They light out for Oregon an' their tail's afire 'til they get thar. Then they spend the rest of their days milkin' fool cows an' steerin' a plow. I don't know why any of you bother to leave Mizoury."

"The ground's softer in Oregon," Joe grinned. "It makes for easier plowing."

"Pah! If the Lord meant men to plow, they'd of been born with a plow in their hands."

"And if He meant them to shoot, I suppose they'd be born with a rifle in their hands?"

"'Tain't the same thing. 'Tain't the same thing at all. Sounds like your young-un's shot at somethin'."

Up on the ridge, the rifle cracked, and its echoes died in the distance. Joe listened for a second shot but heard none. Twenty minutes later Tad appeared, dragging a timber wolf by a rope around its neck while Mike trotted proudly beside him. Tad panted to a halt.

"There was three of 'em!" he gloated. "They was goin' to jump old Mike an' they didn't even see me! The other two cootered off like scared rabbits when I shot this one! Plunked him right in the ear!"

"Was he runnin'?" Snedeker inquired.

"Nah!" Tad said scornfully. "He was just trottin'."

"Did you aim at his ear?"

"Sure. Figgered that'd put him down to stay."

Snedeker said dryly, "Well, don't be shootin' at my ear no matter if I'm walkin' or gallopin'. You'll be a right handy man with a rifle after you've growed a mite."

"You should have hunted something we could eat," Joe said.

"Don't be preachin' thataway," Snedeker protested. "Meat's to be had for the takin', but wolf pelts ain't. Pelt that critter, cure the pelt, an' some Oregon-bound emmy-grant will pay fancy for it."

"Do they buy such things?"

"They spend money for what takes their eye. An' what takes their eye is ever'thing. You could sell 'em a full-sized steamboat if you had one to sell. They couldn't haul it along, an' even if they could they wouldn't know what to do with it in Oregon. But they'd buy it. Young'un, you mind that short rifle in my rack?"

"Yes."

"Want to swap your wolf pelt for it?"

"Gee!" Tad gasped.

"Pelt this critter out an' the rifle's your'n, 'long with the horn an' bullet mold. Bullets you got to mold yourself."

"Oh!" Tad was walking on clouds. "Can I have it, Pa?"

"Mr. Snedeker says so."

"I'll pelt the wolf right away, just as soon as I've looked at the rifle!"

Tad dragged the wolf toward the store. Joe watched him go, then turned to Snedeker.

"No pelt's worth a rifle."

"Not usually it ain't. But any sprout that size who can aim at a trottin' wolf's ear an' hit thar can swap the pelt for a rifle with me any time. It's wuth it."

Joe shook a puzzled head; he'd thought he understood Snedeker thoroughly and found that he did not. However, the old man had conceived a great liking for Tad.

The gentle wind blew all day, turning everything in a sea of slush. The younger children had played outside until nearly evening because their playing ground was reasonably dry, and Emma had been relieved of watching them. She met Joe smilingly, and was gay, when he went in for the evening meal. But not all her high spirits were induced because the children hadn't harried her. Much as she feared the open plains, they seemed less worrisome now, in the bland spring weather, than the everlasting walls of their cabin. All winter long she had been confined in or near the cabin, and now release was in sight. That promise was borne on the warm wind, and in the melting snow. They had come this far and Oregon no longer seemed a great distance away.

"It won't be long before grass grows," Joe assured her.

"I know. I can feel it."

The warm spell continued and every day more snow melted. Here and there, where the sun shone all day long, a patch of bare, wet earth appeared. The aspens sprouted fluffy buds and a flock of northbound geese honked over. Emma's hens, that had been shut in their shed all winter, could go out and scratch in the earth and they began to lay again.

Joe, Ellis and Jim Snedeker, continued to work on Snedeker's new building and Joe knew that the old Mountain Man hoped he would stay until it was completed. He said nothing; Snedeker had always gone where he wished when he wanted to go there and he never asked any man's permission. It went without saying that everybody else had the same freedom of choice and he would not try to hold Joe. But Snedeker was old. He could not erect the building himself and there was no certainty as to when he would find another emigrant willing to trade his labor for money or supplies. Snedeker needed help now.

Because he wanted to help him, and because he found in hard work an anodyne for growing restlessness, Joe drove himself and Ellis furiously. Ellis kept his mouth shut and followed Joe's orders. They laid sills on the site Snedeker had chosen and used skids to roll logs on top of them. When the walls were as high as they must be, the roof was made of poles overlaid and braced with more poles. Joe showed Ellis how to split shakes from a block of cedar. One blow of the ax did it, and though the shakes were not uniform in size they were a better roof than the mixed clay and mud that thatched the other buildings. Snedeker had covered his roofs with the same material he used for chinking.

But, even as he worked, Joe fretted. The fuzzy aspen buds gave way to tiny leaves, and only in places that the sun seldom touched did snow linger in dirty gray patches. A pregnant earth was taut with labor pains and about to give birth to all its fullness.

They worked from daylight to dark, but after they were finished Joe and Emma could not stay in the cabin. The Trail wound past Snedeker's post and disappeared in the west. At the end of the Trail was a dream come true, and every night, hand in hand, they walked down it. In the darkness Joe got to his hands and knees to feel for grass, without which there could be no travel. Only when he had assured himself that there was not yet enough did his soul know any peace.

Joe's impatience mounted and he controlled it only by working furiously on Snedeker's new building. It was to be half again as big as the present store which would become a warehouse for buffalo robes, and Snedeker had made more concessions to comfort. In the post he and Ellis slept on the floor, using buffalo robes as a mattress and more for covering, but here there would be bunks. There was also to be a fireplace in Snedeker's private quarters, and that was a real revolution because never before had he had one. Snedeker and Ellis rose and dressed in their freezing quarters at the post.

A good carpenter himself, Snedeker was working on the roof beside Joe when Joe suddenly threw his hammer to the ground. In the pines a song sparrow was pouring its heart out, and from somewhere an early-arriving sparrow scolded. A covey of small clouds winged across the sky, and Joe sat watching and listening. Snedeker stopped working and looked at him curiously. Joe looked down at the greening grass around the post and followed the Trail with his eyes. He said,

"Just figured something, Jim."

"Yeah?"

"The Trail isn't too soft and my animals are in good shape. They won't need much eating for a while, and in another week the grass will be tall."

"Yep. That's right."

"So we're leaving tomorrow."

"Wait a mite an' there'll be a wagon train through that you can jine up with."

"We came this far alone. We can go the rest of the way."

"Reckon you can. Sort of don't like to see you an' your missus an' all them kids light a shuck from here, though. The place has been right sociable all winter long."

"Since when did you have to have things sociable?"

"Must be gettin' old," Snedeker confessed. "You know Ellis ain't lettin' that girl child of your'n outen his sight? He'll go with you."

Joe looked gravely at the horizon. He had already told Ellis that he was Barbara's father, not her master, and that he had no intention of choosing a husband for her. But he worried greatly about the pair. Young love was a glorious thing, a bright and glittering ride on a rainbow. But all too often young lovers saw only the glitter and the rainbow, and Ellis was still unstable. Joe thought of men he had known, Claude Garson, Thomas Severence, Arnold Pulaski, who had been unable to face the problems marriage brought and had simply walked out on their families. Suppose Ellis married and deserted Barbara? The prairie was an easy place in which to disappear. But all Joe said was,

"I figured he'd go."

Snedeker sighed. "If I liked farmin', which I don't, I'd go too. But I don't guess I'd like it anyhow. Oregon's civilized by this time."

"You can finish the building yourself, can't you?"

"Yeah. 'Tain't naught to do but finish the roof, chink her, an' finish the innards. Ain't no hurry nohow. Injuns won't be down for a spell yet an' emmy-grants will be later. If I lag too far behint I'll get one of 'em to help me. Do you know whar you're goin' in Oregon?"

"No. I'll have to decide after we get there."

"I ain't tellin' you what to do, but if you want real good country whar you can take your pick, thar's some a mite beyond Fort Boise. Preacher named Whitman used to have a mission near thar until he an' ever'body elst in the mission was kilt by Injuns, mebbe a dozen years back. Army post, Camp Axton, not too far away. About half a day west of Axton you'll come to a crick. Clear as a bell she is, an you can't go wrong on account the white stones in the crick. Turn north on the east bank an' you'll come to some medders whar the grass grows high's a pony's head. Emmy-grants haven't liked to stop thar sinst the Whitman massacre, but it's a good place if you've a mind to look at it."

"I might just do that," Joe decided. "How are the Indians now?"

Snedeker shrugged. "Like they allus are. You can get along with 'em if you want to. Just let 'em know your rifle's loaded an' you can shoot it, but don't shoot unless you have to. You, Ellis an' that sharp-shootin' kid of yours won't have too much to trouble your heads about. Besides, thar's goin' to be more emmy-grants findin' them medders an' a settlement will go up thar. If you do like it, an' want to stake out some of them medders, build away from the crick. She can be a real rampagious thing when she gets high."

They climbed down the ladder. Ellis sawing apertures for windows, came out of the building to join them. His eyes sought and found Barbara, who was washing clothes on a bench beside the cabin. A little smile lighted his face, and Joe thought curiously that, when he looked that way, he was not at all like Percy Pearl.

"Tuck your shirt tail in an' hitch up your belt!" Snedeker called. "You're shovin' off in the mornin', so let's get the wagon loaded!"

They started in the early dawn, while a light drizzle dripped from a cloudy sky and wispy tendrils of mist lingered like the dresses of ghosts in every sheltered nook and gully. Barbara remained in the wagon to look after the little ones, and Ellis rode up ahead on King. The hat Barbara had knitted for him planted firmly on his head, Snedeker stood in the doorway of his post and waved good-by. They waved back, and all were light-hearted and gay. Their stay at Snedeker's had been pleasant, but they were going to Oregon and Snedeker would not be lonely for very long. While the lost wagon hit the trail west, other wagons were starting from various points on the Missouri. Snedeker would have company and he would fit in nowhere except here.

They rounded a bend and Snedeker's post was lost to sight. Nobody looked back any more, but only ahead. Ahead lay Oregon.

CHAPTER FOURTEEN

The Mule

THEY HAD been a month on the Trail. Behind them lay a land of startling contrast and grim beauty. They'd forded or ferried rivers and creeks that wound out of fastnesses so remote and silent that they seemed to have no end. Weird formations of vari-colored rocks had formed desolate little wildernesses all by themselves. Cloud-stabbing peaks with snow-whitened summits had loomed in the distance. It was not a gentle country nor was it a place for timid people. But to the hardy of soul and the strong in heart who were able to face the challenges it flung, it was good.

Tad loved it, and Joe responded to it. Emma did not like it. For her it was too vast, too big and too grim, and while she appreciated its beauty she hoped that Oregon would be more soft and gentle. Little Joe frowned while he sought answers to problems which he felt must exist here and the rest of the young children were merely curious. Tired of the day-after-day riding, they wanted little now except to find the end of the journey and to be suitably diverted en route.

Barbara and Ellis, aglow with love for each other, saw the land they were passing through in a sort of happy daze. Each day was marvelous because each day they could be together, but the most imposing scenic view or the most majestic mountain meant less to them than a moon or star-lit evening when they could walk beneath soft light and be away on the magic wings that are granted all young lovers. While they were with those in the wagon they were at the same time apart from them. To each, the most important thing in the world was the other. A word, or a gesture, which in ordinary living would be commonplace, acquired a meaning and a significance all its own. Their private world was a wonderful place which no one else could enter.

They had seen no Indians but they were in Indian country. The mules and the cow were always staked close to the wagon and were never left unwatched. Guard duty was a source of special delight to Tad who always took the first watch in the first couple of hours after nightfall. Mike beside him, the rifle Snedeker had given him clutched firmly in both hands, Tad investigated every small sound that occurred and when there weren't any he invented some. To Tad's great disappointment no Indians had appeared yet, but he hadn't lost hope. Each night, at ten o'clock, Tad went grudgingly to the bed while Joe took over until two. The third watch was Ellis's.

Ellis lay prone in the grass, his head resting on cupped hands and his rifle beside him. Near by, the mules had eaten as much as they wanted and were standing close together. The tethered cow had lain down to chew her cud, and the wagon's stained cover seemed pure white in the night's unreal glow. Ellis's big horse stamped a hoof and switched flies with its tail. Ellis raised his head to look at the horse and settled back to watch the star-studded sky.

It seemed to him that his life had had three phases. The first was his childhood, and he remembered his gay and gentle mother. She had soothed his cut fingers, skinned knees, heartbreaks, all the little tragedies of childhood that are unimportant to almost everyone except a child. Vividly, Ellis remembered riding with her, she on a spirited horse while he bestrode a pony. It had always seemed to him that they could ride forever.

The second, which Ellis thought of as his sterile phase, came after his mother died. His father was affectionate and kind, and in his own way he had been proud of Ellis. But he had been too preoccupied with gambling and his numerous enterprises to give enough attention to his son. Ellis had been grief-stricken when he died, but it was not the complete desolation he had known when his mother passed away.

The years when Uncle George had been in charge of him were the worst of all—Uncle George, the sanctimonious cheat who had come into possession of most of the family fortune, and by methods so legalistic and clever that even Ellis's friends, who wanted to help him, could do nothing. But that was all in the past. Ellis had hated George at the time, but later events had made that hatred seem somehow dim and unimportant.

The third phase, a short one, had centered about Mary Harkness, a vivacious, pretty, intelligent little brunette. Ellis had thrown himself heart and soul at her feet. He knew now that she had never wanted him there and had tried, as politely as possible, to tell him so. But Ellis's whole world had crashed when Mary married another.

Now, Ellis felt, he was entering upon the fourth and most worth-while phase of his life. It seemed to him that, until he met Barbara, he had never known his capacity for feeling. It was almost like living for twenty years without ever having been fully alive. In Barbara lay fruition and in her was the only possible life. Ellis knew, and he was grateful to Mary Harkness because she had helped him now. Ellis knew also that Emma trusted him pretty much, though not entirely, and he had a feeling that Joe trusted him not at all. At the thought of Joe's worried and suspicious eyes watching him, Ellis felt the familiar rage and resentment beginning to surge up in him, and he clamped down hard on it because conquering his temper was the one thing he was determined to do.

Suddenly he sat up and grasped his rifle in both hands. Out of the night had come a sound that should not be. A moment later a shadow moved before him and Ellis's heart leaped.

"Bobby!"

"I couldn't sleep," she said softly. "I came out to see you."

He rose, encircled her slim waist with his arms and kissed her.

Their lips parted but their arms remained about each other while they looked at the stars and for the moment they were the whole world.

Ellis said, "I wish we were in Oregon."

"Why?"

"So I could marry you."

She said dreamily, "I wish we were there too." Then she smiled. "Mother and Daddy were funny about insisting that all of us be settled in Oregon before we could get married."

"Settled, *and* with a roof over our heads," he reminded her. He grinned dryly. "Guess maybe they're still not sure I'm capable of putting up a roof."

"Oh, they think you're capable, all right." She giggled. "I guess they think you might take a fancy to some other girl. You know, an impulse. You've got lots of impulses, Ellis Garner!"

"You're absolutely right," he agreed. "I've got an impulse right now to kiss you twice." He did so. "And to build a big, beautiful home for us and our twenty children." His voice settled into a soft, crooning rhythm. "I'll build a palace for my queen," he promised, "all of pure white marble. But the colors inside will be warm and beautiful, like you. And every day I'll bring you milk and honey, and all the rest of the time I'll be happy just to look at you."

She laughed gently. "Oh no, Ellis. It will be a nice log house, with a big kitchen where I can make the things you like, and every day when you come in from the fields you'll bring me wild flowers. Except in winter, of course. Then you can bring me evergreen branches with bittersweet to trim them so I can always have everything looking just the way you want it to look."

They stood together while the night wore on and dawn came. Ellis turned with a guilty start.

"I shouldn't have kept you up!"

"I *want* to be up. This is more fun than sleeping!"

"You aren't tired?"

"Truly I'm not."

"Do you want to ride ahead this morning?"

"Oh yes!"

Hand in hand they walked back to the wagon. Ellis built a fire and heated water. Coming from the wagon, Joe stretched and went to look at the mules. A moment later, Emma had a gentle greeting and a caressing look for the two young people. They sat side by side and ate breakfast. Then Ellis saddled his horse and both mounted.

This was part of their ritual, something they did every day, and they told themselves that they were scouting the trail. But in reality, the wagon was slow and the horse was fast. He provided the wings which their fancies created for them. Barbara, no more than a feather's weight, encircled Ellis's waist and they were off. They would ride perhaps four or five miles, then walk together, leading the horse, until the wagon caught up with them. But this morning they were scarcely out of sight of the wagon when they saw them.

They were coming up the Trail, a dozen men mounted on tough, wiry little horses, and Ellis needed no second glance to know that they were Indians. He clenched his long rifle and whispered,

"See them?"

"I see them," she whispered back.

They were walking their horses, but when they saw Ellis and Barbara they broke into a trot. Barbara's arms tightened about him, and Ellis said gently,

"Don't be afraid."

She shivered. "They—they're coming."

"But they can't catch us."

He wheeled his big horse and let him thunder back the way they had come. Barbara's fear ebbed. Ellis, she told herself, would know what to do. He always knew. They came in sight of the wagon and Joe stopped the mules. Ellis reined alongside.

"Indians," he said quickly. "We'd better be ready."

Tad, who had wanted an Indian fight but who was now shaken at the prospect of one, leaned against the wagon wheel with his rifle in his hands. He stopped shaking and looked to the priming of his rifle while his jaw set grimly. Joe sat on the seat, his rifle ready. Ellis and Barbara remained on King. Just before the Indians came, Ellis spoke sharply and with authority. "We're outnumbered, Joe. We don't want a fight. We won't raise a gun unless they do—and then we'll shoot to kill. But remember, and you too, Tad! Don't raise your gun unless I say so."

The Indians came.

They stopped about twenty feet away, twelve grim men whose garb and coloration revealed that they were Indians and whose faces revealed nothing. Two had rifles, the rest bows and arrows. They were looking at the mules, the horse, the wagon and Barbara. As though he never had thought that he could be stopped, as though nothing could stop him, a brave on a black pony rode up to Ellis. But he ignored Ellis and examined Barbara gravely. Joe's hand clenched over his rifle stock, waiting for a signal from Ellis. Ellis made no sound.

The Indian lifted his hand as though to touch Barbara's hair. Tad froze and nearly cried out. Joe leaned tensely forward, the lining of his throat dry.

Still there was no sound or movement from Ellis.

The Indian's hand touched Barbara's hair. She did not flinch. With his hand still on her hair, the Indian now turned to look full into Ellis's eyes. It was a long look, silent, mysterious and compelling, and Ellis returned it without moving, without blinking. The silence was intense, and through it the only sound was the quick, harsh breathing of Emma inside the wagon, clutching baby Carlyle to her breast. Barbara gritted her teeth and thought that in one more instant she would scream.

The Indian's hand stroked her hair gently, as though the feel of it was something strange and wonderful. Then his hand fell away. He reined his horse around and, without a sound and without a change of expression, the twelve men turned and galloped back the way they had come.

Still encircling Ellis, Barbara's arms went limp. Joe sat silently on the wagon seat, not yet fully comprehending what had happened because it had happened too fast to permit full comprehension. But this much he knew. Ellis, the hot-tempered one, the impulsive one, had showed the greatest nerve and steadiness of them all. Ellis had saved them from a bloody and losing battle. Tad, too, recognized this. His eyes, fixed on Ellis, were adoring and would forever adore.

Tad looked at his sister, the luckiest of all girls.

The sun was warm and good on the wagon cover, and green grass that had not yet reached the fullness of its maturity grew in and on both sides of the Oregon Trail. It was grazed a little but not heavily, for the few travelers they'd met had been coming east from Oregon. There were Mountain Men with sometimes only the horse they rode, the clothes they wore, and the rifle they carried. Others had from two to as many as thirty pack animals, loaded either with furs or with goods that they were taking to Fort Boise. But the Oregon Trail, probably the longest, widest, and most heavily traveled in the history of the world, had not yet known the great press of traffic that it would know as soon as land-hungry emigrants reached this place. That would be months; the fastest-traveling wagons wouldn't get here until the last part of August or the first part of September.

Ellis and Barbara, on Ellis's horse, had gone down the Trail together. Carrying his short rifle proudly, Tad walked beside the wagon and Mike padded at his heels. The back flaps were open to allow free passage of air and the youngsters crowded at the back, looking out. They were in Oregon, the Promised Land, and they remained so interested that they played their games only at sporadic intervals. Sitting beside Joe, Emma had taken off her bonnet and a soft wind played with her silky hair. Emma knew a great peace and a quiet happiness. For almost a year they had been homeless wanderers and now, soon, they were once again to have a home.

"Look at the land here!" Joe gloated. "Look at the grass! A man wouldn't have to be much of a farmer to grow crops in land like that!"

"I love it, Joe!"

"So do I!"

Joe drew a long breath. He had his ax, his rifle and his tools. The mules were his and so was the cow. Everything a man could possibly need was at hand, but it was different because complete freedom was present here too. The next time Joe plowed a field he would be plowing it for himself and not for Elias Dorrance. Joe slapped the reins over the mules' rumps to make them walk a little faster. Then he eased all rein pressure while a little fright rose within him.

Both mules had started out briskly that morning, and he had given them only cursory attention, but now he saw that the mare mule was walking with her head down and ears drooping. She was unsteady on her feet, and when Joe slapped the reins she swayed from side to side. Emma saw it too, and the alarm she felt was plain in her voice,

"What's the matter?"

"I don't know."

The team halted as soon as he spoke, and the horse mule turned a questioning head toward his mate. He sniffed softly at the mare, and Joe hopped from the wagon seat to walk to the head of the team. The horse regarded him anxiously, but the mare stood tiredly in harness with her nose almost touching the Trail. Gently, Joe took hold of their bridles and led them into grass. The mare gasped for breath.

"She's sick!" Joe said. "We'll have to stop!"

Tad came over. His rifle, that had not been out of his sight since he'd owned it, hung in the crook of his arm and concern was written on his face.

"What's wrong, Pa?"

"I don't know."

As gently as possible he unhitched the team, and stripped their harnesses off. The horse mule he picketed, but the mare was left unhampered. She walked a few uncertain steps and halted. The horse followed anxiously, and stood very close to her. He moved aside when Joe came in for a closer examination. Soothing the sick beast with his voice, he lifted her flabby lips and looked inside her mouth. Her tongue was hot, her breath foul.

Joe stepped back. He had considered himself familiar with mules and the diseases of mules, but he was not familiar with this. It must be something peculiar to western country; maybe last night or this morning the mule had eaten something that poisoned her. Or perhaps it was the result of some poisonous insect's bite. It was not snake poison; Joe was familiar with snake-struck mules and he knew that, if they were rested, they would recover. He filled a bucket at the water barrel and held it under the mare's muzzle, but she took only a few sips and staggered away. The children watched concernedly and Emma asked,

"Is she going to die, Joe?"

Suddenly the distances again seemed vast and the Trail forlorn. For the first time Joe realized completely just how dependent they were upon the mules and how lost they would be without them. A broken wagon might be repaired, but one mule couldn't pull it. Joe turned to the medicine he carried in his tool chest and he shook the brown bottle. But even as he did so he felt the hopelessness of it. This was Missouri medicine and the mule had an Oregon ailment. Tad called,

"She's down!"

Joe turned to see the mule fallen in the grass and making a valiant effort to hold her head up. But even as he looked her head lowered, so that she lay prostrate, and the heavy rasp of her labored breathing was terrible to hear. Breath rattled in her throat and there were a few short gasps. Then silence. The horse mule raised his head and tail and delivered an ear-splitting bray. Very gently, walking slowly, the horse went to his dead mate and touched her with his muzzle.

Emma looked to Joe, and she saddened, because more than at any time during the entire trip, Joe now looked distraught and worried. She knew that these were not the rich, flat, well-watered meadows that Snedeker had talked about. They must travel farther, and to be forced to stop now, and thus lose precious plowing and planting days for the first season's crop, was a bitter disappointment. They were more helpless, actually, than they had been at any time before for how, in this vast uninhabited wilderness, did a person go about buying a mule? Joe squared his shoulders and tried to conceal his own worry. They could not stay here but, obviously, neither could they go on.

"Ellis will be back soon," he said. "We'll hitch his horse with the other mule."

The horse mule lingered near his dead mate, looking fixedly at her, and Joe turned away. For seven years the team had worked together in harness. They knew each other as no man can hope to know a mule, and mules are sensitive. The horse knew what had happened and there was none to share his grief. Emma said pityingly,

"Poor beast, poor faithful beast."

Joe muttered, "I wish Ellis would come."

But another hour passed before Ellis and Barbara came riding back up the trail down which they had ventured so happily. Ellis drew the horse to a walk and the laughter that had been his faded.

Joe saw quick hurt flood Barbara's face and tears glisten in her eyes. She slid from the horse and stood for a moment looking at the dead mule. Then she disappeared around the wagon. Even while his heart went out to her, Joe knew misgivings. Barbara had never been able to see anything she liked hurt, but this was a new country where some things were bound to get hurt. How many more hurts would she have in the west?

"Lost a mule." Joe could not keep the worry from his voice. "I don't really know what happened. Let's hitch your horse in with the other one and get out of here."

"Right."

Ellis slid from his horse and unsaddled him. The horse stood quivering, a little afraid, when Joe approached with the mare mule's harness. He was a saddle mount and had never worn a harness, but he had complete faith in Ellis. The horse pushed a trusting muzzle against his master while Joe adjusted the harness to fit. Joe said,

"Bring him over."

Joe leaped just in time to avoid the mule's lunge, and the bridle was jerked from his hand. The animal went berserk. His ears were back. Eyes blazed and his awful mule's mouth was savagely open as he leaped at the horse. Coming to the end of his picket rope, he was brought up short and reared to paw the air with furious hoofs while he squealed his rage.

The horse was plunging too, dragging Ellis as he sought to avoid the fury coming at him. He snorted and reared, and allowed himself to be halted only when a hundred yards separated him from the enraged mule. The horse rolled his eyes and shivered. He eyed the mule, ready to run again should it come again. But once the horse was chased to a safe distance the mule merely returned to his dead mate and stood quietly near her. He did not resent Joe's presence and he made no protest when Joe stroked him softly. But the horse could not come near.

Joe said, "We'll have to get another mule."

"Do you think he'll work with one?"

"He won't work with the horse."

"I'll get a mule," Ellis said.

"Where?"

Ellis set his jaw. "Ride down the Trail until I find one."

He took the mare mule's harness from his horse and put the saddle back on. Barbara came from behind the wagon and Joe looked wonderingly at her. There had been tears, but there weren't any now. She walked straight, her shoulders braced as Tad braced his. Joe had a curious feeling that he no longer knew this lovely youngster. She had left Missouri a young girl; now she was a young

woman. Joe knew suddenly that she would never again throw herself, sobbing, into his arms. She had learned to cope with her own
fears and heartbreaks. There was a touch of almost wifely solici-
tude in her voice.

"You be careful, Ellis."

"Don't you be worrying about me."

"Here." Joe took out his wallet. "You'll need money."

I've got some."

He kissed Barbara, mounted, and set off down the Trail.

Joe watched him go, and as the young figure sitting jauntily
astride his horse disappeared over the horizon Joe knew a twinge
of apprehension. If Ellis found a mule pretty soon, he'd likely bring
it back. But if he had to go very far, and a mule was too hard to
find, and if he came upon some other traveling family in which
there was a pretty girl and he received a warm invitation or a
good offer—No, no, Joe told himself. Ridiculous. Ellis was made
of better stuff than that. And then, in order to reassure himself, he
turned to Barbara and said, 'He'll be back, Bobby."

Her voice was calm. "Of course he'll be back. And he'll bring a
mule."

Joe turned away. Bobby's love and faith shamed him but frightened him, too. If anything went wrong between Ellis and Barbara
—but nothing could go wrong. Nothing would dare to go wrong.
He felt himself fully capable of wringing Ellis's neck if he were to
cause Bobby any unhappiness, and at the same time he recognized
that wringing Ellis's neck was not likely to insure Barbara's happiness.

Joe set himself to the tasks in hand. "I'll get firewood," he said.

Their meal was a silent and listness one, for the loss of the mare
was deeply felt. For endless miles she had been one of their party,
and now she was no more. She had helped pull the wagon all this
way, but she would not share the home they were to have at the
end of the Trail.

Darkness fell. Emma and the children sought their beds in the
wagon. But Joe was restless and he had no wish to sleep. He stood

under the star-dappled sky and let the soft spring wind caress his cheek. The wind whispered to him and the earth seemed to pulse around him. There were no other sounds save the cow moving about and the occasional shuffle of the horse mule's hoofs. He still stood watch over his dead mate and Joe felt sorry for him. But such things did happen and there was nothing anyone could do about them. People had to weather their own misfortune and prove stronger than ill luck, because if they did not they were lost. Mules, Joe supposed, must do the same.

He sat on the wagon tongue feeling himself in tune with this new land that he had decided to call home, and knowing it for a good land. Mike padded up to crouch beside him, and Joe reached out in the starlit night to pet the dog.

There came the sound of hoofs from down the Trail and Joe reached inside the wagon for his rifle. He stood quietly, the rifle ready, and waited for Mike to bristle or challenge. But the dog remained quiet and Joe relaxed. An enemy would not approach openly. He heard Ellis's,

"It's me."

He came slowly on his horse, and by the light of the stars Joe saw that he was leading a black mule. The horse mule called softly, walked to the end of his rope, and stared. The mule knew what was coming and he would welcome one of his own kind where he would not tolerate a horse.

Joe said, "You got one, huh?"

"I got one."

"Where'd you get him?"

"Stole him," Ellis replied tersely.

Joe stood rooted in his tracks. Ellis's statement hit him like a thunderbolt. He licked dry lips.

"That's right," Ellis said. "A couple of trappers have about forty mules in a corral up the trail. When I asked them to sell me one they didn't seem interested. I waited until nightfall and took one." He fixed Joe with a tired and angry glare. "Any complaints?"

Joe's jaw worked. The boy's headstrong action, and the cool way he told about it, frightened Joe anew. What other willful and dishonest actions was he capable of? What was his Bobby getting into?

He tried to control himself. "You shouldn't have done that, Ellis."

Ellis squared around to face him. "I expected you to say exactly that," he muttered. "Just how did you expect us to move on without another mule?"

Joe had no immediate answer. He stood quiet, staring unhappily into Ellis's sullen face. "We'll take him back," he said.

"If that's the way you want it," Ellis said.

In the darkness, Joe walked to the black mule and laid a hand on his powerful neck. The mule smelled him over and nibbled Joe's arm with his lips. Ellis had brought no bronco, but a harness-broken mule. Joe tied a rope to his halter and picketed him in the grass. The horse did not protest when he was led away from the mare and picketed near.

Joe said shortly, "Better turn in, Ellis."

"All right."

Ellis spread his bedroll beside the wagon while Joe sought his bed inside. It was true that they had to have a mule and, in Ellis's place, he didn't know what he might have done. He supposed he'd have continued on farther until he could buy a mule, even if it took another day or two. But it wasn't only the stealing of the mule—it was Ellis's calm way of reporting it that shocked him. The calm way, he knew, was a cover-up for real anger. But why the anger? The whole thing worried him and it was some time before he could fall asleep. When he awakened the soft light of early dawn had found its way into the wagon. Joe lay quietly for a few minutes. They must return the stolen mule, or else arrange to pay for it, but they might as well hitch both and drive down to the trappers' corral. Joe climbed out the rear of the wagon and made his way to the front.

He heard the crack of the rifle, and felt the bullet smack into the ground at his feet. Shocked with surprise, Joe stood still and for a

moment his mind was incapable of directing his body. Still half
asleep, Ellis sat up in his bedroll. There came a voice.

"Don't neither of ye move thar! Stand right still thar!"

They came from behind a huge boulder whose arched back
lifted from the earth about sixty yards away. They were two men
dressed in greasy buckskin and with long black hair brushing their
shoulders. The man who had shot carried a rifle in the crook of
his arm but there was a pistol in his hand. They advanced pur-
posefully, menacingly, and the morning wind ruffled their shaggy
hair.

"Move," the smaller one said, "an' I'll drill ye clean. Bring him
up, Pete."

Holstering his revolver, the tall man untethered the black mule
and brought him up to the wagon. Joe had a glance for the mule, a
powerful beast that had not yet shed his long winter hair. The
brisk wind played with it, laying it back along the black mule's
flank and ribs. The smaller man looked at Joe's horse mule.

"Mought's well have 'em both. Git that one too."

"Now wait a minute—" Joe began.

"Don't 'wait a minute' me. My finger's right oneasy on this trigger an' I'd just as soon shoot a mule rustler."

"We were going to bring him back."

The smaller man laughed jeeringly and another rifle cracked as
Tad shot from behind the wagon. There was a sodden "splat" as
the bullet struck the muzzle of the rifle covering Joe and Ellis. It
snapped out of the short man's hands, dropped to the ground, and
as it did the black mule began to rear. The man holding him
reached frantically for his revolver, but he needed both hands on
the rope. Ellis dived to his bedroll and rose to a kneeling position
with his own rifle.

"Suppose," he said almost pleasantly, "that you two take a turn
at not moving! I can shoot, too."

Rage overspread the smaller man's face. The mule quieted, and
the man holding him tried to slip beside him. But Joe had his
rifle and Tad was reloading.

Joe said quietly, "Get the mule, Ellis."

Ellis walked up to take the black mule. He led him aside, and Joe remained quiet.

"You two drop your guns."

They let their firearms fall to the ground. Joe ordered, "Now get out. You can pick up your guns after we leave. But if we see either of you again, we'll shoot to kill."

They strode back toward where they'd left whatever mounts they'd ridden here. Pale and shaken, Emma got out of the wagon to stand beside Joe.

"Joe, those men will give us trouble!"

Ellis, standing beside the black mule, spoke to Joe. "How come you didn't give them back their mule?"

"Because it isn't their mule," Joe said. "Those men are rustlers. All they'll do is hightail it back to wherever they left their other stolen stock and get out of the country."

"Exactly," said Ellis. With his hand he parted the hair on the mule's side, revealing a brand. "This is an army mule. It can be returned when we get to Camp Axton, which is probably where it was stolen in the first place."

Joe stared at him in astonishment. "You knew this all the time?"

"I know the army brand when I see it," Ellis said.

"Then why in tarnation didn't you tell me!"

Ellis gave him a straight look. "Because I knew you would put the worst possible interpretation on anything I did. I knew if I stole a mule, you'd be ready to blast out at me before I had a chance to explain." He clenched his teeth. "So I didn't feel like hurrying to explain."

Joe was flustered. "Too proud to explain, is that it?" he said. "By not explaining, you hoped to make a fool of me, is that it?"

Ellis ignored the accusation. "The way I figured," he said, "this mule will take us to Axton, and once we're there we stand a better chance to buy a mule than we do out here in the middle of the prairie."

"Very true," said Joe. Ellis and Joe exchanged a long, silent look, in which Ellis accused Joe of judging him too hastily and Joe accused Ellis of making a fool of him by not explaining.

Bobby went to stand at Ellis's side. Her movement was a shock to Joe. It made him question himself. Was he looking for trouble with Ellis, perhaps more than he had any need to?

Joe swallowed his pride. "I been doing too much judging, Ellis," he said. "And I'm sorry."

Ellis grinned. "Forget it," he said. "When I get mad, I get ornery. I got plenty of work to do on my temper."

CHAPTER FIFTEEN

The Meadows

THE BLACK mule was a big, powerful animal and a willing worker. Like all mules, he had his own ideas and regardless of what the driver liked he would put them into effect if an opportunity presented. For the most part he was tractable, though Joe knew enough about mules to know that any of them would kick unexpectedly and he watched himself when hitching or unhitching. In addition, the black fitted in perfectly with the other horse mule. He lacked the horse's rugged character and was willing to follow his lead. He was an ideal replacement for the dead mare.

Nevertheless, Joe worried a great deal about the mule. It belonged to the army, and they must go to Camp Axton to return it. Joe had a hunch the army would take a dim view of anyone found with one of their mules. Likely they'd be able to convince the commandant that they were not themselves mule thieves. The real problem, though, was that the army was always on the lookout for more mules, but didn't sell any.

He confided his worries to Ellis one night after the children were asleep and Barbara and Emma were washing dishes by the fire's leaping light.

"First off," he said, "it's going to take them some time while they investigate us to make sure we're not rustlers. Then it's going to take some more time until someone else comes through that can sell us a mule. And meanwhile the best plowing and planting time is getting away from us every day that we wait."

"They'll sell us an army mule," Ellis said, with the bland optimism of youth.

"Not a chance," said Joe glumly. "Those army men are only interested in one thing—regulations."

"Just the same," said Ellis, "we can explain to them about plowing and planting time. Obviously we can't make a crop if we can't reach our land on time. Even an Army man can understand that."

"Army regulations," said Joe, "do not concern themselves with the planting time of strangers."

Ellis chuckled. "Army men can be human, like anybody else." He smiled softly, because Barbara had just slipped over into the circle of his arm. "I'm for looking on the bright side of things," he insisted.

"Naturally," Joe grinned. He left them and walked over to the wagon. By the fire's light he examined the plow. Joe ran his fingers over the implement, and in his soul felt a vast longing to take it off and use it. A plow meant to him what a rifle meant to Jim Snedeker. It was part of his life, a tool he had been born to use. Joe left the wagon and sat on a block of firewood very close to Emma. Emma's face was upturned to the sky, and she breathed deeply of the fragrant prairie breeze. Joe's hand stole out to hers, and she turned eagerly to him.

"It's like being born again, isn't it?"

"Are you glad we came, darling?"

"Oh, yes I am! Now I am! Lots of times along the way I had regrets. And then, I was cowardly at the beginning."

"Cautious," Joe corrected.

"No, *cowardly*," insisted Emma. "Afraid to take a chance on anything. We took such a big chance, starting so late, with all the children. But Joe! I wouldn't undo it, not a single moment of it, not even the moments when I was miserable and angry and scared half to death! It's taught me so much about—about what courage can do." She turned to him. "I want to say something from the bottom of my heart, darling. I wouldn't have come if you hadn't *made* me come. And now, Joe, I want to thank you for making me come. Thank you, Joe." Her eyes were swimming. He laughed deep in his chest and blotted up her happy tears tenderly with the corner of her own kerchief.

"You weren't the only one who was scared half to death," he said simply. "I had a lot to learn about courage, too."

She put her head down on his shoulder and he drew her close. They sat, in harmony, watching the dying fire and making plans. Not far away sat Barbara and Ellis, clinging together, making their own plans, thinking ahead to their own home and their own children.

Inside the wagon, baby Emma cried out and they heard her turning restlessly in her sleep. The child cried again, and alarm mounted in Joe. He loosed Emma's hand and turned to listen. Emma spoke softly,

"She's been very fretful since noon, and didn't you notice that she ate very little?"

"No," and somehow Joe felt a great shame because of the admission. "I didn't. Is it the same fever?"

"Not yet, but I'm afraid it will be."

'It always came on in a snap of the fingers before."

"I know. But this is a little different."

They sat silently, the happiness they had known tempered by melancholy. Oregon was a bright, shining promise, a new land where they could build a new life and leave the withered husks of the old one behind. So far it had given something to Barbara, something to Tad, and it would have something for Joe and Emma and the other three children. Of them all, only a wisp of a child must still bear the same cross she had borne in Missouri. Joe shivered. This was a good country but it was also one where violence could reign. He said with a confidence that he did not feel,

"I don't believe it's anything much."

"I hope not!"

But the next morning, when Joe got up and peered behind the curtain, Emma sat with her back braced against the trunk, holding the child in her arms. Baby Emma's cheeks were blazing, her eyes dull and listless. She looked at her father, but the smile that usually flashed across her whole face when she greeted him in the morning was absent now.

Joe turned away from the wagon and built a fire so Barbara could prepare breakfast. A mighty weariness rode his shoulders, and a great despondency. He ate without tasting the breakfast Barbara made, and helped her wash the dishes. Ellis stood helplessly near, without the least idea of what must be done in a situation such as this one. Only a woman's wisdom and tenderness could cope with it. Ellis saddled his horse, glad to be doing something.

"I'll go down the Trail a ways and scout what's ahead."

He looked wistfully at Barbara, but she shook her head. Her mother, busy with a sick child, would have time for nothing else. She must have as much peace as it was possible to find inside the cramped wagon, so Barbara would watch the other three youngsters. Ellis must ride alone today. She watched him ride his horse down the Trail.

Joe harnessed the mules, hitched them, and climbed into the wagon seat. It was lonely, forlorn, because Emma was not beside him. For the first time in days the Trail was a tedious one, utterly lacking in inspiration and joy. Joe drove the mules at a fast walk. Two hours later Ellis rode back up the Trail and reined in beside the wagon.

"The camp's ahead," he called. "I told them you were coming."

"What did they say?"

"We're to see the commander, Major Dismuke."

The camp was built on top of a hill, probably for better defense, and the timber around it had been cleared. Primitive compared to Laramie's splendor, Camp Axton consisted of log buildings and a log stockade. There were a few tents, probably erected by recently arrived troops because the camp itself did not have accommodations for them. But the flag waved proudly and the sentry at the gate was very brisk and military. He stood aside to let them enter.

For a moment, Joe wished mightily that Sergeant Dunbar could be here. Dunbar, who knew the army, would probably know how to cut any red tape that might be involved and certainly he'd know just what to do. But Dunbar wasn't here and Joe had to do the best he could. He drove to a single big pine that had been allowed to stand inside the stockade and brought his team to a halt in its shade. He tied them to an iron ring imbedded in the tree for that purpose, and looked back at Emma. Her face was taut with anxiety.

"She's very warm, Joe. I'll stay with her. Barbara can let the youngsters out to stretch their legs."

"Keep them near the wagon, will you?" Joe addressed his daughter. "We'll be back as soon as possible."

"Yes, Daddy."

Joe turned to confront a trim young sergeant. "Mr. Tower?"

"That's right."

"This way, sir."

He led Joe to one of the log buildings and stood aside to let him enter. With a disarming grin, Ellis entered too. Joe looked at the man who sat behind the desk.

Major Dismuke was perhaps forty-five, and his was the bearing that only a lifetime of soldiering can impart. His hair was short, graying at the temples, and it surmounted a face that seemed chiseled out of solid granite. Cool eyes appraised Joe and Ellis, but never for a second was there any departure from military briskness or any indication that the taut mouth could smile. Major Dismuke was a good and efficient officer but he was also a stern one. He knew all the regulations by heart and he enforced them as they were written.

"Mr. Tower?"

"Yes."

Major Dismuke leaned forward on the desk and rested his chin lightly in his right hand. "You have an army mule in your possession?"

"Guess you're right."

"You guess? Don't you know?"

"We have one."

"Where did you get it?"

"From a couple of trappers."

"*Where* did you get it?"

"Maybe sixty miles down the Trail."

"Describe the trappers."

Briefly Joe described the two men while the officer listened. He looked searchingly at Joe.

"Did you know, when you received this animal, that it was army property?"

"Yes."

"Did you know also that the army isn't selling any mules?"

"I did."

"Therefore you knew that this one was stolen from the army?"

"I had that idea."

"Why did you take the mule?"

Joe's anger flared. "Blast it, man! I lost a mule and had to have another! What did you think we'd do? Sit there?"

"Control your temper, Mr. Tower. If you knew these two men were thieves, why did you not take them into custody?"

"It was none of my business. I'm no law officer."

"Do you have proof that what you've said is true?"

"I have my word, Ellis's here, my wife's, my daughter's, and my oldest son's."

"Do you realize, Mr. Tower, that we shall have to take the mule and detain you until we have investigated?"

"You can have the mule!" Joe roared. "But nobody's detaining us! We're going on as soon as we can get another!"

"I've already advised you to control your temper. Do you have this animal with you?"

"Yes."

"We'll look at it."

He rose and walked past them. Ellis and Joe fell in behind as he strode toward the wagon. Ellis nudged Joe with his elbow. "Joe Tower," he said solemnly, "your explosions of temper are going to get us all into trouble."

Joe turned angrily to him and then, at the quizzical set of the boy's eyebrows, Joe grinned.

"Let me handle this," Ellis pleaded. "You can argue with a human being, but that man is no human being. He's a bundle of army regulations. Let me try, Joe." And then, before Joe could say yes or no, he called out, "There's a sick youngster in that wagon and you're not to bother her or her mother."

Major Dismuke halted. "What's the matter with the child?"

Joe was about to explain when Ellis took over. "It isn't smallpox" he said vehemently. "Don't get the idea that it's smallpox because it isn't!"

Major Dismuke whirled on Joe. "Did you bring a case of smallpox here?"

"I just told you it isn't!" Ellis remained vehement. "But if you're going to detain us we'd like to move her to the hospital, and get quarters for ourselves, until the youngster can travel."

Joe said bewilderedly, "Ellis—"

"I'm just telling him it isn't smallpox," Ellis asserted. "You know that yourself."

For the first time, Major Dismuke was uncertain. As every rightthinking soldier knew, regulations covered every situation connected with the Army. But these were civilians, they might have a case of smallpox with them, and he had no facilities to cope with a possible epidemic. For a long moment he was completely nonplussed. He said finally,

"This is a United States army post, and it exists for the convenience and benefit of United States citizens. It is our duty to offer you such facilities as we afford. On the other hand, if you want to go on, I shall neither detain you nor confiscate the mule. The choice is yours."

"Do you mean to tell me," Ellis demanded righteously, "that you will not offer hospitalization to this sick child?"

Major Dismuke's nervousness became clearly visible. "Gentlemen," he said, "I beg you to take the mule and leave camp."

"Well," said Ellis, with a fine show of reluctance, "of course if you insist . . ."

"I will be grateful," said the major.

"Well, in that case," said Ellis.

Joe looked from one to the other in honest amazement. Never had he seen a ticklish situation so quickly resolved.

But what about payment? "Look here, Major," he said, "if you'll just tell me how much you want for this—"

"The Army doesn't sell mules," Major Dismuke barked.

"Regulations," said Ellis politely.

The major threw him a sharp look. Then he added some hasty advice.

"It is my duty to advise you that the Indians in this section are restless. If you go on, you risk meeting hostiles."

"We'll still go on," said Ellis.

Major Dismuke halted and when they had drawn away from him Ellis said softly, "Sorry, Joe, but we have to get out of here."

"Yes, we have to get out."

"It wasn't really a lie."

"Ellis, let's face it. It was a lie. But we had to tell it. As soon as we get set, we're sending that mule back."

"All right with me. But let's get set."

The youngsters scrambled back into the wagon. Joe untied the team and climbed up on the wagon seat. He was not happy, for the baby was still feverish, but he was relieved. Emma wouldn't care to stay anywhere near this fort as long as the baby was ill. It was too rough, and the wagon was better. Somehow and somewhere Joe would get another mule and send this one back. He shook his head. Ellis's quick wit in raising the smallpox scare had averted what would have been an intolerable situation.

They stopped for lunch, and drove on. Ellis rode ahead to scout and Joe's sick heart throbbed when the baby babbled in delirium. A few minutes later, Emma spoke softly,

"Joe, we must stop. She's very bad."

He was about to swing the mules to one side of the Trail when Ellis rode back. Ellis swung his horse in beside the wagon and looked up at Joe.

"How is the youngster?"

"Emma says bad. We have to stop."

"There's a good creek about a quarter mile ahead and a meadow only a little ways up the creek. It's a better place than this if we're going to camp."

"Hear that, Emma?" Joe called. "Want to go there?"

She said, "I think it will be better. There'll be no interruptions if we're off the Trail."

The mules plodded down the Trail to the creek. Sparkling, clear and cold, it trickled out of a shallow little gully and flowed across the Trail to lose itself in trees on the other side. The west bank was tree-lined, but tall grass grew on the east bank and laid a soft carpet back to the line of trees. Joe saw trout lingering in a pool.

Ellis swung his horse from the Trail up a grassy embankment. "Follow me," he called. "The wagon can get up here."

The mules walked unhesitatingly after him, and Joe held them to a slow walk in order that the wagon might take gently any hidden obstructions. Tall wild grass brushed the bellies of the mules and of Ellis's horse. A cool and gentle breeze breathed down the creek, and ruffled the slender tops of trees on the west side. The wagon listed a little, and there came the rattle of a falling bucket.

As they proceeded upstream, the meadow widened and the trees on the west bank gave way to grass. Save for one towering pine that grew halfway between the creek and the forest on top of the gently sloping hill, as far as Joe could see there was only meadow land. Three nervous cow elk, probably with calves hidden somewhere back in the forest, edged cautiously out of sight. Joe guided his team to the big pine's shade and stopped. He turned to Emma.

He unhitched and picketed the mules while Tad tied a picket rope to the cow and staked her in tall grass. Used to traveling, and accustomed to grazing different grounds every night, all three animals fell to cropping grass. Though the Oregon Trail was only a few hundred yards to the south, for centuries these meadows had been the haunt of wild things. Probably an occasional horseman had ventured here, but as far as Joe knew theirs was the first wagon that had ever come up the creek. He took a moment to look around, and breathed deeply of the pine-scented air. Jim Snedeker had known what he was talking about when he spoke of nice country.

Ellis swung Emma's crate of poultry to the ground and opened the gate. The rooster jumped to the top of the crate, flapped his wings, and crowed lustily. Four of the hens scurried here and there in the grass, catching bugs and picking up fallen seed. The other two, wings spread, clucked fussily and avoided the rest. Those two were broody and had been for more than a week. Even confinement in the crate and traveling all day was not enough to make them forget age-old instincts. One of them stalked secretively into the grass, searching for a place to nest.

Joe took his snath from the place where it had lain since they left Missouri and fitted a scythe to it. He tested the blade with his thumb, and through the coating of grease that covered it and prevented its rusting he felt its keenness. With a hand full of grass he wiped the scythe clean and went to work.

Strength flowed into his arms, and in spite of the pall that overhung all of them he felt a little song spring into his heart as he mowed the first swath of grass. There had been times when he wondered seriously if the long Trail would not make him forget all he had known about farming, but he fell automatically into the rhythm of what he was doing. The scythe ceased to be a mere tool and became a part of him as grass toppled beneath his attack. He mowed to the big pine, and all around it, then kicked together armfuls of soft grass and arranged it in a pile. Joe covered the bed with a buffalo robe and went to the wagon.

"Bring her out now," he said gently.

Baby Emma lay weak and listless in her mother's arms, lacking either the strength or the will to hold her head erect. But hope sprang anew in Joe's mind and his heart was not quite so leaden. The child smiled at him, and she had not done that earlier. Joe took his wife and daughter to the couch he had made them and watched Emma lay the baby down. He looked again at her flushed cheeks and dull eyes, and wished mightily that he knew as much about sick babies as he did about driving mules.

Emma said, "May we have some fresh water, Joe?"

Barbara called, "I'll get it."

She had lifted the other three youngsters from the wagon and they were tumbling around in the grass. Joe watched them closely; he had never been here before and he did not know what to expect in such a place. Then the children found the place he had mowed and played there. Joe relaxed. He had just covered that ground himself, and knew there was nothing harmful on it. The youngsters showed no inclination to go elsewhere. The tall grass was as high as their heads and they became entangled in it. This was more to their liking.

Tad exclaimed, "Look yonder!"

Joe followed his pointing hand. On the far side of the creek a buck deer, his head heavy with grotesque clubs of velvet-covered antlers, was gazing at them. The buck stretched its neck toward them, then stamped its forefeet and flicked a short tail. Tad looked hopefully at Joe.

"We need meat, don't we?"

Joe shook his head. "Not that much meat. We'll be going on in a couple of days and we can't waste time curing what we don't use."

"Shucks!" Tad said dejectedly.

"But I'll tell you what you can do," Joe said. "I saw trout in the creek. Suppose you take a hook and line, cut yourself a pole, and see what you can do about bringing in a mess for supper."

"You betcha!"

Mike at his heels, rifle in his hands, Tad went whooping toward the creek and Joe watched him go. Joe turned back to the tasks at hand, for there was much to be done. But even as he worked he had a curious feeling that this was no routine halt.

They had had many different camps under many different conditions, and some were so ordinary that Joe could not remember them at all. Others, such as the one where they'd eaten their first buffalo and the camp where they had forded the creek after he replaced the broken wagon wheel, he remembered clearly. But this one had something that was all its own. Joe tried to pin down the elusive quality it possessed and could not. Perhaps, he thought, it was partly his determination to make it the best and most comfortable stopping place they had yet known. He had a hazy idea that, if he could do everything right and work everything right, baby Emma's fever would depart.

He worked furiously with the scythe, cutting more grass and letting it wither in what remained of the afternoon sun. He carried stones from the creek and arranged a fireplace while Ellis cut wood in the fireplace. Tad came in with four big trout dangling at the end of a willow stringer.

"Threw back all the little ones!" he boasted. "Caught 'em on worms that I found under rocks! Do we need any more, Pa?"

"These will do," Joe declared. "Let me have them and I'll take the bones out."

"I can do it myself. I watched you with the bass."

He sat down to fillet his catch and Joe raked up the partially dried grass. He arranged a bed, turning all the stems downward so that only wispy grass lay on top. This he covered with buffalo ropes, and built a small fireplace near it. Joe and Ellis made beds for the other youngsters, but Ellis declared that he could sleep on the ground and Joe threw down only a couple of armfuls of grass for himself. He built a cooking fire and a small fire near where Emma and her sick daughter were to spend the night.

They feasted on broiled trout and fresh bread, and Joe watched with hope in his heart while baby Emma sipped at a bowl of warm milk. Her fever seemed to have lessened, but Joe worried because it was not following its usual pattern. Always before it had struck suddenly, burned its course, and left just as suddenly. This time the child was very ill, with a fluctuating temperature.

The darkness deepened. Joe lay on his bed near Emma and the youngster, watching stars so near that it almost seemed he could touch them. Out in the forest wolves yelled, and there were soft shufflings and gruntings as the things that ordinarily used these meadows by day—but no longer dared do so because there were humans near—moved about at night. Mike growled a warning whenever anything came nearer than he thought it should, and three times during the night Joe rose to visit the couch of his wife and daughter. On one of these visits he saw that his wife's eyes were open, and he heard her whisper. He bent close to hear her message.

"When we're settled and have a roof over our head, Joe—" He waited.

She added softly, "I'm going to miss the open sky and the stars."

Morning brought mists that swirled upward from the creek and spread like gossamer spirits over the meadow on both sides. The mules and the placid cow were half hidden by it, and the air had a distinct chill. Joe rose to throw more wood on the fire, and when he walked over to see if Emma was awake he found her staring at him.

"How is the baby?" he whispered.

"She had a difficult night," Emma said softly, "but she's sleeping now. Joe, I'm—"

"Yes?" he asked.

"I'm afraid she won't be able to travel for a while."

Joe looked toward the other side of the creek. The three cow elk, sure that the night was a cloak of safety, were grazing unconcernedly. Joe looked at the tall grass that could have grown only in fertile soil. He thought of last evening. Barbara and Ellis had gone wading in the creek. Barbara's legs, bare to the knee, had flashed in the setting sun, and through the clear water small stones that either were white or appeared to be white due to some trick of the water's reflection were plainly seen on the bottom of the creek.

Out in the meadow, a meadow lark piped its greeting to the rising sun. The lark was Joe's totem bird and always a symbol of good luck.

He said with sudden decision, "She won't have to travel. This is the place we came so far to find."

CHAPTER SIXTEEN

The Farm

A HUNDRED and sixty-five measured yards from the big pine in the meadow, there was an icy spring. It bubbled out of sand so white that it seemed to have great depth, and the overflow made its own little watercourse that trickled into the creek. The spring was four feet wide by two and a half deep, and Joe and Ellis made the watercourse a dividing line to separate the land they took for themselves.

Joe went to the south, so that the great pine was on his property, and he chose very carefully. A man needed enough land, but not too much and Joe fronted his hundred and sixty acres on the creek. He wanted eighty acres of the meadow for crop and pasture land, and he ran his property back to the top of the slope so that he had eighty of timber. In addition, he allowed ten acres for the road that would one day parallel this creek. Snedcker had been right. The creek headed out two and a half miles away and throughout its length was natural meadow land that needed no clearing. Emigrants hadn't claimed it as yet because of the Indian danger, but nothing could keep them from coming here when the threat subsided. Some, sure of their ability to defend themselves, might come anyway.

Ellis laid out his claim just as carefully, with a judicious selection of meadow and timber, and between the two of them they owned a half mile of timber and a half mile of meadow. It was much more land than they needed for the present and as much as they were likely to need in the future.

Joe worked with a happiness and contentment he had never

known before, and his pleasure was complete when baby Emma made a slow recovery. She remained frail and she could not be as active as the other children, but Emma nursed her carefully and watched her closely. She might have traveled on, but all of them had lost all desire to travel. They had chosen their home and they were happy with it, and the fact that it meant working from the time the sun rose until it set again was accepted as a part of things. There was a vast amount of work and never enough time. However, next season there would be only routine farm tasks and more leisure.

He stood back on the ridge and chopped cleanly a slender pine whose ruffled top towered fifty feet above him. Joe chopped the last strip of wood that held the pine erect and rested his ax on the needle-carpeted ground while the pine swayed on its stump and fell. He wiped his sweating brow. A little distance away he heard Ellis chopping a tree, and Joe grinned.

There were as many trees as anyone could possibly want, but many were centuries-old giants with massive trunks. They were too big for two men to handle or for mules to drag, and splitting the trunks would mean a great deal of work and require a lot of time. There was simply no time to spare, so they had to search through the forest for trees that needed no splitting.

Expertly, knowing precisely where to strike, Joe trimmed the branches from his tree and cut the trunk in half. He fretted as he did so, and wished that he were two men so he could do twice as much. They were still camped in the meadow and a house was of the utmost importance. But crops were necessary too, and every day at two o'clock Joe had stopped all other work so he could plow. He let the felled tree lie where it was and went to seek Ellis.

Joe had distrusted this slender young man at first, but he had come to love him as his own. Ellis was still inclined to be reckless and impulsive, but reckless impulse was the birthright of youth. However, Ellis rose when Joe did and worked until it was too dark to work any more. Ellis was striving toward a cherished goal. He and Barbara had set no definite date but they wanted to be married before the summer was over. But rather than build two houses when there was so much to be done, it had been agreed to build just one with a room for the young couple. They'd build a house for Ellis and Barbara when autumn brought some relief from other work.

Ellis was trimming another pine when Joe found him. For a moment Joe watched, taking sheer delight in the supple rhythm of the youngster's physical efforts. Ellis had the rippling grace of a cat, and Joe thought of his lovely daughter. Their marriage was right and good, as it should be. Ellis turned to Joe and grinned.

"Loafing again, huh?"

"If you did half as much work as I do, the house would have been finished yesterday."

"You and Hercules!"

"That's right," Joe agreed. "How about hauling some of this timber while I work a bit more on the foundation?"

"Sure thing."

Axes swinging from their hands, they left the timber and descended into the meadows. They had already selected the site for both houses, with Joe's and Emma's on one side of the spring and Ellis's and Barbara's on the other. However, due to the slope it had been necessary to level the sites and the only tools they had for such work were picks and shovels. Joe glanced down at his new farm.

Since this was to be a permanent home, and not just an overnight stop, Emma and Barbara had busied themselves making it a comfortable one. They'd rearranged the fireplace, made a table from a log Joe had split for them, and even cushioned the chunks of logs that served as chairs. Now, while the children threw stones into the creek so they could watch the resulting splashes, Emma and Barbara were planting more vegetables in the garden Joe had plowed. Tad, Joe thought wryly, was probably fishing.

A vegetable garden had been first in order of importance because there was little need to worry about the animals. The grass was tall and rich and their discarded beds, thoroughly dried, as well as other grass Joe had mowed already made a respectable hay stack. As soon as they got time, if they ever did, Joe and Ellis would cut more. This season the mules, the horse and the cow, could winter on hay. Next year there would be grain.

Joe had plowed his vegetable garden near the creek, and it had been a back-breaking job. First he had mowed all the grass as short as possible, let it dry, raked it up, and added it to the hay stack. Then it had required all the strength in Joe's arms and all the power the mules had to turn the tough sod. Joe had plowed and cross plowed, turning the sod under. But all the labor had been worth while.

The earth was rich, with very few stones, and already seedlings were sprouting in it. Joe had purposely made the garden big enough not only to supply his family, but also to provide a surplus which he hoped to sell at Camp Axton. He couldn't imagine Major Dismuke planting any gardens. Regulations didn't cover them.

Joe and Ellis walked down to the garden. Kneeling in the soft dirt, patting a hill of corn in with her hands, Barbara might have been some lovely young wood sprite as she glanced up at Ellis. Joe left them alone—young lovers are not partial to sharing even one moment with anyone else—and walked over to Emma.

There was something new about Emma, a deep and enduring quality rising from both strength and happiness. She had conquered her shattering fears, and her face showed the sweetness of her new self confidence. Joe smiled down on her.

"By this time next week, darling, you'll be a housekeeper again."

"Oh Joe! I can hardly wait!"

"The logs are all cut. We can start building this afternoon. Of course the furniture will be rough at first; Ellis and I will have to make it. But if our crops are good next year, and I don't see how they can fail here, we'll go into The Dalles or Oregon City and buy everything new. That's the money Elias Dorrance would have had if we'd stayed in Missouri."

She said, dazedly, "It's—it's hard to believe, isn't it? We've been through so much, and now we're *here!* We're here, Joe—all of us!"

He bent to kiss her. "Well, this isn't building a house. I'd better get busy."

He turned back toward the building site and as he did Ellis went to bring the mules in. Joe felt a little sorry for him. Remembering his own courting days, he knew that nothing was as fascinating or as important to Ellis as Barbara, but Ellis was aware of the necessity for getting things done. He was young in years but he had a sense of responsibility. Joe caught up his pick and shovel and went to work.

They had planned a combined kitchen-living room and three bedrooms; one for Ellis and Barbara, one for Tad and his brothers, and one for Joe and Emma. Baby Emma would share with her parents until Barbara and Ellis moved into their own house. Then she would have their room.

The main room would be in front, facing the creek, and the only door would also be there. The rear would be divided into bed rooms. Until there was time to lay puncheons, the floor would necessarily be dirt and Joe had taken a cue from Snedeker's post. Though they would not have Snedeker's advantage in looking through small windows from a raised floor, the windows would be small and so placed that everything around the cabin could be seen from them. Thus, in the event of an attack, they would be able to shoot in any direction.

They had dug into the slope at the rear and leveled it out to the front, but it was not exactly level. Joe drove stakes at either end, stretched a cord between them and laid his level on the cord. He loosened dirt with the pick, scooped it up in the shovel and threw it down the slope. Ellis came with a drag of logs, left them beside the excavation and went back for more. Joe got down on his hands and knees, leveled a small hump and was satisfied. He leaned his pick and shovel against the wagon, took his ax out of the tool box and began notching logs.

Once the building started, it went swiftly. Still working from dawn to dark, Joe and Ellis built up the walls, laid the roof poles, and covered the roof with shakes. Joe made a stone boat, a flat sledge and hauled clay from a bed that was about a mile up the creek. While Joe and Ellis worked on the inside partitions, Emma and the children started chinking. The youngsters worked so enthusiastically on the lower cracks that in places there was more clay than log.

Summer was well under way when they had their first visitor.

He came riding up from the Oregon Trail, a thin sliver of a man on an enormous white horse. But though he was thin, he was a strong man. Muscles rippled smoothly beneath his homespun shirt, and his smile was pleasant. He slid from his big horse and spoke with a pronounced New England twang.

"Howdy, folks."

"Hello!" Joe said warmly.

The thin man extended his hand. "My name's Winterson, Henry Winterson. I live—" with a gesture of his thumb he indicated the entire west "—about four miles out there."

"We're the Tower family," Joe introduced the individual members, "and this is Ellis Garner."

"Glad to know you!" Winterson acknowledged. "Glad to know you!" He came to Barbara. "Woo-hoo! Double glad! If I wasn't already married to Martha, you wouldn't get away!"

"Careful," Joe grinned. "Barbara and Ellis are figuring on being married before very long."

"Well, strike me down! We not only got close neighbors but there's going to be a wedding! Martha will be plumb out of her mind when she hears that! When's the big day?"

Ellis said, "Soon, I hope."

"We'll come," asserted Winterson, who hadn't been invited but took it for granted that he would be. "Martha and me will be here and you can bet on that! Yup! You can just bet on it! Sure is a lucky thing I rode into Axton this morning! Otherwise I might never of known we had neighbors! Yup! Worth losing a horse to find that out!"

"You lost a horse?"

"Yup. There's some half-witted Indians prowl about here and

they must have run it off. Figured I'd report it to Axton. Never can tell. Those soldier boys might be shot through with dumb luck some day and find something they're looking for."

"Indians bother you much?" Joe queried.

"Nah!" Winterson said scornfully. "Martha and me came through last year, right at the tail end though we started at the fore. Wagon broke down five times this side of Axton. Finally I said, 'Martha, if this blamed thing breaks down again we're setting up right where it happens.' Those were my very words. That's exactly what I said to her. So the blame thing broke down again and we set up right there. This is the first time Indians pestered us even a mite; mostly they're too lazy to scratch when they itch. You don't have to trouble your head about 'em."

"They told us at Axton to watch out for hostiles."

"And why wouldn't they tell you that at Axton? As long as that iron-faced major can keep up an Indian scare, he can set around here and enjoy life. If they transfer him to some other post he might have to work and I doubt if he could stand the shock. This country's every bit as safe as Vermont. Sure do like these meadows. If we'd known about 'em we probably would have come here."

"Come anyhow," Joe urged. "There's plenty of room."

Winterson grinned. "Martha'd bend a skillet over my head. We've got our buildings up and our crops in. The day we moved in Martha said, 'Henry, I moved from Vermont to here. That's enough moving for one lifetime.' Those were her very words. That's exactly what she said to me. She meant it, too. I know she'll be fretting to come and visit, though, soon's she knows you're here. She hasn't seen a woman since last year."

"Please bring her," said Emma, who hadn't seen a woman other than Barbara since they'd left Laramie. "We'll be delighted to see her. Come prepared to stay a while."

"Do that," Joe seconded. "We've plenty of room."

"I can see that." Winterson eyed the house. "You sure built as though you aim to stay here a spell."

"We'll be here," Joe assured him. "We've had enough moving too."

"Guess everybody has, time they get to Oregon." Winterson eyed Emma's chickens. "You wouldn't want to sell or trade a couple of those hens, would you?"

"That's my wife's department," Joe said.

"I don't believe so," Emma told Winterson. "We have only four left. There were six, but two of them were broody and went off to steal their nests. I haven't seen them since, and suppose some animal must have caught them."

"That's our trouble too," Winterson said sadly. "We fetched three hens and a rooster all this way and they all went in one night. Martha tells me often, 'Henry, the sound I'm most lonesome for is a clucking hen.' Those are her very words. That's exactly what she tells me. I do have a right nice bunch of little pigs. My sow littered eleven, and I know that a piglet for a hen is giving a lot but I'd be willing—Hey, look!"

Joe had mowed a wide swath to the creek, and as Winterson spoke one of the missing hens appeared in it. About her feet were a cluster of fluffy baby chicks, and the hen moved fussily around them. With a little squeal of joy, Emma ran forward. She knelt to gather the chicks in her apron, and clutched the hen beneath her arm. When she returned, her cheeks were flushed with pleasure.

"Fourteen! Just fourteen! Joe, we must keep them in the house until you can build a coop where they'll be safe! I can't have anything happening to them!"

"Boy, oh boy, oh boy!" Winterson breathed. "Would Martha like to see them! You have fourteen more chickens than you thought you had!"

"Yes," Emma agreed happily. "You may take a hen now, Mr. Winterson."

"Obliged to you," Winterson declared. "Right obliged, and Martha will just kick up her heels for pleasure! She's been so lonesome for a hen, and I'll bring the piglet when I fetch her to visit."

Emma put her chicks in the living-room corner and the hen,

feathers fluffed, clucked about them. Then she settled down on
the floor and the babies ran beneath her feathers. Joe glanced at
them and made a mental note to build a chicken coop as soon as
possible. They needed a stable, too. But the mules, the cow, and
Ellis's horse, were in no danger from prowling predators. The
chickens were, and they must have a safe place.

"This is right nice," Winterson eyed the interior of the house
approvingly. "Right nice and big too. But I reckon you need it
for that clutch of young ones you have. Martha and me, we built
only one room and we're making out in that."

"Don't you have any children?" Emma asked.

"Not yet, but it won't be long. Martha and me, we were married
the day before we left Vermont. The next day she said, 'Henry, I
want three boys and three girls. We can start on them as soon as
we're in Oregon.' Those were her very words. That's exactly what
she said to me. Looks like we can expect the first one in about two
months."

Emma said, "I must be there."

"Good of you, right good of you, and I know Martha will be
pleased about it too. I cudgeled and cudgeled my brains wondering what I could do for her, and all I could think of was the
hospital at Camp Axton. But Martha will be glad to have you
around and she'll feel better about it too. I know she wants the
little one born in her own house. It will be sort of lucky."

"Hope you don't aim to keep all six of 'em in one room," Joe
said. "Young ones can be right lively at times."

"I know," Winterson laughed. "I have five brothers and six
sisters. We'll build on as we need more rooms. We plan a sizeable
house."

Emma and Barbara prepared dinner, and after they had eaten
Winterson mounted his vast horse and rode away with one of
Emma's hens tucked tenderly beneath his arm. He dropped the
horse's reins and turned to wave good-by.

"I'll bring Martha over next week," he called.

They watched him until he was out of sight, sad because he

was going but happy too. They were not alone. There was a near
neighbor and Joe speculated on the fact that in Missouri anyone
who lived four miles away would have been reasonably far. This
country was different. It had depth and breadth, but wasn't that
what they'd hoped to find? But Joe had another man to plan with,
and Emma went a little more briskly about her work because
there was a woman near. Barbara's dreamy eyes reflected only
that there would be extra guests for her wedding.

Joe and Ellis went to fell saplings for Emma's chicken coop
and Joe looked wistfully at his fields. There was so very much to
be done and so little time in which to do it. He wanted to plow
again, to see the rich earth turn and feel it beneath his feet, for
he had a kinship with the earth. For the present, plowing must
wait. But before winter, Joe vowed, he would have at least ten
acres plowed and sown to wheat and rye. He didn't hope to do
much more than that because here plowing was difficult. But
once the land was worked it would not be hard to work again,
and in the years to come he would have as much plow land as
he wanted. We wondered oddly why he thought of this in terms
of years. In Missouri he had seldom planned beyond the next day.

After the evening meal, Barbara and Ellis slipped out. The
children slept, and by the light of an oil lamp Emma mended
clothes. Utterly tired but completely happy, Joe sprawled on a
wooden bench that would serve as a sofa until they had enough
money to buy a better one. The money he had and all he would
get must be saved, for during the winter to come they would still
have to buy a great deal of what they needed. Emma's needle
flicked back and forth, and she added one of Tad's shirts to a pile
of already-mended clothes.

"A penny for your thoughts," she said.

"They're worth a million dollars," Joe asserted. "I'm thinking
about you."

She smiled knowingly, "Do you miss Missouri, Joe?"

"Can't say I do."

"Wouldn't you like to do other things?"

"What are you driving at?"

"In Missouri you used to go to Tenney's store nights and have a talk with the men. Here all you do is work from dawn to dark. Isn't it monotonous?"

"Why no," he said. "No it isn't, and the only reason I have to work sixteen hours a day is because there's much to do. Next year we'll be pretty well set and I can go hunting or fishing now and again with Ellis and Tad."

"But don't you miss your friends in Missouri?"

He thought of the men he'd known in Missouri: John Geragty, the Garrows, Pete Domley, Les Tenney, Percy Pearl, Tom Abend, Fellers Compton. No doubt they were still gathering in Tenney's store every night to discuss whatever the current topic might be. Here there were no near neighbors, but there was, instead, the nearness of each member of his family. The warm and wonderful togetherness that had been cemented during their long journey. This was better, this was more real, and Joe knew he'd rather be here.

"I'd like to see them, if that's what you mean. But I wouldn't go back."

Barbara and Ellis came in, hand in hand, Joe smiled. They were so young, so in love, and so obviously happy. Joe said with mock severity,

"Better give her hand back and get to bed, Ellis. Tomorrow we start on the stable."

"Tomorow," Ellis said, "you'll have to work on the stable yourself."

"Are you running out on me?"

"Just to Camp Axton. I must see a man there."

"What man?"

"The chaplain." Ellis's whole face smiled and Barbara blushed. "We're getting married on the fifteenth."

"Honey!"

Emma rose and crushed her daughter in a maternal embrace. Joe sat bolt upright, sobered and a bit anxious, and wondered why he should be. He had known since New Year's that Barbara and Ellis would be married, but it hadn't seemed real until now. Then he grinned happily; he'd always wondered how it would feel to be a grandfather. He rose and wrung Ellis's hand.

"Good for you, son! Hey! The fifteenth! That's only a couple of weeks!"

"We know."

They stood together, a little abashed and a little uncertain but wholly proud. Joe sat down to think. The father of the bride had certain duties but he hadn't the faintest idea of what they were. As soon as they were alone he must ask Emma; she'd probably know. But Joe was certain that a wedding present was in order. He racked his brains wondering what he had to give, and could think of nothing appropriate. Then he thought of Henry Winterson's huge horse. Ellis had his Kentucky thoroughbred, but except in emergency such a horse should be saved for saddle work only, and Ellis needed a team. Maybe Winterson would sell his or perhaps he had spare horses that he would sell reasonably. If not, Joe would promise the youngsters a team of mules and buy them as soon as he sold some crops and had enough money. Right now neither of the young people looked as though they were worried about wedding presents, and they could get along. Ellis was welcome to use Joe's mules.

The next day Joe worked alone and Ellis returned shortly before twilight. The chaplain had promised to come on the fifteenth and some of the soldiers were coming too. They'd seen Barbara during her short stay at Camp Axton, and they wouldn't miss a chance to kiss this bride. There was sure to be a party and Barbara and Emma made great preparations for it. Mere men around the house became very unimportant, but that, Joe decided, was the way things should be.

The next week, as he had promised, Henry Winterson brought his pretty young wife for a visit. They came in a light wagon drawn by the huge white horse and another, smaller animal. Despite the awkwardness of her body, there was a calm assurance and easy poise about Martha Winterson that Joe warmed to at once. He knew that he would always be at ease with her.

"So glad you could come," he greeted, "and Emma will be happy to see you. Come on in—"

Before he finished speaking, Emma came out. She put a motherly hand around the other's shoulder.

"I'm Emma," she said warmly. "And I know you're Martha. Your husband told us all about you. Now you just come right in and make yourself comfortable while I fix you a cup of coffee."

They entered the house. Winterson went to the wagon and from it took a small, frightened pig with its legs trussed.

"Brought it," he said cheerfully. "Martha was so tickled to see the hen that she said, 'Why don't you take them two pigs, Henry? Why be stingy?' Those were her very words. That's exactly what she said to me. But I told her a bargain's a bargain, and here's the pig. What are you going to do with it?"

"Keep it in the stable," Joe decided, "until I can build a pen. Say, you don't have a team of horses or mules to sell, do you?"

"What for? You have a team."

"The kids need it. They're getting married next week."

"Glory be!" Winterson breathed. "I have a black horse at home. He's not as big as the white but he's sound and a good worker. You can have him for fifty—No! Forty dollars. This is a special occasion and those kids have to be started right."

"It's a deal."

"You don't have to pay cash," Winterson said. "I have enough money to see me through and my crops are good. Pay for him next year after you've made a crop if you want to."

"That will be a help."

"We'll leave it that way. You can get another horse easy when the emigrants start coming through. They always have stock that's footsore and needs only a little rest to get in shape again, and besides they'll trade. You'll have vegetables to trade by that time. Sorry we can't stay the night. I told Martha we were invited but she has a lot to do. Besides, she's made a pet of that hen and she isn't letting anything happen to it. Darn thing sleeps in the house with us."

"Come on in. Might just as well make good use of your time while you're here."

Tad hadn't come in from fishing. Ellis was up in the timber cutting firewood and Barbara was with him. The younger children, overawed at seeing two strangers at the same time, stared at them. Martha Winterson was seated at the table and Emma bustled about.

"She'll wear my wedding dress," Emma was saying. "When I had to pack it to come here I was worried. I feared that it might turn yellow, but it only shaded to a soft ivory. I think it's even more beautiful that way."

"Isn't it badly rumpled?"

"No. I packed paper around it and between each layer, and then wrapped it in my curtains. After it's hung out to air for a few hours, the wrinkles will blow out. The sun will get rid of the camphor odor, too."

"I'd love to see it!"

"I'd show it to you, but Ellis might come in any minute and he mustn't see his bride's dress before she wears it. You'll see it at the wedding."

"What's it like, Emma?"

Emma's voice was soft. "It's white satin with short puffed melon sleeves, over which I wore full long sleeves of white silk gauze fastened at the wrist. My cape was of Swiss muslin, with rich foulard patterns stamped on it. There are short white gloves with embroidered tops; there's a small mend but it won't show. I sewed it carefully. The neck line is low. The waist line is tiny, too tiny for me now but right for Barbara." Her eyes glowed with the warmth of remembering.

"Will she wear a bonnet?"

"Oh yes. I have a Pamela bonnet with a blue ribbon and a colored plume. I suppose it's out of fashion now, but it's very beautiful."

Ellis and Barbara came in and Emma hurriedly changed the subject. Martha Winterson rose to embrace Barbara, and turned a laughing face to kiss Ellis lightly on the cheek. Ellis blushed, and Joe grinned. He remembered his own wedding, and how embarrassed he had been when Emma's best friend, Sarah Townley, had kissed him. They had dinner. The Wintersons left, and the house was given over to preparations for the wedding.

Joe shrugged away any thought of work; there would be time for that later and Winterson was right. The youngsters had to be started out correctly and Emma wanted lots of decorations. But still Joe found it impossible to sleep after the first light of dawn.

Hatchet in hand, he wandered up the slope into the woods. It was too late in the season for most wild flowers, but there were fragrant, cone-laden evergreen boughs. Emma wanted the whole living room decorated with them, and Barbara would carry a bouquet of cloth flowers scented with Emma's precious perfume. About to enter the woods, Joe turned, as he always did, to look proudly over his land. His heart skipped a beat. To the west, about where he thought the Wintersons' home was, an ominous plume of thick yellow smoke reached far into the sky.

CHAPTER SEVENTEEN

Besieged

JOE STOOD still, studying the smoke and trying to analyze its meaning. Fear tugged at his heart, and his lips had gone dry. He could see only the smoke, and it was not a forest fire because it was not traveling. Winterson would hardly be burning brush at this season, either. The obvious answer was that Winterson's house itself was burning, but why? Was it an accidental fire? Or had the Indians, whom Major Dismuke respected and Winterson scorned, finally attacked? Joe walked back into the clearing and turned to look nervously at the forest. If the Indians were on the warpath, they would come from the woods.

He felt and checked a rising fright. Whatever the situation was, it must be met coolly. Panic would help nothing. Joe entered the house and Emma, cooking breakfast for the rest of the family, looked questioningly at him.

"There's things afoot," Joe said quietly. "I think Winterson's house is burning and Indians might have set it. We'd better get ready for whatever it is."

Horror was reflected in Emma's face. "That poor woman!"

Ellis still slept outside and he had not yet come in. Joe went to his bed and shook his shoulder.

"Ellis."

Ellis, who had a happy faculty for coming awake all at once, opened his eyes and sat up.

"What do you want, Joe?"

"Things might be stirring. I believe the Wintersons' house is burning and we'd better be ready for visitors. Come on in."

"Right away."

Ellis sat up beneath his blankets and started pulling on his clothes. Joe formulated a plan of action. The house was a strong fortress, and all the grass for a hundred yards on every side had been mowed. Tad was a crack shot and Ellis was good, and anyone with the wrong ideas who came in range would have reason to regret it. Joe went back into the house. His eyes shining with excitement, Tad accosted him.

"Are they comin', Pa? Are they really comin'?"

"I don't know. But get your rifle ready."

"It's all ready!"

Barbara asked anxiously, "Is Ellis coming?"

"He'll be right in. Come on, everybody. Get everything that will hold water and fill it."

They filled the buckets, Emma's pots and pans, and even some of the dishes and stored them in Joe's and Emma's bedroom. Joe went to the garden, and filled a basket with lettuce, radishes, onions, and peas. He put the filled basket in the pantry along with the food already stored there and Ellis came in with his arms full of firewood. He dropped it into the wood box. Now, in the event of a siege, they had water, food and fuel.

Barbara and Emma were nervous, but not so nervous that they were unable to discharge their tasks efficiently. Ellis and Tad, except for Tad's excitement, seemed to grasp the situation and the younger children, not understanding, were merely curious. Joe fought his own rising nervousness.

"Bring Mike in the house," he instructed Tad, "and watch him carefully. If he growls, barks, or even bristles, watch for whatever might be." To Ellis he said, "Watch the dog. Keep the kids down and make the rounds of every window. Pay very close attention to the rear; they'll likely come from the woods if they come at all. If they do, both of you shoot—and shoot straight. I'll be back as soon as I can get here."

There was a rising note of alarm in Emma's voice, "Where are you going?"

He said quietly, "To find out if the Wintersons are in trouble and help them if they are. Don't anybody stir outside the house until we know just what it is."

Ellis said quickly, "You stay here, Joe. I'll go."

Barbara paled, but said, "Let him go, Daddy."

Joe hesitated, but only for a moment. His children deserved a chance, and Barbara was going to be married within the week. Barbara and Ellis were young and the world was theirs. Ellis, Joe felt, would help take care of Emma and the children if he didn't get back. Besides he was older. He'd picked up a few tricks that Ellis didn't know. Joe said,

"It's no time for fussing. I'm going."

Emma said worriedly, "You be careful, Joe."

"I will, and don't you fret about me. Likely I'll bring the Wintersons back."

"I will, and I want to tell you again not to worry. King can out-run any Indian pony. Now remember, stay in the house, keep your eyes open, and fight if you must. I won't be gone long."

Rifle in his hands, hatchet at his belt, Joe left the house and closed the massive door behind him. He listened for the wooden bar to fall in place, and after he heard it drop he started toward the stable. They'd built it down the slope, far enough from the house so that stable odors would not be offensive but near enough to defend. Anyone who tried to get into the stable would be within rifle range. Joe swerved to lock Emma's chickens in their coop and he scooped the piglet up under one arm. The pig had only a rail fence enclosure; there had been no time to build a house for him.

The mules looked questioningly around and Ellis's horse nickered a welcome. The placid cow chewed calmly on hay, and Joe put the piglet down. It scooted into the cow's stall and hid beneath the manger. Joe bridled Ellis's horse but did not saddle it. He was used to riding bareback and he preferred to ride that way. Joe led the horse from the stable and bolted the door.

For a moment he stood still and a faint smile curled the corners of his mouth as the incongruity of the situation occurred to him. He, Joe Tower, was riding forth to help repel Indians. For some reason he remembered Bibbers Townley and his fancied fight with the eight Apaches in Arizona, and he wondered what Bibbers would be doing if he were here right now. Probably, Joe guessed, he would be riding as fast as possible toward Camp Axton.

Joe would have been happy if Jim Snedeker was here for Jim would have known exactly what to do. That, Joe had to admit, was more than he knew. He had come to Oregon to farm, not to fight Indians. But if they were attacking he'd have to fight them, and Joe was an experienced hunter who knew how to skulk through brush. If necessary, he would abandon the horse and take to the woods, and he wasn't sure that Ellis would do that if he had ridden to help the Wintersons. Joe pondered the best method of reaching their place.

He'd never been to their house, but now he wished mightily that he had visited it because there might be a short cut. He was riding a horse, and horses do not have to stay on trails. But all Joe knew was what Winterson had told him; he'd built where his wagon broke down the sixth time. It stood to reason, therefore, that he had built beside the Oregon Trail and the surest way to find his house was by riding down that. Joe urged Ellis's horse into a gallop.

The trees on both sides were deceptively peaceful, as though nothing violent could possibly occur here. But not too far away a man and woman who had traveled three thousand miles in order to find new hopes and new dreams were seeing them go up in smoke. The horse slowed a bit and Joe urged him again.

He rounded a bend and saw the approaching team. They were Winterson's big white and the smaller horse, and they were being driven at full gallop by Martha Winterson, who, somehow, still managed to hold her precious hen. Winterson crouched on the wagon seat, rifle in hand and looking backward. Trailing the wagon by a few yards ran an unhampered black horse. Without breaking astride, Joe swung his own mount around the onrushing team and fell in behind.

"Keep them moving!" he shouted. "We're all ready for you!"

He said no more because this was not the time to talk, but now he knew. Major Dismuke had known what he was talking about when he spoke of hostiles. The plume of smoke, the racing team, the fury on Winterson's face, and the blood on his arm, were ample proof that the Wintersons had been attacked. Joe glanced backward down the Trail, as though he expected to see warriors pounding in pursuit, but he saw nothing.

Expertly, Martha Winterson turned her racing team from the Trail and into the meadows. She brought them to a plunging halt. The black horse, rolling frightened eyes, edged very close to Joe as though it sought his protection. Ellis, Barbara and Emma came from the house, and Emma took charge of Martha Winterson.

"Are you all right?"

"Of course I'm all right!" Martha's eyes were blazing too. "I'm not going to faint on you or anything like that! Oh, I'm so glad I could bring my hen along!"

"Well, you just come right in the house! We have everything we need there and the men will be along!"

Winterson, Joe and Ellis unhitched the team and led them to the stable. The black horse followed and crowded in as soon as the door was open. They put the mules in one stall and two horses in each of the others. Ellis filled the mangers with hay and Joe turned to Winterson.

"What happened?"

"They came at dawn!" Winterson said savagely. "The hen started cackling and woke me up! I saw this one looking in the window and threw the first thing I could lay my hands on at him! Happened to be the chamber pot! Time I got my hands on my rifle, he was gone! I took Martha with me, and time we got harnessed there were more of the skunks in the woods! They nicked me in the arm and we were gone!"

"Did they have horses?"

"Probably they had some somewhere! I suppose they left them back in the woods when they came to get us! Yes, there must have been horses! These Indians are too blasted lazy to walk anywhere! I got off one shot, but think I missed!"

"How many are there?"

"I saw anyhow six, but there are more than that! Blasted mongrels probably wouldn't fight at all unless they were anyhow fifteen to one! Wish I'd had another rifle! I—There's three of us now! Let's go back and tear into them!"

Joe said gently, "Leave the women and kids here unprotected?"

"You're right! Guess you're right! It's just that I'm so lashing mad I'd do about anything! I'm never going to like an Indian again if I live to be five hundred years old!"

"They burned your buildings. I saw the smoke."

"That's probably why they weren't hot on our trail; they were too busy looting! I suppose they got my cow and pigs too, but I saved the horses and Martha got her hen out. That's some hen! I wouldn't swap her for a farm!"

"Better come up and get a dressing on that arm."

"Just a scratch," Winterson assured him. "It doesn't amount to anything. What are we going to do now? Send somebody to Camp Axton to bring the soldiers?"

"Too dangerous," Joe decided. "One man alone could be ambushed and we have four rifles now. We'd better figure on making a stand right here."

"Who's the fourth rifle?"

"Tad, and he'll be a good one. That kid can shoot the whiskers off a cat at a hundred yards. Did you bring plenty of bullets?"

"Just what's in my pouch. We didn't have time to grab as much as we'd have liked."

"Well, we have lead and molds. We can rig a mold to fit your rifle. Let's go in before the womenfolk decide we've all been scalped."

Still more angry than frightened, Martha Winterson had taken

Carlyle on her lap and was relating the story of the raid. Barbara and Emma listened closely, while the three younger children stood silently near. Too young to appreciate exactly what had happened, they knew it was something out of the ordinary and they digested it as such. A look of eager excitement on his face, Tad was sitting in front of the fireplace melting lead in a ladle and molding bullets for his rifle.

"That's enough," Joe ordered. "Leave some lead for the rest of us."

"But what if there's a whole mob of them?"

"Everybody still has to shoot."

Martha rose and, despite her swollen body, there was a supple grace about her as she moved across the floor to her husband.

"Now I'll fix that arm, Henry," her voice was faintly apologetic. "There wasn't time to do it before."

She unbuttoned his shirt, removed it, and bared the bloody arm. The bullet had torn through one side, missing the big muscle and the artery, and leaving only a flesh wound. Martha washed the dried blood away and put a cold compress over the still-bleeding wound.

"Would you have some whisky?" she appealed to Joe. "This should really be sterilized."

"Don't have a drop," Joe admitted. "I didn't bring any."

"I did," Emma announced. She reached into her trunk, brought out a brown bottle, and glanced aside at Joe. "I brought it for emergencies only."

"Thank you, Emma." Martha Winterson pursed her lips, dampened one side of her cloth with whisky, and said, "Now this may sting a little."

While her husband gritted his teeth and made a face, she applied the antiseptic. "The bullet wasn't that bad!"

"Now don't be a baby," Martha chided. "You won't feel it in a little while."

"Probably won't be able to feel anything," he grumbled.

Martha applied a clean bandage and Henry put his shirt back

on. He wandered restlessly to look out of a front window. Anger flared in his face. Henry Winterson cherished his house. Nobody was going to destroy it and go unpunished.

"Wish they'd come," he said nervously. "Wish they would. The day I left Vermont my brother Enos said, 'Henry, what are you going to do if Indians attack?' Those were his very words. That's exactly what he said to me. 'If the Indians attack,' I said, 'I'm going to shoot them dead in their tracks.' And by gosh, I didn't. But I aim to."

Joe said worriedly, "You might get a chance soon enough."

This was not real, he thought curiously. It was a charade that all of them were acting out, and as soon as they were finished acting the Wintersons would hitch their horses and go home. Jim Snedeker might have waited in a house such as this one while Indians prepared to attack it, but such things did not happen to Joe Tower. Then he reminded himself forcibly that they *were* happening to Joe Tower. A cold shiver ran through him.

"Hey, Pa!" Tad breathed. "Look at Mike!"

The dog was standing very still, ears alert and nose questing. He moved a step, as though to verify some elusive message that was reaching him faintly. His hackles rose and a low growl rumbled in his throat. He was looking toward the rear of the house, and when a door was opened for him he padded into a back bedroom. At the same time they heard the crack of a rifle and a sodden "splat" as a bullet thumped into an outer log.

Joe's fear and nervousness departed and he knew only a terrible, white-hot anger. This was his house. He had built it with his own hands and now it was threatened. At all costs he must avert that peril. No enemy could enter. Rifle ready, Joe peered through one of the rear windows.

He could see nothing except the mowed swath, the tall grass beyond, and the green trees on top of the hill. It was as though a real bullet had been fired by a ghost. Then the tall grass rippled slightly. Winterson leveled his rifle through another window, shot, and the grass stopped rippling.

"What'd you shoot at?" Joe queried.

"I didn't see any Indian," Winterson assured him, "but you don't see the critters. Still, that grass wasn't moving itself."

"Think you got him?"

"Nah," Winterson said sadly. "I dont think so. We'll—"

"Joe!"

There was cold fear in Emma's voice, and when Joe moved to the front of the house he saw the women looking out. Across the creek and up on the opposite slope, sixteen Indians stood in the meadow. There was something insultingly contemptuous about them as they either leaned on their long rifles or held them in their hands. They were dressed in buckskin save for one who wore a black suit that probably had been plundered from some settler. Of the rest, some wore fringed shirts and some were naked from the waist up. They stood so openly because they were out of rifle range and knew it.

Henry Winterson breathed, "There they are!"

He rested his rifle across a window sill, took an interminable time to sight, and squeezed the trigger. One of the sixteen jerked awkwardly, as though he had stepped on something that slipped beneath his foot, and sat awkwardly down. The rest ran back into the shelter of the woods, and after a moment the wounded man rose to follow. There was a savage satisfaction in Winterson's voice.

"Winged me one anyhow! Wish I'd killed him!"

"How high did you hold on him?" Joe asked.

"About a foot over his head. Still probably caught him too low down. Wish I'd given it another foot!"

There came five quick shots from behind the cabin. Ellis took two slow forward steps, turned to smile at the others, and managed only a fatuous grin. Blood bubbled down the side of his head, giving his hair a seal-sleek look and reddening his cheek. Joe caught him as he slumped backward while Winterson plucked the rifle from his hand. Barbara gasped and knelt beside her lover. Her face was pale and terrible fear and shock glittered in her eyes. But there was hot anger in them too as she took Ellis's head tenderly on her lap while his blood reddened her skirt. Emma came with a cold compress and Barbara took it from her hand. Her voice was dull and trembling, but at the same time she showed her inner strength.

"Let me do it, Mother."

She applied the compress to Ellis's head while she bent tenderly over him. Barbara, who had always hidden when anything she liked was hurt, rose to the occasion when one she loved was injured. Joe said awkwardly,

"Let's move him to a bed."

And Barbara said fiercely, "Leave him alone!"

She sopped up the bubbling blood and Emma brought her a clean compress. Joe, Winterson and Tad went to the rear, but again all they saw was the mowed area, the tall grass and the forest. Up in the forest one of the attackers shouted, probably advice to someone on the opposite hill. Joe furrowed his brow.

They were doing things wrong, with everybody rushing to wherever an Indian appeared. That left three walls unguarded all the time, and they must inject some system into their defense. Besides, there was another and very deadly peril that could be lessened. No bullet could tear through the logs, but one might penetrate the chinking or the windows.

Joe called, "Emma, get the kids on the floor, will you? You womenfolk had better get there, too. Lie behind the sill log and you can't get hit."

Emma said, "I'll get them down."

"We'd better do things a little differently, too. Tad, you watch the north side. Henry, do you want the front or the rear?"

"The front for me!" Winterson bit his words off and spat them out. "They might have another pow-wow and I know I can reach 'em the next time. How about the south wall?"

"One of us'll have to slide over there now and again to watch."

Barbara said steadily, "Mother, will you bring me a pillow?"

Emma brought it and, very gently, Barbara transferred Ellis's bandaged head from her lap to the pillow. She stood and for a long moment looked down at him while Ellis moaned fretfully and moved. Then she took his rifle and went to the south wall.

"Bobby!" Joe protested.

"Ellis showed me how to shoot, Daddy, and I will."

Joe looked vexedly at her but said nothing. The children lay prone on the living-room floor, curled tightly against the bottom log. But Emma and Martha Winterson sat quietly at the table. These women had men defending the cabin. If one of the men needed help suddenly, they did not want first to have to get up from the floor. Joe took his post at a rear window.

He had disposed his force in what he considered the wisest fashion. When the Indians came, as he was sure they would come, it would probably be out of the forest at the rear and down the slope. It was right that Joe should be there to draw at least their first fire. This was his house; he was the one to defend it. Joe worried about Barbara and Tad, but the least likelihood of attack was from either side. Winterson was well placed in front. He had already proved his ability to gauge distance and to hit what he aimed at.

Out in the mowed area, a grasshopper took lazy wing and settled fifteen feet from where it had started. A robin that probably had been sitting on the house swooped on the insect and bore it away. Gophers scurried back and forth, and a crow alighted in the field. The fields hadn't changed and the day was like any day. It was hard to believe that, just beyond the mowed area, lay men who would kill everyone in the house if they were able to do so. Joe's eyes roved the tall grass farther up the slope. He concentrated on one place.

He thought he saw the grass sway there. It moved ever so slightly, then was still. Joe relaxed taut muscles. He had never shot at another man with the intent to kill and until now he had considered himself incapable of doing so. But the terrible anger still had him in its grip and he could kill these men. The grass moved again, and Joe knew without a doubt that there was something in it that should not be. He stepped back, sighted and shot. A crawling Indian threw himself upward so that his whole torso was revealed and fell back. The grass stopped moving.

"Did you get him?" Tad called excitedly. "Did you get him, Pa?"

"I don't think so."

He tried to keep his voice calm, but it was taut and strained. He felt surging joy because he had killed one of the enemies who had come to destroy them. He remained too much the civilized man to speak of that to his son.

"I thought I heard a shot!"

The bloody bandage contrasting oddly with his dark hair, Ellis was sitting up. For a moment he did not move, but stared at something that only he saw. Plowing a furrow beside his head, the bullet had shocked him into unconsciousness. Leaving her post, Barbara knelt and put her arms around him.

"Ellis! Lie down!"

"I—Bobby! Where did you come from?"

"Please lie down!"

"I—Oh! I know now!"

Her arm remained about him as he rose to shaky feet, swayed and recovered his balance. He reached up with one hand to push the bandage a little farther up his head and looked wonderingly at the blood on his fingers. He said, as though that were an astonishing thing,

"They nicked me!"

Emma and Martha Winterson hovered anxiously about, and Joe said, "Better stay down, Ellis."

"I—I'm all right now. Bobby, my rifle!"

She choked back a sob. "Ellis, no!"

"I'm all right now. I'll watch the south wall."

She said determinedly, "We'll both watch the south wall," and she stood very close beside him in the event that he needed her suddenly.

Time dragged on. Rifle cradled in his arm, Winterson came back to stand beside Joe. He peered at the tall grass.

"See anything?"

"Nothing's moved for a couple of hours. Do you think they've gone?"

"No, I don't," Winterson declared. "They don't like hot lead and they aren't going to expose themselves to it. They're out in the brush cooking up some new kind of deviltry. When they get it cooked, they'll serve it to us."

"They might try something, but I doubt it. There's some hea- thenish nonsense about their having to die in the daylight so they can see their way to the spirit land. But—and I'll bet on it—we haven't seen the last of them. Think one of us should try slipping out to Camp Axton tonight?"

"It's a pretty long chance, what with so many of them being out there. We can hang on for one more day. The day after tomor- row's the fifteenth, and the chaplain and some soldiers are com- ing from Axton anyway. No sense in being foolish if we don't have to."

"That makes sense," Winterson conceded. "Well, I'll go rest my eyes on some of your scenery again. Might get a shot."

All through the long afternoon nothing appeared, and the women prepared and served dinner in the last lingering hour of twilight. They ate, while the embers of the dying fire cast a ghostly glow into the room. Again Joe wondered if this were ac- tually real. None of it fitted his preconceived notions of an Indian fight, with bullets flying thick and fast and deeds of derring-do. So far not a dozen shots had been fired.

Then he glanced soberly at Ellis's bandaged head. It was real enough.

They took the mattresses from the beds and laid them on the floor. Sleepy, and somewhat bored, the children curled up where bullets could not reach them. Joe walked back to his post at the window, and he saw a thin sickle of a moon hanging as though from invisible wires in the sky. It shed a faint light, and Joe stiffened when he saw an Indian crawling up to the cabin. But closer scrutiny proved that it was only a shadow.

"Haven't seen a thing!" Tad wailed. "Do you suppose they'll come tonight, Pa?"

"I don't know. Hadn't you better knock off for a while and get some sleep?"

Winterson called softly, "Joe."

Joe went to the front of the house, and down at the stable he saw a flickering, tiny light. It grew, and within seconds it was a leaping fire. Joe felt his body grow taut, and fury mounted to new heights. But he could do nothing except stand helplessly by and watch.

"The stock won't be there," Winterson assured him. "The devils'll run that off with them."

"I—" Joe gritted.

"I know what you're thinking. You don't have to say it."

They watched the fire grow and heard its crackling, and the entire space between the house and stable was lighted by it. Sparks floated skyward and winked out. Fire broke through the shake roof, and transformed it into seething, liquid flame. Then the roof fell in and there was a vast shower of sparks.

"They're real playful," Winterson commented. "Real nice people."

"Where's the wagon?" Joe asked.

"What did you say?"

"They've taken the wagon!"

Winterson grunted, "They'll take anything they can lay their hands on."

Joe walked back to the rear window and stared into the darkness. He had not slept but he was not sleepy. Flaring rage still consumed him, and he peered intently at every shadow.

The slow hours of the night dragged endlessly. Dawn came softly and Tad called,

"Pa."

"Yes?"

"There's the wagon."

Joe peered past his son's shoulder. Far up the valley, hopelessly out of rifle shot, the wagon's canvas top was sharply white in the lightening morning. Mounted Indians were pulling it with ropes, and Joe felt sick to his stomach. This was the wagon that had brought them all the way from Missouri, over prairie, hills, rivers and mountains. This was the wagon that had been their home. Now it was stuffed full of hay from the haystack, and the raiders must have worked all night to get where it was. Now all they had to do was drag it up the slope, find a position directly behind the house, set the hay on fire and send the wagon rolling down. Without exposing a man they could burn the house, and its defenders would be at their mercy.

Winterson and Ellis came to stand beside Joe, and they looked at this thing that could not be but was. The wagon turned and stalled sidewise and Joe's heart gave a great leap. But the Indians righted it again, kicking savage heels into their mounts' ribs as they forced them to pull. Slowly the wagon moved up the hill. Joe swallowed a hard lump in his throat. He looked at Emma and the children, and at Martha Winterson, and strode grimly to the rear of the house.

The wagon did not appear, and for a moment he cherished the wild hope that it had broken a wheel or become snagged in the trees, and that the Indians would be unable to move it. The sun rose, warming the meadow, and still Joe stared up the hill. After an eternity he saw what he had prayed he would not see. The upper third of the wagon's canvas top was silhouetted against the trees, and smoke was pouring from it. Joe turned to find Winterson and Ellis at his elbow.

He said vaguely, "It might miss the house."

But he knew that it would not. The besiegers had their one great opportunity and they would not waste it.

Joe's hand tightened around the breech of his rifle, and for a second he thought he must have shot. But the shot came from the top of the hill, near the wagon, and it was followed by a volley that was in turn followed by the barking of revolvers.

They waited, wondering, and after fifteen minutes, while the burning wagon continued to smoke, they saw the horsemen come down the hill. They were nine men, riding at a walk, and they herded Joe's mules and Ellis's and Winterson's horses ahead of them.

Joe breathed, "God Almighty!"

It was a prayer, not a curse, and he flung the door open to go out and meet these horsemen who had appeared so providentially.

"Told you I'd come!" Sergeant Dunbar called. "Told you I'd come as soon as my hitch was up! I brought a wagon train through with me and they told us at Camp Axton that you were here. We smelled smoke and figured the rest."

His arm around Martha, Henry Winterson stood just behind Joe and both their faces wreathed in smiles. Emma came, and the younger children ran with open arms toward this man who had been their playmate at Fort Laramie. Joe looked through the cabin's door to see Barbara and Ellis in a lovers' embrace. He grinned; they thought they could not be seen.

"Get down!" Joe sang out. "Get down and come on in! Where are your wagons?"

"Left 'em back along the Trail when the Sarge here smelled Indians," a lanky Kentuckian on a brown horse said. "Say, this looks like good land. Is it all taken?"

"Not near. There's room for all of you if you want to come and we have everything here. Everything but our wagon. That's lost, but we'll get another." He glanced again through the open door and shouted joyously,

"All of you just better stay right here, at least through tomorrow. There's going to be a wedding!"